AVID

READER

PRESS

THE GREATEST POSSIBLE GOOD

A Novel

BEN BROOKS

AVID READER PRESS

New York   Amsterdam/Antwerp   London
Toronto   Sydney/Melbourne   New Delhi

AVID READER PRESS
An Imprint of Simon & Schuster, LLC
1230 Avenue of the Americas
New York, NY 10020

This book is a work of fiction. Any references to historical events, real people, or real places are used fictitiously. Other names, characters, places, and events are products of the author's imagination, and any resemblance to actual events or places or persons, living or dead, is entirely coincidental.

Simon & Schuster strongly believes in freedom of expression and stands against censorship in all its forms. For more information, visit BooksBelong.com.

For information about special discounts for bulk purchases, please contact Simon & Schuster Special Sales at 1-866-506-1949 or business@simonandschuster.com.

The Simon & Schuster Speakers Bureau can bring authors to your live event. For more information or to book an event contact the Simon & Schuster Speakers Bureau at 1-866-248-3049 or visit our website at www.simonspeakers.com.

Manufactured in the United States of America

1 3 5 7 9 10 8 6 4 2

Library of Congress Control Number: 2025933760

ISBN 978-1-6680-8946-0
ISBN 978-1-6680-8944-6 (ebook)

"The children are always ours, every single one of them, all over the globe; and I am beginning to suspect that whoever is incapable of recognizing this may be incapable of morality."

—JAMES BALDWIN

Part One

A Pair of Shoes

1.

Around a lacquered oak dining table made from looted church pews, below a bulkhead lamp that had once belonged to a Polish fishing trawler, the four members of the Candlewick family were picking distractedly at clay plates of salad. The dish was a delicately improvised medley of charred root vegetables and crumbled feta, doused in manuka honey dressing and crawling with ant-black sesame seeds.

One side of the six-hundred-year-old room had been punched out and replaced with a triple-glazed wall of tinted glass, revealing a pale moon hung in the dimming pink sky. It was late April and the magnolia in the centre of the lawn waved its clenched buds like winning tickets. Beyond the back fence, lights flickered on in the leaded windows of neighbouring cottages.

At fifteen, Emil Candlewick was the youngest of the family and eating in sporadic bursts while listening to an AirPod lodged in his left ear. The clove of white plastic was relaying a conversation between two Canadian professors about Max Tegmark's theory that the universe might be a mathematical structure—something Emil had come to believe was possible but not probable, and so painful to consider that it gave him migraines he once described on a physics forum as feeling "like absolute ass."

Emil's bloated, badger-bearded father, Arthur, was transfixed by the presence of a housefly that had settled on a framed photograph of his family, taken on a beach in the Maldives. In the photograph, the four Candlewicks are ankle-deep in rags of surf, spaced so far apart that they look like a band being shot for a magazine.

Below the table, Yara Candlewick's thumb traced the heartbeats of a stock portfolio on the screen of her phone. The copper bracelet on her right wrist meant to subdue arthritis clinked intermittently against the rim of her plate as she ate with the other hand. A shaft of dusk light tethered her face to the vaulted glass ceiling.

Rounding out the ensemble, Yara's seventeen-year-old daughter, Evangeline, was engrossed in a slim, red paperback, propped open behind her food. She read with the urgency of an actress searching for her own name in a bad review. Still chewing, she lifted her eyes from the page and aimed them at her father.

"Did you know that every year in the developing world, thousands of children lose their sight because they don't have access to Vitamin A?"

"Very interesting, dubbin," said Arthur, watching as the fly abandoned its post on the picture frame and crept across the richly veined marble-top of the console table.

"It's not interesting," said Evangeline. "It's a tragedy."

Arthur reluctantly switched his gaze from the fly to his daughter. "Something can be both tragic and interesting, I'd imagine. Look at the *Titanic*, or *Macbeth*."

"Or MK Ultra," said Emil, a narrow frond of lettuce flopped out of the corner of his mouth like a cigarette.

His father pointed a bone-handled knife at his son approvingly. "Exactly. The US government injecting prisoners with hallucinogenic drugs. What's more interesting than that?"

"Literally everything," said Evangeline.

"Sorry we're not talking about dead babies," said Emil.

"Emil," said Yara, digital mountain ranges reflected in the mirror-coated lenses of her Prada sunglasses. "I'm warning you."

Evangeline lifted the book again, trying to refocus the discussion. "I really think you should read this," she told her father. "He explains this idea called 'effective altruism.' It means using mathematical models to work out how a donation can do the most good. One hundred pounds, for example, could either train one fiftieth of a guide dog in Britain, or save the sight of one thousand children through vitamin supplementation in sub-Saharan Africa."

Arthur sighed. "That's not quite how the world works, dubbin."

"It's how charity works," pointed out Evangeline.

Yara re-entered the conversation without moving her eyes from the screen. "If we sent money to everyone who needed it, what would we have?"

Emil imagined himself saying "each other" and almost choked with laughter on a mouthful of salad. Evangeline frowned so deeply that three parallel waves appeared in her forehead.

The eating resumed for a full minute. One of the voices in Emil's left ear wondered whether the fact that an unyielding David Hilbert had failed where Einstein succeeded was proof that pure mathematics would never be sufficient to explain physical reality. Evangeline read that easily reparable fistulas caused by lack of access to medical interventions during childbirth left women ostracised from their communities. Having lost track of the fly, Arthur began twisting in his seat to see whether it had taken up residence elsewhere in the minimally furnished, light-flooded kitchen-diner. Yara considered reallocating a portion of her Disney shares to an index-linked developing markets fund.

A spoon chimed against the lip of a bowl. Evangeline was finished.

"May I be excused?" she said.

Yara sighed and placed her phone facedown on the enviable patina of the table. She surveyed her family with the downcast air of someone turning up at a restaurant and realising they've been catfished. A nest of almonds and white cheese remained at the bottom of her daughter's bowl. "You haven't finished," she said.

"I don't feel like finishing," said Evangeline. "I'm finding this atmosphere to be hostile."

"I'm finding this atmosphere to be full of farts," said Emil.

Yara gripped the stem of her wineglass like a pen. "Emil, that's not clever and it's not funny."

In response, Emil mumbled something unintelligibly quiet. A private grin spread across his face and a chuckle bubbled up and stalled in his throat.

"What did you just say?" said his mother.

"Nothing," said Emil, hastily tidying away his smile. "Can I go too?"

"No, you cannot." Yara tipped her head toward Evangeline. "Evie, you can get down from the table. Emil, you're staying here. Your father and I have a bone to pick with you."

On hearing this, Evangeline's desire to leave rapidly evaporated. "Why?" she said. "What did he do?"

Emil drew his face down into his shoulders like a turtle.

"That's none of your business," said Yara. "Do you want to get down or not?"

"I'll find out anyway."

"She has a point," said Arthur.

"No, she doesn't," said Emil.

Evangeline leant toward her brother conspiratorially. "Did you get caught planning to shoot up school?" she whispered.

"If I did," whispered Emil, "I'd start with you."

"Emil!" said Yara, her voice managing to spread and linger like a pungent gas occupying the sixty-square-metre room. The outburst provoked a period of silence in which the only movement came from Arthur, straining his neck to try and discern whether the fly was now examining the base of a Yankee Candle, or he was waiting for a stray coffee bean to take flight.

Through gritted teeth, Yara said, "What's wrong with you?"

"Sorry, poppet," said Arthur. "There was a fly."

"Christ," said Yara. She cradled her face in her hands and breathed deeply until she felt ready to resume the proceedings. "Evangeline, go up to your room. Emil, take that fucking thing out of your ear and sit up straight."

Evangeline rolled her eyes and carried herself out of the room like a phantom. Emil removed the AirPod from his ear, placed it in the shadow of his bowl, and became desperately interested in his food. He chased a single flake of almond in circles with his fork. His heart was beating maniacally and the full sleeve of custard creams he'd eaten an hour earlier clotted painfully in the pit of his stomach.

"I didn't do anything," he said, quietly.

Yara produced a padded manila envelope from beneath her seat like a magician. It was a level of preparation that made her son wince with irritation. Why make them all suffer through dinner when she was literally sitting on his death sentence the entire time? Emil believed his mother revelled in doling out misery because her parents had been poor: not in a jolly, noble, at-least-we-have-each-other kind of way, but in a miserable Dickensian ordeal of filth and hunger. Until a few years earlier, when he'd been shown photos of a glum-looking family outside a low terraced house with only two front windows, he'd genuinely harboured the belief that she'd been raised in something akin to a Victorian workhouse, with soot smeared across her brow and a stingy cup of unidentifiable goop for each meal.

"Do you know what this is?" Yara said, looking first at her son, then at the envelope, then at Arthur, who was trying to appear as though he wasn't more interested in locating an errant fly than reprimanding his wayward son.

"An envelope?" said Emil.

"Yes," said Yara. "An envelope, addressed to you. With a label saying it's come from a place called Gary's Computer Parts."

In that moment, Emil felt the same way he did when he watched videos of people clinging to the edges of impossibly tall buildings without wearing safety equipment. He pictured the lumpy thumb of hash in his underwear drawer the way someone else might picture a saint—luminescent and reassuring.

Yara tipped the envelope forward until the contents fell with a hushed tickle on the table. It contained a foil packet, the size of a paperback book. A small white sticker in the corner read: TTLXX Graphics Card. Emil felt a tentative rush of hope, then realised the foil packet had been slit open at one end. His mother lifted it and the incriminating evidence toppled out.

Fourteen tabs of 80 mm acid. Two grams of crystal MDMA. Bought and paid for with the cryptocurrency Ethereum, vacuum-packed, and shipped in packaging the seller had promised would be "unbelievably discreet."

Yara lifted the perforated sheet and the clear bag of murky crystals and held them toward her son on an outstretched palm.

"What are these?" she said.

Emil hesitated.

"That wasn't rhetorical."

"Um," said Emil. "I don't know." He made a show of squinting at the items in her palm. "It looks like maybe some very small stamps and some powder?"

"Yes," said Yara. "It does look like that, doesn't it?"

Emil swallowed. "Uh," he said. "Yes?"

"That one *was* rhetorical, Em," said Arthur.

"Not helping," said Yara.

"No," said Arthur. "Sorry, poppet."

Arthur reached forward and picked up the sheet of "tiny stamps," made a tiny "oh" with his mouth, and put them down again. "Where does one *order* drugs?" he said.

"The dark web," said Yara.

"Mum," said Emil, embarrassed. "No one says 'the dark web.'"

"Well," said Yara. "Pardon me."

Emil grunted, realising that he wasn't helping himself.

"It's not the drugs that upset me," said Yara. "It's the lies."

"That's a lie," said Emil. "And I didn't even know they were drugs."

"You did know they were drugs."

"No, I didn't. I thought they were Gary's computer parts."

"You said they looked like small stamps."

"I thought they were computer stamps."

"Don't be cheeky," said Arthur. "You've ordered drugs to our house. That's not just reckless and unusual, it's a crime."

"A victimless crime," said Emil.

Evangeline, who had been loitering around the corner of the frame like James Bond, reappeared urgently at the head of the table. "Actually," she said. "The drug trade causes untold—"

Yara rose a few centimetres off her chair. "EVANGELINE PHYLISS CANDLEWICK, GO UPSTAIRS TO YOUR BEDROOM NOW."

Evangeline Phyliss Candlewick crossed her arms, tucking her hands into her armpits. She was almost eligible to vote. She knew how to make a negroni. She'd sent tasteful nudes to boys who'd promised not to disseminate them. It wasn't appropriate for her to be dismissed like a petulant Labrador, she was an adult and ought to be treated as such.

"I'll go," she said. "But when I'm upstairs, I might call the police."

Emil shot her a look. "Then I'll tell them you drew that swastika on the library door."

"Evangeline!" said Yara.

"Mrs. Duglett is a Nazi," said Evangeline, calmly. "She stocks books by TERFs and incels."

"I can't do this tonight," said Yara. "I just can't."

Yara left the kitchen through the bifold patio doors and blundered blindly into the garden, onto a flagstone path that meandered around three stone cherubs hoisting basins of moss, a cluster of acers guarding a miniature waterfall, and a hexagonal granite enclosure of pastel-shade wildflowers. Near the bottom of the garden, where a wall of beech trees peered over the fence, an old vardo wagon had been restored and set on blocks. It was fitted with a wood burning stove and a standing desk and a half-size fridge, and had served as Yara's office until two years earlier, when she'd taken early retirement. Yara called it "my gypsy wagon," Evangeline called it "literal cultural appropriation."

"Should I go and talk to her?" said Evangeline.

The blinds fell closed behind the windows of the wagon.

"I shouldn't think so," said Arthur.

"She's probably going to smoke cigarettes," said Emil.

"I expect you're right," said Arthur.

"Does she really think we don't know?" said Emil.

"I think she thinks there's a chance we might not know," said Arthur.

"She's utterly delusional," said Evangeline.

Once the two children had made their way upstairs and Yara had returned to the kitchen smelling of Marlboro Golds and spearmint chewing gum, Arthur got up from his seat and limply tried to loop his arms around his wife's waist. She batted him away, blubbed, then drew him close.

"I'm sorry," she said. "I don't know what's wrong with me."

"Nothing's wrong with you," said Arthur. "You're wonderful. It's the kids who are defective."

"If that's true," said Yara, "aren't we to blame?"

"Quite possibly. Should we ship them off to boarding school?"

"It would be cheaper to give them up for adoption." She backed out of his embrace and shook her head like a dog emerging from the ocean. "I can't even think of a punishment that makes any sense anymore. We used to be told to stay in our rooms, I think for him the bigger punishment might be to go outside."

"He could re-do the patio."

"I don't think so, Arthur," said Yara, realising only after she'd responded that it had been a joke. Arthur laughed and Yara took hold of his elbows as though afraid she was going to be dragged away before she had the chance to relay a message of utmost importance.

"How about we sleep on it?" he said.

"Fine," said Yara. "But I'm going to look into that rehab again."

"I really think he's just dabbling, poppet."

"He's been dabbling for months."

"Is there a time limit on dabbling?"

"He's fifteen years old, Arthur."

"My point exactly. At least give him a chance to get addicted."

"That's not funny."

"No, I know."

"We could still talk to the rehab, ask for their advice."

"I'm not sure that'd be for the best, poppet. It feels as though it might be crossing some sort of a line."

"Because you think he's dabbling."

"Everyone dabbles."

"Did you?"

"It was only you who didn't."

"You wouldn't have either."

"Not if I'd had your parents, poppet, no."

With a final kiss, she was gone.

Arthur stood looking around the kitchen, which had cost close to sixty thousand pounds to plan, 3D model, manufacture, and install. It elicited virtually no feeling from him. When they'd bought this house, it had felt inconceivable that anyone could live in such an architectural marvel and be discontent. Who could be unhappy in the rolltop beaten copper bathtub positioned beside a bay window overlooking a koi pond? Who could be depressed among the floor to ceiling bookcases of the attic library, in a hammock slung between lovingly restored cedar beams? Who could be anything but blissfully, bottomlessly happy, living in £1.3 million of Cotswold stone, with views like Constable paintings, and a personal orchestra of turtle-doves, honeybees, and clip-clopping draught horses to play out the end of each summer day?

Arthur used his foot to prise open the wine fridge beside the dishwasher and pulled out a red without bothering to check which country had produced it. He carried the bottle to the dining table, uncorked it, and filled his glass to the brim.

The book his daughter had been reading lay sprawled between his son's drug haul and a pair of obelisk-shaped salt and pepper shakers, bought during a family trip to the National Gallery several years earlier. He remembered that trip because Emil had gone from picture to picture, pretending to very seriously study the information plaques, then turning to his parents and loudly announcing things like, "Apparently this one was painted with poop."

Did he care if Emil took acid? He supposed not. He wanted his son not to hate him, that was the main thing. He wanted his son not to look at him and see the kind of people Arthur had grown up under: disconnected, self-interested, hysterical. (Did people really still take acid? Had it not fallen out of fashion with moonboots and the SodaStream?)

Arthur picked up the book Evangeline had been reading and skimmed the first sentence.

The average citizen of a western democracy today lives a life of luxury that would have been unimaginable to even the richest king of two centuries ago.

Arthur looked around himself at the William Morris tiles running behind the bronze sink and the lights secreted beneath the Shaker-style cabinets, illuminating the zinc countertop as though it were a museum exhibit. The calendar on the wall was split into four columns, three of which were crowded with jottings and crossings out. On the chalkboard, someone had written "SUGAR FREE!! soy milk" and someone else had drawn an ejaculating penis. A glowing blue cube on the LCD panel of the double-doored fridge requested a top-up of water for the icemaker.

Three hours later, Arthur got up and left the house.

It would be another four days before he returned home.

2.

The following morning, when Yara Candlewick saw her husband's large electric BMW iX missing from the driveway, she assumed he'd left for work early. She was relieved. Since she'd shipped her final project—a piece of data management software designed to streamline genomic research—Arthur had begun to disengage from the timber business where he was joint director and speak about the possibility of joining her in early retirement. Riverwild Timber was already in the process of closing out its acquisition by a larger Scottish firm and Yara was still trying to talk her husband into accepting their offer to stay on as a consultant. Arthur was tempted to decline.

"And do what?"

"Enjoy life."

"How?"

"Notice things, poppet. Eat slowly. Visit National Trust properties."

Those were not the things Yara spent her days doing and she pressed him to continue working. She needed her time alone in the peace of the house and she wasn't ready to give up at least one steady stream of income. She was the worrier: she shouldered the family fear. In order to feel even remotely at ease, she built excessively wide safety margins into as many areas of their lives as possible. In reality, it didn't matter how much the sale of Riverwild brought in, Yara would find a way to calculate its insufficiency: what if they wanted to cruise the fjords when they were eighty-five? What if neither of the kids could afford to buy their own home? What if hyperinflation rendered all cash virtually worthless, or a global stock market crash wiped out their investments?

Yara was the reason they arrived at an airport four hours before the scheduled departure time. She was the reason they both had bi-annual dental check-ups, even in the years when nothing cracked or throbbed. And she was the reason they owned four rental properties, five private pensions, investment portfolios with three brokerages, a case of Krugerrands held in a safety deposit box in Solihull, and several contemporary works of art that couldn't have been bought for any purpose other than investment.

The Candlewicks had as many safety features as a Boeing 747. Unlike Arthur's two brothers, who had frittered away their inheritances and now subsisted with the help of lodgers, handouts, and pawnshops, they were financially robust and prepared for a future in which almost anything could be weathered.

During one late night a decade earlier, after watching a documentary about the disappearance of Lucie Blackman in Tokyo, Yara had sat down to work out how much it would cost if either Emil or Evangeline were to go missing abroad and they were forced to relocate and hire a private investigator to pursue leads the local police would inevitably fail to pick up. Depending on the country, the costs of such an endeavour would quickly mount. Of course, a certain amount of money could be recouped through book deals and exclusive tabloid interviews, but these would depend upon the circumstances of the case and the level of public interest. Yara had thought, guiltily, that if one of her children had to go missing, it would be better for it to be Evangeline, because that would generate more publicity, allowing them to raise more capital for plugging the inevitable holes left in the inept investigation by corrupt local detectives.

But the shape of her worries had altered since then. They were out of the woods and into the other woods—the woods through which her two children approached adulthood. And what kind of adulthood would they arrive in? Would there be any joy left in the world, or any jobs not usurped by AI, or any country that was possible to bear for more than ten minutes in the summer? Would there be enough light at the end of the tunnel for them to want to bring children of their own into existence? Or would the world simply continue to feel as though it was about to end until it finally did?

Yara waited in bed until she heard the door slam and slam again, and she peered over the stone ledge of her window and watched her children drift along the driveway. They walked a precise, unchanging ten metres apart, as though they were the security detail for an invisible celebrity who existed somewhere in between them. Emil was sipping from a steel thermos filled with black coffee. Evangeline was holding a hand-painted placard under her arm, which read: "Hawthorne Money is Blood Money—This Science Lab is a War Crime!"

Yara saw herself flinging open the window and shouting at her daughter to bring the sign back inside and she saw her daughter showing her the middle finger and she couldn't summon the energy to go through with it. There were times, generally during particularly vicious rows, that Yara saw herself as though from above, like a dying patient having an out-of-body experience, and she wondered what it was she was trying to achieve. It certainly didn't seem to be harmony, or at least if it was, she was pursuing it in the least effective way possible. "You're doing what we all do," her therapist had once said. "You're trying to inflict a version of your own childhood on your daughter."

Yara couldn't believe that was even remotely true.

Evangeline disappeared around the corner, followed by the invisible celebrity and a bleary-eyed Emil.

Presumably, a call would come from the school later that day, and Yara would be instructed to come and collect her unrepentant daughter. It had happened before. She could always tell them she was at an unusually long dentist's appointment or out of the country for work. She could simply say she was "otherwise engaged." They were paying more than a university education for that school, after all, and it wasn't just so the children could eat nigiri rolls for lunch and go on VR strolls of the Colosseum during history lessons. It was because they had wanted them to have an unusually gentle on-ramp into the world, without cause for protest and without being provoked into doing anything that warranted Yara having to collect them before five o'clock.

Downstairs, Yara was irritated to see the debris from dinner hadn't been cleared away. There were hardened punctuation marks of rocket on the plates and a stagnant pool of salad dressing had become a designated meeting spot for tiny flies. At least Arthur had bothered to stow the packet of drugs somewhere. Unless he hadn't, of course, and Emil was now walking to school with a bag full of illicit narcotics, in which case it was likely she'd be reunited with both of her children before lunchtime.

The coffee machine had long been awake and was awaiting instructions via a touchscreen panel hosting a police line-up of Candlewick avatars. Yara pressed her face on the screen and its internal workings cranked into action to create her double-shot Americano, which she drank while sitting among the red acers and the gentle water of the Japanese-themed enclave in the garden.

Once she was sufficiently caffeinated, Yara would meditate using an app that gave her increasingly little guidance as she became more adept at stilling the waters of her mind. She would perform thirty minutes of vigorous exercise in the form of a CrossFit AMRAP workout. She would eat a bowl of soaked chia seeds, ispagula, Brazil nuts, cacao nibs, and kiwi fruit. She would take a cold shower until her skin was coarse with goosebumps.

This routine wasn't a lifestyle choice but a combination of medical recommendations. During the end stages of the last piece of software she'd built, Yara had experienced something terrifyingly akin to psychosis, gone without sleep for three nights, and contracted hypothermia after spending an entire January night hugging her knees in the garden. The word "breakdown" had been used only once, by her son, in the midst of an argument about whether or not it was acceptable to refuse a school vaccination on the advice of an American podcast. Yara preferred to see her "tough time" as a simple sign; a sign that she ought to refocus her energies. She had achieved a great deal professionally and now she was ready to step away. It was time to begin pickling the harvest in anticipation of the winter.

At quarter to ten, while Yara was sitting in the lotus position and serenely riding the present moment toward the unreachable future, her phone rang with a call from Brian Clinks, one of the three directors at Riverwild Timber. Yara couldn't remember ever receiving a phone call from Brian and hadn't even been aware he had her phone number. The circular photograph attached to his name on Whats-App was of a bald man in a linen shirt, grinning behind a frosty pint of beer while a Mediterranean sun set behind his shoulders.

"Yara?"

"Brian?"

"Where's Arthur?"

"What do you mean?" said Yara.

"He didn't come into work this morning. Phone's off. We have an audit with the bank in ten minutes."

Yara stood up and went nowhere.

"But he left before I woke up," she said.

"You sure?"

"His car's not here."

"Have you spoken to him?"

"No."

"Where is he?"

"He doesn't have a meeting somewhere?"

"Yes, he bloody well does. He has a meeting here, now."

She hung up and tried calling Arthur sixteen times, first the usual way, then through WhatsApp, then again the usual way. There was no response. Yara couldn't even begin to assemble a list of possible explanations. She knew, at least, that it wouldn't be anything nefarious on his part. Arthur wasn't like the adulterous men she saw in domestic thrillers on Netflix. He wasn't viciously handsome, manipulative, or cunning. He didn't have a secret life or the latent potential for assembling one. Arthur was straight-forward and toothless and endearingly, clumsily, apologetically upper-middle-class. He slipped in the vicinity of swimming pools and fell asleep in armchairs and compared mundane activities to historical incidents. He wore his dead father's camel-colour cardigans to fidget with half-dead tomato vines in the garden. He frothed milk for hot chocolate using a chrome wand that he left unwashed in the sink.

For the rest of the morning, Yara rang around hospitals, growing somehow both more relieved and increasingly worried with each failure to locate her husband. She briefly allowed herself to fantasise that he was arranging a surprise trip for the two of them in an attempt to restore the intimacy that had waned over the preceding years. She knew how likely this was. Arthur's unwavering predictability went both ways.

Brian Clinks called back an hour later.

"Nothing," said Yara.

"He's seriously left us in the shit," said Brian.

"Do you think he's hurt?"

Brian audibly swallowed as though the thought hadn't occurred to him until that moment. "Couldn't say," he said. "Do you?"

After hanging up, Yara went to the bathroom and flung open the cupboards, pulling down half-empty blister packs of omeprazole and paracetamol, pro-biotics and pre-biotics, turmeric capsules and cod liver oil capsules and capsules that contained homeopathic doses of belladonna, arsenic, and crushed bees. She soon found what she was looking for: citalopram, 20 mg, unopened. It was the packet she'd picked up for him two weeks ago, when the repeat prescription had come in the post.

Arthur had been taking anti-depressants for as long as she'd known him. He'd been taking them since before they'd become a national pastime, since before a full half of BBC documentaries were about mental illness, before there were posters in schools and notifications after the credits of soap operas and rap songs in which depression was added to the list of luxury goods that young men bragged about possessing.

Yara called 101 and explained the situation, stressing that this kind of behaviour was utterly out of character for her husband, who had only recently phoned her from the toiletries aisle of a Waitrose to ask whether she thought he ought to switch deodorant.

"He's vulnerable," she said.

"In what way?" asked the operator.

"In every way," said Yara.

At lunchtime, Evangeline and her closest friend, Ada van der Volk, shuffled along the salad bar in the dining hall of St. Isidore's College, helping themselves to scoops of romaine lettuce, cherry tomatoes, sweetcorn, kidney beans, and a mixture of organic pumpkin seeds and chopped walnuts. They ate exactly the same lunch, from Monday to Friday. No croutons. No dressing. No breaded chicken bites or seared pads of halloumi.

A piece of advice Evangeline had once absorbed: don't eat anything your grandma wouldn't recognise as food. She had met her maternal grandma twice, that she could remember, and the woman was living in a nursing home and subsisting on wedges of lemon cheesecake covered in double cream. Evangeline mentally altered the maxim accordingly, so that it became: don't eat anything Virginia Woolf wouldn't recognise as food. This had the consequence that, whenever confronted with a choice of food, she tried to picture the very dead writer being offered a selection of ultra-processed supermarket meals. (Had Virginia Woolf ever eaten pizza? Or Kettle Chips? Did she know what spaghetti carbonara was? Could she identify that a square of Galaxy chocolate was something meant to be ingested?)

The two girls ate at a table in the back corner of the refectory, watched over by a stained-glass window of a monk tenderly washing the feet of another monk. The hammerbeam roof of the millennium-old hall hung ten metres above their tightly wound plaits like the ribcage of a fossilised dinosaur, draped in an oil painting of stars. All around them, the smell of hot meat hung in the air, absorbing the hushed chatter and occasional screeching gale of laughter. Some days, Evangeline envied the kids who thoughtlessly piled their plates high with glistening pucks of deep-fried gristle. Other days, her sense of superiority more than made up for the calorie deficit. I feel significantly better than they do, she told herself. My brain is developing as it should. My bones are growing stronger. With each mouthful of this bland and nourishing food, my ability to emotionally self-regulate strengthens.

"I'm kind of scared," said Ada van der Volk. "Not because I don't think this is right, because I totally do, obviously, but I really don't think my dad is going to be as chill about it as you say he is."

"You told me he was a punk at our age."

"He was," said Ada. "But he's not anymore. He wears Skechers and listens to Adele. Plus he thinks Victoria's dad is like, important, or whatever."

Ada couldn't bear to look Evangeline in the face and instead shifted her gaze to the bell-shaped pit between her friend's collarbones. Evangeline rolled her eyes and kept eating. Once they'd both consumed half of what they'd taken from the salad bar, they carried their bowls to a conveyor belt and set them down to be carried away into unknowable darkness. Tomorrow the bowls would be stacked up by the entrance once again, gleaming, and ready to be filled with identical heaps of fresh greenery.

"Maybe we could do it another day?" said Ada. "Like after exams, maybe?"

Evangeline rounded on her friend and puffed herself up, expanding with righteous indignation. "Fine," she said. "I'll do it on my own."

"Evie, I didn't mean it like that. I just meant, you know, maybe we should focus on our exams now, and then do this after."

"Do you know who can't focus on their exams? Everyone who's home has been destroyed by a Rheinmetall drone."

"But at least Victoria's dad is doing something good with the money—he's giving us a science lab."

"You're a fucking idiot, Ada."

"Hey," said Ada, her face collapsing into something that was dangerously close to a sob. "No, I'm not."

"Our parents pay more for tuition than most people earn in a year. If they wanted to build a new science block, they could just build one. If Victoria's dad wanted to do something actually good, he'd build facilities for a school that doesn't have a literal spa."

Ada swallowed. "I know that," she said. "But maybe someone here will, like, discover a cure for cancer or whatever, because of the lab, and then it'll be good."

"Ada," said Evangeline. "If anyone here discovers a cure for cancer, it'd be because they were working for big pharma, and big pharma don't want to cure anything, because it would mean they couldn't make money selling chemotherapy drugs anymore."

Cowed, once again, by her friend's aggressive logic, Ada flapped her hands gently, sighed, and surrendered. "Fine," she said. "Let's just do it."

The two girls excused themselves near the end of a Politics lesson on the Singing Revolution of the Baltic states and retrieved their signs from the art cupboard. (Ada had not wanted to take Politics for A-Level and Evangeline had talked her into it. Everything is politics, she'd said. Your clothes are politics. Your house is politics. That app you use to make your nose smaller in photos is politics.) Evangeline was not pleased to discover that Ada's sign, which she'd been given clear instructions regarding, was a lilac piece of A5 paper, supported at each end by a taped-on plastic straw, with the words "Love Conquers Hate" scrawled across it in neon marker pen.

"What does that have to do with anything?" said Evangeline.

"I thought it was good," said Ada. "I saw it in a photo of a Pride march in Portland."

"But how is it at all relevant to what we're doing?"

Ada looked back and forth between her sign and her friend. "Well, because we're love and they're hate, and we want them to, you know, we want them to show more love to other people."

Evangeline sighed.

The "o" in "love" was a wonky heart.

They ducked under the blue ribbon that fenced off the doors to the new science lab and hid beneath one of the lab tables in the centre of the room. Evangeline used a butter knife brought from home to prise the lid off a tin of red paint described on its label as "vermillion autumn." She held the sign in one hand and the open pot in the other. The smell from the paint made Ada nauseous. She pressed her forehead to the cool metal leg of the table.

"Evie, I changed my mind again. I don't think I can do this."

"Don't be a little bitch, Ada. Zoom out, see the wider context. A small amount of discomfort for us now could lead to huge changes in the lives of other people, voiceless people, people who need us to speak for them."

Ada tried zooming out but only got as far as a bird's eye view of the town, from which she could see her father, spinning on the chair in his study, waiting with red-rimmed eyes for her to knock so that he could say what he always said: "Who the hell do you think you are, Ada van der Volk?"

"Yeah," she said. "Okay. Sorry."

The two girls remained huddled beneath the lab table for ten minutes, watching as polished pairs of handmade brogues, loafers, pumps, and kitten heels shuffled in and massed behind the ribbon that stretched across the doorway. There was a mercifully brief speech from the headmaster about the pride he took in the facilities their school was able to offer to their students, before Victoria's father, Alan, was given a pair of comically large scissors and instructed to cut the ribbon.

"I officially declare this science hub open," he said.

The two girls leapt out from beneath the table. Evangeline tried to throw the paint out of the tin but instead she threw the entire tin, which clunked against a stool on the opposite side of the room. Alan dropped into a squat and threw his hands over his head.

"This lab is a war crime!" shouted Evangeline.

"We're sorry," said Ada, lowering her sign. "Please don't call our parents."

When school was over, Emil caught the bus into Stroud, the nearest town big enough to have a Cineworld, and parked himself at the back of a Starbucks to continue reading a reference book on geometric algebra. Despite the telling off he'd received earlier in the day, Emil was in relatively good spirits, at least in part because of the triple-shot Frappuccino he was drinking through two paper straws. He'd paid for it with his neon pink Monzo card. Every month, two hundred pounds were added to the account by his father. Emil moved one hundred and ten of those pounds across to a separate account used for buying cryptocurrency and spent the rest on cinema visits, cheap sweet things, and large elaborate coffees. He ordered most of the books he wanted from the library in Gloucester and torrented pdfs of anything that was too esoteric to be in their system.

Emil checked his phone. There was no message from his mum, which he presumed meant Mr. Wyndham had flaked on his promise to call her. If it did eventually happen, Emil wondered whether his mother would care twice as much because of Gary's Computer Parts or whether the seriousness of Gary's Computer Parts would eclipse this transgression entirely. He wondered what had actually happened to Gary's Computer Parts. Emil wouldn't put it past his mother to have dropped them off at a police station, along with a note begging for forgiveness on his behalf.

He sighed at a page of rotation matrices, irritated not for what he'd done at school, but for the fact that it would probably drive his mum slightly more insane. His crime was starting a German essay on his personal hero with the sentence: "Ein mann das ich sehr bewundered heisst Ted Kaczynski, oder 'der Unabomber.'" His other options, which had included Aphex Twin and Kurt Gödel, would have probably gone down with significantly less friction.

"What are you reading?"

Emil glanced up. The woman standing over him was short and broad-shouldered, in a tank top that was frayed at the edges as though it had been cut out of a larger piece of clothing with blunt scissors. Her cheeks were pierced with studs, as were both sides of her top lip and both nostrils. A sharply cut bob of blue-black hair framed her face asymmetrically like a Norman helmet worn sideways.

"Um," said Emil. "Sorry?"

"I said, what are you reading?"

Emil flashed the cover of the reference book. It was written by three men with Polish-sounding names and the design was of a series of concentric cubes constructed from dotted lines.

"That sounds crazy complicated," said the woman.

"Yeah," said Emil. "Or no, not really. Not when you get it."

"Is it for school?"

"No."

"It's for fun?"

"Um. Not really."

"Go on then, what's it for?"

"I'm building a geometric algebra library."

The woman took a seat beside Emil. She smelled of cheap, solvent-like perfume, Golden Virginia tobacco, and pickled onion Monster Munch. "Couldn't you just go to one?" she said.

"It's not really a place," said Emil. "It's a thing. Like, a tool."

"Right." The woman nudged his shoulder with hers as though they were two friends sharing a fond memory. "You don't have a little spare change, do you?"

"No," said Emil. "Sorry." The woman sighed and turned her scarred hands over in her lap. "I have my card though. I could buy you a coffee?"

The woman perked up. "That's sweet," she said. "You're sweet."

Emil took this to mean yes. As they queued at the counter, he tried to ascertain whether the woman was homeless and whether or not that meant she injected heroin. For as long as Emil could remember, his mother had explained every refusal to give loose change to beggars by announcing to her children that it would only be spent on heroin. *What's heroin?* Emil could remember beginning to ask, somewhere around the age of six. A waste of good money, his mother would reply, every time.

Heroin was still on his bucket list. Emil wouldn't want to inject heroin but he had long ago decided he would happily snort it, given the opportunity. People got given morphine in hospital, after all, and you couldn't say the same for cigarettes or sauvignon blanc, which weren't considered beneficial under any circumstances. Emil had dedicated numerous hours to reading incredibly detailed "trip reports" of various drugs online. He'd memorised the half-lives of ketamine and DMT. He knew about naloxone, machine elves, and the cold-water filtration method of separating codeine from paracetamol. He could name five kinds of opiates, eight kinds of uppers, and ten kinds of psychedelic substance. Once, he'd split a full cereal bowl of magic mushrooms with Deepesh Patel and convinced himself that he was communicating with an extra-terrestrial intelligence bent on relaying the truths of the universe to him. He'd awoken the next day to find his phone filled with indecipherable notes, punctuated with exclamation marks.

Cones to the heavens! Cones. Cones into the earth! It goes on and on!

He thought of alcohol the way other people thought about George Eliot novels or croquet: a largely dull, outdated form of entertainment that had been surpassed a thousand times over by more interesting innovations.

The woman ordered a double-shot Americano. She didn't add sugar or sweetener or the powdered cocoa from the glass shaker. Emil glanced around to see whether anyone could see him interacting with this terrifying, heavily pierced, grown-up woman. A cluster of year eights from Marling were sat around a single, small hot chocolate at a table beside the window. An elderly man nervously stuffed a Ziploc bag with pink paper sachets of sweetener from the table of hot-drink accoutrements.

Emil's phone vibrated with a message from his mother: "Get your arse home now." .

His joy evaporated at once, replaced by a dread so all-consuming it felt as though the particles of his body were now vibrating at a different frequency. He loved his mother—he thought she was intelligent and impressive and, generally, fair—but he could also recognise that something was profoundly imbalanced about her. She had been so totally consumed by doubts and anxieties during his teenage years that the other, better parts of her had been forced out. Emil had once discovered a warped copy of his mother's 2003 PhD thesis in the loft, titled "Trust Issues: Self-Enforcing Automatic Contracts Between Computers," and when he'd asked her to explain it, she'd dismissed the whole thing as being so outdated it would be like going over a fax machine instruction manual. Sometimes, while zoning out on dissociative drugs, Emil thought that they offered exactly the kind of cognitive reset his mother would benefit from. A hallucinatory voyage into the unknown might remind her of the person she'd been before the drab yoga shorts and medicinal jewellery.

This, he knew, was an unusual degree of analysis to perform on your own mother. Sam Batuman's only assessment of his own mum was that she was "a trophy wife who got fat." And Deepesh once confided in them that his mum "sucks off old men." Emil could enjoy incredibly violent Atlanta trap lyrics and watch porn in which women were trussed up with intricate spiderwebs of rope, but hearing his friends speak that way about their mothers caused the hairs on the back of his neck to twitch. He wasn't sure what to do with the feeling. It wasn't like he was going to intervene. Hey, he sometimes imagined himself saying, *You two ought to be nicer to your mothers. Don't you realise that they brought us into existence?*

By the time Emil returned to the village, his fantasies about the impending punishment had taken several forms. His mother might take away his electronics or curtail his liberties or, worst of all, confiscate his Monzo card. What if she went looking and somehow found his savings? She couldn't. She wouldn't know how to. It didn't matter if she'd researched the "dark web," there was no way she would locate his crypto wallet and the endless string of random numbers and digits that unlocked it. If she asked him, point-blank, to offer it up to her, what would he do? He was an enthusiastic but unconvincing liar and he crumbled easily under parental pressure. It was why he'd taken German for GCSE, not French, and it was why he wore patent leather loafers to school and applied benzoyl peroxide to his cheeks every morning. By and large, Emil did what he was told. The problem for his parents was that he did many other things too.

When Emil arrived at home, Yara greeted him halfway down the drive, barefoot, the polished river pebbles hissing as they slid beneath her feet.

"What's wrong?" he said.

"Your father's missing," she said.

Emil came to an abrupt halt.

"What do you mean?"

"No one knows where he is."

Before he could begin to worry about his father, Emil breathed a sigh of relief for himself.

"Did he say anything to you?" said Yara.

"About what?"

"About where he might have gone, Emil. What do you think?"

"Um," said Emil. "No. I don't think so."

Yara used her teeth to tear a wiry strip of cuticle from her left thumb. Emil followed his trembling mother into the house and found his sister rearranging souvenir fridge magnets while speaking into the landline. "He's six-foot-one," she was saying. "When he walks, his arms barely move. There's a birthmark on his back in the shape of Peru."

3.

For the four days in which Arthur Candlewick was missing, a heavy, inescapable weather filled The Old Rectory at 87 Drybrook Lane. The 56-inch TV in the living room remained off. The botanical-print curtains remained drawn. Nobody read news through the restored walnut cabinet of the radio. Nothing was cooked on the eight glass segments of the sheer black induction hob.

The three Candlewicks who were not missing remained cloistered in their separate bedrooms, pursuing their own avenues of distraction. Without anything needing to be said, the two children simply decided that they would not go to school until their father had returned home. When St. Isidore's called to inquire as to their whereabouts, Yara impatiently announced that they were in the midst of a family emergency, put down the phone, and returned to her Peloton bicycle and its two-hour-long spin class. The video on the screen of her bike alternated between a handsome, stubbled instructor, and an oncoming rush of seaside pathway. She was both in her bedroom and making her way along the Amalfi coast. Garish villages passed her by, watching themselves in the water. Flustered groups of tourists photographed each other along precarious ledges.

After receiving a visit from two disinterested police officers on the evening of the first day, Yara completely withdrew from the effort to locate her husband. This was on the advice of her Lacanian therapist, Dr. Ash Weber, who had promised Yara, on behalf of the police, that there was nothing she could do that they wouldn't be doing, and that the most important mission she could embark on for the time being was the preservation of her own health and sanity. Yara drank hot mugs of lemon juice, apple cider vinegar, and black pepper. She rowed while listening to lectures on the illusory self. She stood on her head for minutes at a time.

Meanwhile, Emil was smoking dark tobacco mixed with strong weed, eating truffle crisps, occasionally masturbating, and watching YouTube videos explaining various mathematical theories of varying degrees of repute. One welcome side-effect of the pot was that it endowed him with a concentration span long enough to sit through entire fifteen-minute explainers on screw theory and homotopy. Without being stoned, the most he could manage was a minute or two, before his mind was drawn toward something that required opening another tab, and another, and another, until the video playing in the background had finished, unnoticed, and Emil was trying to decide whether or not he could summon the energy to wank himself off one more time before he went to bed. There had been a time when he would wade through biblically proportioned sci-fi novels over the course of weekends. He couldn't pinpoint when exactly he lost this ability to exit the world through a paperback escape hatch. He missed it. He knew he'd lost something valuable but every attempt he made to recover his ability to read properly ended with him pacing like a zoo animal, hands fluttering like moths in his pockets.

Evangeline was the only one of the remaining Candlewicks who left the house to look for Arthur. She packed a rucksack with bottled water, green bananas, mixed nuts, and a blanket from the airing cupboard, and walked south out of the village, reasoning that there was a slim possibility her father may have been heading for the late-night supermarket in the Slad Valley when he disappeared. She walked for four hours, listening to an audiobook about the life of Jane Austen, hoping that it might give her something vaguely original to say in her English exam. She walked along the side of a road without pavement, pressing herself into a spiny box hedge when she could hear cars approaching. By eight, the sun was almost gone from the sky and a Tudor-style pub rose out of the hills, its crumbling white façade peppered with iron horseshoes and x-shaped tie rods. Groups of bleary-eyed men sat around low picnic tables, their bellies pressed into the slatted wood. Evangeline wondered whether her father had never had friends or he'd just lost them somewhere along the way, and she wondered too whether her brother had inherited the same disease. She went inside and ordered a gin and tonic and drank it in several thirsty gulps before using an app on her phone to summon a taxi home.

On the second day of the disappearance, a mild-mannered cleaner named Patrice let himself into the house. He found a note on the kitchen island: *Just downstairs today please, Patrice.* There were three twenty-pound notes weighed down by a crystal whisky tumbler beside the slip of paper. Patrice carefully folded the notes and slipped them into the breast pocket of his blue cloth shirt. He covered his ears with headphones and pressed play on a podcast about the life of a CEO that he had queued up on his phone. He worked for half a day, scrubbing stubborn orbs of limescale off the shower doors, hoovering crumbs of brittle cheese crackers out of carpeted corners, and scratching the residue of organic vegetables off the grill racks in the double oven. Once he was done, Patrice sat on a wall outside the house and ate leftover spaghetti from a plastic takeaway carton. There were restless silhouettes in two of the mullioned windows. Some of the other cleaners at the agency talked about finding the lives of their clients endlessly fascinating. Patrice couldn't have been less interested in the people he cleaned up after.

Several hours later, when night had descended on the quaint and prohibitively expensive valleys of the Western Cotswolds, Emil Candlewick shuffled into his kitchen, wearing a pair of boxer shorts and an untied dressing gown. He only vaguely recognised that something about the house was different, though he couldn't put his finger on what it might be. His pupils were swollen and sluggish and the whites of his eyes were cross-hatched with red. Barely lifting his feet from the limestone tiles, he made his way across the kitchen and threw open the fridge doors, recoiling from the cool blast of light, and pawing at his eyes like a newborn baby. The fridge was fully stocked with things his mother considered life-prolonging: washed blueberries in Tupperware pots, furred fruits ferried halfway across the planet, roasted chunks of root vegetable, vats of organic yoghurt, kombucha, kefir, sauerkraut, smoked tofu, edamame beans, mastic, hairy fingers of parsnip, and grotesque purple tomatoes. Emil closed the fridge, crouched, and pulled open the freezer doors. The lower half of the fridge was filled with impeccably labelled glass tubs of leftovers. "Lentil Curry 06/04/2017, spicy." "Carrot and Coriander Soup 10/12/2018." His litre of Ben and Jerry's Half-Baked was still tucked behind a bag of frozen Hokkaido pumpkin, where he'd left it two days before. Emil lifted the tub out and rolled it between his hands, trying to soften the contents.

"Hey."

Emil turned around to find his sister lounging against the door-frame. She was smiling in a weary, sophisticated, grown-up way, that Emil realised was the result of drunkenness. There were moments in which he felt they were still both sun-creamed, knee-scraped children, giggling at a kids' club in Tenerife, and other moments in which he felt like Evangeline had gone on somewhere distant and left him behind.

"Where do you think he is?" said Emil, holding the ice cream to his chest, as though afraid his sister might snatch it away from him.

"He's probably just stuck somewhere."

"Stuck where?"

"I know as much as you do," said Evangeline.

Evangeline opened the wine fridge and scanned the bottles, head tilted, as though she were browsing a bookshelf.

"Are you allowed to take wine?" said Emil.

"Why, are you going to tell Mum about that too?"

Emil wasn't. He'd immediately regretted blurting out his knowledge of his sister's library vandalism, not necessarily because it would get her into trouble, but because it would exclude him from her future confidences. Contrary to how it often seemed to Evangeline, Emil genuinely wanted to remain in his sister's good graces. Though he felt certain he was frequently right in the face of his parents' misguided ideas, he was sure he'd never once won an argument with her. She knew more than he did about everything from the Russian Revolution to the correct way to hold chopsticks. Emil occasionally helped his sister with her maths coursework but was under no illusion that she believed mathematical ability had any relationship to real intelligence.

"Sorry," he said.

"It's not like she cares," said Evangeline. "Dad's actually a convenient distraction. Maybe now we can get on with our lives."

"Aren't you even a bit worried?"

"No."

Evangeline dug a corkscrew out of the drawer below the cutlery, where the kitchen implements too large to live anywhere else had been banished. She uncorked the bottle with a competence beyond her years and proceeded to fill a turquoise enamel coffee mug to the brim. She held the mug two-handed, as though it was a cup of hot tea on a cold day.

"Are you high?" she said.

"Yeah," said Emil. "Are you drunk?"

"Quite possibly."

The two siblings sat opposite each other at the dining table. Emil continued to chip curls of ice cream out of the tub with an antler-handled teaspoon, bought by his father as a souvenir in Helsinki airport on the way back from a meeting with timber suppliers. Evangeline glugged the wine without even bothering to take notice of the taste. She'd read a year earlier that sommeliers were all frauds and the taste of a wine came almost entirely from the expectations and preconceptions of the drinker. It had been even more proof that the world she was due to inherit was built on a web of ridiculous fictions.

"Why is Mum so angry at you?"

"We staged a protest against the new science lab," said Evangeline. "Victoria's dad donated the money and he runs an investment fund who own huge swathes of oil companies and Rheinmetall."

"What's Rheinmetall?"

"They make weapons."

"Oh. So are we not getting the science lab?"

"The science lab's already there. Didn't you see it?"

"No," said Emil. "Maybe. I don't know."

"It's in the Rhodes building, at the end of the tech corridor."

"Oh."

"It's important that men like that know they can't distract people from the fact they're destroying the planet by buying people off. They're like the Sacklers."

"Who are the Sacklers?"

"They own Purdue Pharma, which invented oxycodone, convinced doctors it wasn't addictive, and caused the opioid epidemic."

"Oh," said Emil, who could remember reading a trip report in which someone described oxycodone as causing "ineffable bliss" and made a mental note to see whether he could acquire some. "That's fucked."

"It's not even us who'll feel the brunt of their greed. It's the generations who follow us."

"Yeah," said Emil, glancing around, as though he'd been trapped with an over-talkative stranger at a party where he knew no one else.

The two siblings indulged their vices. A creeping sense of unreality took hold of Emil and he rolled the ice cream tub back and forth across his forehead. Evangeline picked at the label on her wine until it came away from the bottle.

"I think I might know his computer password," said Emil, partly because he wanted to prove he had some knowledge of his own to share.

"What?"

"I think I know Dad's laptop password."

"How?"

"Two weeks ago, I saw a Post-it on his monitor which said Maximus383."

"Go and get his laptop."

"Why do I have to get it?"

"Because alcohol has more of an effect on coordination than weed does and I'm liable to drop it."

Emil rolled his eyes, set the ice cream tub down on the table, and dragged himself out of the room. Left alone, Evangeline's thoughts ranged from a boy at school she'd considered trying to initiate conversation with, to a video she'd seen online of a teenager attacking a fast-food worker in Philadelphia, to her father and the fact of his disappearance and the possibility that he was lying facedown in a ditch with blood leaking out of his ears. Could he have suffered a stroke? Or a heart attack? Could he now be experiencing some form of locked-in syndrome, so that his mind wandered hysterically inside a body that refused to take any more orders? She imagined time-lapse footage of his body decomposing in a forest of primeval trees. She remembered Cancún, four years earlier, and the way he'd picked her up and carried her back to their five-star beachfront hotel after she'd been stung by a jellyfish. The smell of sweat through the silver hair of his back had made her think of cattle.

"Here," said Emil, slinging a MacBook Pro onto the dining table. It was the latest iteration of the model, with the largest screen and near-bottomless memory. A long, deep scratch bisected the upper half of the shell. Evangeline pushed the ditch and the beach from her mind, flipped open the computer, and typed in the phrase Emil had recited minutes earlier. It worked. With a digital chime, the ocean-front of the lock screen was replaced by a photograph of Tutankha-mun's death mask.

"Holy shit," said Emil.

Faced with her father's desktop, Evangeline felt a surge of guilt. She wasn't betraying him, she told herself. Quite the opposite, in fact. She was doing everything in her power to track him down. If they were to find anything, she'd report it directly to their mum, who would alert the police, who would purse the information in accordance with official procedure. It was in her father's interest to have her be the first line of investigation. Evangeline could be trusted to hide anything embarrassing and pass everything relevant further up the food chain.

She opened the browser and navigated to its history.

- Houses for sale in Bourton-on-the-Water
- Houses for sale in Nailsworth
- How to remove badgers from garden
- Badger deterrent
- Can badgers feel anything
- Cheapest rehab Gloucestershire

"Why was he looking at rehab?" said Emil, pointing to the screen, as though Evangeline might be looking at something else.

"Why do you think?" said Evangeline. "Because you're an invet-erate junkie."

"No, I'm not."

"Yes. You are."

"You're an alcoholic."

"That's an ad hominem argument."

"So?"

"So it means you've already lost."

"I'm not a junkie, Lean."

"It's not me you have to convince."

Emil knew he wasn't addicted to drugs, he was *interested* in them. It was different.

They continued reading.

- McLaren 765LT
- McLaren 765LT resale value
- McLaren 765LT extras
- McLaren 765LT paint cost difference

"This is embarrassing," said Evangeline, scrolling down for a full second until they were out of McLaren territory.

- Good gifts for woman
- Good sports gifts for woman
- Sports gifts for woman, luxury
- Gift for woman meditation
- Is a clarinet a good gift for a woman
- DVD Blackadder full set
- Interracial, anal

"Nope," said Evangeline, slamming the computer shut. Both she and Emil sat bolt upright in their seats as though they'd just been caught cheating on a test.

"Did you read it?" Evangeline said, after three seconds had elapsed.

"Yeah," said Emil. He pushed the tub of ice cream to one side on the table, leaving behind a ring of water on the lacquered wood. "Why was there a comma?"

"I don't know."

"Interracial *comma* anal."

"Don't repeat it, Emil."

"Do you think it might be a clue?"

"I truly hope not."

"Did you look further down?"

"No."

Evangeline turned back to the computer. "I'm going to have to open it back up," she said. "So I can close the browser. Try not to look at it, okay? I'll just close the browser then shut it down and we won't talk about this again."

Emil nodded, swallowing.

Once again, Evangeline typed in the password and was welcomed into the inner sanctum of her father's digital world. She closed the browser window, slammed the computer shut, and shunted it away from her. Emil let out a low whimper.

"What?" said Evangeline.

"I saw the next thing," he said.

"Don't tell me what it was."

"I can't hold it in."

"Yes, you can."

"Can I tell you?"

"No, Emil."

Evangeline stood up and held herself around the throat as though acting out an assault she'd previously been subjected to. Emil tried desperately not to think of his father's erect penis. He tried not to think of his father leering over an elderly couple engaging in frenetic, grunting sex. He remembered an Ursula K. Le Guin story he'd read where the inhabitants of a planet named Gethen only became sexual beings for two days every month, and as a result the planet was devoid of war or disorder, and no-one's father looked at morally dubious porn online.

"I'm going to bed," said Evangeline. "Put this back where you got it."

"Why do I have to put it back? I got it."

"I'm liable to drop it."

Evangeline slunk off upstairs, bottle of 2014 Châteauneuf-du-Pape swinging like a censer in her shooting hand. Emil briefly considered going back into his father's computer and taking another look around, more out of curiosity than a belief it might turn up anything that would help to pinpoint his whereabouts. He dismissed the idea, while the words "interracial, anal" rolled across his mind like a news ticker. It was no worse than anything he'd looked at, he supposed, but he'd never even entertained the idea that his father was participating in the same kind of seedy, blue-lit voyeurism he felt compelled to indulge in almost every night of the week. When exactly was his dad jerking off? And where was his mum while these multicultural masturbation sessions were taking place? They weren't watching porn together, surely? If that turned out to be the case, Emil thought that he would probably have to leave home. He'd get a job washing dishes at a dingy pub in Stroud and sleep round the back of the condemned office block where the homeless people hung out.

The ice cream had melted into a sweet sludge and Emil lifted the paper tub to his mouth and drank from it, feeling the icy weight as a relief in his stomach. He carried a kombucha with him upstairs and tried to read a book of Freeman Dyson essays, before opening his computer and masturbating into a sock over a video of a forty-year-old Japanese woman dressed as a bus driver.

It was four hours before anyone else interrupted the lonely rattle of the giant refrigerator. The sun was arriving over a crop of coppiced beech trees, casting its glow across the countertops and revealing shoals of fingerprints on the glass cabinet that held the wineglasses. Yara bounded into the room having taken the stairs two at a time. She refilled three glass bottles with filtered water, carbonated them, and sat at the kitchen island, rehydrating. She had slept for three hours and been plagued by dreams in which she was an exam invigilator, overseeing clones of her husband, while they stared blankly at a test all of them appeared to be totally unprepared for. If she exercised enough, she'd pass out again. She had another call with Dr. Weber at three and she was planning to nudge her therapist toward prescribing sleeping pills. She'd been given them back when she'd had her "trouble," and it had felt like being sent on a holiday. Even now, she looked back on those fuzzy, elastic days as a kind of second adolescence, in which everything had felt so alive and tender that it was as though she was experiencing the world for the first time.

She sliced a lemon into hot water and ground pepper over the *Hallo! Ni Hao! Bienvenido!* mug. Through the mindfulness app on her phone, a man with a faint trace of Edinburgh in his voice asked Yara to envision herself as a sphere of selflessness, expanding to include every human being on earth. He was cut off violently by a default ringtone.

"Mrs. Candlewick, this is DC Samnani. We've found your husband."

4.

On the evening of his disappearance, Arthur Candlewick left his house in calfskin slippers, climbed into his unusually large electric car, and drove for twenty minutes along a single-lane country road, before parking outside a timber-framed pub and climbing over a rickety kissing gate into a field of quivering barley crooks. The reason for taking along his daughter's book, his son's drug stash, and an uncorked bottle of mid-price Bordeaux were not clear to him. Nothing about what he was doing was particularly clear to him.

Arthur drank as he walked and quickly gained momentum. In the thin, crisp light of the early morning, he crossed fields filled with wheat and disinterested cattle and he waded through chicory and poppies and lavender. The slippers on his feet accumulated snowshoes of dark mud. He passed a former kiln, now a holiday let, and a former mill, now a holiday let, and a former pub, now a restaurant where pressure-cooked tumours came adorned with tangy foam and priced as though food had become a scarce commodity. He climbed through a long hedge tangled with white flowers of stitchwort. A tractor hauling a trailer loaded with storm-damaged fence-panels honked its horn as he crossed the narrow road without pausing to check for oncoming traffic.

The sudden burst of energy had caught Arthur off guard. He hadn't walked so far for several years. His knees creaked and caught like rusted hinges. He brought the wine bottle to his lips, found it empty, and tossed it to one side. He felt possessed and unstoppable.

Striding across the awakening countryside, Arthur was not a person who had recently discovered that his wife had been assembling a large digital trove of diverse pornography. The pornography had not featured painfully handsome, impeccably groomed men, so low in body fat that rippling fans of muscle visibly undulated beneath their skin as they moved. And Arthur had not masturbated along with these men as they ejaculated onto the faces and breasts of doe-eyed women. And he had not carried on about his life as though none of this had taken place. He had not continued to ask after his wife's Pilates sessions and assured her that the choice of new border plants for the front garden had been a stroke of genius. He had not helped set up the direct debit to her new gym or bought her an anniversary bangle engraved with lyrics from the song used for the first dance at their wedding.

Arthur had caught a glimpse of himself reflected in his reaction to discovering his wife's porn habit and he was disappointed in the face he saw. Was he weak and terrified or just forgiving and understanding and modern? Was he being a good person or a doormat? What would Brian Clinks have done, if he'd found that his wife had been hoarding pornography like a teenage boy? What about Arthur's brothers? Or his father?

His father would have slapped his mother so hard she'd stagger into the wall like a drunk and collapse into a snivelling heap. He would, quite possibly, have—

The thought was interrupted when Arthur walked directly into a disused mineshaft and fell fifteen metres to the ground, breaking his right leg and his left ankle, gouging open the back of his scalp, and herniating a disc in his lower back. He lost consciousness for three seconds. When he opened his eyes, he saw a constellation of hazy, pearlescent orbs, bobbing around in front of his face like a cluster of helium balloons. He wondered if he was being abducted by aliens. Two separate species of pain raced up his legs and rattled his brain and Arthur tried to haul himself to his feet with his hands but was forced to accept that this was not possible.

There would be no walking. There would be no lower body movement. He called out but his voice was thinned to nothing by the cavernous darkness around him.

Arthur Candlewick had no idea how far he was from civilisation. He couldn't tell whether he was on someone's land or on anyone's jogging route or a well-used dog-walking trail. There were no cars in earshot. If he scrunched his eyes shut and strained his ears, all he heard was his own heartbeat, ticking ominously in his skull like a clock.

The days that followed were, Arthur would later explain to anyone who would listen, the most important days of his life.

But in a grey-panelled hospital room, overlooking a multi-storey car park, Arthur Candlewick was still piecing himself back together. He was dressed in a hospital gown and draped in a starched white sheet. His eyes were slow to react to the light. An untouched plastic tray of breakfast lay in his lap: two slices of white bread, a square of cheddar cheese, a rectangular tub of strawberry jam, and a foil-wrapped pad of butter. Arthur had at least drunk the cup of tea that accompanied his underwhelming meal, though it had been luke-warm and tasted faintly of soap.

The heavy door swung open without warning.

"How are we feeling, Arthur?"

Arthur turned to the woman who had been looking in on him at regular intervals since he was admitted. She was the person who'd cleaned out his wounds with stinging swabs and laced his scalp back together with fifteen dissolvable stitches. A crude tattoo of a blue whale occupied her forearm and she smelled of a sweet and uniden-tifiable vape flavour. The black Crocs on her rainbow-socked feet were splotched with purple.

"Very well," said Arthur.

"Not hungry again yet?"

Arthur shook his head. When they first brought him in, six hours earlier, he'd been unable to speak, and had eaten nine tuna and sweetcorn sandwiches left over from the previous lunch service, be-fore falling into a sleep so deep that it became clear the force needed to wake him would veer into cruelty.

"You'll be going in for X-rays soon. Dr. Chandra thought you might want to hold off until you've seen your family."

"They're here?"

The nurse took a step back and leant into the door, so that it opened, revealing the three idling Candlewicks. Arthur's family bustled into the room, dressed as though they'd been hastily evacuated from the path of a hurricane. Evangeline was wearing Emil's Norwegian army surplus jacket over silk pyjamas. Emil was in combat boots, tracksuit bottoms, and a Christmas T-shirt. Yara wore cycling shorts, a blouse over a sports bra, and a pair of fleece-lined wellies. She threw herself onto her husband like a wrestler and Arthur smiled into her hair, his hands polishing the canyon between her shoulder blades.

"The call button's there," said the nurse to Yara, lifting a controller attached to the metal bedstead by a pigtail of cable. "Just press it if you need anything. I'll give you some privacy."

Yara ignored the nurse and held Arthur at arm's length, scrutinising his face.

"What the hell were you doing, Arthur?"

"I'm not sure, poppet."

"Where were you trying to go?"

"I honestly could not tell you."

The two children moved awkwardly toward the foot of the bed, unsure of the protocol for such a situation. They were both relieved but also confused and both privately felt as though something about the scene was anticlimactic. Not that either of them had wanted anything more serious to have transpired, just that the consensus had been that they were in the midst of a major crisis—that either Arthur was running away or mentally ill or involved in some kind of crime—so the revelation that he'd just fallen over and not managed to get back up felt somehow like discovering the mundane secret behind an astounding magic trick.

"Hey, Dad," said Evangeline, lowering her face until it brushed his. The accumulation of hair on his jaw was unkempt and greasy.

"Hello, dubbin."

Emil raised one hand in greeting and his father mirrored him.

Yara stepped back, as though trying to fit them all into a photo. Arthur was still beaming, his teeth the yellow of foxed paper. It was the first time in several months that he'd looked at his wife and not imagined her hunched over pornography, picturing herself with men who weren't him. What he saw was a beautiful, radiant human being, filled with love and worry.

He beamed. Yara frowned and turned to the two children.

"Could you two leave us alone for a moment?" she said. Neither of the children moved. Digging into her vintage Louis Vuitton handbag, Yara produced a sleek teal wallet and extracted a ten-pound note, which she held toward Evangeline. "Go and get yourselves something from the vending machine."

Evangeline stared at the note with open hostility. "We're not children from a Roald Dahl book," she said. "We don't want sweets."

Interracial, comma, anal, thought Emil.

"I want sweets," he said, accepting the note from his mother's hand, and turning and leaving the grey room. His sister followed, after a final, sympathetic look at her gaunt father. Yara sat on the edge of the firm bed and lifted her husband's hand. There were seams of dirt in his fingernails. A thorn lay embedded in the plump curve of his palm.

"Arthur, the nurse said they're testing you for dementia."

"I don't have dementia, poppet. I've told them that."

"Did you take Emil's drugs?"

"Of course not."

"Then tell me what's happening. I don't know what to think. They said someone found you lying in a hole."

"I believe it was a mineshaft."

"Christ, Arthur."

"I fell, that's all."

"But why were you there in the first place?"

Arthur looked Yara directly in the eyes. There was something foreign in his gaze, a new energy that alarmed her. "Poppet," he said. "It hardly matters now, does it?" Yara withdrew and relocated to the window, where she watched a grieving father fume at the list of charges on the signpost above the parking meter. A new-build estate of red-brick houses offered a footnote to the vast tank of cerulean sky. She drew her blouse up over the lower half of her face and blew her nose into the fabric. If it wasn't dementia, it had to be some other kind of mental degeneration. But what came on so quickly? And how rapidly would he degenerate? Was it irreversible? Terminal, even? Or was she being overly dramatic? The doctors didn't seem concerned and Dr. Weber always said she had a tendency to catastrophise.

I'm catastrophising, she told herself. My husband is well. My children are well. I am well and I am whole and I am present.

"Poppet?" said Arthur.

Yara turned hopefully toward her husband. "Yes?"

"I'd like you to imagine that you're walking to work one day and you come upon a child drowning in a pool of water."

Yara pressed the call button.

5.

Yara carried a mattress downstairs and built a bed for Arthur in the living room, using sofa cushions as a headboard and a corduroy pouffe as a bedside table. She placed a thermos of chamomile tea on the improvised table, along with a bowl of chopped fruit and a selection of history books from her husband's to-read pile in the study. Arthur lay on his back with his casts propped on travel pillows and wriggled his toes contentedly.

"Are you sure you're comfortable?" she said, stepping back like a sculptor to admire her handiwork.

"Extremely," said Arthur. "Thank you, poppet."

On the first evening of his return, the family ordered from an Italian restaurant in the neighbouring village and sat in the living room watching a documentary about the Khmer Rouge, chosen by Evangeline and seconded by Arthur. Yara had a Caesar salad, Evangeline opted for burrata, Arthur ate two slices of vegetable pizza, and Emil consumed three quarters of his diavolo at a savage pace before telling his mum he was heading upstairs early to prepare for a mock exam the following day. Yara accepted this without questioning its believability, too busy observing her husband, who was watching the TV with the rapt awe of a toddler. His eyes were wide and unmoving. His mouth hung loose as he chewed, displaying revolving clumps of cheese and dough in a manner far removed from his usual closed-mouth, hamster-like nibble.

"Don't stay up too late revising," she told the closing door.

In the documentary, talking heads recounted the atrocities they'd committed decades earlier. Arthur paid so little attention as he ate that the front of his baggy T-shirt became stippled with grease and tomato sauce.

Later, on the upstairs landing, Yara met her daughter coming out of the bathroom. A chalky comet of toothpaste extended from the corner of her mouth like the remnants of a clown's make-up.

"Is he honestly okay?" said Evangeline.

Yara hesitated. She'd read books about the developmental stages of the adolescent brain. She understood that her daughter hadn't yet assumed cognitive size but she wasn't entirely sure how to use that information. There were many respects in which Evangeline had already surpassed her mother: she could calm herself, quell her anxieties, make an omelette that was as fluffy as cottonwool.

"The doctor says so," said Yara, after a pause so long she knew it would negate whatever followed.

"But you don't agree?"

"I think he might be in shock."

"Shock about what?"

"He's been through a traumatic experience, Evie."

"Do you think he has PTSD?"

"I don't know."

"Or something else?"

"I'm telling you, I know as much as you do."

She signalled to Evangeline that there was a daub of toothpaste on her top lip and Evangeline shrugged at her mother and carried on to her bedroom.

Before she went to sleep, Yara did something she had never done before: she locked the front door and took the key upstairs. She ran a bath and sat in the tub as it filled, watching the woodland below, stock-still in the fading light. She had no idea what had happened to her husband. They had an appointment, the following week, with a neurologist at a private clinic. Yara didn't even know what she ought to be hoping for. Her husband insisted he was fine but he said it with the preternatural serenity of a cult leader. She was certain something had happened to him, something that needed to be rectified.

Neither the scans nor the cognitive tests they'd done at the hospital had shown any abnormalities. According to the doctors, Arthur was as healthy as he'd ever been. He wasn't dropping things or forgetting names. He could tell you what year it was, recall the German word for "in between," and name the incumbent Home Secretary. There were no signs of concussion or trauma, no mood swings or irrational outbursts of anger, no signs of memory loss or loss of motor function.

With her laptop on a tray that fitted over the width of the bath, Yara searched the internet for clues about her husband's state. She tried "large fall personality change." She tried "personality change brain injury." "Brain injury broken legs." "Brain damage, fall." "Injury, head, mental illness." "Husband changed after hitting head."

She read about cases in which people had resurfaced from comas speaking in foreign accents. She read about patients who forgot everything but their childhoods or their mothers or how to play the cello. In one article, on a gossip news site, a man said his wife had inexplicably crashed into the side of a primary school and regained consciousness with an unflappable determination to engage in extreme sports. He looked on helplessly as she threw herself out of planes and scaled mountains. "It's like she's a different person," he told the journalist. "And now I'm learning to love her all over again."

Emil left the house via the trellis that guided clematis up to his bedroom windowsill. He tramped into the village across a hump of unused farmland and caught the bus into Stroud, where he met a friend called Lewis, who he'd sat next to in junior school, and who now attended a comprehensive with a reputation locally for breeding criminals and driving teachers to abandon the profession. Lewis's parents both worked in the old people's home in Minchinhampton, smoked Superkings, and grew chillies in tiny pots on every windowsill of their house.

"Hey," said Lewis. "What's up?"

"Not much," said Emil. "You?"

"Same."

The two boys sat on a low drystone wall, overlooking a valley of patchwork fields, their feet kicking at heads of cow parsley. Lewis had stolen a cigarette from his dad and they shared it while also sharing a pair of headphones through which Lewis played a new mixtape by a grime rapper whose name sounded to Emil like a lazy email password.

"I think my dad might have brain damage," said Emil.

"Will you have to feed him through a tube?" said Lewis.

"No," said Emil. "It's not like that."

"Does he go like this?" said Lewis, pressing his chin into his shoulder and grunting and letting bubbles of saliva form and burst in the corners of his mouth.

"Don't do that," said Emil.

"Why not?"

"I don't know. It's not cool."

Lewis burped and patted his belly like someone who'd just finished a large meal. Emil wished he'd brought weed but he didn't have much left and didn't want to share it with Lewis because he'd become afraid of ordering more online. A woman moved past them, holding two jute tote bags that could barely contain her shopping.

"Nice melons," said Lewis.

The woman came to an abrupt halt and shuffled ninety degrees until she faced the boys, her cheeks pulsing with anger. Emil wanted to apologise. He couldn't understand why he still hung out with Lewis, who didn't even live particularly nearby, and who had once confided in Emil that he'd had sex with a ham sandwich. The woman with the shopping decided against reprimanding them and she walked away, the calloused heels of her feet slapping against her flip-flops.

"Those weren't even melons," said Emil, quietly. "They were papayas."

Evangeline waited for half an hour after her mother's bedroom light had turned off before creeping down the stairs and peering into the living room, where her father was lying awake, staring at a point on the opposite wall with no discernible attraction.

"Dad?"

"I'm awake, dubbin," said Arthur. "Everything okay?"

From a perch on the sofa, Evangeline could see that her father's eyes were twinkling, as though he'd either been crying or was on the verge of doing so. He'd pulled the duvet up over his chest and arms, which made him look like a sick child, swamped by his bedding. He still hadn't trimmed his beard and the hairs of his moustache hung over his chapped top lip like a fringe.

"I read your book," he said.

"Which book?"

"The red one." Evangeline waited. "It was beautiful," said Arthur. "I'd never thought of things that way. It really moved me." Evangeline wasn't sure what to say. "I'm sorry for being dismissive."

"Forgiven," said Evangeline, who didn't know whether she ought to feel afraid or proud or patronised. Her father didn't sound like her father. "Mum's worried about you," she said.

"I know, dubbin. But she's a worrier, you know that."

"So you don't think she should be worried?"

"I know she needn't be. I feel better than ever."

"She thinks that might be a symptom of something."

"Dubbin, a symptom has to be a hindrance in some way, I'd imagine."

"And you're saying you don't feel hindered?"

"Quite the opposite."

Arthur gazed at the length of starry sky unfurled like a deep blue banner above the bottom of the garden. The silhouette of a squirrel moved along an oak branch in sprints.

"There's a big old world out there," he said.

"I suppose," said Evangeline.

"Do you have any more books like that?"

"How do you mean?"

"Well, about 'effective altruism' and aid and so on?"

Evangeline hesitated. "I might have a few more," she said. "I can bring them down. But maybe it's best that you rest and recover first."

Arthur nodded and swallowed in the heavy, lip-twitching way that indicated tears might be forthcoming.

"We're very lucky, aren't we, dubbin?"

"Yes," said Evangeline.

"Yes, indeed," said Arthur.

It had been ten years since Evangeline last curled up beside her father and fell asleep but he smelled like he always had, of old leather

and electricity. His breaths were so deep and long that when she
tried to match her breathing to his, she grew dizzy and gave up.

Emil came home after sharing a three-litre bottle of white cider
with Lewis, bought for them by an elderly man who accepted their
three-pound bribe because he needed money for his electricity
meter. The door was locked. Emil dropped into a squat and carefully removed the pins holding the brass flap over the letterbox. He
slid his hand through the letterbox, bent it to the left, and scrabbled
against the keyhole. The key wasn't in the lock. Emil groped desperately at the empty keyhole. He didn't understand. The key was
always in the lock.

Emil traipsed around the side of the house and peered in through
the living room windows but the curtains were drawn. There was
no way he could climb back up to his room. He weighed his options.
He could always ring the bell, hoping that somehow it was his sister
and not his mother who woke up to let him in. In the excitement of
Arthur's disappearance, Yara seemed to have agreed to abandon her
fury over the drugs, but he had no doubt that if he committed another transgression now, while she was obviously so worried about
their father, he would be subjected to a thorough and painful series
of punishments.

He closed his eyes and pictured his room, as though by imagining
it vividly enough, he would transport himself there. He mentally
reconstructed the shelf of sci-fi books and glass desk of monitors and
replica of Paul Atreides's crysknife from *Dune*. He opened his eyes
and shivered. He started typing "how to pick a lock" into the search
engine on his phone but gave up halfway through the sentence and
sat on the front step with his hands tucked into his armpits.

In the end, he walked back into the village and caught the night
bus into Stroud. A town that had appeared harmless and roman-
tic as the sun set was now an underworld of roving shadows. The
streets were haunted by shuffling junkies and drunken football fans.
Beneath a lamppost where Emil paused to light a cigarette, a brothy
trail of kebab meat and pitta chunks led toward the doorstep of a
vape shop.

Though the pubs cast an inviting glow onto the steep, cobbled streets of the town centre, Emil knew it would be pointless and humiliating trying to get served anywhere. He walked quickly and aimlessly, past closed charity shops and garish outposts of American coffee chains and window displays of crackle-glazed mugs and plastic zoo animals and laser-cut plywood models of local landmarks: Gloucester Cathedral, Woodchester Mansion, barges floating on the Sharpness canal. Emil kicked a Styrofoam burger box uphill. It occurred to him then that the door had been locked to prevent his father going on another unsanctioned night-time excursion. It was his father's fault that he was alone on the street at night. His father was now someone who had to be looked after.

"Master Emil?"

It was the woman from Starbucks, sitting on a doorstep, wearing a hoodie so large it pooled around her like a puddle of ink. She was rolling a cigarette in her lap. There was a man beside her, dressed in an absurd number of clothes, and jabbering excitedly while trying to draw her attention to something on his phone. Clocking Emil, the man gave him a brief nod, before limping away in the direction of the train station.

"You okay up there, Master Emil?" said the woman. "You look a little lost."

"I got locked out," said Emil.

"Bummer. What are you going to do?"

"I'm not sure."

The woman motioned for Emil to sit beside her and she removed an origami wrap from inside her bra, made from a leaflet for a techno club night at a former rectory in Bristol. She unfolded the wrap to reveal a thumbnail-size pile of white powder. She kissed the tip of her cigarette and rolled it in the dust. When she lit it, the end of the cigarette flared green, and she drew on it so forcefully that a full quarter of the cigarette became ash.

"How old are you?" said Emil.

"Nineteen," said the woman. "You?"

Emil wondered what he could get away with. The translucent threads on his chin weren't particularly convincing but he was broader than most of the other boys in his class and he sung, when forced to, in a gravelly baritone.

"Um," he said. "Seventeen."

The woman laughed and passed him the cigarette. He drew the smoke as deep into his lungs as he could and held it there, until it felt as though his face was expanding outwards. When he exhaled, a faint voice in his mind swore joyfully and his mouth turned numb. He'd done cocaine twice before but even he had been able to tell that a significant part, if not all, of the contents of the bags were washing powder and crushed-up Fisherman's Friends.

"Can you pick up?" said Emil, trying to affect a casualness that he didn't feel.

The woman laughed again. The studs made dimples in her cheeks and Emil wondered what it would be like to kiss her. She smelled, wonderfully, of body odour. "Pick up what?" she said.

"More of this."

"You want white?" She blinked. "Do you have any money?"

"I have my card."

"Of course you do." She stood up and brushed sprigs of tobacco out of the folds in her hoodie. "You go and fetch us eighty English pounds, Master Emil, and I'll make the call."

"Um," said Emil. "Okay. Thank you."

Two hours after passing her eighty pounds in cash, Emil hadn't seen the woman again. He lay down on the corrugated tiles of the office building entrance and tucked his knees into his chest, the smell of stale urine catching in the back of his throat. The AirPod in his right ear relayed an old Isaac Asimov story about a man who buys a dead version of planet earth in a parallel world in order to have enough space to raise his family. Emil imagined himself on that parallel earth, alone, and free to do as he wanted. How would he spend the days? He would watch all the films ever made and then he would watch them again. He would learn combinatory logic. He would teach himself how to cook elaborate desserts and then gorge himself on them until he couldn't move.

Emil woke up at five a.m., shivering. Someone had thrown a ragged fleece blanket over him and there was a stubby bottle of mineral water lying on its side by his head. A metre away, a man dragged a Pomeranian in a quilted jacket away from a black coil of faeces.

Emil caught the first bus back to Bourton and surveilled his own house from a distance until his mum took two wine bottles out to the recycling bin and went back inside to wash under the rain shower in the mosaic-tiled downstairs bathroom. He let himself in and pressed his avatar on the coffee machine. Four sludgy shots of espresso began trickling out of the chrome spout. When his sister entered the room whistling, Emil was sat at the dining table with his face flat against the wood as though he'd been shot through the back of the head.

"Morning," said Evangeline.

"Yeah," said Emil.

6.

During the weeks that Arthur spent recovering in the living room, he voraciously read books on moral philosophy and applied ethics provided for him by his daughter or ordered, with her help, from the internet. Upon arrival, these new books were hastily shucked out of their brown card envelopes, which piled up in accordion-like stacks on the utility room countertop. Some were patronisingly readable pop-science airport fare, while others were dense, academic texts that Evangeline had heard mentioned in other, less dense academic texts, and assumed would lie beyond her grasp. Whether or not he understood them, Arthur consumed every one of the books in their entirety, unmoving, in his makeshift bed.

He had Evangeline teach him to make use of the smart TV's features so that he could watch videos on YouTube. He sat through hours-long lectures on utilitarianism and consequentialism and the TED talk of a man who had discovered a way of training rats to detect landmines. He took in explainers on vaccine uptake and malaria transmission. He watched documentaries on Chuck Feeney, Bill Gates, and the philanthropists of the industrial revolution.

"Did you know," he asked Evangeline one morning, as they ate overnight oats in front of breakfast TV, "that by inventing disease-resistant wheat strains, Norman Borlaug is estimated to have saved over a billion lives?"

"Yes," said Evangeline. "I did know that."

"Did you also know that he was a very, very good wrestler?"

Evangeline grinned. "No," she said. "I didn't."

When Yara asked what he was doing, Arthur unconvincingly

insisted he was helping Evangeline with the personal statement she was writing for her Cambridge application. Yara had become so worried about her husband's mental state that she attempted to accept this, because it at least felt like a reasonable thing to be doing, especially compared to the fact that Arthur was now refusing to engage in the completion process for the sale of Riverwild Timber, an event he had been labouring tirelessly toward for nine months.

"There are papers to sign," Brian Clinks told her, over the phone. "I understand he's ill, but he can't fuck this up, Yara." He pronounced her name Yawa, like a two-year-old. She wasn't sure he'd ever asked her a single question about herself; not how she was or where she was or whether she was coping okay since her husband had returned from an inexplicable jaunt into the countryside with a life-altering head injury and several broken bones.

Arthur gently refused to give Yara power of attorney. He said he wanted to think about how things would move forward.

"What's there to think about?"

Arthur smiled and shrugged.

Five days after he'd come home, Yara drove her husband to a Victorian manor house in Cheltenham, for a private consultation with a neurologist who wore his hair in a ponytail and looked how she imagined a black jack dealer might look, despite having never set foot in a casino. The doctor talked slowly and explained terms that made Yara feel patronised, though she understood there was no way for him to know that she'd already conducted hours of online research into the responsibilities of the various brain regions and the ways in which traumatic head injuries could thwart them.

At first, the neurologist performed a series of tests similar to those Arthur had been subjected to at the hospital. Reflexes, simple maths, general knowledge, pattern recognition. Arthur passed them all. He could correctly predict subsequent numbers in a logical series and identify the odd one out in sets of pictograms. His reflexes, too, were on top form, as were his eyes and lungs and heart. Even his sense of proprioception—a word Yara had been grateful for a definition of—was utterly intact, with Arthur able to pick up and put down a plastic beaker with his eyes closed, move his outstretched fingertips to the end of his nose, and navigate through a series of cones without looking down at his crutches.

The neurologist signalled the end of the tests and they all took seats.

"Day to day, what does your life look like at the moment, Arthur?"

"I've been laid up because of my legs," said Arthur. "Usually, I'd be out of the door by six, off to work."

"And do you plan on going back to work?"

"I shouldn't think so."

"He just sits there and reads," said Yara, pointing to her husband in frustration.

"I understand your frustration, Mrs. Candlewick, but that's not really reason to believe there's something wrong. Sometimes, after a significant traumatic event, the body just needs some time to rest and recover."

"It's a massive personality change. Doesn't that mean he's had a brain injury?"

"Poppet," said Arthur. "I am present."

"Not necessarily," said the doctor. "People are often profoundly altered by significant life experiences. It needn't be medical."

"He fell fifty feet into a hole," she said.

"A mineshaft," clarified Arthur.

"He had fifteen stitches across the top of his head. How can that not be responsible for all this?"

"It's true that severe concussion patients can experience some mild personality changes, but these generally take the form of mood swings or bursts of anger and tend to pass within a few weeks." The neurologist smiled reassuringly. "People hit their heads very often," he said. "And most of the time, provided nothing breaks through the skull, we don't see any real damage. We're very resilient creatures. Well-designed." He rapped on the side of his head. "Nature gave us helmets."

The doctor stood up, indicating that he considered the consultation to be over and that his patient ought to be relieved by his lack of concern. Yara felt a rising panic in her throat. She wanted to throw out an outrageous, undeniable accusation—to claim that Arthur could no longer count or cry or tie his shoelaces. In the car, Arthur suggested that they go and find somewhere to have lunch, and Yara gripped the steering wheel of her Porsche Macan so tightly that her knuckles glowed in her hands like blanched hazelnuts.

"Why didn't you tell him how you've been feeling?" she said.

"I feel great, poppet."

Exactly, thought Yara. It doesn't make any sense.

When they got home, she leafed through Arthur's address book and found the number of a psychologist he'd been seeing up until a decade or so ago. She wasn't sure who else to call.

Contrary to Ada's fears of activism taking precedence over studies, Evangeline became unfailingly strict with herself in the run-up to exams. She printed up revision timetables and Blu-Tacked them to her bedroom walls, crossing out the thirty-minute-long chunks with a green highlighter once they'd been completed. If she missed a revision session, because of lateness or tiredness or the period pains that felt like hostile parasites in her stomach, she carried the missed session over and forced herself to slot it in elsewhere, during a school lunch break or by waking up earlier than usual. She gave herself half an hour of free time per day and she used it to read exiled Soviet poets or talk about global development with her father. She avoided her mother, who haunted the house with spray bottles of detergent in her hands, mumbling about getting to the gym or cooking or washing the towels, as though anyone was paying her any attention.

"You're going to burn yourself out," said Yara, finding Evangeline asleep at the dining table one morning in May. Multicoloured notes on psychological case studies lay spread out around her like unpaid bills. "Clive Wearing." "Little Hans." "Loftus and Palmer."

Evangeline felt torn between wanting to go to university and wanting to go out into the world and begin doing something that felt meaningful. She told herself this was a false dichotomy, that she could and would do both, that continued education would equip her with the means to accomplish all she had planned.

Although there were no more dramatic protests and Evangeline did her best to maintain a veneer of civility toward even her most disagreeable teachers, she continued to assert herself in less visible ways. She stole hardback books from the library and donated them to the Oxfam shop in town. She left radical environmentalist leaflets taped to the backs of toilet doors. In Geography lessons, she made a point of consistently referring to all migrants as "expats." "The response to the Syrian expat crisis has demonstrated our institutionalised selfishness," she wrote. "Expats from the Balkans face numerous challenges when trying to secure employment commensurate with their qualifications."

On a wet morning in early May, she caught a coach to Cambridge with Ada van der Volk for the university open day. The two girls sat with their heels on the seats and their phones wedged between their knees, scrolling. Evangeline thumbed nostalgically through photographs of increasingly far-back times. She curated her photo library, culling the inane and the duplicated, so that every image that remained was a reminder of something that ought to be remembered. Older ex-boyfriends with nose rings, hardcore concerts at the Guildhall, last-day-of-term wine binges with Ada on the terrace of her house.

School was almost over.

The things they'd done every day for the past seven years would never be done again. They would never again bustle through the over-equipped canteen or doze at the back of the science labs. Never again would they loiter at the periphery of scrappy rugby matches or watch French music videos in the computer lab or yawn through endless assemblies bookended with Bible quotes.

Evangeline tried to evaluate how much she'd truly learned during her time at St. Isidore's. The things that stuck with her had not been the things that their teachers had necessarily intended. For now, she could recall how many seats there were in the House of Commons and why the Stanford Prison experiment was flawed, but she knew these facts would fade from memory, as each batch of knowledge always had after each batch of exams.

The most memorable lesson had probably been an English double in year ten with Mr. Frankl-Slater, a young teacher who wore flannel shirts and chukka boots and who Ada had heard from Laura Saunders had a tattoo on his back of a dragon crouched atop a motte-and-bailey castle. Mr. Frankl-Slater was in the habit of prodding and steering his classes toward lively debates and he was one of the few teachers that the Isidore pupils felt confident they could say anything to, knowing that it would be received without anger or judgement.

The year ten class was studying *The Sun Also Rises* by Hemingway and Rhea Chapel put up her hand to ask, "Why do we even have to read this, sir? It's so misogynist. He literally beat his wives."

"That's a wonderful question," said Mr. Frankl-Slater. "Why do we have to study this hideous stuff at all? But I'd ask you, Miss Chapel, how do you expect to appreciate what exactly the patriarchy is unless you possess an awareness of the cultural artefacts that typify it?"

Rhea Chapel rolled her eyes, for the benefit of her classmates. "I don't know, sir, maybe by looking around me?"

Mr. Frankl-Slater affected a look of sudden terror and glanced about him as though he'd just been ambushed by assailants. The class laughed. "Miss Chapel," he said. "I think when you look around yourself, you're much more likely to see the fruits of grievous inequality than the horrors of it." Three weeks after saying that, he was let go, ostensibly for including a reference on his CV that the school administrators suddenly found impossible to verify. There had been other comments, none of which were sackable offences when considered in isolation, but which added up to a teacher who refused to play by the rules of his institution, and who Ada had thought about multiple times while masturbating with the showerhead in the downstairs bathroom, index finger clamped lengthways in her mouth to stifle the moans. In her fantasies, he asked her to stay behind after a lesson and she so impressed him with her knowledge of Marxist film theory that he fell to his knees and used his tongue to trace words on her clitoris.

"Do you remember Mr. Frankl?" said Evangeline.

"Obviously," said Ada. "He was so hot."

"He wasn't that handsome," said Evangeline.

"No," said Ada. "I mean, he wasn't that handsome. But he had something about him. Like, you knew that he would be like a good dad and stuff. He would look after you. He would like, know how to fix stuff."

In Cambridge, they walked with their arms interlinked and their heads tipped back, pausing occasionally to take in flocks of students who looked impossibly older than they were.

"It's magical," said Ada.

As childish as she found the choice of adjective, Evangeline couldn't help but agree. The town was like the cities she'd built in her mind as a child while reading fantasy novels. Although the buildings of Bourton were at least as old as those in Cambridge, it looked like a child's toy compared to the university city. While one part of her was quickly enamoured by the grand stone churches, leafy quadrangles, and leaning medieval pubs, another part of her was repulsed by it all, and fought valiantly to hold in her mind the suffering of those she'd spent her school years reading, writing, and protesting about.

"Imagine living here," said Ada. "Imagine that this is actually where you lived. Like when you went home, it would be to here."

Evangeline knew it was unlikely Ada would ever live here, at least not as a student of the university. Not only was she a private school pupil, but she played no instrument, read nothing she wasn't forced to, and believed that Atlantis was a place that had genuinely existed. She had an encyclopaedic knowledge of *Grey's Anatomy* and knew the birthdays of over thirty A-list actresses, but her curiosity was narrow and quickly depleted. Her plan involved going into forensic pathology, which was the result of having ingested so much crime-related TV drama, but her grasp of what the real-world profession might actually entail seemed to Evangeline to be incredibly naive.

"You can tell a lot from the teeth," she said once. "If they turn pink, it means the person drowned or died in a fire or from being strangled."

When the time came, Evangeline wrote two personal statements for her university application. In one, she spoke about feeling a keen sense of justice ever since watching a harrowing documentary about the American penal system. That personal statement was bland and peppy and intended for her mother and the university applications tutor at St. Isidore's. In the other essay, the one she intended to actually send, Evangeline wrote:

Over the course of my life, my parents have spent over £110,000 on private schooling, with the hope that it will help me to gain an advantage over poorer children when it comes to applying to elite universities such as yours. For this reason, I would encourage you not to entertain me as an applicant. It is necessary for my mother's sanity that I apply, but I don't believe it's ethically defensible for me to earn a place ahead of others when my parents have essentially paid for an unfair advantage. I believe you should dismiss all applications such as mine. By turning down students from private schools, you will hopefully help to bring about the demise of a system that entrenches inequality.

According to the ethicist Peter Singer, the amount my parents spent on a marginally "better" education for me could have restored the sight of 4,000 people who are blind due to trachoma. Alternatively, it could have saved nearly 8,000 lives through diarrhoea education. It could have nutritionally fortified food for 44,000 children for ten years, potentially preventing the blindness caused by Vitamin A deficiency or the intellectual disability caused by lack of iodine, among other things. In short, there are many ways my parents could have chosen to make the world a better place for thousands of people; instead they decided to send me to a school with a Steinway, a squash court, and a falafel station in the canteen.

So thank you for reading this far but I don't want to go to your university. I have spent more than enough time surrounded by inappropriately wealthy children, feeling humiliated by the level of unearned privilege afforded to me. All my life, I felt like I was in the wrong place, doing the wrong thing. I am ready to leave this bubble behind.

Again, thank you for your time and apologies for wasting it,

Evangeline Candlewick

The next time Emil saw the woman, he was in town after school, making his way toward Starbucks, where he was planning to blast himself awake with caffeine and try reading a book on the life of Kurt Gödel for at least half an hour before he could no longer resist checking his phone. He was passing The Hope and Anchor when the woman emerged, using a lighter to seal up a joint like a welder working in miniature.

Without thinking, Emil turned and broke into a run, feet folding inwards beneath him like a puppet being dragged by its strings. Unlike his mother or sister, Emil was not physically fit, and he had the feeling as he was moving that what he was doing might not look like running, but like some other, less athletic verb: ambling or shambling or even limping with haste. He hadn't participated in school sports for the last year and a half. Every time the allotted hour came to strip off the school uniform and don school-issue navy shorts, Emil came down with a sharp pain in the belly that rendered him unable to move. In any other place, this might have been immediately seen as a ruse, but at St. Isidore's Emil was sent directly to the school psychologist, who said that his stomach issues were a psychosomatic symptom related to a valid and indisputable phobia of engaging in group activity. In this way, Emil gained an extra hour and ten minutes to himself each week, which he generally spent tapping into his computer in the back corner of the library or leafing through books on the Manhattan Project or set theory.

"Why are you running?" said the woman, who appeared to be gaining on him with minimal effort.

Emil wasn't entirely sure why he was running but guessed that it was partly due to having been humiliated at a moment when he'd been feeling both particularly vulnerable and slightly cool. He didn't want to face the cause of his humiliation. He thought she might do something else to humiliate him even further.

The woman caught up with him outside a Cash Converters, its window stocked with forsaken trombones and christening bangles. Emil was bent in half, hyperventilating, his shirt ridden up to expose the pale knuckles of his spine.

"I'm sorry," she said.

Emil allowed himself to be rotated by the woman. Her hands around his wrists felt electrifyingly intimate and Emil wondered if she felt anything in return. The woman's hair framed her face in spikes like an anime character. Her ears were so laden with piercings they hung low on her head.

"I'm sorry, okay? What I did was shitty, but I had some of my own stuff going on, and I got caught up in it, and that was shitty of me. I didn't mean to screw you over." She raised her eyebrows as though daring him to suggest otherwise. "Do you accept my apology?"

The woman looked genuinely apologetic. Her nails had been chewed down to bloody slivers.

"I don't even know your name," said Emil, quietly.

"What?"

"I don't know what your name is," he said.

"I'm Alice," said Alice. "And once again, I'm sorry."

Arthur's casts came off, his stitches dissolved into his scalp, and the makeshift bed in the living room was disassembled, its components returned to their rightful places. Yara opened every downstairs window in the house and hoovered up the clots of dust and fluff that had accumulated beneath the mattress while it lay on the living room carpet. Her last act of tidying was to stow her husband's new collection of books beneath the television. She handled them with the reluctance of a dog-owner picking up after an unwell pet.

The books had titles like *Doing Good Better* and *The Aid Trap* and *There Is No Charity*. One caught her eye because the cover was a blurry photo, the font a curlicued kind of seventies writing that made her think of disco music. The title was *Reasons and Persons* by Derek Parfit. She flipped open the book and read a sentence: "... my existence was such a further fact, I seemed imprisoned in myself. My life seemed like a glass tunnel, through which I was moving faster every year, and at the end of which there was darkness. When I changed my view, the walls of my glass tunnel disappeared. I now live ..." She closed the book and arranged it with the others in a neat stack beside the old DVDs under the TV. These were the films the kids had watched religiously when they'd been small: Disney and Pixar and Studio Ghibli. These were the stories that they had watched again and again, learning the lines and the songs and the dances, memorising the jokes, acting out the action sequences by leaping off the coffee table and onto arrangements of sofa cushions.

As a teenager, Yara had always imagined that her family, when she had one, would be an inseparable band of bantering adventurers, going forth into the world together, on road trips and holidays and outings to restored castles or spangly caves. She had never expected that they would be four people conducting four entirely separate lives out of the same building, like businesses sharing space in a shopping arcade, their owners nodding to each other as they arrived early to roll up the shutters.

7.

One afternoon toward the middle of June, as the lavender fields came alive and tourists jostled for space along the riverbank, Arthur returned home without his car. When Yara asked where it was, he claimed to have dropped it off at the garage for some "minor repair work."

"Which garage?" she said.

"Oh," said Arthur. "You know."

Yara didn't know and couldn't tell what was happening. Online, she continued to devour articles about post-concussion syndrome and brain injuries and detailed accounts written by people whose spouses, children, or parents had emerged from accidents acting eccentrically.

One woman said that her sister had bashed her head while skiing in Chamonix and returned home with an unquenchable desire to create obtrusively large pieces of abstract art. Someone's husband had been mugged in an alleyway behind an Irish pub and become obsessed with visiting the zoo. One young father, who couldn't tell whether his son's problem was the result of a skateboarding accident or heavy drug use, said his fifteen-year-old boy had started ingesting paper clips, pencil shavings, and copper coins.

None of them bore much of a resemblance to what Arthur had undergone. They were all too clearly symptoms of illness. The personality shifts were always so obviously negative, and though Yara viewed her husband's transformation as fundamentally problematic, she knew there were others who would perceive it as being a cause for celebration. No one else knew Arthur Candlewick well enough to understand how categorically this new person wasn't him. He didn't chew like Arthur, didn't laugh like Arthur, didn't speak or walk or think like Arthur. But what more could she tell medical professionals? He didn't get lost, didn't leave the oven on, didn't wander into the living room clutching a whisk without being able to explain why. He read books that belonged in the reference libraries of prestigious universities. He watched three-hour-long lectures given by left-wing politicians and UNHCR representatives.

No longer able to rely on finding peace in the house, Yara retreated to a twenty-four-hour gym in Stroud, where she completed gruelling back-to-back CrossFit classes until she could barely muster the energy to depress the pedals in her car. She sat in the car park watching Korean soaps on her phone and drinking cans of Red Bull until she had the strength to drive home. As she made her way from the Porsche to the front door, her legs trembled like a newborn calf.

Arthur occasionally left Bourton on the Gloucester bus, with an old thermos filled with herbal tea and a plastic takeaway carton of mixed nuts and dry crackers. After a call with Brian Clinks, Yara was relieved to hear that he seemed at least to be allowing the Riverwild sale to go ahead. Occasionally, while heading out to the gym or the bank or to meet with Oscar La Mesa, the handyman who took care of the three rented houses in Brockworth, Yara would catch a glimpse of Arthur sitting on a bench in the village or watching himself in the stream, and feel as though she was in a kind of horror film, where her husband had been replaced by an automaton or an alien, or possessed by a spirit that was biding its time before revealing the extent of its horrific designs.

She tentatively posted on one of the forums she'd been lurking on, careful not to divulge any personal data. She wrote that her husband had fallen from a great height and become obsessed with reading books on foreign development. She wrote about feeling alone in her marriage and afraid and unable to envisage a future she wanted to head toward. The responses came in almost immediately.

Sounds like hubbie had a tragic accident and wifey wasn't there for him afterwards. He's the one who's been through something harrowing, not you, Mrs. Melodrama.

Was that true? Had Yara been so frightened by the shift in Arthur's personality that she hadn't found the capacity to support him? She didn't think so: she'd taken him to specialists, she'd built him a bed.

> To be actually totally honest that does not sound like much of a problem such as some of us have on this forum, so please check yourself, I would do anything so that my husband just read a lot of books about other countrys but he actually gets so angry its scarey

Yara scrolled further through the meagre selection of replies.

> You just gotta reconnect. Maybe things r a little different now. But accept that. Roll with the punches. Find your husband again. He's in there somewhere.

After returning home from a trip to the Stroud library, Arthur found Yara in the living room, dressed in a black chenille dress she'd bought six years earlier for the Women in Tech Awards in Leicester, the existence of which she found slightly patronising but not patronising enough to decline an invitation to, despite the fact she hadn't won anything and spent the majority of the evening smoking borrowed cigarettes on a terrace overlooking the city.

Arthur stopped in the doorway, with the shocked and slightly put-upon look of someone who's just walked into their own intervention. He was clutching a plastic Tesco bag filled with tangerine peel, two empty water bottles, and a thermos containing dregs of chamomile tea.

"This is ridiculous," said Yara. "We're like ships in the night, Arthur. It's time we went out."

"Out?"

"To dinner. I want to hear what you've been up to, how you're feeling, how things are at work."

"I'm very tired, poppet."

"Then have a coffee."

Arthur tried to protest but was told to go upstairs and put on something "halfway decent," so that they could go and eat and drink together like civilised adults. He returned from the bedroom fifteen minutes later, wearing a rumpled gingham shirt and corduroy shorts with one of the pockets turned inside out. Yara pushed the pocket back into itself.

"Will I do?" said Arthur.

"You'll do," said Yara.

A taxi at the bottom of the drive honked.

The restaurant was an Italian two villages over and Yara had booked a table despite them arriving to find that, aside from an elderly man at the bar frowning at an Agatha Christie novel over a glass of red wine, they were the only two guests. They were shown to seats at a window overlooking a stone weir splitting a shallow stream into levels beside an old mill. The mill had been converted into flats stapled with Juliet balconies, the windows crowded with children's drawings and drying clothes. Two shire horses captained by young women in black velveteen helmets clopped around a bend of blackthorn hedge.

A young waitress in running shoes took their order: tap water and a bottle of 2019 white Bordeaux, selected by Yara because the name had been dimly familiar, as though she'd encountered it once before in a dream.

"This is nice," she said, lifting her open menu until it obscured her face.

"Yes, poppet," said Arthur, straining his neck to watch the tail of one of the horses swing in the air one last time before disappearing round the corner.

The waitress reappeared and uncorked the wine and placed Arthur's tap water down onto his paper placemat so clumsily that it spilled.

"I'll take the carpaccio to start," said Yara. "And then the tagliatelle with venison."

"And I'll just have the bread," said Arthur. "The free bread, that comes in the basket."

The waitress hesitated, pen hovering over a pad that wasn't really a pad but a block of wheat-yellow Post-it notes.

"Arthur," said Yara. "You're not just having bread." She paired their menus and passed them over. "He'll have the linguine and he'll enjoy it very much."

Arthur sighed.

"They're doing a big *Vanya* again in London," said Yara, once the waitress was out of sight. "It's that kind of seedy actor from *Game of Thrones* playing every part."

"Really?" said Arthur.

"I thought we might find time to make a trip over and see it."

"Maybe, poppet."

They'd seen *Uncle Vanya* together on their second date, thirty years earlier, and had both got so drunk on champagne that the play had felt like a religious experience. Afterwards, they'd walked aimlessly around the West End, smoking and laughing and marvelling at how something written so long ago by someone so far removed from their own experiences could conjure such emotion in them both.

The wicker basket of bread arrived, along with a ceramic dish shaped like a serrano pepper split into two sections, one holding olive oil and the other balsamic vinegar. Yara smiled at her husband, waiting for him to speak. Arthur smiled back, squinting to get a better view of a man outside wrestling with a mud-struck Labrador, before realising that he was expected to say something.

"This dish is shaped like a pepper," he said.

"Arthur," said Yara.

"Yes?" said Arthur.

"Let me start: I realise I might not have been too sensitive to your needs since the accident. I was so caught up trying to make sure you were okay, that I forgot to even ask how you were feeling."

"Oh," said Arthur. "Well, thank you, poppet. I know you're just worried."

"Is there anything you'd like to say to me?"

Arthur tore a scrap of bread in two and steeped it in vinegar. "I do have something to tell you," he said. "And I'd like to say, first of all, that I know I must have seemed slightly strange to you since the accident and I'm sorry, I can see it scared you."

"It did, Arthur. It does."

An ember of hope began to glow in Yara. If her husband could see that he was malfunctioning, then surely he wasn't really malfunctioning at all. The pilot light was still on. The safety features were operational.

"I confess, I've been rather preoccupied. Part of this is because I stumbled into a world I hadn't been previously aware of."

"This stuff in Evangeline's books?"

"Exactly," said Arthur, beaming at the apparently unexpected expression of understanding. "It's all about how much good we're in a position to do."

"We?"

"The well-to-do, you know. It's a matter of assessing where a pound might have the most impact. For you or me, one pound goes essentially nowhere. It's something that we might lose without noticing down the back of a sofa. But when given to the right organisation, that pound might pay for a malaria net that could save the life of a child. And the same goes for ten or a hundred or a thousand times that amount."

"Right," said Yara, nervously.

"There's this organisation, well several really, but groups of people who aim to live by some of those principles. One is called Giving What We Can."

"Okay," said Yara. "And what does that entail exactly?"

"Well, everyone who takes the pledge promises to give at least ten per cent of their income to a group of charities that have been selected by the organisation based on how effective they are at helping people. They use these remarkable things called QALYs to break it all down. One QALY is equivalent to one year of good, healthy, human life, with all a person's needs met, and you can use them to compare the value of various interventions. Fixing a cleft palate, for example, might give someone eighty QALYs at a cost of two hundred pounds, while supplying iron to someone deficient in it might provide thirty QALYs at a cost of ten pounds. Isn't that wonderful?"

Yara took a moment to absorb the information. It felt so irrelevant to what she was feeling about her husband that she wasn't sure what to do with it. "That's a very noble idea, Arthur, but I'd suggest we wait a few months before making any big decisions. We've got a lot on at the moment."

"Well," said Arthur. "Okay, but I've already joined."

Yara set down her knife and fork and pushed the half-eaten plate of carpaccio to one side. "You've pledged to give away ten per cent," she said. "Of what?"

The waitress returned to their table holding two steaming dishes of pasta.

"That was too fast," said Yara, abruptly.

The waitress looked terrified.

"We like this plate," said Arthur, pointing to the pepper. "Very snazzy."

"Should I take your mains back?"

"No," said Yara. "They're here now. Just leave them."

The waitress lowered their plates with trepidation and performed an almost imperceptible bow before moving away.

Yara ignored her food. "Tell me now, Arthur, have you already given away ten per cent of something?"

"Well, poppet," said Arthur. "Ten per cent is kind of a minimum. The spirit of the thing is that you give as much as you can without really impacting your own life. It's amazing the amount of—"

"Arthur, what have you done?"

Arthur moved his glass of tap water in a slow orbit around his plate. "Before we get too much into the weeds on this, I'd really like to explain some of the fundamental principles of the movement."

"Arthur, I'm seriously not in the mood. Just tell me what you've done, now."

The waitress was back and clutching a mottled brick of parmesan and a microplane grater with the uncertainty of a squire bearing his master's heavy weaponry.

"Fresh parmesan?" she whispered.

"Will you give us a fucking moment?" said Yara.

"Yara," said Arthur.

"Sorry," said the waitress.

"Sorry," said Yara.

The waitress departed.

The tap water made another lap of the linguine.

"I've given the money away," said Arthur.

"I'm sorry?"

"The proceeds from the sale, I've given it away."

"From the sale of Riverwild? You've completed?"

"Yes."

"And you're trying to tell me you've given away the money to charity?"

"My share, minus taxes due, yes."

"No, Arthur."

"Sorry?"

"No, you haven't done that. I'm sorry, but that isn't what you've done."

"Well, I'm sorry, but it is."

"To who? Who did you give it to?"

"That's what I was trying to explain. How to Save a Life is an organisation that distributes funds to the most effective charities operating globally."

Yara genuinely felt as though she might throw up. She whipped the red serviette from the breadbasket and held it against her mouth.

"You're joking," she said.

"I'm afraid not, poppet."

Arthur struggled to read the look that came over his wife's face. He knew it was not a look that he'd ever seen before and never wanted to see again.

"Wait here, Arthur. Don't move, okay?"

Arthur nodded and shook open the origami swan that had been perched beside his plate, spreading it across his lap. He wasn't hungry and the bowl of linguine sat untouched before him, the half-opened clams staring at him like tired eyes among the heap of buttery pasta, garnished with dried heads of pansy flowers.

In a blood-red bathroom decorated with tin signs advertising olive oil and motor scooters, Yara called Brian Clinks.

"What?" he said, evidently in the middle of his own meal.

"Was the sale completed?"

"Yeah, last week. Arthur not tell you?"

"Which account was his money sent to?"

"I'm sorry?"

"Where was it paid?

"I dunno, Yawa. You'd have to ask Sammy. I'm not the accountant."

"Can you ask?"

"What, now?"

"Yes, now."

Brian grumbled and sighed and said, "I could check in the thing," without elaborating on what the thing was. She heard him heft his weight from one room to another and type painfully slowly into a keyboard that clicked too loudly to have been made this decade. "He changed the details for his transfer from the usual," he said. "It's to some other account, NatWest, under his name, last numbers is 8919."

"And you didn't think to tell me?"

"Why would I tell you?"

"Because he's lost his fucking mind, you asshat."

"Alright, there's no need to get nasty. How am I supposed to know you wasn't in the loop?"

"Because you've interacted with him. You know what he's like."

"He's gone a little off-piste but I'm not about to try and get between the man and his money. I'm not his doctor."

Yara hung up and watched her reflection in the bathroom mirror. Was there a way to undo a donation to charity? What if the donor could be proven to be suffering from severe mental illness? Surely, in that case, the charity couldn't hold onto the funds? Unless they'd already spent the money? She wasn't sure if she was allowed to be angry, she couldn't tell if her husband was out of his mind.

She returned to their table in the empty restaurant and drained her glass of wine and poured another and drained that.

"Are you okay?" said Arthur.

"Do I look like I'm fucking okay, Arthur?"

"I'm sorry, poppet."

"If you call me poppet one more time, I will climb across this table and shake you." The threat seemed strange and hollow and Arthur bit his lower lip. "You didn't even tell me you completed," said Yara.

"Oh, well, we did, yes. Last week. Signed and sealed."

"You didn't ask me about any of this."

"In my defence, you would have said no."

Yara clutched the tablecloth with both hands as though preparing to drag it off the table. "Yes, Arthur, I would have said no. Because you don't just sell the company you spent your life building and give away the money, not when you have a family to look after, not without consulting your fucking wife."

"At the risk of sounding silly, poppet, why not?"

"Because that's not the promise we made for each other. Because I had a plan. Because you consult your family on a decision that affects your family. We have to live, Arthur. We have to survive."

"But we'll survive regardless of whether we're still millionaires when we're eighty."

"Grow up, Arthur."

"What does that even mean, poppet?"

"You know exactly what it means. It means not having some kind of teenage communist freak-out when you're fifty-five years old. Go to India if you want to. Sit in a fucking ashram and meditate on how we're all connected children of the universe but do not drop us in the shit when you have your funny five minutes. You're a grown man who has to look after his fucking family."

"But you're all looked after. None of you are sick or starving. We have a beautiful home and wardrobes full of clothes and two cars and we won't lose any of that. Why do we want so much more than we need?"

"We have enough to be comfortable and safe and to leave the children with enough to be comfortable and safe too."

"Why leave them something? Why deprive them of the opportunity to make something for themselves?"

"What if something happens, Arthur?"

"What would happen?"

"Anything! Anything could happen. The climate is going insane and robots are taking over and fucking plagues are spreading across the planet."

"What could happen to us?"

"Who the fuck knows, Arthur? What kind of jobs will there be left for our kids? How will they afford houses? How will they afford to have lives of their own or children or weddings with cake and food and music?"

"I'm not sure wedding cake is the most important thing in the world."

"You don't get to decide that. So what if I want our children to have fancy cakes at their ludicrous weddings? Don't I get a say?"

"Yes, but what if Emil said he wanted a five-hundred-pound wedding cake while there was a child standing beside whose life would be saved by a five-hundred-pound heart operation?"

"Oh, get a grip, Arthur. There is no choice because there is no other child. There are our two children, who we created, who we are responsible for, and who you are fucking over by making this ridiculous decision without so much as a single word to me."

"I'm hardly fucking them over."

"We're comfortable, Arthur. All anyone wants is to be comfortable."

"We own four houses beside our own, poppet."

"Because we both worked damn hard for years."

"A lot of people work very hard. Cobalt miners in the Congo work very hard."

"What does that have to do with anything? We're not cobalt miners."

"No, poppet, but only through sheer dumb luck."

"You're ill, Arthur."

"I don't feel ill, poppet."

"You fell and you hit your head and now you're brain-damaged."

"I don't think I am, poppet. I think you're just upset."

"Arthur, I'm a lot fucking more than upset." For the first time, Yara looked away from her husband and toward the saloon doors leading into the kitchen, wishing for some inexplicable reason that the inept waitress would return. "I knew I should have done something," she said. "I shouldn't have let those doctors tell us you were okay. You shouldn't have been let out of the hospital. I should have forced them to keep you in. To keep scanning or testing or what have you." The wine had reached her brain now and she could feel the machinery of thought flailing. "I should have made them put you in a mental ward."

"But I'm okay, poppet."

"You're not okay, Arthur. You're out of your mind."

Yara picked up her knife and put it back down again, not trusting herself to not do something stupid.

"We've helped an awful lot of people," said Arthur.

"Shut the fuck up, Arthur, okay? Just shut your fucking mouth."

In the taxi on the way home, Yara clutched the window-winder as though afraid she was about to be launched through the roof by an ejector seat. She didn't know who she was meant to call. She didn't know how to fix what was happening.

8.

On the last day of each term, it was customary for the majority of St. Isidore's students to catch buses into the town centres of Cheltenham, Stroud, or Gloucester, and loiter in parks and alleyways, stuffing their school ties into their pockets before trying to talk strangers into buying them cheap alcohol. Evangeline had never participated in the tradition, choosing instead to retire either to her house or to Ada's, where the two girls would steal a bottle of wine or champagne and drink it while watching *Gilmore Girls* or *Ally McBeal* or *Grey's Anatomy*, which they commentated over as though they were watching ironically, but which they both in reality felt deeply emotionally connected to, the American actresses in these decades-old programmes having accompanied them now through almost half of their lives.

Emil usually went alone to the cinema in Stroud to watch whatever film was set the furthest in the future. At the end of year eleven, he had two weed gummies in his left pocket, which he was planning to consume while entering the new Marvel film, despite knowing that it would leave him feeling like a child who had been given the wrong present at Christmas.

He peeled a damp sock off the back of his locker and dropped it into his rucksack.

"Emil?"

It was Imogen Enderby, a girl from an adjacent form who tramped through school in fleece-lined boots, with gel pen drawings of eyeballs and burning churches sketched onto her forearms. She was wearing a Breton jumper over her school shirt and her hair was massed in a loose bun atop her narrow, porcelain head.

"Um," said Emil. "Hello?"

"You coming into Gloucester with everyone?"

"Um," said Emil. "I don't think so."

"There's a hill party afterwards, up Robinswood. Me, Luca, and Kaya are going. We have a tent and everything, but I don't know if we'll really sleep there."

Emil glanced over her shoulder at Luca Henderson and Kaya Patel. He'd never spoken to either of them, beyond awkwardly discussing exothermic reactions with Kaya when they'd been partnered up during a chemistry lesson.

"Okay," said Emil.

"Come," said Imogen. "Unless you have other plans. I know Deepesh is away."

She was right, Deepesh had left school three days earlier, to catch a flight to Bali with his dad so they could trek up the side of an active volcano. Lewis was flying to Ibiza with his family, who he claimed had won their holiday through one of the online competitions his mum entered while bored at work.

Emil wondered whether the invitation was some kind of trap, whether he'd be led out to the wilderness, talked out of his clothes, and left to hitchhike home, shivering, with his testicles flush against his body like limpets. But Imogen Enderby didn't belong to the stratum of students likely to inflict cruel pranks on anyone and Emil didn't belong to the group of recurring victims likely to be chosen as targets. She was looking at him with something like curiosity. She had the peaceful, harmless gaze of a dairy cow and a mole on the tip of her nose. During last year's school production of *The Crucible*, she'd actually made herself cry on stage and it had given rise to a brief and bizarre strain of rumours—"Did you hear about Imogen Enderby?" "Apparently she actually cried in the play." "Apparently she was knifing herself with a corkscrew through the pocket." "Apparently she was thinking of when Daniel Dickinson broke up with her because he asked her to shave off her pubes."

"Emil?"

Emil nodded, thinking that if necessary, he could ditch them in Gloucester and try to catch a screening of something at the cinema in the Quays instead. They rode together on the top deck of the 94 and Emil was surprised to find the conversation relatively painless. He sat with his feet pressed flat on the front window and one AirPod in, playing an old Flying Lotus album that sounded like a rush of clicks and glitches. This was a pre-emptive attempt to look as though he wasn't at all bothered about being in their presence and would barely even notice if they decided to spontaneously abandon him. Although it stemmed from a place of deep insecurity, this calculated nonchalance gave Emil an undeniable air of enviable aloofness.

"Is it true you hang out with older kids in town?" said Kaya.

Emil shrugged. "Sometimes," he said.

"Your sister's friends?"

"No," said Emil. "Evangeline only hangs out with Ada and Leona and their dickhead boyfriends."

"I can't believe she threw blood onto Victoria's dad. That was so insane."

Emil felt an unexpected surge of pride. "It wasn't blood," he said. "It was paint. They thought it was acrylic but it turned out to be oil."

"Insane," repeated Kaya.

"Batshit," said Luca.

"Was it really a protest?" said Imogen.

"Yeah," said Emil. "Against the investment company Victoria's dad runs. They make money from weapons and drugs."

"That's clapped," said Kaya.

"Total bullshit," said Luca.

In town, they stopped for paper-wrapped bundles of soggy chips and carried them through the uneven, half-empty high street to the grounds of the cathedral, where delegations of pupils from several local schools were mixing drinks and smoking and vaping. Some were tangled together on the threadbare grass, sucking at each other's faces or giggling at each other's phones or wrestling with half-hearted seriousness, their white shirts tiger-striped with dirt and grass.

Someone passed Emil a bottle of supermarket cola mixed with half a bottle of supermarket vodka and Emil glugged from it, dislodging a little of the tension in his shoulders. He felt like a zoo animal, unexpectedly released into the wild and expected to function as nature had intended him to. He sat between Imogen and Kaya with his back against the cold stone of the cathedral. Kaya pointed out a tall boy in a Marshfield Lane uniform and said that his name was Aaron Reyes and that his brother had ploughed into a toddler in his Mondeo last summer. Luca aimed her finger at a girl in a pink balaclava and asked when balaclavas had become a thing.

A Bluetooth speaker was produced from a bag, set atop a rucksack, and tasked with blaring Bad Bunny at the blank blue sky. On the path leading through the grounds, a pair of community support officers glanced warily at the assembled teenagers.

Imogen tugged on Emil's sleeve and asked if he'd go with her to buy Sprite as a remedy for her slight vertigo. As they walked, she pulled strands of hair across her lips as though she was licking an envelope.

"Why didn't we ever hang out before?" she said.

"I don't know," said Emil.

"Actually, I do. You know, people are kind of scared of you."

"Scared of me?"

"There's a rumour you've smoked crack and you're in Mensa."

"I haven't smoked crack," said Emil. "My mum made me and Imogen take the Mensa test when we were younger. I didn't want to. I think it's stupid."

"But you passed?"

"So would you," said Emil. "It's not hard."

"I don't think so," said Imogen. "The only thing I can do is art and that's a different thing. I don't have the right kind of brain for that other stuff."

"Brains can change," said Emil. "Especially our brains, while we're young. They just need to practise."

"Maybe," said Imogen. "But don't they choose the things they want to practise?"

The comment caused a fuse to burn out in Emil's mind. It was the same kind of glitch he experienced when he tried to imagine an infinitesimally small point or an infinitely large universe, or when he thought about black holes swallowing light, or how consciousness was matter observing itself.

"What do your parents do?" said Emil, which sounded like good, solid ground to return to.

"Mum used to work for the RSC," said Imogen. "Now she's on some boards for stuff and helps with the literature festival in Cheltenham." Emil didn't know what RSC stood for. It sounded some-how close enough to RSPCA that he assumed it was something to do with animals. "Dad's a barrister, the boring kind. He has his own chambers. What about yours?"

"My mum's retired, she used to be a programmer. My dad sold his company."

"What was his company?"

"Just wood."

Why did he say "just"? What wouldn't have been preceded by "just"? Just diamonds? Just shock collars? Just nuclear weapons?

"At least wood is sustainable. You know Kaya's parents both work in marketing for AbinBev?"

"What's that?"

"They own like every alcohol brand you've ever tried."

"Oh," said Emil. "I guess that's worse than wood."

"Way worse than wood."

They walked on and Emil felt both safe in the silence and afraid that he was proving himself to be insufficiently exciting for Imogen to want to continue with their time alone. "My parents are getting a divorce," he said, hoping that this was an interesting fact to reveal about himself.

Imogen came to a sudden halt, as though remembering she'd for-gotten to perform a crucial safety procedure. "Emil, that's awful. I'm sorry."

"It's okay," said Emil. "I don't mind."

"Of course you mind. It's an incredibly traumatic thing for you to be going through. You have to make sure you don't blame yourself."

"I don't blame myself," said Emil. "I blame my dad."

"My aunt and uncle got a divorce and now one of my cousins is in prison for punching a waitress at Pizza Express."

"And I already smoke crack," said Emil.

Imogen grinned and slapped him across the back of the shoulder.

By the time they returned to the cathedral grounds, something tentative existed between them, and in the fuzzy warmth of the vodka, Emil let his fingers dance near Imogen's, until she breathed a sigh of impatience and took hold of his hand.

Later, the 94 bus took them out of town and onto the Golden Valley, past the angular Evangelical church on the roundabout, and the huddle of discount supermarkets opposite the crematorium, and the conifer plantation, the bowling alley, the industrial park, and the recycling centre, until they were free of the city, passing fields where bales of hay were parked at regular intervals like limbless creatures sleeping against the stubbly ground.

They got off the bus at the Tuffley stop and hopped a fence into a field overgrown with brambles and sheaves of fluffy-headed meadow grass. By the time they reached the crop of trees at the top of Robinswood Hill, there was already a fire burning in a rusted barbecue. Groups of kids were smoking and drinking and scrolling on phones, some lounging in half-erected tents, some crouched on yoga mats and flattened rucksacks.

Emil took the two weed gummies from his pocket and passed one to Imogen.

"I've never done drugs before," she said.

"It's okay," said Emil. "I'll take care of you."

It was Brian Clinks who'd pushed for the renegotiated Riverwild deal to be closed before the summer holidays began, so that he could leave for an all-inclusive three weeks in Mallorca without his four children, who would be attending a free, residential Christian camp in Wiltshire; not because they were Christian but because it was free and Brian Clinks couldn't stand the squawking of his offspring in the sweaty fog of his hangovers.

He'd barely spoken to Arthur since his business partner had last returned to their premises on an industrial estate at the edge of Gloucester. During a meeting with the company accountant, in a room scattered with crushed Relentless cans and decorated with pages torn from porn magazines, Arthur sat smiling like a stoned teenager while the accountant, Samuel Ahmed, danced his mouse across a flickering monitor. Though neither Brian nor Arthur would be accepting the offer of staying on as consultants, Ted Markow had, at the last minute, opted to remain, and they were attempting to revise the share settlements to reflect this.

Arthur was sitting on his hands.

"You doing okay, Arthur?" said Samuel.

"Oh, yes," said Arthur.

"Good to hear. Sounds like you took quite a tumble."

Arthur picked up a Newton's cradle from the desk and promptly dropped it on the floor. Samuel looked up from the screen.

"Samuel," he said. "I'd like you to imagine you're walking past a child drowning in a pool of water."

Samuel looked over at Brian nervously and Brian held an open hand up to Arthur's face. "Arthur, will you give it a rest?"

"What's he talking about?" said Samuel.

"It's some kind of pyramid scheme."

"It's not a pyramid scheme," said Arthur. "It's an analogy that illustrates the moral case for donating a portion of your income to non-profit organisations."

"Right," said Samuel. He pointed to the screen. "I'm just going to finish with this, okay?"

"You go ahead, Sam," said Brian.

After the meeting, Arthur went down into the warehouse where planks of rosewood were being cut into bungs for whisky barrels and asked one of the workers to vacate his seat on a forklift truck. Brian Clinks watched him from a safe distance, anxiously rotating the Divemaster on his chubby wrist. The hijacked forklift careened dangerously close to a tower of pallets loaded with planters destined for a garden centre. Brian called Yara.

"Can you come and pick up your husband?" he said. "He's scaring the lads."

A month later, the deal had been finalised and Arthur's portion of the proceeds had entered his new bank account and promptly left it, after he had visited his branch to request a temporary exemption to the transfer limit. He had spent the preceding weeks with a donation advisor discussing, at length, how best to split the money he was gearing up to donate through the umbrella organisation How to Save a Life.

During the first stages of his divorce from Yara, which took place in a sequence of dark solicitor's offices in soulless buildings, it would transpire that the proceeds of the takeover weren't the only thing Arthur Candlewick had given away.

The BMW had been sold.

The Krugerrands had vanished from the safety deposit box in Solihull.

One investment account had been entirely emptied.

And three relatively valuable signed prints by New York abstract
expressionists were no longer in the attic.

All of the money had gone to the same organisation, who had split
it between several more organisations, who had either spent or begun
to spend it, on projects and programmes clustered mostly around sub-
Saharan Africa, Central South America, and Northeast India.

Arthur came to one of the early meetings with a list written in
pencil on an endpaper torn out of *Great Expectations*. He'd written:

*One year of education for 300 girls in Kerala. Removal of poisonous lead
from six hospitals in Malawi. Direct monetary aid for 100 families living in
extreme rural poverty in Guatemala.*

He was trying to show his wife what good they'd done. Yara accepted the note and promptly threw it into a wire bin.

With Yara insisting that Arthur was mentally unfit to have given
away all of the assets listed solely under his name, and Arthur insisting that he was sane and pleased with his decision, there was no
resolution in sight. A court date was set. Arthur slept in a sleeping bag
on the floor of the vardo wagon at the bottom of the garden. He ate
baked beans from the tin and cold pouches of pre-cooked rice. When
Yara left the house, he let himself in through the kitchen, to use the
toilet and the shower and to make himself a new thermos of floral tea.

Ada van der Volk's house was a stack of glass cubes perched on the
side of Ruscombe Valley, with views of vast fields sparsely grazed
by sluggish cows, the boxy steeple of Whiteshill church, and clusters of cream-stone houses much older and smaller than the van der
Volk mansion. The front door had a fingerprint scanner and a welcome mat that sent warning signals to a surveillance system housed
in the utility room. The glass wall of the master bedroom could turn
opaque at the touch of a button.

In Ada's suite of two rooms overlooking a hill crowned with lanky
pines, the two girls were flicking through the Instagram account of
an American girl who'd got into Cambridge and documented her
experiences with Californian glee. She posted pictures of crumpets

and Cornish pasties, presenting them like a botanist reporting from a newly discovered land.

"Why are we still looking at this?" said Evangeline, who was the one in control of the iPad.

"It's fun."

"It's depressing."

Evangeline let the iPad fall facedown onto her stomach.

"Can you imagine if we both got in?" said Ada. "It would be literally insane."

Evangeline hadn't told her friend about the essay she'd submitted and she wasn't planning to. Some nights, she fell asleep imagining herself wandering the streets of Cambridge, at the centre of a group of people engaged in a debate about the viability of rebranding communism using social media. She saw herself smoking, sophisticatedly, while discordant music played from a group of morose jazz musicians. She saw herself elbow-to-elbow with floppy-haired men at a long mahogany desk in a cathedral-like library. Ada van der Volk was not present in any of these daydreams.

"You shouldn't get too invested in one outcome," said Evangeline.

"I'm not," said Ada. "I'm just saying. It would be nice."

"We ought to commemorate today," said Evangeline. "We don't know how our paths might diverge from here."

Ada flopped onto the floor and crawled under her four-poster bed like a marine, returning with a stuffed donkey, unzipping its stomach, and holding out a baggie containing two pink pills.

"My cousin gave me these," she said.

"Why?"

"He says I need to have some fun."

"He sounds like a creep."

"He's actually really nice. He's going to be a vet."

"Isn't it repulsive to think that animals have doctors, while there are humans suffering in the world?"

"It's just a job, Evangeline."

The pills looked very small in the palm of her hand. Evangeline had, for some reason, pictured ecstasy tablets as being around the size of a two-pound coin and consumed in several bites, like a cookie. The only time Evangeline had taken drugs before was during a house party at the end of year eleven, when she'd inhaled too ambitiously from a joint of pure weed and thrown up into her own lap. It was the kind of episode that for a lesser mortal would have resulted in social exile but Evangeline had only sighed and pulled her T-shirt off over her head so that she was sitting in her underwear, her eyes melting down her face.

She plucked the pink pill off her friend's hand and held it a few centimetres from her right eye, twisting it in the crude halogen light like a jeweller.

"I think they're meant to make you, like, feel connected to the world."

"They're entheogens," said Evangeline, who had researched the most popular recreational drugs after overhearing a conversation in which her parents argued about whether to send Emil to a residential rehab centre. "If they're too heavily contaminated with cutting agents, we could be poisoning ourselves. Also, we should hydrate properly and leave a note for our parents saying what we've taken."

"In case we die?"

"In case we pass out and become unresponsive."

"So we're taking them?"

"You're the one who just got them out, Ada."

"I was just going to show you."

"It's our last day ever, we might as well make it eventful."

Evangeline threw her pill back with the last of the acidic wine from her mug. Ada followed suit before promptly clasping her hands over her mouth in horror.

"Oh my god," she said.

"Calm down," said Evangeline. "No-one's going to know."

"No," said Ada. "I think it might, like, interreact with my other pills."

"You're still taking those?"

"Yeah."

"Why?"

"Because you're not my doctor, Evangeline, and you don't get to tell me what to do."

Evangeline raised an eyebrow and smirked at her friend, amused

by both her outburst and the obvious pride she took in finally standing up for herself. Seeing that Evangeline found her protest funny
rather than admonishing, Ada's pride ebbed away, and was replaced
by a desire to go into the bathroom and make herself try to puke the
pill up, so that she could claim to be feeling ill and tell Evangeline
she had to go home.

"Alright," said Evangeline. "I'm calling a taxi."

They found Arthur Candlewick sitting in his garden, with a blanket spread out across his lap and *Capital* by Thomas Piketty cradled
in his hands like a Bible. He was reading by the light of a motion-
activated patio light that meant he had to get to his feet and swing
his hands over his head once every three minutes.

"Mr. Candlewick?"

Arthur looked up. Despite having no idea who the two people
in his garden were, he waved at them. One of them waved back,
became self-conscious, and clenched his hand into a loose fist before lowering it to his side. Both men were in their early forties and
wearing chinos with fleeces. Arthur wondered whether they might
be Jehovah's Witnesses.

"Hello, Mr. Candlewick. My name is Will, this is Clive, we're
community psychiatric nurses from the Gloucestershire Crisis Resolution Team. We've had reports from someone who's concerned you
might be experiencing a mental health crisis."

"Ah," said Arthur. "Have you really?"

"How are you feeling, Mr. Candlewick?"

"A little tired, to be honest. But in general, very good."

The truth was that Arthur Candlewick felt better than he had since
he was a teenager. For the first time in his life, he woke up knowing
exactly what he wanted to do and found himself possessed of all the
energy he needed to do it. He was discovering his place in the world,
excavating his own context, like a burial chamber yielding layer after
layer of mythology.

"Do you mind if we ask you a few questions?"

"Be my guest," said Arthur. "Could I get you something to drink?
Tea? Coffee?"

"We're okay, thank you, Mr. Candlewick."

One of the nurses glanced around the garden and dragged two wrought iron chairs across the patio, their feet screeching on the stone. He set them up in front of Arthur and both men sat down.

"You were seeing a therapist, a number of years ago."

Arthur nodded. "She was very nice," he said. "But we ran out of things to discuss. There are only so many ways to say one's childhood could have done with a few improvements."

"And you were taking citalopram on her recommendation?"

"Correct," said Arthur. "For a number of years."

During those years, Arthur had not once cried at the correct moment. He had not cried on his wedding day or when either of his children had been born. He had not cried when Yara had suffered a miscarriage or when his father had been cremated and shaken out of a cardboard urn and into the Aegean sea. He had, however, cried in the cinema watching *Monsters, Inc.* and he had cried during Eurovision 2007 and he had cried when BBC News announced that Princess Margaret had died following a series of strokes.

"Can I ask why you stopped?"

"I stopped," said Arthur, "because I was still depressed, and I'd been taking tablets named anti-depressants for quite a number of years."

"You didn't think they were helping?"

"Oh, I was quite sure they weren't helping."

"But you can never know how you might have been feeling if you hadn't been taking the pills?"

"No," said Arthur. "I suppose not. But if you were taking cold medicine for a decade and your cold didn't go away, you might start to wonder if it wasn't a cold you had after all."

"What else might it be?"

"A general dissatisfaction, I suppose, assuming we've left that metaphor behind and are talking about me again."

"The medicine might still have been keeping your illness at bay."

"Yes," said Arthur. "Or it might just have been making someone else richer." He looked into the faces of the two people in front of him, trying for the first time to discern exactly what their presence in his garden meant. "Am I being sectioned?" he said.

"Do you think you need to be sectioned?"

"I shouldn't think so, no, but I daresay my wife would disagree."

"Can you tell us why you decided to give two point one million pounds from the sale of your company, Riverwild Timber, to a charity named How to Save a Life?"

"Yes," said Arthur. "I can." He straightened his back. "I'd like you to imagine that you're walking home from work one day and you spot a child drowning in a pond."

The two nurses glanced at each other.

"Okay," said one.

"Presumably, you'd plunge directly into the pool in order to try and save the child?"

The two nurses nodded uncertainly.

"But imagine that someone refused to jump in after the child on the grounds that it would ruin his three-hundred-pound pair of John Lobb loafers. We'd consider them utterly immoral, would we not?" One of the nurses glanced down at his shoes, which were a nondescript pair of pleather winkle-pickers. He nodded again. "Now, if it's possible that we can save the life of a child in the developing world for three hundred pounds, then what's the difference between buying the shoes instead of donating the money, and walking past the child drowning in the pool?" Arthur glanced up at the sky, as though searching for confirmation that he'd relayed the analogy correctly. "That was the argument put forward by an ethicist named Peter Singer, in a 1973 *New York Times* article. It was reiterated in a book I borrowed from my daughter and I have to say, I found it utterly compelling."

The nurses shifted in their seats, caught off guard.

"You're saying you read this article and decided to give away all of the money you made from selling your company?"

"More or less," said Arthur. "It was a gradual process, though the article was my jumping-off point."

"But to clarify, you did receive a head injury?"

"Oh, yes," said Arthur. "I had fifteen stitches but it didn't affect my ability to think. I consented to see two specialists and neither could find any cause for concern."

"You can understand why your wife might be concerned?"

"My wife has a wonderful, generous heart, but I'm afraid she's spent it all on our family."

"You and your two children?"

"That's correct."

"Can you tell me their names?"

"Evangeline and Emil."

"And can you tell me if you've had any thoughts about hurting yourself or those around you?"

"Quite the opposite," said Arthur.

"Okay, Mr. Candlewick. Thanks for your time. We'll see ourselves out."

Upstairs, Yara Candlewick pressed her face to the glass, watching her husband wave away two slightly bewildered-looking mental health nurses.

As the last day of term gave way to the morning after the last day of term, Emil was sitting beside Imogen Enderby, her head rested on his shoulder, both with phones in their free hands. They had kissed and it had felt momentous. They had swapped phone numbers and spent most of the evening sending each other messages while sitting knee-to-knee, watching the hill party unfold around them.

Need to wee, wrote Imogen.

Be careful, wrote Emil.

She got up, tapped Emil on the top of the head, and moved away into the darkness.

The night had long since taken on the texture of a dream. Emil was drunk and stoned and the huge mass of people who had accumulated in the woods on Robinswood Hill were growing increasingly rowdy. Other fires had been started, in holes dug into the ground, and there were competing speakers blaring different genres of rap. Two men in Navajo print jackets had set themselves up on a fallen log, selling balloons they filled with nitrous oxide using a whipped cream dispenser.

Emil stared into the flames, thinking about Imogen Enderby.

Through the flickering shadows of the fire, Emil saw his sister. She was draped across a man in his early twenties with a Burberry cap on his head and a too-small polo shirt exposing neon yellow boxers. There were two other similarly dressed men with them, all wearing gold chains around their pencil-thin necks. Ada van der Volk was between the two men, rubbing the grass with both hands as though she were petting a dog.

Emil wondered if the edible had been a lot more potent than he'd imagined. He moved slowly around the fire, dabbing at his eyes, waiting for the vision to resolve itself into something that made more sense.

"Evangeline?" he said.

"Emil?"

His sister extricated herself from the arms of the man in the cap and floated toward him with her arms limp at her sides.

"Why are you here?" said Emil.

"Same reason as you, I expect."

"But you never come out."

"Neither do you."

"Then how would I know you never come out?"

Evangeline signalled for her brother to wait one moment and she ducked back to Ada and the three men, swiped a cigarette from behind someone's ear and plucked a brown glass bottle of Weston's cider from a carrier bag. She led the way and Emil followed until they were free of the trees.

They sat on the crest of the hill beside the thicket and Emil opened the cider with the tail of a lighter wedged in the crook of his thumb and forefinger. Evangeline swiped the lighter and lit the pilfered cigarette.

"You don't smoke," said Emil.

"I'm a social smoker," said Evangeline. "And today I'm being social."

The city spread out at their feet was low and unimpressive, clustered with orange orbs of light linked by streams of red and white traffic. Only the tower of the cathedral punctured the sky with any conviction.

"Do you have to go?" said Emil.

"To university?"

"Yeah," said Emil. "I don't know. I can't be alone with Mum. I don't know what we'll do."

"You don't have to do anything," said Evangeline. "Just finish your last two years and get out. You're so smart, you'll do incredible things."

Emil looked over at his sister. "Are you high?" he said.

"Potentially," said Evangeline. "But that doesn't mean what I'm saying has no merit."

"You don't get high."

"Perhaps I'm a social drug user too. And we're marking the occasion of our last day."

"You told me the illegal drug trade kills innocent children."

"Not the trade in this drug."

Emil wasn't sure he wanted to know which drug his sister was on. It threatened to revive the same disconcerting feeling he'd experienced on finding out his father also masturbated over niche porn. These things were disruptions to the normal order of the world. His family members were not behaving in character.

"Will you come back to visit?"

"Of course," said Evangeline. "I'll come back all the time. And it'll be much more congenial, because we won't all be so sick of each other."

"Do you think Dad's going to be okay?"

"He'll be fine. You'll be fine. I'll be fine. Mum'll be fine. Because we're all, in our own ways, really wonderful people who have a lot to offer the world."

"Oh my god," said Emil, grinning. "You're so high."

Evangeline hugged him and went back to Ada and the three boys with gold chains and Emil lingered where he was, trying to imagine both himself and his sister as elderly people in rocking chairs, before rejoining Imogen at the mouth of the tent and slipping his hand back into hers. *Was that your sister?* she wrote. *Yeah*, Emil wrote back. *She's so pretty*, wrote Imogen. *Gross*, wrote Emil.

A court order attempted, unsuccessfully, to retrieve Arthur's donations from the charities they'd been split between. The money was tumbled together with other funds given through the umbrella organisation and there was no real way of telling what had come from where. Yara agreed to an out-of-court settlement. Alone in the dark of her bedroom, she chain-smoked cigarettes and drank warm chardonnay while Arthur loaded his books and blankets and cardigans into the back of an open-top Riverwild Timber truck and drove out of Bourton-on-the-Water, toward Gloucester.

Part Two

A Place to Sit

9.

It was the year Emil turned seventeen and since the population of
The Old Rectory had halved, it now felt twice as big. With a life
swirling around her at Cambridge, Evangeline very rarely ventured
back down to the village, and Yara was keeping herself occupied
on Dr. Weber's orders, by working part-time at a start-up incuba-
tor attached to a university in Birmingham. She enjoyed the work,
which felt, at least occasionally, like she was involved in something
meaningful. It was enough to distract her but not to wear her out,
given that the stakes were so low, and her only real responsibility
was to help guide young people toward the most realistic goals for
their software projects. After some initial caution, the budding en-
trepreneurs had realised how much she had to offer and Yara found
herself in high demand.

Unlike his sister, Emil received almost no pressure to revise for
A-Levels and wasn't sure whether this was because his mother
didn't care how he did or simply believed that it was a foregone
conclusion. He knew she didn't see the same level of potential in him
as she did his sister, which confused him given that his own talents
more closely resembled Yara's. His mother had rarely tried to relate
to him through their shared love of computers, and although it was
probably true that he'd quite aggressively rebuffed any attempts to
do so during his teenage years, as the end of school loomed into
sight, he found himself wishing that the slightly more anxious, in-
trusive version of his mother would return. The times he had tried
to get her talking on the relative merits of various programming languages, her responses bordered on the patronising. They very rarely

ate together and it became common for entire days to pass in which the two remaining Candlewicks saw nothing of each other at all.

Sleep still crusted in the corners of his eyes, Emil tripped down the stairs, fumbling with a pouch of tobacco and a packet of cigarette papers that had become glued to each other in the humidity of the bathroom while he showered the previous night. He was surprised to find a man standing at the open cutlery drawer clutching a dish-cloth, until his brain cranked into action and he realised that this was the person who'd cleaned their house every week for the majority of his life.

"Hi, Patrice," said Emil.

"Morning."

Emil flung open the fridge door. He had begun to stock it with things he actually liked eating: pre-made fried chicken wraps, Parma ham, cocktail sausages, Babybels, iced tea. Yara hadn't yet commented on this development. She occasionally left businesslike notes on the living room table, asking him to take the recycling bin out or hang up the washing, but she no longer seemed interested in policing his behaviour. Packages of drugs arrived without customs checks. Ultra-processed midnight feasts were assembled and con-sumed in the cosy, indirect light of the kitchen.

"Is Mum here?" Emil asked Patrice.

"Haven't seen her," said Patrice. "Your dad neither."

"Yeah," said Emil. "They got divorced like a year ago."

"Ah," said Patrice. "Your dad find a new lady?"

"Um," said Emil. "I don't think so. He lives in Gloucester now. In a flat by the docks."

Emil closed the fridge. He had been on his way into the garden to smoke and he lifted his tobacco tin to indicate he was going to move on.

"Mind if I join you for a fag?" said Patrice.

"Um," said Emil. "No. I have weed too, if you want it."

"Why would I want it?"

"What?" Emil turned the colour of a radish. "I don't know."

Patrice grinned. "Just fucking around. Sure, if you got a little weed, I'll smoke it."

Patrice and Emil went out into the garden and sat on the stone steps leading down to the lawn, which had withered and sprouted spiky clumps of crabgrass and thistle. There were unnaturally blatant spiderwebs in the windows of the wagon, as though it had been decorated for Halloween, and thin trails of cat shit streaked across the flagstones. Dandelions and threads of moss had grown to occupy the narrow slivers of space between the patio slabs.

"Do you think we're bad people?" said Emil, lighting a crooked joint and passing it immediately over.

"Nope," said Patrice.

"Really?"

"Nope," said Patrice again.

"Me and Evangeline always used to try and guess stuff about your life."

"On school holidays, you two used to follow me around the house, from room to room, thinking I couldn't see you."

"I remember," said Emil. "We were bored. Sometimes you'd do like a funny dance or something and we'd think you were nuts."

"It passed the time," said Patrice. "What was it you two were guessing?"

"Evangeline thought you had two daughters who were her age and she thought they were probably really good at school. I thought you were maybe a singer." Patrice chuckled. Emil filled his chest with smoke and held it there until his eyes watered. When he exhaled, it felt as though he was shrinking. "What did you think about us?"

"I clean twenty-odd other houses," said Patrice. "I didn't think anything about you."

"Really?" said Emil. "Nothing?"

"Maybe I thought you seemed like sad people," said Patrice. "And the food you ate looked kind of sad too."

During Evangeline's first weeks at university, she had been plunged into a whirlwind of grand, unfamiliar buildings, and drunken parties, and introductions to people whose names she promptly forgot. She forgot a total of sixty names in the first month, signed up to twenty societies and organisations, jumped into two fountains, listened to someone recite the entirety of *The Waste Land* while playing a hang drum, drank Pernod for the first time and threw up Pernod for the first time, into her very own flip-lid bin in her very own, slightly mildewed bedsit.

Predictably, to Evangeline at least, Ada hadn't managed to gain a place at any of her top four universities. Less predictably, Evangeline had been given an offer from Corpus Christi, Cambridge. When she'd gone for her preliminary interview with a tutor, he'd smiled and shaken his head as he retrieved her statement from the worryingly tall pile beneath his seat.

"I was impressed by your essay," he said. "But I have to ask how much of it is genuine and how much of it is a somewhat clever ploy to endear yourself to us."

At that point, Evangeline herself had no idea what it was she wanted. She had beliefs about how a person ought to be and beliefs about how her life ought to be and she was finding, more and more, that it was a struggle to reconcile the two. She did not believe, for example, that young women ought to be concerned about the physical space occupied by their bodies, yet she subsisted largely on undressed salad and handfuls of Jordan almonds. She also did not think women should allow themselves to be defined by men, yet she emotionally prostrated herself before all the boys she fell in love with. And she did not believe anyone ought to let themselves be manipulated by social media platforms engineered to steal time and sell it to advertisers, yet she lost hours to soul-destroying binges of contentless content that left her feeling as though she'd just been robbed in broad daylight, of something small but of great sentimental value.

"I'm conflicted," she told the tutor. "Of course, I want to study here and of course I recognise that doesn't mean I deserve to, or that I don't believe it might be worth under-representing private school pupils for a period of time if it's how we redress the societal imbalance."

The tutor smiled to himself and stowed the paperwork back in his drawer. He sat with his legs crossed, twitching his ankles uncontrollably, flashing Argyle socks. Evangeline liked him immediately and saw in him the person her father ought to have been—a benevolent, teddy-bearish academic, who could have existed in exactly the same form thirty or sixty or ninety years ago.

"And what is it you'd like to go on to do once you leave us?"

"I'd like to work in the non-profit sector or at a start-up developing radical technology," said Evangeline. "Whatever has the most impact."

"And where does it stem from, this desire to do good?"

"Does it have to stem from somewhere?"

"No, but often these things can be traced."

"I think it can be traced to my parents," said Evangeline. "I watched them spend their entire lives never thinking about anyone other than themselves. My father's biggest dream was always to retire and buy a supercar and my mother wants to stay as rich as possible for as long as possible. None of it makes them happy. Not that happiness is a goal, just that I imagine it might be a by-product of a meaningful life." She screwed her hands into fists and cricked her neck, a fighter gearing up for the next bout. "I'd like to have children eventually," she said. "And when they realise how the world has been arranged and ask why, I'd like to be able to tell them that I didn't lie down and accept it as it was."

On the return journey to Stroud that day, Evangeline purposely bought her train ticket from a machine and not the app on her phone, so that she could keep it in the shoebox reserved for physical tokens of treasured memories. She'd unpacked the shoebox first, on arriving in her ten-square-metre bedsit equipped with its own micro-kitchen and a window overlooking a meandering street of secondhand bookshops and Fairtrade cafés. Aside from clothes, she'd packed a pair of borderline inappropriate silk pyjamas Yara had bought for her as a going-away present, a selection of the books her father had left behind when he moved out, and the yellow-check blanket she'd slept with since she'd been born. The blanket had been a gift from her paternal grandmother, about whom Evangeline could remember nothing, but onto whom she projected all of the qualities she missed in her own parents. Her grandmother was wise and selfless and physically powerful. Her grandmother, she fantasised, had fought for women's suffrage and black rights and marched alongside homosexuals and miners. Evangeline's other grandmother, the one who died on a cheesecake diet in a cheerless nursing home, had spent her entire life as a housewife, though Yara always said "homemaker," which made Evangeline think of an elderly woman in a dark garage, painstakingly constructing a miniature town.

Evangeline met Ahk Srisuwan, the man who would go on to become her closest friend at Cambridge, after tagging along with two girls to a sketch revue staged by the university's comedy group. The two girls were studying social sciences and were, to Evangeline at least, depressingly unremarkable. They reminded her of the girls back at Isidore's, who recorded themselves performing viral dances and wore Ralph Lauren polo shirts with culottes and patent loafers.

Ahk was playing a bumbling Winnie the Pooh, trying to keep the residents of the Hundred Acre Wood from turning on him by offering them a referendum on remaining part of the A. A. Milne estate.

"If we leave," said Pooh, "we can form lucrative merchandising deals of our own."

"And the estate can't let Disney force stupid new characters on us," said Owl. "Like Beaver or Turtle."

Later, when Ahk wandered back onto the stage, mumbling hungrily and patting his padded belly, Evangeline laughed so hard that the social sciences girls frowned at her, as though laughter wasn't the appropriate response to comedy, as though she ought to have sat there posed like *The Thinker* while six tipsy students dressed as animals plotted a referendum of independence.

After the performance, Evangeline found Ahk smoking a cigarette on the kerb, feet in the road and a bottle of Bacardi at his side. He'd changed into a straw boating hat, cut-off shorts made from 501s, and an Acapulco shirt, two sizes too small. There were tiny fine-line tattoos on his hands of birds and butterflies. He was texting with the speed of a court stenographer.

"That was incredibly funny," said Evangeline.

"It was cheap," said Ahk. "But I have a soft spot for Pooh."

Evangeline lingered, hesitant to disappear into the night. She was alert to the idea that her opening week of university would chart the course of the rest of her life. She was cripplingly aware that this was the last opportunity for her to assemble the group of friends she may prove to be stuck with for years to come. Her friendship with Ada had been born out of nothing but a seating plan that had forced them together and she was determined not to allow chance to play such a pivotal role in proceedings again.

"First-year?" said Ahk, realising his admirer was still there.

"You can tell?"

"Always. What grand plan have you got lined up for yourself?"

Evangeline squatted beside Ahk. "I'm doing Human, Social, and Political Sciences," she said, not knowing how else to answer the question.

"Ah," said Ahk. "The connoisseur's PPE. And what do you hope to use it for, selling the NHS to American investment firms, or trying to scare all the billionaires over to Ireland?"

"Are those the only two options?"

"You could stand as a Lib Dem, I suppose."

"I'm not sure British politics is an effective vehicle for real global change," said Evangeline.

"That's the spirit."

The ensuing pause caused Evangeline to grow anxious.

"Are you from Cambridge?" she said, to break the silence.

Ahk laughed. "Nobody's from Cambridge," he said. "I'm from Thailand, but everyone's wonderfully terrified to ask these days." He pulled his head high, tipped his chin back, and affected a hoarse, posh voice. 'Are you originally from here?' they say, as though I'm talking to them with no trace of an accent."

"I don't think you have an accent."

"And I don't think that's the compliment you think it is."

"I'm sorry."

"Don't be sorry. Sit down, stop squatting there like you're about to take a dump."

Evangeline laughed and took a seat next to Ahk, who passed her the bottle of Bacardi, as well as a fresh cigarette, lit from the tip of his own. His aroma was an expensive, organic blend of lavender and patchouli. Almost as soon as Evangeline had sat down, he leapt to his feet, slapping his calves as though they were being attacked by mosquitos.

"Let's go," he said. "If I sit still for too long, my legs fall asleep. And there's a party that I'm sure won't be worthy of the name currently taking place six minutes from this very spot."

They walked together along the cramped, sheer stone facades of Trinity Lane, until the looming spectre of King's College Chapel appeared. Ahk walked some way out ahead of Evangeline, lighting cigarette after cigarette, and whistling along to a snatch of reggaeton leaking from a window several storeys above them.

The party that Ahk brought Evangeline to consisted of a smoke-filled living room, in which six third-year students of Physics and Pure Mathematics were arranged around a fibreglass coffee table shaped like a giant staple. One of them was slumped in an armchair with a wool blanket draped over his lap, his eyes barely open. A girl in a Hessian cassock sat cross-legged on the floor in front of him, hiding her face behind a reference book the size of a broadsheet newspaper. The other four were engaged in a heated debate that had evidently been underway for some time, fuelled by cigarettes of various foreign brands, bottled Italian beer, and three bottles of mid-price chianti.

"They have some interesting things to say," said Ahk, as he ushered Evangeline into the room. "But every time they tell me they're having a party, I get here and find I'm the only normal human who was invited."

Two of the boys were seated on opposite sides of the coffee table, a large plate of cigarette butts equidistant between them like a chessboard.

"What you're arguing is market fundamentalism," said Thayyab Raheem. "And we know it's not true. Free markets don't balance themselves, they lead to increasing concentrations of wealth."

"Just because something leads to something else," said Leo Gaskill, "that doesn't make it the logical, inevitable, final endpoint."

"Look at Boghosian's yard sale model."

"Look at my nuts."

"I'd rather not, Gaskill, and you can't argue that Ehrenreich wasn't right, that it's objectively expensive to be poor, and if it's more expensive to be poor than it is to be rich, then how can it not be the case that wealth invariably flows in one direction?"

Evangeline was immediately entranced. When the spotlight finally swung around to them, Ahk introduced her as a first-year HSPS student, his biggest fan, and his new personal assistant, capable of elaborate latte art and shining even the most neglected shoe to a mirror-like polish. Evangeline blushed, realising only as it happened that this sensation of being on the bottom of a pile was utterly unfamiliar. Even as a year seven back at St. Isidore's, she'd strolled the corridors with her head held high, already aware that she could intellectually outmanoeuvre most of the people she encountered.

"Prime minister or investment banker?" said Leo Gaskill.

"Neither," said Evangeline.

"That's a good start," said Thayyab Raheem. "How was your pantomime, Srisuwan?"

"The performance of a lifetime. Thank you all for attending in support."

"We were busy," said the girl behind the book, her voice a creaking hinge.

"Were we?" said the boy who could barely keep his eyes open.

"What happened to the wild party?"

Toby Nagle shrugged.

"We imagined a party might materialise, but everyone else seemed to have other ideas."

With that settled, they returned to the discussion on free markets and Evangeline accepted a cigarette from Ahk, declined to light it, and sat twirling it over and under her fingers like a drummer as she tripped along behind the rambling argument, trying to keep up.

It was nearly five when Evangeline got back to her room and sleep wasn't even a remote possibility. Instead, she made a cup of tea using the travel-sized kettle in her tiny kitchen and carried it into her single bed. She thought about messaging her brother and didn't. She thought about Ada and felt a stab of regret at how impatient she'd always been with the girl who'd ended up being her single close friend throughout their school years. She scrolled to her father's name in her phone and wondered if it still worked—he seemed to change his phone number every week by then, though she had no idea why. Later she'd learn that he periodically gave away his phone to strangers that he met on the street.

Evangeline wasn't sure how she felt about her father in the months after his personality shifted and the divorce took shape. She felt, somehow, that he'd cheated and become exactly the kind of person she wanted to be, overnight, and with no effort whatsoever. On the pretext of having sided with her mother during the divorce proceedings, she avoided seeing Arthur during the summer after his accident and her first year of university, which added to a growing guilt she felt that her father was doing the one thing she'd always claimed to want him to do and yet she was ostracising him because of it.

Once her guilt had settled like silt at the bottom of her new life, Evangeline began sending her father fortnightly emails, in which she relayed repetitive, unemotional information about her existence. She talked about the types of cuisine she was experimentally cooking, the books she'd read, the documentaries she'd watched in bed, laptop balanced on her belly like a newborn baby. Arthur replied to each email within an hour, deploying exclamation marks with alarming frequency, and bookending his missives with curt declarations of pride in his daughter. *You're doing so well, dubbin!* He never engaged with anything she said directly, never asked further questions or probed, just wrote at length about how he was acting as a kind of pro bono business consultant for several international charities while volunteering at local projects involving the homeless, the lonely, and the addicted.

The speed of Arthur's replies meant that Evangeline generally told herself she'd reply at some point in the future and never did. She'd wait another two weeks and send another two paragraphs about how she'd burnt shakshuka or learned about the Silk Road, and Arthur would immediately write back to tell her about a Congolese NGO trying to rescue children from the pit mines where they painstakingly sifted for minerals to build the smartphones and iPads that would distract children of the same age, a thousand miles away, when their parents wanted peace in speciality coffee shops.

It began to feel to Evangeline as though they had signed up to newsletters about each other's lives. On the rare occasion she replied to Arthur's replies, she did so briefly, telling her dad that she was glad he was doing something worthwhile, and that she looked forward to seeing him, without offering any concrete plans about when she might be able to do so. It had been nearly a month since she'd sent a message and so it had been nearly a month since she'd received one in return. The mug warmed her through and she shivered in the silky cocoon of her duvet. "Dear Dad," she imagined writing. "I'm so tired, I think I might combust. University seems as though it might be a rare occasion of something living up to all expectations. It's five in the morning and I'm watching the sun come up above the street outside my room. I can't imagine why you left here early but it must have been a difficult decision. I think I'm going to be unexpectedly happy. I hope you are too."

In the end, she didn't write anything.

On Fridays, Emil would catch the bus out to his father's flat and eat whatever mixture of tinned foods Arthur had decided to rinse and salt in the single serving bowl he owned, a scratched Bakelite container he'd bought at a jumble sale in aid of the community centre's new guttering. Emil soon developed a morbid fear of these visits. He wanted to see his father and continued to harbour vague daydreams about being the one who would restore his sanity, but he also hated the stale vegetable broth smell that clung to the cramped flat and the terrifyingly old neighbours and the windowless communal hallway that felt like a hospital wing.

Dread had become his predominant feeling. He dreaded school, dreaded meeting his mother in the corridors of the house, dreaded small-talking with his father in his bizarre and depressing flat. He dreaded the passage of time, in general, and the end of his school years and the thought of the life that was to come. The only thing he didn't dread was time spent with Imogen, which was also increasingly fraught with its own set of problems, but which at least involved sex, which was gradually coming into focus for Emil as something that offered a temporary relief from monotony, the same way drugs or stories set in space sometimes did.

Arthur answered the door in a pair of unflattering, supermarket-brand jogging bottoms, with an XXL T-shirt advertising a decorating firm draped over his shrinking frame. This was another unfortunate consequence of his transformation: Arthur now dressed like someone who'd just suffered a painful break-up and was refusing to leave the house—except he did leave the house, often to wander aimlessly around the area, saying hello to everyone he passed and stooping to pick up crisp packets and cigarette butts from the ground.

"How are you doing, Em?"

"Fine."

"Tea?"

"Thanks."

"You can have any flavour you like, as long as it's chamomile."

Emil nodded. Over the preceding months, he'd grown used to the bitter, floral teas his dad had switched to consuming. Arthur no longer imbibed caffeine. The one bad habit he seemed to have retained, aside from a general lack of cleanliness and a total disinterest in how he appeared to others, was that he would drink at least one glass of red wine with each meal, regardless of whether the meal was a flimsy tray of microwave lasagne or a cone of chip-shop chips.

"You say you're doing okay?" Arthur repeated.

"I'm fine," said Emil. He put his hand into his pocket and gripped his phone like a talisman.

"Just fine?"

Emil shrugged, watching his father potter around the grimy kitchen. There were cigarette burns in the countertops, revealing the fibrous plywood beneath the unconvincing veneer. "Worried about exams, maybe. Everyone says they're getting harder. And my mocks weren't that good, except maths."

Arthur motioned for his son to sit down at the dining table. Out of everything in the third-floor flat on Honiton Lane, the table struck Emil as one of the saddest. It was a grey plastic rectangle with hairpin legs, and it bore the scars of having served years in a secondary school: long nicks from bored kids sawing at the perimeter with rulers and protractors, pointillist portraits of classmates done with compasses, strings of expletives and out-of-fashion first names and declarations of love or lust or hate. Emil sat behind the school table, sliding the edge of his phone up and down the scars left by years of bored rulers.

"Em," said Arthur. "Think of it like this: in one hundred years, strangers will live in our house, and everything we've ever owned will be rotting away on a landfill site."

"What?" said Emil, startled.

"Our descendants, if there are any, won't have the foggiest clue who we are. People who feel as much like the present moment belongs to them as we do now will sip their drinks at their tables, feeling the sun on their skin and wondering why the universe bothered to cobble them together."

"I guess," said Emil.

"So you understand that you needn't get yourself het up about these tests?"

"That's not what you said to Evangeline."

"Well," said Arthur. "Maybe not. But things were different then."

Yeah, thought Emil. You weren't mental then. "So you don't want me to go to university?"

"In all honesty, Em, I just want you to find something that means something to you."

With some difficulty, Emil lifted his face and nodded to his father, recognising that it was a good thing to have said, even if it felt like a burden. Didn't everyone do something meaningful, even if the meaning was that they needed not to starve? Emil knew what interested him—the philosophy of mathematics, theoretical physics, hard sci-fi—but the thought of spending years sitting through lessons on any one of them wasn't necessarily an exciting one. He was already free to watch Stanford lectures online and there were a coterie of YouTubers who explained even the most obscure mathematical concepts with elegant simplicity, visual aids, and cringe-inducing attempts at humour.

Emil waited for his dad to go to the bathroom and took half an alprazolam pill from his pocket with a swig of the chamomile tea. He'd made a promise to Imogen that he would stop taking any kind of drug until after their exams were finished, but he had succumbed almost immediately after a particularly vicious row with his mother over whether or not artificial intelligence would ever be capable of creating genuine works of art. (Yara had never changed her mind in front of her son. There were times she would leave a room and return with a different opinion, but it would never happen in full view of Emil.)

With the pill dissolving into peace in his belly, Emil took a photograph of the flat on his phone and sent it to Evangeline. This was a running joke between them—one of the few things that continued to tie them together, a constant excuse for contact. Emil would send pictures of their father's dismal home and Evangeline would send back a shot of some imposing church, vaulted ceiling, or congregation of po-faced students. This back-and-forth acted on Emil as an unintended propaganda for the general idea of going to university. Although the prospect of continuing to be a student didn't excite him, the glimpses his sister offered into a world far removed from the place he was in was undeniably compelling.

When Arthur returned from the bathroom, he insisted on showing Emil an article about a charity who were managing to effectively offset carbon emissions by training Amazonian tribes in more lucrative trades than selling the trees around them for timber. The words tumbled out of him with the rabid excitement of a coked-up City trader.

"That's cool," said Emil.

"It is rather cool," said Arthur. "Isn't it?"

Emil pulled away from the computer screen and swung on the back two legs of his chair. The chairs too were made of the kind of textured plastic that Emil recognised from school classrooms. He'd once asked where the furniture had come from and his father had shaken his head and shrugged, as though it were a total mystery to him.

"Dad, do you ever get scared you'll get bored of this and want to have a normal life again?"

"What's a normal life?"

"You know, just, being with Mum and living at home and going to work."

"A lot of people don't have 'normal lives' to go back to, Em. They don't have access to clean water, let alone steady work."

Emil sighed. "Yeah," he said. "Okay."

The sudden sound of violent flushing emanated from the bathroom and Emil jumped out of his seat as though it had just tried speaking to him. A man dressed in blue canvas work trousers emerged from the toilet, scratching at his armpit with a curved, nicotine-yellow fingernail. Tight curls of silver hair framed his jowly face like a chainmail hood.

"Morning, lads," said the man.

"This is Tony," said Arthur. "He was thrown out of the shelter on Barton Street."

"Got a temper on me," said Tony, apologetically.

"Oh," said Emil. "Okay."

"Tony's staying here for a few days, while he gets himself sorted out."

Tony helped himself to a Nationwide mug from the cupboard and rinsed it under the cold tap before adding a teabag. "Your old man's a star," he said. "Saved my worthless arse more than once."

After excusing himself from a sofa where his dad and Tony were discussing the relative merits of colonising Mars, Emil caught the bus to Imogen's, which was a four-storey Regency townhouse hemming Pittville Park in Cheltenham. It was built of giant sandstone blocks and made Emil think of the Banks' house in *Mary Poppins*. The hallway floor was a strip of black and white diamonds and the walls were adorned with gilt frames housing sepia-tinted ancestors, playbills, and several of Imogen's early but relatively successful gouache landscapes. The taps and towel rails were burnished brass and the rooms were painted dim but cosy hues of mossy green.

Imogen's parents were rarely at home and when they were, they welcomed Emil with a fierce, unearned affection, as though he were a close friend they hadn't seen in years. They were the wealthy, open-hearted, bohemian guardians who Emil had imagined only to exist in Christmas films, and who allowed their daughter extensive freedoms, safe in the knowledge that she wouldn't abuse them.

Imogen was an only child and had accepted her position at the centre of the universe with humble seriousness. Roughly half her sentences started with "I." She'd seen more plays than Emil knew existed.

"How's your dad?" she said, tangling her legs in Emil's.

"Fine," said Emil. "There's a homeless man living in his flat."

"Seriously?"

"Yeah."

"I think that's very kind of him."

"Yeah," said Emil. "I guess."

The walls of Imogen's room were decorated with her own giant charcoal sketches of large-breasted women lying atop burning buildings, as well as scraps torn from magazines and printouts and genuine signed prints, by Miró and Chagall and Dalí, given to her on birthdays in earlier years, when her taste in art had been straightforward and largely based on the artists they'd been introduced to in lessons at school. Since then, Imogen had developed an interest in the kind of art that couldn't be framed: women who puked and pissed and masturbated in front of audiences, video projections that lasted for days, hand-poked tattoos of misogynistic YouTube comments, photographed and blown up in size beyond all comprehension.

Walking the perimeter of his girlfriend's room during his visits, picking up ornaments and candid photographs and handwritten letters from great aunts, Emil would wonder whether he'd be another kind of person if he'd inherited Imogen Enderby's life. Would anything have been different? Would he have navigated the world with the brash, charming confidence of the boys at school who captained rugby teams and riffed with teachers? Would his acne have been more muted? Would he have masturbated as much as he did? Or would he still, in spite of everything, become exactly the person he was?

"I've got something for you," said Imogen.

She left the room and Emil picked up and put down a picture of Marina Abramovic and Ulay holding a drawn bow between them. He found most of the art Imogen liked incredibly embarrassing. She thought maths was a chore. When he tried to communicate certain mathematical ideas to her, she glazed over, as though these unparalleled discoveries couldn't come close to rivalling the profound truths explored by people who expelled their bodily fluids onto the floors of art galleries.

Imogen returned with a cube-shaped box which she set on Emil's lap. He made no move to open it, so she lifted the flap and removed a shiny plastic tomato that fitted neatly in the palm of her hand.

"It's called a pomodoro timer," she said. "You set it for twenty-five minutes, then you work non-stop for that long, then take a two-minute break. It's a way of being more productive."

"Oh," said Emil. "Cool."

"I thought it would help you to learn to concentrate again. So you could get some revision done. It helped Mum when she was addicted to Candy Crush. She started reading Simenon instead."

Emil looked apprehensively at the plastic tomato in his hand and felt the familiar surge of dread. Somehow, Imogen had taken it upon herself to fill the gap that his mum had left behind. Imogen had a clear plan of her own. She would complete her A-Levels, focusing most of her energies on Art but easily passing her other subjects, then she would undertake a year-long Art foundation course in Cheltenham College, before applying to Central Saint Martins, in London, where she would attempt to network her way into finding a gallerist and launching a career as an artist. She thought this career path would prove challenging but not impossible. Her parents had friends who were artists, real ones, who made real money and used it to buy real houses with excavated basements and glass-walled studios nestled in their landscaped gardens.

She'd told Emil she was realistic about the likelihood of their relationship extending beyond the bounds of their secondary school years, but was willing to try, if he was, because she felt like they had something special and she didn't want to lose him.

"Why?" said Emil, his tongue loosened by the pill it had flicked to the back of his throat a few hours earlier.

"You don't want to?"

"No, I mean, why do you want to, with me?"

"You're asking me why I like you?"

"I guess so."

"Because you're smart, Emil. Smarter than you know. And kind too. And funny, when you're not so anxious."

"I'm not anxious."

"Then why are we having this conversation?"

It felt to Emil like an act, as though they were participating in a play written by someone who had experiences that neither of them could comprehend. He thought, sometimes, of precocious seven-year-old children he'd seen on TV talent shows, auditioning by belting out songs about unrequited love or unyielding grief. Emil knew he hadn't been in enough relationships to judge whether or not the time he spent with Imogen was special. Imogen, on the other hand, had been robbed of a full piggy bank by her previous boyfriend and flagrantly cheated on by the boyfriend before that, so Emil's relative lack of cruelty did make it feel as though their relationship was something that ought to be preserved.

Emil twisted the timer and placed it on the desk beside the bed, where it ticked like a bomb.

"Don't you like it?" said Imogen.

"I like it," said Emil. "Thank you."

She lay on her back beside him and ran her nose up and down the side of his neck. His facial hair was arriving in frustrating tufts and patches that aggravated his acne and made him look as though he was attempting a look he hadn't yet accepted he couldn't achieve. He'd begun to shave, tentatively, with an electric Gillette trimmer, but he needed to avoid his spots, which meant he'd been forced to adopt a slightly unhinged style of facial hair.

"How do you learn how to shave?" said Imogen. "Did your dad show you?"

"No," said Emil. "I watched this thing on YouTube."

"Are you sure you're meant to shave it in that shape?"

"I don't know," said Emil. "I think so."

Emil was reminded of a night when Evangeline had come home drunk and eager for someone to talk to. She'd used the opportunity to confess that the first time she'd tried shaving her legs, she'd taken one of their mum's razors into the shower and peeled a curl off her calf like potato skin.

Emil looked down Imogen's hairless leg. "How did you learn?"

"Mum took me into the shower one morning when I was eleven and let me try it on her. She told me I shouldn't feel the need to shave if I didn't want to, but that I'd probably get shit for it at school if I didn't."

"Do you want to?"

"Right now, I think it's more revolutionary to embrace tradition. Growing your leg hair is just as much of a statement as shaving it. Anyway, I don't think there's anything wrong with customs. The Vikings used to dye their beards with lye, did you know that?"

"No," said Emil.

"Well, it's true."

When they had sex, it was almost silent and Emil held at least one of Imogen's hands, which was not something he'd ever seen in porn, but which he liked nonetheless because it reassured him that he wasn't doing anything wrong. To keep himself from finishing too early, Emil conjured mental images of the worst things he'd ever seen: a Mexican cartel beheading video, *The Human Centipede 2*, the open casket that preceded his grandmother's funeral. This rarely had the desired effect and instead turned their intimate moments into confusing cinematic montages of pain and pleasure.

"Sorry," he'd say, each time he ejaculated into a rapidly wilting condom, soon to be sheepishly tugged off his penis and swaddled in a sheaf of tissue paper then tucked into the bottom of the bathroom bin.

"Don't be sorry," Imogen would say. "It was nice. I liked it."

Yara met Luke Tapper beside the giant mirrors in the gym, where he was attempting to take a selfie that best captured the rippled slabs of muscle he'd worked tirelessly to cultivate. His hair was shaved down to a blonde fuzz, his beard shaped meticulously into sharp angles that accentuated the line of his jaw. He moved with a cowboy-like gait, which Yara at first assumed was an affectation, but which she later learned was the result of having quadriceps so developed that they chafed against each other as he walked.

Luke was a bodybuilder who made the majority of his income through sponsored Instagram and YouTube posts but would square up to anyone who dared suggest he was an influencer. He drove a convertible Mazda and listened exclusively to Radio 1 or workout playlists consisting of nineties rap and Euro trance classics. He gave life-coaching sessions on the internet to young men without girlfriends. His flat was listed on Airbnb and when anyone booked it, he slept on the sofa of an ex-girlfriend who was still in love with him.

Yara glanced at him for two seconds too long on her way to the elliptical trainer with the TV screen, and Luke nodded, and Yara nodded back.

"Body Pump with Marcus, right?" he said.

"Sometimes," said Yara. "If my knees are co-operating." She instantly cursed herself for saying this, realising how old it made her sound and quickly feeling embarrassed for caring how old she appeared to a man half her age. She was not an insecure middle-aged ghost who thought it was beyond human possibility that any man would find her attractive, but she also wasn't deluded enough to imagine that the kind of person who drank buckets of powdered protein and unashamedly took selfies in the gym would be looking for a woman with two teenage children.

"I hear you," said Luke. "We gotta look after our bodies if we want them to look after us."

At the time, this had struck Yara as intriguingly succinct, and it would be a month before she discovered it was something Luke had heard on a weightlifting podcast. It would take a long time for her to learn a lot of things about Luke that were immediately apparent to almost everyone she introduced him to. Not all of these things were bad but they did all point toward the uncomfortable truth that Yara had been at least somewhat blinded by the way Luke Tapper looked.

"I have this guy, a chiro out in Longford, he can work wonders with anything. Tore my ACL last year, he had me up and running again in no time."

"Does he have a time machine?"

"As good as," said Luke. "Pass me your phone, I'll slip his number in."

"Slip his number in" seemed too much like a line from a *Carry On* film to Yara, who then realised that this man standing in front of her may very well have no idea what a *Carry On* film was. Yara took her phone out of the transparent pouch that kept it wedded to her tricep, so that she could listen to eighties synth pop while she worked out. Luke typed into it with a speed closer to Emil's than her own.

"I popped my number in there too, I'm Luke."

"Yara," said Yara.

"What is that, Mexican?"

Yara laughed ridiculously and immediately glanced around to see if anyone had seen her so thoroughly shed her principles in the face of a handsome man. "No," she said. "My dad was half-Portuguese."

"Nice," said Luke. "I went to Portugal for a stag last year. Wild place. Didn't get on with it at all."

Their relationship developed quickly, with a few relatively expensive meals along Cheltenham Promenade and subsequent nights spent in Luke's caricature of a bachelor pad. He owned a WWEthemed pinball machine and a wooden rowing machine and a machine that ironed shirts by inflating itself within them like a headless man. Pull-up bars were installed across three separate doorways. There were posters in his bedroom of Tony Soprano and Tommy Shelby. Old plastic rugby trophies were arranged along the bathroom windowsill, filled with loose change and crumpled receipts.

Luke's neighbours occasionally doorstepped Yara as she left his house to stress how sweet he was. They told her about how he'd carried Audrey Tyreman on his shoulders through last year's floods so that she could be at her grandson's christening. They told her that he baked unparalleled cupcakes for street parties. They told her that when bailiffs took the Elliot family's TV, he'd given them his own, casually saying it was time he ordered something bigger anyway.

She had no idea why they told her these things and occasionally imagined she was being mistaken for a potential employer or parole officer.

Sometimes, early on, Yara wondered what she was doing with Luke Tapper, and at other times, she allowed herself to like him. She allowed herself to laugh at the way he frowned and scratched his ear while watching bad news on the TV. She allowed herself to be impressed by the fact that he could strip and rewire a house. She allowed herself to enjoy his confusion during sci-fi films and his lack of interest or understanding in the constantly reshuffled teams of government.

She pushed away her guilt as snobbery. Luke Tapper had worked alongside his dad as an electrician from the age of fifteen. His friends wore Timberland boots and ate bacon butties and there were LED lights fixed to the chassis of their cars. He told her they made fun of him for making money on the internet but that he knew they were secretly envious and at least one of them, Ryan McCormick, had tried to follow him into the realm of fitness influencing and failed, because he was too self-conscious to feign excitement in the face of a camera.

Yara couldn't quite decipher her feelings. Wasn't she enjoying being around someone with so much energy? Hadn't she just had her entire future stolen out from beneath her, and wasn't she entitled to a spree of mindless sex? There were things Luke wanted to do and he did them. He kept a list on his phone of hiking trails, restaurants, and obscure combat sports. Sometimes, he'd pick her up for lunch and decide that they ought to go to the dry ski slope in Matson or the climbing centre or to sail boats in South Cerney, and they'd actually go, right then, as though there was no need to plan or prepare anything at all, as though life was just a matter of deciding which fun thing to do next. The trips doubled as social media content for Luke Tapper but Yara found she didn't mind. She was having too much of a good time to care that her boyfriend insisted on monologuing into a camera every time they went anywhere.

"We're about to get wild," he'd tell a tiny action camera, clipped to the front of a kayak in the Forest of Dean. "Hold onto your hats, fitness freaks."

They drove to Snowdonia, stayed in a yurt, had sex in the accompanying hot tub, and climbed the mountains in bobble hats. Luke asked her questions like: what are your goals? And, where do you see yourself in five years' time? They weren't original questions but they were original to Yara, whose entire purpose for several years had been her family and their finances.

As Luke spent more and more time at the house on Drybrook Lane, he also asked questions about Emil, and Yara grudgingly supplied the answers, becoming acutely aware that it sounded as though there was something profoundly wrong with her son. No, he never had friends over. No, he didn't play any sports. Yes, the tiny sausages and the precooked chicken goujons in the fridge belonged to him. Yes, he did well at maths but lazily scraped passes in everything else. Yes, school occasionally called to say he hadn't turned up. And yes, she thought he might have a girlfriend, but the few times she'd dared to ask, he'd responded with such hostility that she'd finally vowed never to ask again.

Yara came to think that Luke might be exactly the kind of person Emil needed exposure to. Someone who lived relentlessly in the real world, who was capable and powerful but gentle underneath it all. Someone who didn't overthink and retreat. Someone who was practical, strong, and single-minded.

She forced Emil to spend at least a couple of hours with her and Luke on Friday or Saturday evenings. Usually, these compulsory hang-out sessions were spent in front of the TV, eating Indian food and watching things chosen by Luke: boxing matches or Formula One races or films starring The Rock or Mark Wahlberg. They allowed Emil to choose the viewing material once, and he picked a Yorgos Lanthimos film, which Luke watched for ten minutes before reaching for the remote and turning it off.

"You've spaffed your shot up the wall there, mate. Let's watch that new Kevin Hart job."

It depressed Emil to see how much of Luke his mother absorbed, and how little of his mother Luke could even see. He once asked Emil where the Cloud was and on several occasions Emil was roped into helping edit some of Luke's YouTube videos. Emil sometimes imagined the two of them participating in one of the games designed to illuminate how well a couple knew each other. Did Luke even know that Yara had once, for fun, designed a computer game based on Conway's Game of Life? That she had created a database solution capable of storing all the genomic data of a human being? That future advances in certain areas of genetic research were likely to be aided at least in part by the groundwork his mother had done?

Their meals had become even more austere and flavourless. Luke ate mainly slabs of poached salmon and tins of mackerel and heaped portions of brown rice, quinoa, and bulgur. He cooked these meals himself, without regard for seasoning or spice, and to rapturous praise from Yara, who was used to her ex-husband's refusal ever to attempt anything more ambitious than a spaghetti Bolognese.

Without officially moving in, Luke annexed one of their mug cupboards and used it to store five-kilogram sacks of protein powder and glittery tubs of creatine and taurine and other supplements that sounded to Emil like construction materials. He claimed it was necessary, given the fact that he often drove Yara home from the gym, and that the human body had an anabolic window of thirty minutes, beyond which any of the potions and powders he poured into himself would prove less effective in adding to his bulk.

His books appeared on the hallway bookshelf: biographies of Elon Musk and Ronnie Coleman, *Outliers* by Malcolm Gladwell, *Unfuck Your Life* and *Twelve Rules for Life* and *Life Lessons from Hip-Hop*, *Rich Dad Poor Dad*, *The Power of Now*, *The Power of Positive Thinking*,

The Power of Letting Go, and, inexplicably, two copies of *The Alchemist* by Paulo Coelho. Once the books had arrived, they never seemed to move. Emil wondered what their purpose was. To prove to Yara that Luke could read? To stake out territory, like a dog that pissed self-help paperbacks?

Yara, for her part, tried not to take their relationship too seriously. She told herself she was just enjoying something casual, and that Luke was just enjoying something casual in return. She still offered to help with his endeavours, still spent hours going over his sloppy tax returns and misspelled business plans. This was just kindness, she told herself. Nothing else.

Luke was building his social media presence into what he called a "proper business." He sold merchandise with his logo emblazoned on it: a fanged bear lifting a barbell over its head. He wanted to expand into protein-enriched frozen pizzas and branded electrolyte powder. He had an entire scientifically dubious empire planned out.

There was still, undeniably, a voice in Yara's head that told her straying with Luke beyond the territory of casual dating meant settling, but there was no arguing with the way he made her feel—desirable and confident and capable of achieving things she'd long ago given up on, even if Luke couldn't understand the precise nature of those things. His company may not always have been challenging or particularly engaging but Arthur had barely been any kind of company at all over the last years of their marriage. And her kids were no company. And her sister was no company. And the friends she'd once got cocktail-drunk with at weekends were no longer any company. Besides, she wasn't marrying Luke, she was spending her mornings and evenings with him, and having sex with him, and learning how to lift increasingly heavy objects in the gym with him.

In the evenings, after coming home from the gym, Luke would slouch across the entire width of the sofa, his thighs spread at a hundred-degree angle, a phone in his calloused hands jingling with the encouragements of an ironically 8-bit roleplaying game. This was where Yara quickly drew a line: she told him, early on, that at least during films or TV, he'd have to keep his phone in his pocket, otherwise it would drive her to distraction. Luke complied. He continued to play on his phone in the toilet and under the dinner table when he inevitably finished eating before Yara did. He played on his phone between sets at the gym. He played on his phone at traffic lights and in supermarket checkout queues.

One night, several months into their relationship, Yara and Luke and Emil were arranged around the living room, watching *Good Will Hunting*, which Luke had announced was in his "all-time top ten movies." They came to a scene in which Matt Damon's character, a working-class janitor with an undiscovered aptitude for mathematics, is sweeping a corridor and pauses for a moment to consider the problems chalked up on the blackboard.

"You watch," said Luke, shaking his head in pre-emptive disbelief. "This is fuckin' incredible."

"That's actually quite simple maths," said Emil.

Luke glanced down at Emil with undisguised irritation.

"Don't be a tosser, mate," he said, pointing to the TV. "He's a genius."

"He's Matt Damon," said Emil.

"I know he's Matt Damon but he's also a fuckin' maths genius, and I'm sure they got some real maths genius in to write some real maths genius problems. This is a bit different to you doing your little A-Levels."

Emil reached for the remote, paused the film, and disappeared off upstairs. Luke threw his arms up in the air like an exasperated footballer trying to challenge the decision of a referee from across the field.

"What's he doing now?" he said.

Yara shook her head, wary of the row that was about to unfold, but curious in spite of herself about what her son was plotting.

Emil returned moments later, carrying an A3 pad of recycled paper he'd been using for revision purposes. He tore out a page and Blu-Tacked it to the living room wall, removing a marker pen from the right-hand pocket of his combat trousers. He grabbed the remote, rewound the film a few frames, then paused it.

"The first question just wants the adjacency matrix of the graph, which says whether the pairs of vertices are adjacent or not. It's simple."

He hastily filled in a grid of numbers on the paper.

"The second question wants the matrix that shows the number of length-three walks between vertices."

Again, Emil hastily scrawled several numbers onto the paper.

"And the third problem—"

"This could just be a load of old shite," said Luke.

"It's not," said Yara, quietly.

Luke shot her a look of disbelief, getting to his feet and staring at Emil with such ferocity that he backed away from the crumpled sheet of paper as though trying to deny any responsibility for it. With a deep grunt, Yara's boyfriend left the room, the clinking welcome melody of his game already playing from his phone. Emil smiled at his mum, certain that she was about to offer him praise. Instead, she lowered her face into her hand and pinched the bridge of her nose.

"Don't embarrass him like that again," she said. "It's not kind."

Upstairs, in his bedroom, Emil crushed an alprazolam under a Le Creuset mug and snorted it in two fat lines that trickled down the back of his throat like glue. He lay on his bed with AirPods buried so deep in his ears that it hurt and he imagined a landscape of fractal patterns, spinning and dissolving into endlessness.

10.

There was more work than Evangeline had been expecting and it was potentially bottomless, with ten books branching off every other book she read, like a family tree of theories, approaches, and movements, many of which seemed like common sense ideas Evangeline herself had once had, dressed up in unnecessarily intimidating language, bolstered by footnotes and appendices that doubled the weight of every printed text she picked up. During tutorials, held in a bookcase-lined room that was always either blisteringly hot or achingly cold, she learned never to be sure of herself. She learned that as soon as she dared to state anything with confidence, someone would point out why it was too simplistic or too convoluted or just plain wrong. Her classmates never accepted each other's opinions, every statement was turned inside-out and shaken, as though it was a suspicious package being ferried across a border.

She elected not to take the paper on moral philosophy. For the philosophy requirement of her degree, she studied logic, jurisprudence, and aesthetics. She tried not to think about why she'd taken the decision to avoid the one thing she'd been convinced was her true calling for the majority of her teenage years. It didn't, she felt, paint her in a very positive light. She didn't approve of her own reaction to her father's transformation but that didn't make it any easier to surmount.

Evangeline had been robbed of the thing she'd built herself in opposition to and as a result, her obsession with the mechanics of charity receded into the background over the course of her first year at university. Compared to her father's unimpeachable saintliness, she found herself lacking, and instead vowed to foster other virtues that she swore would be put to good use at a later date.

"Study now," said Ahk, when Evangeline confessed to feeling as though she was betraying her younger self. "Save the world later."

This was all the excuse Evangeline needed to throw herself into her studies. The books on applied ethics and global inequality that she'd brought with her from home were quickly lost below her bed, along with the childish-seeming poster of Frida Kahlo and several photos of family holidays that she thought might be a comfort but in reality had become both awkward to look at and a slightly boring reminder of a time that Evangeline felt had been lived through by someone else, someone who had told her about it at length while she wasn't really paying attention.

When the group of friends she'd acquired through Ahk argued, everything became abstract. They spoke about the economics of poverty and populism, and none of them ever came into contact with anything more real than a book or a pint of beer. The world was a thought experiment, devoid of feeling beings, and existent only in as far as it presented a series of problems to be mulled over. They argued unendingly and with such great conviction it was as though the fate of the world depended on the conclusions that they felt their way toward in the dim corners of sticky pubs. With the exception of Ahk, they didn't participate in activities or sports or go on trips anywhere further afield than the edges of town. They drank in one of three pubs, ate in one of two restaurants, and spent cloudless days dozing in the same spot beside the same stretch of canal, where a ropey willow tree touched fingertips with its reflection in the water.

It was several months into her first year before one of the third-years she'd encountered that first night asked Evangeline if she wanted to go with him, alone, to see the new Michael Haneke film at a dingy cinema on the edge of town. Leo Gaskill was the son of two people who had money, who were the children of four other people who'd had money, and so on, in a geometric sequence of inherited wealth. His parents owned a large house in rural Lincolnshire as well as a smaller house in the London borough of Richmond upon Thames, and a three-storey building containing six flats in Walthamstow. She learned the specifics of this much later but had already come to sense that while Leo's family may have possessed a similar amount of wealth to her own, they possessed it in an entirely different way, a way that had become familiar to her through some of the kids at St. Isidore's who carried themselves as though they were wardens of some great secret that imbued them with profound importance.

They met in the courtyard of Corpus Christi, surrounded by a towering medieval patchwork of stone buildings, some resembling tenement cottages, others cathedral cloisters or country inns, all punctuated by mullioned stained-glass windows. A marquee was in the process of being set up on the lawn. Leo Gaskill had a slim book conspicuously pinned under his arm and he was dressed like a Cornish fisherman in rubber wading boots, turned-up chinos, a blue flannel shirt, and a waxed jacket with arm patches. The majority of his wardrobe, Evangeline would learn, consisted of items of clothing meant for professions Leo had no relation to: canvas chore coats, flak jackets, multi-pocketed utility trousers, a brown leather Stetson with a braid of black leather around the brim.

They walked and talked and smoked.

"Have you seen any Haneke before?" said Leo.

"No," said Evangeline.

"This one's life-affirming. I've already seen it twice."

"And you want to go again?"

"I want to watch you watch it. You'll love it."

She wondered how he could know what she'd love. He didn't know anything about her, except for the fact that she spent a lot of time with Ahk and often perched on the sofa in his shared flat getting very drunk and saying very little.

But she did love it and she wasn't even sure why. It had made her feel part of a shared experience and unexpectedly fond of human beings, of their fumbling, unpredictable feelings and their misguided attempts to acquire the things they thought would make them happy.

They spent a Lebanese meal of grilled lamb and griddled flatbreads dissecting their favourite moments, recalling them in all their glorious detail, like football pundits deconstructing a miraculous goal. After the food, they decamped to a pub and Evangeline told Leo Gaskill that she was afraid she might be the least capable student in the entire university. Leo told her that everyone apart from psychopaths felt that way and that the first year was generally a process of learning how everyone else was managing to get by. There were a few real geniuses, sure, but these were dwarfed by the number of people who'd simply learned how to present themselves as more intelligent than they really were. He told her most of the students were "midwits" who had been taught by elite institutions to talk with confidence and authority about things of which they knew nothing, like pigs trained to play chess.

"And what are you?" said Evangeline.

"I'm Socrates," said Leo Gaskill. "I know that I know nothing but have been taught to do a convincing impression of someone who knows an awful lot."

"Also," said Evangeline, "you don't wash."

"That too. Shall we settle up and move on?"

The flat she'd visited the night she met Ahk, Evangeline learned, belonged to Toby Nagle, who Leo claimed was from a family worth more than the rest of them combined. The Nagles owned the four-bedroom flat and arranged a cleaner who came twice a week to erase the sins of its residents: the overflowing ashtrays and mossy fruit, the drunken spills and splashes of blood and spit on the carpets and rugs. The flat had hosted several generations of Nagles as they slurred and stumbled their ways through Cambridge degrees, each accompanied by their own group of freeloading friends.

After her first night sleeping with Leo in his complimentary room at Toby's flat, Evangeline sought out Ahk, and found him drinking shandy while reading a biography of the American comedian George Carlin at the back of a green-tiled pub. She asked outright what he thought of Leo.

"He's clever and he's pretty," said Ahk. "But he's that weird kind of posh that has big dark secrets. Not like you or me."

"What are we?"

"We're interlopers," said Ahk. "We're the unwashed masses who conned our way into the castle."

Evangeline wasn't sure why or how Ahk had misunderstood her background and she was too grateful to bother correcting him. She told herself it wasn't entirely untrue—her mother wasn't from money and her father had given all of his away. She wasn't like Leo, she was sure of that. Any vestiges of upper-classdom that her father had possessed had been knocked out of him during his fall. Even his accent had slipped since his injury, from a gently musical Radio 4 newsreader, to the indecipherable neutrality of someone who had grown up in so many different countries that none of them had left a discernible mark.

The relationship with Leo developed gradually into an intense, serious thing that involved long dinners and nights that stretched until dawn with great quantities of wine and cigarettes. There was a world Leo wanted to show her: the films of Akira Kurosawa, the music of the Kronos Quartet, the poetry of Rimbaud. Some of it she loved, some of it she found excruciatingly dull, to the point where she'd feign illness to excuse herself from having to experience any more. Evangeline did not show Leo many of the things she cared about. She was afraid of how he might respond to them. She once played Penguin Cafe Orchestra for him, and he'd sniffed and said, "What is this? Music from a car advert?"

And it was music from a car advert, that was how she'd first found it.

Having told the story of her father to Leo Gaskill one night at the end of a languid, hungover dinner, Evangeline expected her boyfriend to be impressed and filled with praise. He wasn't. They were sharing a circular table at the window of an Indian restaurant and both were the slumped, hair-of-the-dog kind of drunk.

"He sounds like a good person," said Leo. "But he probably does as much good as gap-year students building unusable orphanages in Uganda."

"I don't think that's true," said Evangeline.

"It's just another form of white saviourdom, enacted to assuage white guilt."

Evangeline had to restrain herself from standing up. "My dad's not a white saviour," she said. "A white saviour's someone who postures as helping while really putting themselves at the centre of a cause and making things worse."

"You don't think that foreign aid is just rebranded colonialism?"

"No," said Evangeline. "I think it's an attempt to redress it."

Waving his hands over the collection of half-eaten dishes, Leo caught the sleeve of his army surplus jumper in a pool of mutton jalfrezi. "You don't think that the trillion dollars given to African countries who have remained the poorest in the world is proof that aid doesn't work?"

"It might be proof that aid isn't sufficient, but ask the mother of a child whose life has been saved by a non-profit whether she thinks aid works or not."

Leo reached across the table and lifted her chin with the tip of his finger. "I'm not trying to attack your father, Evangeline, I'm trying to have a discussion with you. You can come back at me."

"I know," said Evangeline. "I did."

He let go of her face.

"If your dad really wanted to make a difference, he would do better to volunteer for an organisation who influences international policy."

"My dad's fifty-six," said Evangeline. "And he didn't finish university."

"So? John Major never even went."

"John Major privatised the railways and probably laid the foundations for Brexit."

Leo Gaskill waved dismissively. "Those are just facts from a textbook, Evangeline. We're not talking about what he did, but the fact that he wielded power without a degree."

What did you ever do? she wanted to say. What did you do that meant you're able to cast judgement over someone you've never met?

But she had cast judgement over her father too. She had pushed him away. And somehow, she wanted to hold Leo Gaskill even closer after these debates that veered into domestic arguments and back again. She thought he was absolutely right and absolutely wrong, and she wanted him to calm down and forget and hold her, loosely, with his face in her hair.

Over dessert, Leo seemed to be thawed out by the rush of sugar from a wedge of pecan pie straddled by a melting globe of pistachio ice cream. He sat back in his seat and steepled his hands on his white cotton Henley shirt.

"I'm sorry if I upset you," he said. "I'm so used to debating with the others, I forget it can actually feel pretty emotional."

"It's okay," said Evangeline. "I'm not upset."

"It's nothing personal."

"It was definitely personal, Leo. The person was my father."

"I just want us to be able to challenge each other."

"No, you don't."

"Very funny."

Evangeline wondered whether it was a joke. When she challenged the things Leo said, he generally looked as though she'd been caught trying to literally trip him up.

They rarely spoke about charity again, or about Arthur. Leo was more interested in discussing the possibility of artificial general intelligence and hyper-speed travel and asteroid mining. He wanted to relay the contents of books he'd read by Nick Bostrom and Slavoj Žižek and Mark Fisher. He had an endless supply of borrowed opinions which seemed to find no use other than being hurled directly at the people he deemed least likely to be capable of tossing them back. He considered the protests that formed in town ineffectual and self-congratulatory, the students who prepared themselves for government roles to be deluded, and the university factions of Amnesty International and Oxfam to be embarrassing simulacra of their actual counterparts. He found philosophical justifications for things most people considered inexcusable: terrorist atrocities and sweatshops and eating large amounts of red meat. He derided anyone who dared to share in a popular opinion as being incapable of thinking for themselves.

Leo was all the things Evangeline had imagined her university boyfriend ought to be. Every time she brought up something new and fascinating she'd recently read, Leo seemed to already possess a comprehensive knowledge of the subject. She found herself totally unable to surprise him. If he had any weak spots, he bluffed so convincingly that she never found them.

One night, alone in her bedsit and unable to sleep, Evangeline called her brother. Emil answered after an optimistic number of rings and she was surprised to hear his voice. He sounded delirious, as though he was in the midst of a fever dream.

"Yeah?"

"Are you okay?"

"Yeah," said Emil. "I'm fine. What's up?"

Evangeline thought on her feet.

"Do you know what minimax is?"

"Like game theory?"

"Exactly. Can you explain it to me?"

"It's late, Evangeline."

"It's important."

Emil sighed. "It's kind of the whole foundation of game theory," said Emil. "It came from von Neumann and says that for any two-player zero-sum game—"

"Which is?"

"Just a game where you win or lose."

"Okay."

"And there's always an optimum move. If you're playing by minimax, you'd always choose the highest value payoff move of the worst possible scenarios to avoid the biggest mistakes. Algorithms can do it perfectly, it's why those AlphaGo matches were so brutal."

"I don't quite understand."

"Okay, you know how in Scrabble, we'd both always use our letters to spell the longest words we could on our letter holder things, but then someone else would take the spot you had planned?"

"Yes."

"Playing by minimax, you might try to score the longest possible word, but you also have to take into account the fact that the other person is going to try and score their word too, and maybe try to block you, or get in your way or whatever."

"You don't just work out what your best move is, you realise that the other person is also going to try and work out what their best move is?"

"Pretty much," said Emil.

"Thanks. I didn't know there would be so much maths."

"Isn't that mostly what economics is?"

"I didn't know there would be so much economics either."

Evangeline heard the grind and hiss of a lighter being sparked.

Emil inhaled deeply and sighed like an old man watching a news report on some runaway form of new technology.

"I have a boyfriend," said Evangeline, in a rush to get the words out, without quite being sure why. It had been several months since she'd spoken to her brother and their last conversation had involved him asking her for the passcode that would allow him to alter the settings on the TV.

"Um," said Emil. "Okay. Is he nice?"

"Yes," said Evangeline. "But that's not really the point."

"I'm not asking you if he's hot, Evangeline."

"That's not what I meant."

"What does he study?"

"Physics."

"That's cool."

Emil could sense his sister wanted him to ask more questions but he couldn't summon anything appropriate. What was he supposed to be interested in? The boyfriend's hair? His hopes? His dreams?

"How's Mum?" said Evangeline.

"Fine."

"And her boyfriend?"

"Sorry, Lean, I'm really tired."

"Okay, I know it's late."

"Yeah."

"Are you okay?"

"I'm fine. Just tired."

"I'll let you sleep."

After hanging up, Evangeline opened her computer and booked a train ticket home, thinking that Emil was probably addicted to drugs and her mother was probably being emotionally or financially exploited by a younger man and her father was probably, out of all of them, the happiest, but only because he'd been lucky enough to receive a life-changing head injury that turned him into a kind of shambling angel, someone who ought to be venerated but really was treated with suspicion, not just by his daughter but by a large swathe of the people who came into contact with him. Because who would give away all that he had? Why would someone be willing to go to such lengths to appear selfless? It was like giving up meat or buying an electric car: people began to worry that they ought to be doing the same thing but, knowing that they wouldn't, instead became aggressive and suspicious, trying to put distance between themselves and the source of the unease.

It wouldn't be until several days later, while walking past a pot-bellied dad gently playing football with his eight-year-old son, that Emil realised how unlikely it was that his sister would have failed to grasp such a basic facet of game theory, and that she'd probably called knowing that he had an interest in von Neumann, and thinking that it would be a good way to get him talking. He set out his theory for Imogen while they were lying supine on her four-poster-bed, watching a documentary about Jeffrey Dahmer on Netflix.

"Did you ask anything about the boyfriend?" said Imogen.

"I asked if he was nice," said Emil.

"She probably wanted to tell you about him."

"Why?" said Emil.

"Because she can't tell your dad and she doesn't want to tell your mum."

"But what would she want to tell me?"

"I don't know, Emil. You didn't ask her."

Emil tried to digest this. The possibility that he might be a person whose existence his sister not only tolerated but relied upon had never occurred to him. He had been pummelled, patronised, ignored, resented, berated, and occasionally consulted by his sister over the course of their childhood, but had not been treasured, or at least not outwardly, at least not in any way that he could recognise. He had always been an inconvenience to Evangeline; someone she had been forced to entertain on long flights or bring with her to the church jumble sales where she bought the majority of her clothes and books. He was never the person she wanted, usually he was the person who stood between her and the thing she was trying to do.

"You are revising, aren't you?" said Imogen.

"Yeah," said Emil, his mind elsewhere.

"Do you promise?"

Without being able to explain why, this irritated Emil, to the point where he buried his thumbs in his fists, told Imogen he had to go and meet his mum, and left, after a kiss that barely made contact.

That night, while sitting on the top deck of the 94 on his way back to Gloucester, Emil sent a message not to his sister, but to Alice. *You okay?* he wrote. *Not really*, wrote Alice. Feeling somewhat guilty toward Imogen, he didn't change buses back to Bourton, but walked across Gloucester Park, rowdy with kids drinking and smoking and playing music from their phones in the pollen-heavy summer night. The smell of cut grass hung in the air. There were men in overalls scrubbing graffiti off the bandstand with long-handled brushes by the light of caged halogen bulbs.

Emil went through periods of spending a lot of time with Alice and other periods of barely seeing her at all. She was, in some respects, an antidote to the people he was forced together with at St. Isidore's. Sometimes he thought that Alice was the only real person he knew, and other times he felt irritated by the way she spoke about kids at his school—as though their lives were pure bliss just because their parents had large houses and cars with heated leather seats. He knew that Deepesh's father hit him with a shoehorn if he played *World of Warcraft* too often and Kaya's mum had died from colon cancer and there were at least two kids in his year who were being raised by people who weren't their parents. He'd made these points to Evangeline once, during a debate about privilege, and she'd told him that of course bad things happened to rich people, but the same bad things happened to poor people, and more often, and with the added problem of also having to worry about rent and food and heating while you tried to fend off terminal illness or domestic assault.

Alice was living in a second-floor council flat with two other girls. The flat was on Cromwell Street and stood directly opposite the pathway that had been created when Fred and Rose West's house had been demolished. It was a house, Emil knew, that had once had the skeletons of nine women buried in the cellar and garden. He always imagined the bones of the women cross-legged in front of a big eighties TV, as though they were Pompeiians who'd been watching *Emmerdale* when the volcano erupted.

He was buzzed up and found Alice hunched over a cocktail of

Rachmaninoff and off-brand energy drink, with the translucent lid of a McDonalds cup acting as an ashtray. There were two men playing PlayStation 4 from the sofa. One wore a plastic ankle tag and had a face loaded with piercings. The other was dressed in a thin summer dress under a puffer jacket, his bare feet propped up on an upturned mop bucket.

"Hello," said Emil.

"Hel-low," said the barefoot man, affecting the voice of a pre-pubescent private school pupil.

"Ignore them, Emil," said Alice. "They're jealous of anyone who can read."

"You're jealous of anyone who's not a fat slut," said the man with the piercings.

Alice threw her lighter wide of the man's head.

"I like your anklet," said Emil.

Alice barked with laughter and the man hurled his controller toward the screen. He skittered over to Emil like a cockroach and squared up to him, finding that he didn't physically dwarf the new arrival as obviously as he'd hoped, and flinging out his arms to try and bolster his size.

"You know what a tag means?"

"That you can't be trusted to go outside?"

"Go on then, big man, can you guess why?"

Emil, who was not brave but only dulled with the alprazolam he'd consumed during the bus journey, shrugged, and Alice slipped herself in between them, facing the man, and somehow giving Emil the impression that he would never be taken as seriously as this other person, because he was too small or too young or too posh, because he hadn't been convicted of any crimes, because his face had no holes in it and his location wasn't being monitored by the police.

"It's okay," he said. "I have to go anyway."

"Don't go," said Alice. "We can get drunk and watch *Naruto* in my room. Ignore these pricks."

"Maybe another time."

"Maybe another time," repeated the man still on the sofa, as though Emil had just declined the invitation in the manner of an aristocratic toddler.

"Go on," said the man with the tag. "Fuck off."

Alice beamed an apology at him with her eyes but said nothing and, as he walked past the car park that had once been a death house, Emil had the distinct impression of belonging to none of the worlds that he visited.

11.

Arthur Candlewick slept on a futon that tied his lower back in knots. Each morning, he woke up with a headache powerful enough to blur his vision and he hauled himself to his feet with the help of an aluminium stepladder that he kept stationed beside the bed. He shuffled over to the cheap plastic window in his living room, slick with condensation, and watched the familiar revolutions of the street: the ginger woman who smoked thin white cigarettes and always carried a bullet-shaped thermos into her mint-coloured Citroën 2-CV. The man who jogged daily but never seemed to find it any easier. The pensioner with the telescopic walking stick who steered her bulldog back toward her pebbledash bungalow after a lap of the field beside the dual carriageway.

Arthur waddled through to the bathroom and splashed his face with cold water. There was a Post-it note stuck to the mirror which read: "Jessica, logistics consultation for leaflet distribution." To the right of the Post-it was a printout of an email from the accountant he'd once shared with Yara, and who now represented only Yara's interests, and who spoke to Arthur as though he was a child for whom English was an unmastered second language. Arthur had taken to printing out emails he ought to reply to and posting them in places he frequented—the fridge or the bathroom or the inside of the front door—so that he could formulate replies slowly and precisely, taking time to mentally assemble the right sentences in the right order.

A large part of his time was now taken up acting as a donation consultant for a charity run by one of the ethicists his daughter had exposed him to during his recovery. He would log onto his computer with a headset, like a Samaritan waiting to field suicidal thoughts, and steer those who wanted to ensure their donations did as much good as possible. This generally involved providing them with a list of vetted charities relevant to their interests and passions, while trying to gently suggest that being led by their interests and passions might not be the most effective way to choose how to donate money. The charities the organisation recommended were mostly clustered around sub-Saharan Africa and tended to focus on disease prevention, vitamin distribution, deworming, and public health broadcasts. They were not the kind of charities that would tug on the heartstrings of potential donors, which was precisely why they needed volunteers like Arthur lobbying on their behalf.

"Do you have some recommendations that aren't Africa?" said one man, who seemed unimpressed by Arthur's introduction to the organisation's values.

"Is there a region you have in mind?"

"We thought maybe India."

"We recommend several charities that operate in India," said Arthur. "Do you have a connection to the country?"

"Yes," said the man. "We like the food."

There was a script Arthur had been told to follow and which he frequently deviated from, piling in personal stories about what he'd given and why and how it had changed his life for the better. There were things that he specifically wasn't permitted to say and he very often said them. He encouraged people to give until they felt the strain on their own lives, pointing out that any negative impact on them would be mirrored by a thousand-fold positive impact on those they were helping. This often had the opposite effect, with people growing irritated and defensive, and sometimes abruptly hanging up, which only hardened Arthur's beliefs about what he was doing.

He carried a steaming mug of chamomile tea over to his computer and logged into his Zoom account. The calendar blinked and a woman's name appeared, followed by an option to begin their call. Arthur took a deep breath and clicked. A large, frustrated elderly woman filled his screen.

"Hello," he said. "My name is Arthur Candlewick."

"Hello?"

"Hello," said Arthur. "Can you hear me?"

"I can hear you," said the woman. "Can you hear me? Should I speak louder?"

"You don't have to speak any louder," said Arthur. "I understand you're looking to make a donation and were hoping for some impartial advice on how to choose where you donate?"

The woman sat back in her seat and crossed her arms. "My husband died last December," she said. "He got sick and then he died. Turned yellow as one o' them Sampsons and shrivelled up like a prune. Liver disease, it was."

"I'm very sorry to hear that," said Arthur.

The woman leant to one side so that she was almost entirely out of the frame, except for her left ear, pinned with a lapis lazuli earring so heavy it pulled open her piercing like a tiny, screaming mouth.

"He always said to me, 'Marie, I know you're not goin' to hold onto the trains.' He was a collector, see. He collected model trains. Boxes and boxes of 'em. Mint condition. Now they're mine. He always used to say, 'Cookie, when I kick it, you're to sell them and go swanning off on holiday for a month. Somewhere tropical, one o' them places I always point-blank refused to visit.'" The video feed trembled, as though she'd just kicked the desk her monitor was perched on. "Well, where is it I want to go? My legs are shot and my hips are shot and I need a bog that's four feet off the ground. I'll go down Weston one afternoon for a spot of lunch, but I'd like those bloody trains to end up doing some good. God knows they've made my life miserable enough as it is."

"That's a very generous thing to do," said Arthur. The woman didn't say anything. Arthur glanced at the printout tacked to his wall and read the correct line. "I think it's very inspiring what you've chosen to do."

"Very what?" said the woman.

"Inspiring."

The woman frowned. "What is?"

"What you're doing. Using your husband's collection to do some good in the world."

The woman pushed herself completely out of the shot, so that Arthur could only see a bare wall, painted cornflower blue. "I don't know about that," she said. "I just want to know where I ought to send the money."

"What causes are you passionate about? We have funds for global poverty and disease, non-human animals, and the future."

"What do you mean 'the future'?"

"We believe that by investing in potentially revolutionary projects and technologies, we can help millions of lives in the future."

"But none now?"

"Well," said Arthur. "No. But there are a lot of future people. A lot more than there are of us. And they're our descendants, after all."

"Not mine," said the woman. "Not for want of tryin'. We used to go at it like rabbits. Every corner o' the house, every hour o' the day. No dice. Phil always said it was 'cos mam used to put brandy in my bottle. I reckon he used to stand too close to the microwave in his tighty whities."

"Okay, let's set aside future people for now. How about poverty? There are still billions of people living in extreme poverty and our partner groups have devised some incredibly impressive ways of helping them."

"I don't know," said the woman.

Arthur waited but no further explanation was forthcoming. "What aren't you sure about?"

"I'm not daft and I'm not cruel, I know not everyone can just get a decent job and work to put food on the table, but poverty just seems very ... I'm not sure I could make a dent in it, you know?"

"Well, international aid has already made a huge dent in it, and we have many studies that show certain interventions can work very well."

"If I'm honest with you, I'm not too interested in studies."

"But studies are the only way of evaluating anything."

"Now," said the woman, "I kind of thought we might build a bench and get one of those plaques with his name on it. It could say: 'Phil Culompton, a good man.'"

Arthur gritted his teeth. "What good would a bench do?" he said.

"It'd give people somewhere to sit," said the woman. "And it'd mean his, you know, legacy would live on."

"What if, rather than a bench, his legacy could be ensuring eighty children were dewormed so that they were able to attend school?"

"Dewormed?" said the woman. "No, I don't think so."

"It's an extremely cheap and effective—"

The woman's feed disappeared.

After work, Arthur made himself lunch and left the house. He said hello to everyone he passed on the street and had garnered a reputation locally for being eccentric in a jolly, deranged kind of way. Down at the docks, he sat on an iron mooring post and slowly consumed a sandwich made with two pieces of stale white bread hugging a single, sweaty slice of cheddar. People clambered up and down the narrow ledges of their canal barges, coiling ropes and carrying jerry cans of petrol. The boats were painted the colour of steam engines and decorated with naively drawn roses. Arthur beamed at the bargemen, his mouth filled with cheap, dense cheese.

Arthur had spent surprisingly little time reflecting on the shift in the direction of his life. It didn't feel as though there was much to unpack. He had been lost, the world had come into focus, and now he knew what he ought to do. He was sorry that his marriage had broken down as a result, but if he was honest with himself, his marriage had begun flailing a long time before his fall and had only managed to limp along because the two fully-grown Candle-wicks saw very little of each other while convincing themselves that this arrangement was the best possible way in which to raise their children.

When he moved out of the house in Bourton, Arthur resolved to never inflict himself on Emil or Evangeline, but to be there when they needed him, in any form he could reasonably agree to. He would not call them or write to them or order them round to his house for stilted catch-ups—all things he felt he had surrendered his claim to—but he would pick up and respond and welcome them with open arms when they came to him, because they were his children, and he loved them, and all that had changed was that his love had now extended so far beyond the bounds of his family that it consumed his every waking moment.

Still, Arthur was human, and he allowed himself an hour each week to trawl through the online presences of his children. Neither proved very satisfying, particularly since both Candlewick siblings had developed an aversion to posting pictures of themselves online. Evangeline generally linked to think-pieces and essays about social justice movements and personal trauma. Emil, under the guise of the username DaCumConjecture<>_<>, posted on forums in which armies of foul-mouthed autodidacts argued about obscure facets of mathematics.

There were, of course, moments when Arthur wondered if his brain had been damaged, as Yara had so vehemently insisted, but he assumed that if that was the case, it was a net positive for the people of the world if he remained injured. He had fantasised about having a machine that might administer to others a blow to the exact spot on the brain where he had received his injury. He imagined himself wandering the world, bopping presidents and billionaires on the head with the device, turning them into people more concerned with alleviating global inequality than launching themselves at distant planets. He imagined that the device would look something like a bicycle helmet with a drill bit poking out of the top like an antenna.

Once his lunch was done, he walked up into town, along a high street that had been largely gutted of what Arthur thought of as "proper shops," leaving behind only bookmakers and job centres and empty shopfronts that were temporarily occupied around Christmas, Valentines, or Halloween by opportunistic traders selling crates of loosely relevant plastic bric-a-brac.

He entered the Oxfam shop, the bell above the door tinkling joyfully to herald his arrival. The blue-rinsed woman behind the counter smiled, pausing midway through handing over change for a porcelain Toby Jug with one ear missing. Arthur returned her smile and moved directly through to the back room. He removed a batch of clothes from the industrial washers and used a blue plastic gun to stitch price tags to their labels with threads of plastic. Most of the clothes were of a familiar variety: baggy, sand-coloured chinos, moth-eaten cardigans with brass buttons, thin, V-neck jumpers in shades of autumn. Very often, they were the clothes of dead people, donated by relatives tasked with emptying the homes of their deceased. Arthur would sometimes hold the donated clothes to his face before they were put through the washer, breathing in the last traces of the people they'd left behind.

Two weeks after calling Emil, Evangeline caught the train back to Stroud from Cambridge, wrapped in a cashmere muumuu and trying not to cry. She spent the journey listening to hyper-aggressive hip-hop and drinking pre-mixed gin and tonics from the can. Leo messaged her a YouTube video of Noam Chomsky falling over, and he messaged her about booking tickets to a play she didn't want to see, and he messaged her to ask why she wasn't messaging him back. She told him she was with family, that she'd call later. He didn't respond.

At the station, she caught a taxi home, and when the taxi driver asked where she was from, Evangeline said "here" so quietly that he didn't hear and seemed to decide she was the kind of antisocial passenger who believed themselves above making polite conversation.

From outside, The Old Rectory appeared unchanged, although in place of Arthur's BMW was a tiny, cherry-red convertible Mazda, with a bumper sticker that read: "Lift Heavy, Eat Clean." Evangeline squinted in through the car window as she walked past and saw that the passenger-side footwell was littered with empty protein beakers, *Men's Health* magazines, and a selfie stick that had been snapped in half.

She knocked at the door and rocked from side to side in anticipation. She'd lost weight, which she'd avoided thinking about, and which had left her feeling insubstantial and delicate, rather than confident or beautiful, or any of the other adjectives she'd promised herself would become pertinent if she could just shrink sufficiently. Her hands had begun to glow purple if she went outside without gloves, and after she came in from particularly long walks her lips were zombie-blue and she felt sleepy.

Yara opened the door with an eager squeal and planted a kiss on Evangeline's forehead. Increasingly, when Evangeline returned home, she had the impression that her mother wasn't greeting the real her, but some fictional daughter, a daughter she had not once threatened to slap across the face with an untouched fillet of pan-fried bream.

"Evie," said Yara.

"Hi, Mum."

"This is Luke."

Evangeline took in the gargantuan man at her mum's side and reflexively took a step back.

Luke Tapper was wearing a vest top with the words "Beast Mode Unlocked" written across it in a font that wouldn't have looked out of place on an invitation to a child's birthday party. There were stretch marks on his biceps. His neck was twice the width of an ordinary human's, laced up with arteries like a joint of gammon.

"I've heard so much about you," said Luke.

Evangeline hated when people said that, feeling that it was unoriginal and, most of the time, untrue. He insisted on drawing her into a loose, emotionless hug. Evangeline was conscious of her shoulder blades against his palms.

Yara tipped her head back. "Emil!" she shouted. "Your sister's here!"

The boy who stumbled down the stairs in jam-smeared jogging bottoms and a Brainfeeder Records T-shirt bore only a passing resemblance to the brother Evangeline remembered. He'd gained a puffiness around his face and his eyes were in shadow as though they'd been pressed further back into his head. There were red scabs capping his knuckles and his uncut fingernails were tipped with threads of black.

"Hey," said Emil.

"Hi," said Evangeline. "You okay?"

"Yeah. You?"

"A little tired, but otherwise good."

The two siblings made no move to hug, despite their mother's expectant look. As far as either of them could remember, they'd hugged twice: once when Evangeline was high on MDMA up Robinswood Hill, and another time when a photographer booked by their mother had shepherded them into a weird embrace, backdropped by an abstract canvas of mauve splashes. The resulting photograph had looked like the poster for a horror film in which two children were cowering as an unseen assailant approached. Yara had buried the photograph at the bottom of a plastic crate in the attic, beside the humiliating result of a pottery course she'd once taken during a frenzy of hobby-searching.

"Luke thought we could all go down to Miller & Carter for dinner," said Yara.

"Did he really?" said Emil.

"Emil," said Yara.

"They do gorgeous steaks," said Luke.

"Just gorgeous," said Emil.

"Alright, mate," said Luke. "That's enough."

Evangeline glanced at her brother and looked back over at the man in the Beast Mode Unlocked vest top. An involuntary laugh escaped her and she clapped her hands protectively over her belly. Emil grinned. Luke frowned. Evangeline realised that if they went out, most people would probably assume that this man was her boyfriend. She couldn't understand how her mother, who she had always known as highly intelligent and achingly self-aware if emotionally unpredictable, could allow herself to wander into such a glaring cliche. She laughed and Emil laughed too and for a moment, they were children again, united in their shared opposition toward the invader in their midst.

"What's wrong with you two?" said Yara.

"Nothing," said her two children simultaneously.

Later, in a ranch-style restaurant beside a lively suburban roundabout, Luke ordered a 21-ounce T-bone steak, without bothering to look at the nervous teenage waiter loitering beside their table. When it arrived, he rubbed his hands together like a pantomime villain. He pulled a tiny tripod from his rucksack, slotted his phone into its rubber fingers, and positioned the set-up at the edge of the table. The two Candlewick children watched him with a combination of horror and glee. Emil, who had already witnessed various iterations of the spectacle, was relishing the prospect of Evangeline getting a full blast of Luke Tapper. Part of him thought that if their mother witnessed his behaviour in the presence of her daughter, she would feel such an acute embarrassment that she'd have no choice but to leave him.

The food arrived and Luke set his phone to record. He gave a thumbs up. Across the restaurant, a table of teenage girls eyed him with unconcealed amusement.

"Hey there, fitness freaks," he said, lifting his plate so that it was angled toward the camera. "Just about to tuck into this absolute beast of a steak."

Before he could go any further, his phone started ringing, and Luke excused himself, winding a path through the restaurant, talking so gravely that it appeared he might be giving life-or-death orders to a subordinate.

Evangeline bit down on her lip and focussed her attention on her glass of red wine. She didn't want to upset her mother any further.

Yara smiled politely at her two children, as though they were at a business meeting and her more senior associate had just abruptly excused himself. Emil thrust his knife into his filet mignon, dragged it back and forth for a few seconds, and suddenly glanced up at his mother, as though remembering something of great importance.

"Hey there, fitness freaks," he said.

"Stop it," said his mother.

Emil turned to the empty tripod, gesturing to his meat with his fork.

"Just about to tuck into this absolute monster of a steak."

Evangeline burst into bellowing, open-mouthed laughter that caused the surrounding tables to pause their conversations and look over. Emil wriggled slightly with satisfaction.

Yara dropped her cutlery with a painful chink onto her plate.

"Will you two behave?" she said. "I don't expect you to be scintillating company, but I do at least expect you to be civil. Luke's trying, which is a damn sight more than either of you are bothering to do."

The sharpness of her tone drained the fun out of the situation and both children regained their composure.

"Mum," said Evangeline.

"Mum what?" said Yara, sawing resolutely at a corner of steak she had no interest in eating.

"He's a YouTuber."

"If it pays the bills, what's the problem?"

"He's closer to my age than he is to yours."

"I'm sorry you don't approve of my choice of partner, Evangeline, but I was under the impression that, since your father decided to drive a fucking snowplough through our marriage, it would be up to me who I chose to spend my time with."

"But why him?" said Emil, emboldened by the presence of his sister.

"He may not be in line to win a Fields Medal, but he's kind and he's generous and he's good to me."

"He doesn't even know you," said Emil.

Luke returned, crashed into his seat, and snuggled his phone back into its cradle.

"Aloha, Candlewicks, sorry for the interruption. How's the grub?"

"Lovely," said Evangeline. "Thank you."

Emil nodded. He could feel his mother's eyes lingering on him, pulling him apart, looking into him, and, he thought, hating him.

Arthur Candlewick gave the majority of his monthly income to How to Save a Life. Sometimes, when he felt tempted to buy a slice of lemon drizzle cake or a marginally more expensive bottle of merlot, he Googled photographs of people with disfiguring tropical diseases or bloated bellies or one-roomed homes without toilets or running water. He imbibed the photographs like medicine. He printed them out and stuck them to the walls of his flat. They reminded him that he was doing the correct thing. They filled him with a renewed sense of purpose.

Evangeline stayed in the village for a week, spending most of her time roaming the quaint streets of the place she'd grown up in, now so crowded with tourists that even short journeys could end up taking twice their Google Map estimates. Sun-cream-smeared Americans asked irritated dog-walkers to snap photographs of them among their exhausted families. Elderly couples drank tea on picnic blankets along the banks of the shallow river. Children waded in the water, collecting colourful stones and bottlecaps and wished-upon coins.

She didn't see her father. She got as close as catching the bus into Gloucester, then found herself walking laps of the town centre, noting the disappearance of the big antiques centre and the record shop and the Hare Krishna café, and feeling nostalgic for the tender rush of her teenage years. When she called Arthur to tell him she wouldn't be coming over because she was feeling ill, Evangeline was disappointed to hear him respond so gently, as if he wasn't bothered whether he saw his daughter or not.

Leo called at least once a day, usually just as she was about to tuck into a flavourless bowl of steamed fish and brown rice, courtesy of Luke. She still hadn't told her mother that she had a boyfriend and the gulf that had opened up between them since that meal on the first night had taken the possibility off the table entirely. Her attempts to reach out to Emil, too, largely came to nothing. He didn't ask about her studies or her plans or her life away from home. His eyes were glassy and unfocused. Although he was happy to make jokes at Luke's expense during mealtimes, he generally kept to himself in his room. He didn't want to walk in the lavender fields or get food at the tourist traps or dust off old board games from the cupboard under the stairs. He wouldn't accept her offer of a drink at The Merman. Evangeline broached the subject of drugs with him once, and Emil told her he took them with friends occasionally, the same as anyone else.

And he wasn't lying, or at least he didn't think he was. Emil wasn't addicted to drugs, he just liked them, the same way a person might like Black Forest gâteau or going to the ballet. And anyway, the drugs he took regularly, in the comfort of his room, weren't the kind of drugs he did with Alice or at parties, but drugs that came in perfect oval pills, with letters and numbers stamped into them, ready to be legitimately prescribed by real doctors. The only difference was that he'd prescribed them to himself, for general discontent and hyperactivity. And they worked. They took the hard edges off the world and let him sleep and turned the relentless dread into something like a typical palette of human emotions.

He had dreams that lasted for years. In the dreams, he tried on entire lives for size, becoming a husband and a father and a stalwart of cult-like communities. Sometimes, Emil convinced himself that these dreams were glimpses into parallel realities, where time unfolded at a different rate, and where he was capable of astounding feats of strength and bravery.

Emil was dreaming that he lived on a rocky island of women who dressed in turquoise robes, when he woke to an insistent call. His phone said that Alice had already tried to reach him twice and he'd slept through both attempts. He called her back.

"Emil," she said. "I'm scared."

"What's wrong?"

"Simeon took something he got from Ky and he's gone mental. He's smashed up the whole flat. He thinks I've been spying on him for the police."

"Where are Emily and Michelle?"

"They're at a thing in Lydney. Can't get through to either of them. Even if I could, they can't get here."

"Can you call the police?"

"If I call the police, he'll go back to prison and his mum'll be so lost and, fuck, Emil, I don't know what to do. I'm scared."

"Okay," said Emil. "It's okay. I'll come."

"But you'll be careful?"

"Yeah."

"Can you bring someone with you?"

"Maybe."

"Thank you, Emil."

Emil hung up, took the replica crysknife of Paul Atreides off his wall, wrapped it in a ketchup-stained hoodie, and went through to his sister's room. Evangeline was wearing all of her clothes, asleep on top of her duvet with her phone lying facedown on her chest. Thick woollen hiking socks, several sizes too large, swaddled her feet like bandages.

"Lean," he said.

Evangeline sat up almost immediately, in a way that made Emil think of Dracula rising from his coffin.

"What time is it?" she said.

"Late. I don't know. I need you to drive me into town."

"I'm not going to help you buy drugs, Emil."

"It's not that."

"Then what is it?"

He looked at her pleadingly. "Please, it's important."

Evangeline swung her legs off the bed and got changed while Emil waited outside the door, typing the address into her phone.

Evangeline drove peacefully and calmly through the warm night in her mother's car, the rules and habits of driving coming back to her like the lyrics to a song that had been a childhood favourite. They stopped outside the block of flats on Cromwell Street.

"Isn't that—"

"Yeah," said Emil. "I'll just be a minute."

"Do you promise you're not buying drugs?"

"Yeah. I told you."

He climbed out of the car and used his phone to cast light onto the pavement below the bathroom window, where he found the key that Alice had thrown down, lodged inside a toilet roll tube and held in place by wet wads of tissue. He let himself in the front door of the building and leapt up the chipped concrete stairs two at a time. Pressing his ear to the door of flat six, he could hear pounding techno and the sound of someone slamming cupboard doors. He knocked. The face that appeared seconds later was missing a number of piercings, with the man's face now covered in sore-looking holes. His pupils were solid black stamps on blank paper.

"What in the shitting fuck is Rees-Mogg doing here?" said the man.

The scene in the flat made Emil think of films in which people suspected to be in possession of vital documents returned from dinner to find their homes ransacked. Everything had been attacked. The TV lay shattered on the floor, fragments of the screen scattered like confetti across the cheap laminate. The curtain pole had become dislodged at one end and crossed the window in a way that made Emil think of the sign for "empty set." Thin tracks of dark liquid ran the length of the room.

Emil shook the hoodie off the replica knife and waved it in the direction of the man.

"Give me your key," he said.

"Whoa," said the man. "You really don't want to do that, fuckface."

"Give me your key and sit down on the sofa."

"I don't have a key."

"Then just sit down."

Once the man was sitting, Emil inched over to the bathroom and knocked. There was no answer. He knocked louder, calling Alice's name. He tried ringing her phone. A snatch of Bullet for My Valen-

tine played through the thin door. She didn't pick up. Emil used the
key like a coin to twist open the lock from his side. On the sofa, the
man rocked back and forth, thumbs buried in his fists.

Alice was slouched in the back corner of the bathroom, wedged
between the toilet and the shower stall, her eyes closed. She was still
breathing. Emil lifted her chin and blew into her face and she stirred
slightly, pawing at his T-shirt without much conviction. There were
cigarette burns on her neck. She smelled faintly of apple cider vinegar.

Emil managed to hoist Alice to her feet and half-drag her out
of the bathroom and into the upended living room. He held the
knife outstretched but the man had curled up on the sofa and was
breathing bull-like into a cushion. Emil hurried Alice out of the
door and locked it behind him. She flinched slightly under the
glare of the corridor light and he knew she'd be okay if he could
get her away.

The car radio was still on and quietly playing Latin pop. Emil
flopped onto the back seat and dragged Alice in after him, arranging
her so that she was sitting, with her head supported by his rolled-up
hoodie.

"Who is she?" said Evangeline.

"Just a friend," said Emil.

"Do we have to take her to the hospital?"

"No," said Emil.

"Is she on drugs?"

"Yeah."

"You told me you weren't getting drugs."

"I'm not the one nodding out."

"Nodding out?"

"She'll be fine. Can you just drive?"

"Home?"

"Yes, home. I need to check she doesn't choke on her own puke."

They drove back to Bourton in silence, with Emil sitting in the
back, Alice's head flopping onto his shoulder when they took corners too sharply. She'd told him once that her mother had been the
sweetest, kindest person she knew, and Emil had been surprised,
having always assumed that Alice had been raised by terrifying, ab-

sent people. When he eventually glimpsed a photo on her phone of a young Alice with her mum, the woman had a face covered in open sores, as though she'd been digging in different spots for a treasure buried somewhere under her eyes.

In Bourton, Evangeline helped Emil carry Alice along the drive, into the house, and up the stairs. They lay her on Emil's bed, on top of the duvet. Emil went to fetch a spare blanket from the airing cupboard and when he came back, Evangeline was gone and Alice's shoes had been taken off and set neatly beside each other at the foot of the bed. He draped the blanket over her quivering body and gathered the paraphernalia needed to roll a joint, leaving his room to go downstairs, and bumping into Evangeline on the landing, the handle of her electric toothbrush protruding from the corner of her mouth like a cigar.

"Emil," she said.

"Please don't have a go at me."

She tugged the toothbrush free of her mouth.

"I wasn't going to have a go at you. I wanted to say you did a nice thing."

"Oh," said Emil. "Okay."

In her old bedroom, the walls a palimpsest of Blu-Tack and Sellotape, Evangeline peeled off both pairs of socks and slipped beneath her duvet. What she had wanted to tell Emil, the night three weeks earlier when she'd called to ask about the minimax theorem, was that she had a boyfriend and he was incredible and he scared her. Leo Gaskill was smart and handsome and he said things that made people laugh until they held onto the backs of chairs for support. He made quiet comments when Evangeline ate too little or too much or pre-packaged foods that contained more than six ingredients. He told her she was naive and self-important. He told her she was the smartest person he'd ever met, but that it was a kind of wild, untapped intelligence that needed to be cultivated. When they slept together, he pulled on her breasts like they were clots of gum he was trying to prise off the underside of a table. He made her try—and then try and then try again—things that hurt, saying that it was a learning process, telling her that she'd been misled by a stuffy culture to believe there was only one way of having sex and that she was "vanilla" and needed to undergo a kind of sexual perestroika. She thought this made sense. She wanted to be free. He put his finger in the hollow of her cheek like a fishhook and pulled until she thought her mouth would tear. In the morning, he'd make mugs of thick, Turkish coffee and tell her things she already knew about Sylvia Plath and American politics. The feelings she harboured toward him were all-consuming and so far removed from the way she'd felt toward her pre-Cambridge boyfriends that Evangeline Candlewick assumed this was the thing that other people called love.

Part Three

A Warm Breakfast

12.

The water in Kalutara was a stained-glass blue, so clear that the brindled seabed was visible even when they waded out to chest height. The sand was as fine and white as icing sugar, and the trees that leant toward it were so green that they looked cartoonish against the VHS blue of the spotless sky.

Slotted into the stretch of coast was a French Colonial–style hotel with wooden window shutters, stucco walls, and tiled verandas. Palm trees hung in groups around a Venn diagram of three increasingly deep pools. Thatched-roof bars stocked with garish spirits dotted the complex.

Every day, Yara woke up before Luke did, collected two towels from a pool attendant with a port-wine stain wrapped around his cheek, and swam lengths until the sleep in her eyes had been replaced by a lively hum of energy. She weighed fifty-two kilograms— fifty-two-point-five in the evenings—and did everything she could to keep the needle on the scale from wandering further north. Arthur had never commented on her weight and Luke never did either, instead making frequent allusions to how "healthy" she was. When Yara was eight, a "healthy appetite" meant you ate plate after plate without thinking of the calories, and a "healthy weight" meant you had cheeks and thighs and upper arms that swung a little when you shook them over your head. Now both seemed to mean the opposite, despite the opinion pieces Yara read in online magazines about the beauty of plus-sized women.

While she swam, her mind inevitably drifted toward family holidays, back when the kids had been small and animated by boundless energy and bottomless spirals of questions. Arthur had paraded them along beaches on his shoulders and they'd swum with dolphins and ridden in catamarans and got travel-sick and food-poisoned and robbed by a Moroccan man in Elton John sunglasses, who spoke in a John Wayne drawl. On one trip, to Cancún when the children had still been in what they all called "little school," Yara had gone out on a worryingly small boat with a man who said that he could arrange for her to swim with a tiger. A very large part of her hadn't believed it could be true, until the boat docked at a wooden jetty floating alone, out of view of the hotels, with a tiger chained by the paw to an iron hoop. As instructed, she approached the tiger from the front, swimming breaststroke, her eyes aimed at the sky behind the animal. She passed by its snarling face with her heart thumping in her chest like a solid object in a washing machine. At the guide's instruction, she cautiously took hold of the tiger's tail.

Proudly presenting her children with a Polaroid the guide had taken of the event, Yara experienced one of the first incidents of her daughter peeling away from her.

"I swam with a tiger, Evie," she'd said, pointing to the photograph clasped in Emil's sticky fingers.

"Yeah," said Evangeline, unimpressed. "But did the tiger want to swim with you?"

Evangeline would later confess to her father that she was jealous that she hadn't been invited to swim with the tiger and had reacted by discrediting the idea altogether.

Yara finished her laps and rested her chin on the concrete lip of the pool. A bartender was wiping down the chrome bar, dressed in an Acapulco shirt and a straw boating hat.

"Morning," said Yara.

The bartender smiled and lifted a glass. Yara shook her head.

Yara wondered what Arthur was doing at that moment, which was a moment four-and-a-half hours earlier back in Gloucester. She'd seen photos of his flat on Emil's phone and it pained her almost as much as the thought of all the money he'd thrown away. She couldn't help picturing the money not as numbers in a bank account but as streets of houses or acres of land. She saw the money as boats and holidays and years of security and peace. The stock portfolio, which she had been allowed to keep in its entirety by the divorce settlement, no longer appeared so reassuring. Compared to what it ought to have been, compared to what she'd planned, it felt woefully inadequate.

Climbing out of the pool, she lay on her sun lounger and read *The Times* on her iPad until Luke emerged from the room, dressed in knee-length board shorts and a flowery rayon shirt, open onto the eggbox of his abs.

They ate breakfast on a terrace overlooking the ocean, being served filter coffee out of steel jugs by persistent waiters and perusing steaming vats of meat and rice, heaped bowls of fresh fruit, and towering glass cylinders which dispensed eight kinds of cereal. There was a short, bristly-bearded man in chef's whites whose entire job was to loiter at the sweet end of the buffet, batting away wasps with a miniature whip. Yara usually shook a few spoons of muesli into the smallest bowl available and ate it with Greek yoghurt and half a banana. Luke took two plates each time and piled each one so high with slick twigs of sausage and pink soles of bacon that Yara had to resist the impulse to apologise to the hotel staff on his behalf.

On the first day, she suggested he might want to eat slightly less, or at least in a more staggered fashion.

"Holidays are for bulking, babe," he said. "Why else go all-inclusive?"

She looked at the blue plastic wristband encircling her wrist, remembering the same wristbands looped around the tiny arms of her children, and how they'd used them to gorge endlessly on virgin piña coladas and mounds of salty chips.

By the end of each breakfast, Luke's mouth would be shiny with grease, his eyes glazed. Yara forbade him from recording YouTube videos during meals they ate together. She told him that they were on holiday and she didn't want to see the tripod appearing on the edges of tables or sun loungers or tiki bars.

"My life is my job, babe," said Luke.

"I understand," said Yara. "But this is meant to be a break from our lives."

After their fifth breakfast in Sri Lanka, Yara realised they had barely ventured outside the hotel, and announced that they were going on an excursion to one of the nearby temples that had respectable reviews on TripAdvisor. At the marble reception desk, in a hexagonal foyer with a church-like ceiling, a woman with a sleek helmet of black hair smiled humourlessly at a sunburned couple. A constellation of wooden ceiling fans were spinning at different speeds overhead. Yara asked how they ought to go about seeing the area.

"There are many guides outside the hotel gates," the receptionist said. "They have tuk-tuks."

"Outside the gates?"

"Yes, madam."

"We just go outside and see who happens to be standing there?"

"It's nothing to be scared of, madam. It's just how we do it. It's very safe. We know the men."

"Can you call us an official guide? Someone who could be traced."

The receptionist moved her head in a way Yara couldn't decipher. She waited for the woman to offer them a more legitimate way of seeing the area but when nothing else came, she turned to Luke, who was peeling a sliver of burnt skin away from the swollen bulb of his shoulder.

"Come on," she said. "Let's just walk."

Luke, who hadn't realised he was meant to be joining her in indignation, followed Yara out of the foyer and across the ornamental front garden of the hotel, where a wheezing minibus was disgorging a new batch of still-pale holidaymakers, fresh from the airport, their hands clasping bulging duty-free bags of scotch and cigarettes. A security guard dressed like a golfer opened the gate and waved them through.

As soon as they stepped out of the compound, they were met by a wall of young men in shorts and rubber sandals. The men pressed toward them, promising wonderous sights and morally dubious-sounding experiences: they could hold baby alligators or visit wild monkeys or feed giant, carnivorous fish. They could swim on untouched beaches. They could climb to the top of temples known only to locals.

"Alright, lads," said Luke. "Give us a bit of space."

The men retreated slightly.

Luke and Yara walked hurriedly around nearby shops selling souvenirs with little or no relevance to the country they were in: tie-dye T-shirts and plastic buckets and hourglasses of brightly dyed sand. Yara felt hyper-alert and dizzy with the heat, which pressed on her temples like a pair of too-small swimming goggles. The shopkeeper was trailing them, smiling, and she could see that at least a handful of men were still waiting hopefully outside the doors, smoking and chatting in a language that felt threatening to Yara.

They stepped out of the shop and two men moved toward them.

"Let's just go back to the hotel," said Yara.

"Yeah," said Luke. "It smells like shit out here."

At lunch, Luke ate two plates of fish curry with hoppers, and fell asleep on a sun lounger without having applied any sun cream. Yara ordered a beer from the bartender and, as an afterthought, asked if he had a cigarette. He looked at her apprehensively as though it was some kind of trap set by one of his managers. She offered a bank note without any real idea what it was worth and he accepted the offer, extricating a cigarette from a pocket beneath his apron, and sliding it underhand across the bar.

Smoking the strong, unfiltered cigarette, and sipping the ice-cold, local beer, Yara observed her sleeping boyfriend. There was a tattoo below his belly-button of a thistle, which he had told her was an homage to his Scottish ancestry. He pronounced the word "homidge" and, without correcting him, Yara wondered where he'd picked up the mispronunciation, because it would mean that he'd have to have read rather than heard the word, and she had very rarely seen him read anything that wasn't the comments section on a YouTube video.

Luke kicked at an imaginary interlocutor in his dreams. His toenails were thick and opaque, like rhino horn.

She knew exactly why she'd fallen for Arthur. It wasn't long since she'd left home but she'd already stumbled through a sequence of toothless romances to men who reminded her as little as possible of her own father. Arthur was the last in a line of gentle, unassuming men, who placed their hands on her with the hesitation of a bomb disposal expert. Arthur was slight and pale and he sat with his knees bent toward each other, trousers ridden up to expose the patterned socks climbing his hairless calves. His hair stuck up in drunken tufts and he smoked Camels back then, out of a packet that was always so crushed it looked as though it had been put through a mangle. Arthur was the third son of a wealthy family who were in the process of losing their wealth. Although they had urged him to keep on at university and enter into some lucrative, respected, reliable field, his studies were making him miserable, and Yara had been the one to unchain him from that misery, to tell him to quit, quickly, unless he wanted to spend his life miserably walking someone else's path toward someone else's idea of a decent life. Which was why Arthur's family had been against Yara from the start, and how the stage had been set for the arguments that raged over bottles of wine the Candlewicks could no longer afford. Arthur's parents hadn't been at the wedding, hadn't been at Evangeline's birth, and had died without knowing Emil had ever arrived on the planet.

And now Yara was here, at an expensive hotel in a poor country, with an unfamiliar man whose physical presence was a threat to other people. Luke made people nervous and lacked the self-awareness to realise it. He got angry in public: not at Yara, but at baristas, receptionists, and hotel porters. And at the drivers of slow cars. Sometimes, when they were driving, he'd tell her: "I'm going to climb out of this car and teach that prick a lesson." But he never did climb out of the car, just huffed and puffed, storing up his rage for later use on an unsuspecting service worker. (He was kind too, wasn't he? Wasn't he also unexpectedly thoughtful and tender? Didn't he also cook every day? Hadn't he walked Audrey Tyreman through the floods to a christening?)

She'd asked him once, after a missed flight to Paris, why he'd been so angry at the person behind the help desk, who bore no responsibility for them having been late. He stared at her blankly. Was I angry? he'd said. The next time it happened, she touched him gently on the wrist, and he glanced over at her with the startled expression of a sleepwalker being woken up.

What was she doing here? Was there even an answer to uncover? Or was it all just chance, that she'd met Arthur outside the bathroom

of an insipid Rotary Club party in Warwick, and she'd met Luke outside the bathroom in their chain gym, and she was colouring in a life
of chance with causality because otherwise it became too depressing
to think about? She had wondered, often, whether every life was a
series of chance events that one strung together into a story, the same
way a brain managed to concoct the illusion of self from the data it
was given by the eyes, the mouth, and the ears.

The illusion of the self. There was a time when she'd thought about
such things. When she'd first met Arthur, they'd talk until dawn
about what it meant to be a human being in the universe. At some
point, their conversations had become about savings accounts and
estate agents and the company Arthur was starting in lieu of pursuing the kind of career his parents had hoped for. Once those matters
had been settled, their conversations became about Evangeline: about
her height and weight and her climbing abilities and the words she
picked up at random and deployed with equal randomness. (Her first
word had been an original: "dubbin." Neither could tell what it had
originally been intended to convey. Birds were dubbins, adults were
dubbins, bananas and shoes and trees were dubbins.)

Luke woke up on the lounger, itchy with fresh sunburn, and they
walked along the beach, holding hands. He spotted a smear of colour on the horizon and gestured excitedly toward it.

"Babe, let's jet-ski."

"I'm tired," said Yara.

"It's relaxing."

Yara shook her head.

"Fine." Luke pointed to a narrow jetty that looked as though it
had been built out of scrap pallets, laced together with cable ties.
"You can sit there and watch me." He clicked his fingers at the side
of his head as an idea entered it. "You can film me," he said. "You
can actually get some sick shots."

"Luke," said Yara.

"Babe, all you have to do is hold the camera."

"Exactly," said Yara.

"What?" said Luke.

"We're on holiday, I don't want to sit around holding a camera
while you jet-ski. I'm not your cameraman."

Luke's face collapsed in such a spectacular fashion that Yara immediately felt like a mother, trying to lead her distraught child through the dark storm of a tantrum.

"I'm sorry," she said. "I'm just tired."

Why was she apologising? What had she done wrong?

"I just want us to have a nice time," said Luke.

"I know you do," said Yara.

"Maybe we can jet-ski tomorrow?"

"Maybe, Luke."

The next morning, when she woke up, Luke was snoring like a broken motor on top of the duvet, a luminescent rind around his mouth betraying the fact that he'd spent the previous night drinking lurid cocktails in the subterranean hotel night club.

She collected towels from the pool attendant, staked out loungers, and swam her laps. She lay on her back on the sun lounger and unlocked her iPad with a practised glide around the grid of numbers. There was a news article about a group of protestors being arrested for gluing themselves to a stretch of road in Central London. When she zoomed in, Yara could just about make out her ex-husband's round face, his mouth hanging open in surprise as a police officer in a riot vest hauled him away.

Evangeline returned to her room on Aarkell Street with a paper bag from the chemist containing three different brands of pregnancy test. She emptied a third of a bottle of chardonnay into a whisky glass and drank half of it in two gulps. She told herself it was okay, because if she was pregnant, she would get rid of it anyway, and surely there were plenty of women who wouldn't even have been aware they were pregnant by this stage, still drinking and smoking with happy abandon.

She wished there was someone to confer with but Ahk had left Cambridge for New York, and with him several of the other third-years she'd come to call friends. Leo had stayed on to do a PhD. He'd tried to convince her they ought to move in together but she'd demurred, and no amount of reasoning or cajoling had been able to persuade her otherwise. She'd come to love her room above the dry cleaner. The whorled Artex ceiling had accompanied her through countless apocalyptic hangovers. The view from the window of trees that dressed and re-dressed as the seasons rolled around felt like a play staged every year for her alone.

Reading the tiny print of the instructional leaflets felt indescribably lonely, which was ironic, Evangeline thought, considering she was about to find out whether or not she really was alone. Did a foetus count as company? She hoped not. She hoped a foetus counted as much as a peanut or a lampshade, because she wasn't sure she could bear anything else. She knew that if she was pregnant, she would get an abortion, because it would be stupid to not get an abortion. Not getting an abortion would mean becoming a mother, rather than any of the other things she wanted to be.

Again, Evangeline recognised the hypocrisy in herself. She very much believed that women could and ought to have both children and fulfilling professional lives, but she didn't believe that she would be one of them. She could barely cope as it was, without having to raise a baby while coming to terms with Wittgenstein and econometrics.

The first plastic stick, dunked in neon-yellow urine and intently watched for three minutes, told Evangeline Candlewick that she was pregnant.

As did the second.

And the third.

Turning over onto her knees on the bathroom floor, Evangeline thrust her hand down the back of her throat and tickled her tonsils until she'd thrown up as much of the wine as she could manage. Panting and massaging her burning throat, she rearranged herself so that she was sitting with her back against the wall and her knees pressed up against her chest. She slid her hands protectively over her abdomen. She told herself she wasn't drunk, that none of the alcohol had yet managed to seep through her stomach and into her blood.

"I'm sorry," she told her belly. "I didn't know you were in there."

Arthur went to meet his brother, Hugo, at a gastro pub on the King's Road, where he asked for a peppermint tea and a tap water, which he mixed together in a huge metal thermos, and sipped from experimentally before pouring a slug back into the mug that the tea had first arrived in.

Hugo Candlewick-Roper was a serial entrepreneur who made just enough money for his life to limp along in the manner he insisted on clinging to. It was two years since they'd been in each other's presence, which was a comparatively short time by the standards of a family who got married and divorced, moved house and had children, without bothering to inform each other. Arthur Candlewick had only the vaguest sense that the birthdays of his two brothers lay somewhere toward the second half of the year. Hugo Candlewick-Roper wasn't entirely sure whether their eldest brother, Duncan Candlewick, had three children or four. Duncan Candlewick, for his part, had either misheard or misunderstood a piece of news about Arthur Candlewick, and was under the impression that his brother had converted to Catholicism and was working as a missionary in Malawi.

Ten minutes into their unemotional reunion, Arthur set out the analogy he'd first encountered in the mineshaft about the man in expensive shoes walking past a drowning child.

"It would be immoral not to help," he said. "Would it not?"

Hugo shook his head in disbelief.

"Christ on a bike, Artie, she was right."

"Who was right?"

"Your old lady." He corrected himself. "Your *old* old lady. She called to tell me you were getting a divorce a while back, saying you were off your rocker. She wanted to know if you'd said anything to me. I told her no, of course. Then she asked had you ever shown signs of, you know, going off the deep end before."

"I'm not interested in hearing this," said Arthur.

"I told her about the summer you went everywhere dressed as an owl. Remember that? Dad had to drag you out of that ruddy suit, kicking and screaming." Hugo wobbled his head disapprovingly as though the incident had taken place just last week. "That suit smelled like piss, Artie."

Arthur lifted his diluted peppermint tea and turned it, trying to find a symbol in the tiny flakes that had escaped the teabag. He did remember that summer, mostly because it had been the summer that a fully-grown man had pursued him down an alleyway with his penis hanging outside of his trousers. Arthur had run so fast he could taste blood and copper in his mouth and his eyesight temporarily cut out, as though all the available electricity in his body had been diverted to his legs. He had nightmares after that and slept with a steak knife under his pillow for months. He never told anyone because he hadn't been entirely sure what it meant.

"What about the kids?" said Hugo. "You still see the kids?"

"Evangeline's at Cambridge," said Arthur. "She doesn't come back down to us too often. Emil, I see. Emil often pops in for a cup of tea."

"He still spooky?"

"He was never spooky," said Arthur. "He's a little quiet, that's all."

"'Taciturn' is the word you're looking for. He got Grandpa Percy's genes."

"Hugo, he did not."

Grandpa Percy had been their mother's father, a man who savagely wrangled them all onto his lap, to tell them things they weren't yet placed to understand about female anatomy or the sexual proclivities of the ancient Greeks. According to rumours passed between cousins, Grandpa Percy had come home from the Great War with a Luger that could be found wrapped in a silk nightgown in the loft. He had worked in India for several years, violently propping up the ailing empire. One of his toes had been amputated because he'd kicked Grandma Lucille so hard it broke in enough places to be unfixable.

Arthur had arranged to see his brother not out of a desire to catch up or be admonished for having once retreated into the character of an owl, but because he'd recently read a convincing essay about how, by evangelising about direct political action and regular donation, a person could multiply the amount of good they did by entire lifetimes.

"So, will you come?" said Arthur.

"To what?"

"To the protest."

Hugo frowned in amazement. "Artie, I've got my own shit to worry about. Jo moans like a ghost in heat about wanting a bigger place to live, meanwhile I've got two kids who both want a new

iPhone every year and an old Lexus that our friendly village me-
chanic has said couldn't even be stripped for parts."

"You don't think we have any responsibility to those less fortunate than ourselves?"

"Not as much as we have to our families, who we brought into
the world."

"And you don't think we have a moral obligation to look after the
planet those children will spend their lives living on?"

"Artie, I don't know what 'moral obligation' means. Does it mean
I have to do something? Because I don't have to do anything. I can
curl up in a ball and shit my pants, if I want to."

"Hugo," said Arthur.

Hugo had always been the most crass of the three brothers and
Arthur privately believed that this was because he had been slapped
the least. By the time Hugo came along, their parents were either
bored of or no longer interested in doling out physical punishment.
Perhaps they'd just become old, their bodies no longer possessed of
the energy required to wallop misbehaving children.

"Some plucked-out-of-the-air moral argument isn't going to make
me do anything," said Hugo. "None of it can trump the fact that,
day-to-day, the kids need to be dropped off at school and the cleaner
needs to be paid."

"But you would do something if you were literally walking past
a drowning child?"

"Honestly," said Hugo, "I might do, I might not. What if it was a
scam? What if he was only pretending to be drowning so his mate
could nick my wallet after I took off my trousers to hop into the
water?"

"You would stop to take off your trousers?"

Hugo glanced down at the pinstriped pair of chinos he had on.
"Maybe not these trousers," he said. "But a pair that were halfway
decent."

Arthur leant toward his brother, as though about to impart a
threat.

"You don't really mean that," he said.

Several hours later, Arthur was lost in a crush of strangers who
shared his belief about the fate of the planet. He'd once broken his leg

in a spectacular fashion, bone thrust out through his skin like a lamb shank. It had filled him with terror but Arthur later experienced a feeling of deep relief in the hospital, not from painkillers or surgical intervention but because the doctors had possessed intricate compound words for his exact injury, which they hastily put to use forming reassuring plans that let Arthur know that he was in exactly the place he ought to be. It was similar to the way he felt on Byron Road, just off Trafalgar Square, with the palms of his hands glued to the tarmac and people either side of him humming defiantly. This was where he was meant to be. This was what he was meant to be doing.

Emil sat his last exam on a cold, bright May morning. He woke up at seven, jolted out of his decades-long dream by an alarm so merciless it sounded as though it was heralding the local escape of a dangerous prisoner. He padded downstairs, prising apart rolling papers as he went. Being alone in the house was an increasingly common occurrence, and one which had long since lost any sense of novelty or excitement. In an empty house, Emil became unchained, and would indulge in behaviours that left him depressed and adrift. Instead of real meals, he would consume a third of a cheap birthday cake, half a box of Lindt truffles, or a Heinz spotted dick, directly out of the tin. He would chain-smoke in the garden and take pills and play PlayStation in his room, sometimes pissing into bottles that had once contained energy drinks or Lucozade, rather than pausing to go and use the toilet. He masturbated, sometimes for hours, over increasingly extreme kinds of porn. He pushed the age bounds higher and higher, until the women he was watching have sex looked to be in imminent danger of needing medical attention.

He thought he might have done passably on the majority of his exams, though he doubted he'd get the two As needed to secure his provisional place at UCL. He wasn't even sure he wanted to move to London. It held no allure for him. It was Evangeline, not Emil, who had loved *Mary Poppins* and begged their parents to take them to West End shows and the National Gallery, and even she hadn't bothered to consider the capital for her studies. London felt like a story Emil had never really wanted to read. It was someone else's idea of an exciting place.

At his sister's insistence, he'd applied for Cambridge and sat for their boring test and gone for a boring interview in a gloomy, wood-panelled room, where a bald man with a white beard sneered down at him. The man was sixty-two years old and hadn't left the city in a decade, hadn't eaten in eight hours, and was one of the very few men of his age not to have arrived at the university via a private school. Emil hid himself almost entirely, coming across as an aloof but unexceptional kid, with nothing to set him apart from the hundreds of other wide-eyed hopefuls traipsing around the hallowed streets of the university city. He slept on his sister's sofa and the two of them stayed up all night getting drunk at a party that Leo Gaskill decided not to attend. Emil spent most of the night talking to a second-year Earth Sciences student about the use of vector calculus in seismology. When she found out he was a year thirteen and not a student, the girl pretended to need the bathroom and never came back.

No offer came either and when Emil had relayed this news to Evangeline, she told him that he shouldn't worry because he wouldn't like it anyway.

"You told me to apply, Lean."

"Only to give you something to aim for," she said.

On the morning of his last exam, Emil cast a disinterested look over his tangle of revision notes, downed two coffees, and listened to Aphex Twin on the bus to school. He finished his English Lit paper before anyone else and left the exam hall without bothering to read it over.

In Gloucester, Emil tripped off the bus and lit a cigarette, prodding the AirPods back into his ears. As he walked, he parked the cigarette in the corner of his mouth and used his hands to untie his stubby tie, which he balled up and shoved into the side pocket of his bulging army surplus rucksack. As everyone sat their last exam at a different time on a different day, the typical end-of-year celebrations would be taking place the following weekend. Instead, Emil was meeting Imogen in Lily's, a kitschy, low-ceilinged café, in a narrow street shared with a new age shop, a place that sold esoteric instruments, and a T-shirt printing business with sun-faded examples of their work hanging in the window. "Minchinhamptom Ladies

Bowls Club Bowel Cancer Fundraiser." "Gloucester Apkido Federation." "Rory's Stag: Pussy's Beware."

Imogen was wrapped in a violet shawl and wore silk ballet pumps on her feet. She sat as though she was at home in her living room: legs tucked beneath her, cushion clasped to her chest. He could tell immediately that something was wrong. It was like walking into a room and realising everyone there had been talking about you half a second earlier, except Imogen was alone. None of her friends were present, her friends who had become his friends, and over whom he'd had several rows with Deepesh, who said that they were basic and dull and doomed to mediocrity. By basic, Deepesh meant that they didn't like the angry American stand-ups who made jokes about dead babies and transgender people. Emil was in the process of realising that he didn't like those things either, and that he was better suited to the milder kingdom of Imogen's friends, and even the comparatively tame anime that he watched with Alice. He was becoming a different person as he aged out of his acne; milder in some respects, more perverse and uncalibrated in others.

"Emil," said Imogen, with such gravity that he wondered if she had cancer. His eyes flicked back and forth across her head, searching for traces of thinning hair. If she had cancer, he would sit by her side during chemotherapy, clutching her skeletal hand, and reading her dull profiles of pretentious artists from glossy American magazines. "I need to talk to you."

"Oh," said Emil. "Okay."

It was dawning on him what might be about to happen. Although at the beginning of their relationship, he'd frequently convinced himself that Imogen was going to either leave him or reveal that their relationship had been part of a joke or a prank or a bet she'd made with friends, in the last half a year or so, he'd begun to take her for granted. Imogen was always there, always reminding him of the importance of their upcoming exams and deadlines for applications, always pushing him to get a haircut or change out of clothes that smelled of compost.

"I'm sorry," said Imogen. "I do think you're a very special person, but I don't think it makes sense for us to keep seeing each other."

She cleared her throat and shook her head, as though she was at a rehearsal for the break-up, rather than the break-up itself. "For us to keep going out, I mean. I don't think we should."

"Um," said Emil. "Okay."

"Do you want to know why?"

"I don't think so."

"It's just that I always feel like I have to look after you, Emil. Like you don't have any motivation of your own. You don't know what you want or where you're going, and I can't decide that for you. But I do think you should decide, because you're such a special person, it would be a shame otherwise." Imogen paused and looked for something in his face but couldn't find it. "Are you upset?" she said, with a very slight tinge of hope.

Emil shrugged. "No," he said. "I have to go."

"Go where?"

"Just—" He pointed over his shoulder.

Emil left the café and pelted through the streets of town, dodging mobility scooters and pushchairs and arriving at the temporary bus station so out of breath that he slumped to the ticket-strewn floor.

Back in the humid gloom of his bedroom, Emil took three pills and put his fist through his computer monitor. He took another pill and hammered his phone against the wall until the screen shattered. Who would he need to call anymore? There was no one in the house to hear the destruction unfolding upstairs. Only once he'd broken everything of any value in his bedroom did Emil flop onto his bed and wonder what he ought to do next.

He had no way of occupying his bloody, bloated hands, now everything had been destroyed. No computer, no phone, no iPad. No inbox to check, nothing to scroll through, no way of being fed brief videos about things he was tangentially interested in.

Possessed by a sudden peace, Emil went over to his bookshelf. Although he'd stopped buying books for himself years earlier, the collection continued to grow, slowly, thanks to gifts from his parents and sister, who either hadn't realised that he no longer read or were trying to nudge him back toward the habit.

He chose the largest unread book from his shelf. It was a Neal

Stephenson novel from a couple of years ago, bought for him by his sister, and shelved after a stalled attempt to make it through the first chapter. The book was 1,192 pages long and covered a period of ten thousand years. It told the story of a small band of human survivors struggling to make it on an ailing spacecraft after planet earth is rendered uninhabitable. Wrapped in a duvet, pressed into the corner of his room, Emil was at page 261 when he realised that the morning was already advancing from the corners of the sky. He went downstairs and flicked on the coffee machine and, while it rattled to life, he stood beside it with the book open in his swollen hand, stuffing cereal into his mouth. He was gripped and there was no way he was letting go. More important than anything else, was the fate of that lone band of astronauts, traversing the outer reaches of the galaxy.

When Evangeline told a hungover Leo Gaskill that she was pregnant, he turned away from her, hands cupped over his face like a smoker trying to light up in a storm. He was barefoot and there was a length of rope holding up his trousers in place of a belt.

"How far along?" he said, into his hands.

"Five weeks," said Evangeline. "I think."

He paced up and down with his hands twitching behind his back and Evangeline thought of Hitler, in the German film about his last days in the bunker. She was afraid of both potential outcomes: that he wanted her to keep it and that he wanted her to get rid of it. She wasn't sure she could bear either one.

"This is good news," Leo said, finally. "This is good."

"Is it?" said Evangeline.

He turned to her and dropped into a squat, placing his hands on her knees and looking directly into her eyes. "If you wanted to abort it, you would have already aborted it, and you wouldn't have told me."

"That's not true at all," said Evangeline.

"So you do want to abort it?"

"I haven't decided."

"Could you make a moral case for aborting this child?"

Evangeline knocked his hands off her knees and shuffled out of his reach.

"Leo, it's my body. This isn't the nineteen sixties."

"And whose body is the baby's?"

"It's not a baby. It's a foetus."

"Whose body, then, is the foetus's? Or does that body have exactly zero rights? Or does it have some rights, but not enough to trump your right to keep your figure for a few months?"

"You're being cruel," said Evangeline. "And reductionist."

He let go of her duvet and dragged his feet over to the old sash window, hauled it up, and lit a cigarette, which he smoked while half-heartedly attempting to aim the smoke outside. "I'm sorry," he said. "I just hate the idea of a life we've given rise to being flushed down the toilet."

"I didn't say I was going to flush it down the toilet," said Evangeline. "I just wanted to discuss it with you."

Leo let his cigarette fall from his hand into the street. He returned to Evangeline on the bed and took her hand. Her fingers tensed into fishhooks. She always liked his hands. They weren't dainty, they were inexplicably calloused and heavy, the nails slightly clubbed and bitten around the edges so they'd frayed like old denim.

"If we've made a life," he said, "however accidentally, I think it's something to treasure. It can only be a net good in the world, the existence of this child. It doesn't matter if it makes our lives tough for a while, the child who comes will make us forget all that. We won't regret it."

Evangeline bit her lip and relaxed her hand into his. More than once, she'd wondered if her own parents had regretted their decision to have children. While she and Emil had come out of the bargain with existence, Yara and Arthur only really got two fewer bedrooms and two more mouths to feed. Did they enjoy their children? Evangeline knew there were entire years when she'd been unbearable. Years when she'd looked sniffily down on her parents as they fed her and clothed her and sent her to a school with extortionate fees.

"You would have to take a break from studying," said Leo. "Just for a year or two. You'd stay with Mum down in Hykeham, go on walks, take baths."

"Leo, I'm not being banished to the countryside. What decade are you living in?"

"It's not banishment. It's nurturing. You need to be in a peaceful, loving environment."

"You know people have babies while simultaneously leading countries and running multinational corporations?"

"People also eat Coco Pops for breakfast and ride motorcycles, Evangeline, it doesn't mean they ought to. If you keep studying, you'll be stressed, and the elevated levels of cortisol will filter through to the child."

"Cortisol?"

"The stress hormone."

"I know what cortisol is, I just don't understand why you're talking to me about it."

"Because I want us to do this right."

Evangeline spent the next weeks in a daze. There were slight changes in her body, though she couldn't yet tell if they were real or psychosomatic inventions caused by her newfound hyper-alertness. She listened to herself in a way she'd never had cause to before. She pressed the flesh of her ankles and smelled her own breath and pinched her own cheeks in the mirror, searching for signs of the person being built in her belly.

She didn't call her mother, she didn't call her father, she didn't call Emil, and she didn't know why. More than anything, she wanted someone to pick her up and carry her through this. She wanted someone she could confide in about what was happening to her, a disinterested party who would offer reasonable counsel on how to proceed. Evangeline knew that she had faults—she was aloof and unforgiving and judgemental—but she couldn't tell if these were vastly outweighed by Leo's faults or she was just holding him to a higher standard than could be justified. The question wasn't just whether or not she wanted to have a baby, but whether or not she wanted to have a baby with Leo Gaskill, who could dance between making her feel like a Nobel Laureate and a pompous toddler in the same day.

The first person she called, in the end, was Ada, who sounded deliriously happy, and spoke at length about a trip to Ibiza she'd been on with two girls from her uni course, and how they'd got so drunk that they climbed onto their hotel roof and stripped down to their underwear.

"I have some news," said Evangeline, during a pause in the recounting of Ada's escapades.

"Is it a boy?" said Ada. "Is he hot?"

"Kind of."

"Oh, like hot in a weird way?"

"I'm pregnant, Ada."

"Wow," said Ada. "That's a lot."

Ada was studying medicine at a university a thirty-minute drive from home. She still lived with her parents but had accrued a new group of friends on her course, friends who didn't patronise or demean her, and who didn't consider themselves her moral superior. In fact, in an unexpected reversal of fortunes, Ada found herself arguably the most popular member of her fun-loving crew of future doctors.

"Are you going to abort it?" she said.

"No," said Evangeline. "I don't think that would be right."

"Are you joking with me, Evangeline?"

"What do you mean?"

"Is that really your new hot take? That abortion is wrong?"

"Morally, under circumstances such as mine, I think it is."

"What happened to you?"

Evangeline moved her phone away from her ear, holding it in front of her face as though to check it was still in one piece.

"Come to Cambridge and visit me," she said, returning the phone to her ear.

"I'm studying too," said Ada. "I can't just come and visit you."

"No," said Evangeline. "I know. I didn't mean right now. You can come any time."

"I don't know, Evangeline. Maybe. I'm busy."

"Fine," said Evangeline. "Don't worry."

There was a lull and both girls listened to each other's breathing. Evangeline's hands moved down to her belly and lingered there, waiting for some kind of reassurance from the almost-person she was ferrying around.

It was Ada who broke the silence.

"You haven't spoken to me for like years, Evangeline, now you call and tell me you're pregnant. I didn't even know you had a boyfriend. I tried to call you like ten times last year and you didn't answer. I didn't even think you liked me."

"Of course I like you, Ada. We were best friends."

"So? I was best friends with Laura Muller when I was six and I haven't seen her in ten years. People change, Evangeline. Things end."

The only light in the spacious, marble-floored hotel room came from the red eye of the wall-mounted TV and the border of hazy grey around the curtain concealing the balcony door. Yara had been awake for two hours, meditating on the raspy, mechanical breathing of her boyfriend. She took out her phone and thumbed the brightness down to minimum. She scrolled back to the news story about the protestors gluing themselves to the road and she sought out her ex-husband. A part of her wanted to call him and ask for permission to rewind their lives, back to that night when he'd gone strolling through the countryside and fallen into a mineshaft, though she knew, really, that they'd have to rewind further, to a time before the children had crowded out so much of everything else, to before they'd settled so deeply into their lives that they had become numb.

Why had he really gone walking that night? What was he looking for? She'd followed that avenue of thought countless times since it had happened. She still wondered, too, whether she was the guilty party. Whether she should have pushed harder to have him seen by psychologists or psychiatrists or neurosurgeons, or made him attempt other forms of therapy or rehabilitation.

A few minutes later, she was in flip-flops, walking across the hotel foyer with a sarong wrapped around her body like a towel. There was a different person at reception this time, a man with a polished gold chain around his neck, reading a newspaper in a language that looked to Yara like a riddle.

"Can I help you, madam?" he said.

"I'm going for a stroll," she said.

"Outside the hotel?"

Yara kept going.

"Be careful, madam," said the receptionist. "It is late."

It is late, thought Yara, the sentence lingering in her head as though it were a zen koan of great profundity. It is late. In the long day of my life, it is late.

Yara was fifty-two. It was not really late, but it was too late to start again in the way her husband might. She didn't imagine he would do it but if the desire took hold of him, Arthur had the freedom to begin everything again. A new wife, new babies, new family traditions. One or two or three new childhoods to fill with favourite films and songs and manic holidays where everything was bright and new. Would anyone want to start a family with Arthur? Surely, someone would. He was a good person, at least. A brain-damaged but good person, a gentle, generous person, even before he'd taken the entire world on his shoulders.

There were only three men lingering outside the hotel gates now, two of which had motorised rickshaws, the other pausing for a chat on his way to somewhere else.

Without exchanging words, one of the men knew to step forward while the other hung back. He was thin and bright-eyed, dressed in a pair of Newcastle United football shorts and a polo shirt with a logo of a stag's head over the heart. His hair was wound into a chestnut on the back of his head.

"Where you want to go, madam? Pharmacy?"

"No," said Yara.

"Club? Bar? You want to dance? Drink? Eat?"

"What's your name?" said Yara.

"I am Upul."

"Upul, do you think you could take me to a temple?"

"There is one in Colombo open late. I take you there. You are interested in Buddhism?"

"Kind of," said Yara.

"So," said Upul. "Kind of let's go there. It will be a nice ride. Please, take a seat. Do not worry, I will look after you."

Yara climbed onto the machine and gripped onto the chrome handles at her sides. She scrunched her toes in her flip-flops and wondered whether she was being reckless. Was this how it had felt for Arthur? Was she really trying to emulate his spontaneous disappearance? If you emulated a spontaneous disappearance by spontaneously disappearing, didn't it cease to be an emulation and start to be an actual spontaneous disappearance? At what point would she begin to count as having "disappeared"?

"Do you have a cigarette I can borrow?" she said.

"No borrow," said Upul. "You can have. So many as you like."

He passed her a cigarette that looked as though it had been rolled from a scrap of leather stuffed with pencil shavings. When she lit it, the acrid smoke filled her lungs like steam and her eyes watered. The vehicle juddered to life beneath her linen shorts.

They drove past the strip of souvenir shops until the buildings on either side of them were replaced by darkness and foliage and Upul sped up, the swinging lights on the front of the vehicle illuminating the dirt track in fits and flashes. Oncoming tuk-tuks and motorbikes appeared without warning from a hazy ring of night framed by wisps of palm and chandeliers of kithul. As the foliage fell away, the road became a ledge between a slope of stubbled dirt and a body of water heaving with small, low boats. A city stood in the distance, its tallest buildings draped in cables and blinking like Christmas trees. The dirt track broadened and billboards appeared, wire-mesh fences appeared, small buildings with corrugated metal roofs appeared.

Yara felt a complicated braid of emotions, wound around each other as she roared through the sludgy Sri Lankan night, the smell of fruit sugar and petrol heavy in the hot air. Crucified kites of fish hung from the beams of huts where they were hawked alongside carrier bags of cashews and bundles of murunga tied with red string. Men squatted beside steel tankards, pouring tea into plastic cups. FM radios blared cymbal-heavy rhythms from steps and ledges.

There was poverty on the road into the city but it was painted bright colours and bustling with determined life, and it confused Yara, who found herself unsure of how she ought to feel about witnessing the lives of the people hefting canvas sacks along the side of an unpaved road. When she appreciated the sight of the city at night, it felt as though she was fetishising the poverty, and when she tried to take in the poverty, it felt as though she was on a kind of inexcusable, dystopian safari. Yara fidgeted in the worn seat, wondering what her guide thought of her, whether he resented her or was grateful for her custom or thought of her as just another parcel that needed to be moved from one location to another.

She thought of Arthur and his talk of moral obligations and the responsibilities. She thought of her daughter and the arguments they'd once had around the dining table. It was meant to be the parents who stressed that the leftovers on their children's plates could feed the starving for days, not the other way around. She wondered if she was a bad person living an indefensible life. If it was true that we were made to answer for ourselves in an afterlife, would the bird-headed guardian, pagan warrior, or bearded angel recognise that there was more than one way to have lived decently? Or was Arthur's choice the only excusable way to live? If there really was some deity waiting beside a set of moral scales, Yara would point down at her grieving family and explain that if she hadn't looked after them, who else would have done it? We can't look after the entire world, she thought. Isn't that the whole point?

At the temple, Upul parked the tuk-tuk and led her up a set of stairs to a terrace overlooking the traffic-jammed road and the dark ocean beyond it and instructed her to remove her shoes and wash at a water fountain. He led her up another set of steps that wound around a great dome, lit from within by candles as thick as tree-trunks, each with three wicks guttering in a pool of liquid wax.

"Please," he said. "Go inside."

Upul remained in the arched doorway, watching Yara shuffle uncertainly into the circular hall. He knew that when the tourists came, they wanted to see things they believed other tourists would not see, and that they wanted to take photographs others wouldn't have taken. He sensed he wouldn't need to warn this woman against taking selfies against the murals and praying monks. She wasn't old but she moved with the leadenness of someone woken up too early from a much-needed sleep.

The year before, he'd driven around a woman who carried white wine in a water bottle, and who talked in winding monologues about herself and her boyfriend and her father, who she said had bullied and belittled her as a child, which lead to her bullying and belittling other children at school. The woman asked him to take photographs of her with children that they met on the street. The woman had tried to hug a mangy dog with the blood of a rat still coating its maw and she had been bitten in the crook of her hand. At the hospital, she burst into tears and he held her until she calmed down. Sadness hung around her like a perfume.

This other woman didn't seem sad, exactly; she seemed as though she was preparing herself for something. It reminded Upul of when his eldest son had begun the preparations for leaving to study engineering in Moratuwa; a seriousness had come upon him and he'd walked the house, taking in every corner and crack, as though he might never come back.

In the temple, Yara looked at painted panels showing scenes from the life of the Buddha. She could dimly recall the story of Siddhartha leaving behind his life of luxury in the palace of his parents, in order to wander the world and discover the truth of reality. Did he do any good, in the end? Or did he just plop himself down, close his eyes, and start a religion? She felt ignorant and irritable. She sat down on the concrete floor, watching the shadows of other visitors shift against the walls. She had no real idea what she was doing here and wondered if her presence in the temple was offensive or amusing or both. Was she having a mid-life crisis? Or had her mid-life crisis started when she'd begun dating a thirty-year-old bodybuilder? Or had it begun even longer ago, when she'd spent an entire night shuddering in the cold of the garden because she was struggling to normalise the tables on her database?

When she got back to the tuk-tuk, a thin lip of light was visible along the ledge of the ocean, and Upul was lying across the cracked leather seat, typing into a mobile phone. He jumped up when his passenger returned, installing a bright smile between his ears.

"My wife is awake," he said. "She makes very good breakfast. You want very good breakfast?"

Yara's instinct was to say no but she held it back and accepted.

They drove on the tuk-tuk for another fifteen minutes before reaching an area where clusters of tiny bungalows were surrounded by high sheet metal walls. Upul slipped a key from the inside of his shorts, where it had been tied with twine to his belt loop, and opened a rusted padlock. He pushed the tuk-tuk through the gate while Yara remained perched on the flaking leather seat.

The house was a squat, breezeblock box. Wooden shutters were open over small, glassless windows that invited shafts of white light into the dark central space of the house. A bare bulb hung from the centre of the ceiling, held in place by twists of wire. On a low mango wood table, bowls of fruit and curry were draped in squares of kitchen towel.

Upul called out and a woman appeared from a doorless room, dipping her head, smiling in a way that was less straightforward than her husband. She didn't seem at all surprised by the appearance of Yara at breakfast, which led Yara to assume it was a regular occurrence for Upul to invite random strangers over at odd times of the day.

"This is my excellent wife, Kumudu," said Upul.

Kumudu was dressed in a loose-fitting shift and pink Crocs and her features were tiny and detailed except for her eyes, which sat huge and clear in her face like pools of milk. She said something to Upul in Sinhala. Upul translated.

"My wife says you look like the Oscar award winner Cate Blanchett; also the actress Trisha Krishnan."

"I'm not sure who that is."

"You don't know Trisha? How you don't know Trisha?"

"Is she Sri Lankan?"

"No, no. Trisha is Indian. And very beautiful. One of the most beautiful in all the movies."

"Then tell your wife she might need glasses."

Upul and Kumudu both laughed. The three of them ate hoppers and daal and small green mangos, while drinking mugs of sweet black tea in the dark room with the door propped open. The food was rich and warm and it made Yara sleepy. She felt increasingly indistinct, as though she was an inhabitant of a memory that was slowly being forgotten.

As she ate, Yara glanced up at the walls. There were torn magazine photos taped to the flaking plaster of Prince, Obama, Stephen

Hawking, and several other celebrities she couldn't recognise. In cardboard frames on the furniture were earlier incarnations of Upul and his wife, alongside two girls and one older boy. The children sat with the straight backs of military cadets, hands arranged royally in their laps.

"Are those your children?" said Yara.

"Yes, madam. One son, two daughters. He is at university studying to become engineer. The girls they are both sleeping still. They sleep long. And you? You are on holiday with your family here?"

"No," said Yara. "I have two children but they're at home. I'm here with my boyfriend."

"He is at the hotel?"

"Yes," said Yara. "He is asleep."

"He is nice?"

"Actually, yes," said Yara, as though she was surprising herself. "He's very different to my ex-husband, and I think anything different can sometimes feel wrong for a time."

"I understand this," said Upul. "At school I liked very much this girl called Chamila. But things change, of course. But also, I always thought I would marry Chamila."

"Oh," said Kumudu. "Again about Chamila."

"Perhaps I was meant to marry Chamila. Perhaps this would have been an easier life."

"Yes, perhaps it could have been Chamila getting blown out of bed by your backside in the middle of the night."

They laughed and Yara saw a story they'd batted between them so many times they could keep the rally going with no effort at all.

She asked to use the toilet and was directed out of the bungalow and into a communal courtyard where three sheet metal walls stood around a ceramic squatting toilet. Yara blinked at the arrangement for five seconds before realising what it was. She checked none of the neighbours were about to emerge and sidled into the open cubicle, sliding her shorts and pants down and squatting over the fluted hole.

It took a while for the pee to come and when it came it thundered out of her in a chardonnay-yellow jet that bounced sparks of water onto her thighs. She tried to slow herself but couldn't.

A girl, somewhere between the age of four and five, appeared at the open side of the toilet, giggling. The girl was barefoot in a lace-trimmed lilac frock, black question marks of hair punctuating a happy, pebble-round face. Yara tried to cover herself. The girl inched closer, pointing. She was smiling, her mouth crowded with tiny, white teeth, pressed together like pellets of chewing gum. She squeaked a sound with the intonation of a question. Yara shook her head. The girl squeaked again. She looked ecstatically happy. Yara flapped one hand out ahead of her as though she was trying to scare a wasp off a meal. The girl's smile faded and she pointed to Yara once more before shambling away to one of the other grey buildings in the compound. Yara shook herself dry and rushed out. Back at Upul's house, she stood in the doorway, lit from behind by the blazing morning sun.

"I'd like to go back now," she said. "Thank you for the breakfast."

"Everything okay, madam?"

"Fine," said Yara. "Just tired."

It was nearly eight o'clock by the time Upul dropped her back at the gates of the Royal Waskaduwa Hotel. She thanked him and slipped him a wad of cash which immediately cast a strange pall over the memory of the last six hours. He looked from Yara to the money and back again. She felt as though she'd taken something away from him, somehow, but she was in too much of a rush to get away to try and repair whatever damage she'd done.

"Thank you, madam," he said.

Yara had just made herself comfortable beside Luke on the bed when her phone rang. She slid it out from beneath her pillow and held it to her face. She wouldn't have answered if it hadn't been her daughter. She carried it out onto the balcony and watched the pool attendant pass folded towels to a young woman in a bikini with a giant yellow paperback clasped under her arm.

"Mum," said Evangeline. "I'm pregnant. I'm keeping it."

The woman tossed her book and towel onto a sun lounger and dove into the pool.

"Oh," said Yara.

"That's wonderful, dubbin," said Arthur.

"Are you sure?" said Emil.

Part Four

Someone to Hold

13.

The Gaskill house near Lincoln was a sixteenth-century manor stocked with French furniture and amateurish watercolour paintings bought by Lily Gaskill in the market towns she day-tripped to with a friendship group of pensioners inherited from her mother. A four-acre horseshoe of ancient woodland cradled the estate, so that each time they went to visit Leo's mother, Evangeline had the impression they were entering a restricted area, home to the kind of institution meant to guard morbid secrets from an unsuspecting public.

Beyond the cracked concrete tennis court, a slate-roofed servants' cottage had been renovated and was occasionally rented out to Airbnb guests, usually when Lily felt like playing at having an occupation. The reviews left by former guests were terse and off-putting. "Unclean," read one. "Smells weird." "Host kept looking in through the windows then running away."

There were beehives under the larch tree, once the object of Richard Gaskill's pride and now peeling timber obelisks, populated by woodlice and worms.

The first time they pulled up to the house, Evangeline experienced a now familiar combination of guilt and wonder. How could so few have so much while so many had so little? But still, wasn't it a wonderful so much that the so few had? Elmwood made the house she'd grown up in appear almost modest. The main building had wings and crenellations and an orangery that was mostly used as a repository for the childhood toys of Leo and his brother, Jeremy, who worked for an investment bank in Singapore and sent Leo lavish, businesslike birthday hampers containing vintage champagne and Formula One tickets.

Lily was standing on the driveway as they arrived, dressed in muck-smeared dungarees that Evangeline would go on to learn had no real reason to have come into contact with any muck.

"She's like a Disney princess," said Lily to Leo, holding Evangeline at arm's length.

This endeared Lily to Evangeline, against her will, but the initial impression quickly wore away, revealing a skittish, insecure, lonely woman, who had an unusual and unhealthy relationship with her son.

The first time Evangeline and Leo slept over, they received a knock at the bedroom door midway through the night. Lily was outside the door, holding an empty copper pan to her chest like a top hat removed while she offered condolences.

"Leo, darling, there's a frog in the kitchen."

"A frog?"

"Yes, dear. In the kitchen. I wondered if you couldn't help me relocate it."

Over the course of their relationship, Evangeline never once saw Leo say no to his mother. He even dressed to please her when they went to Elmwood: in pleated chinos, golf socks, and polo shirts. He didn't bother to bring the torn flannels or ragged jeans he wore in Cambridge. He didn't smoke in Elmwood, barely drank, and walked dusk loops of the garden, whipping at fox turds with a willow branch. Without knowing anything about the man, Evangeline understood that Leo was doing an impression of his father, for his mother's benefit. His voice even slowed down half a beat in Elmwood and he rolled certain Rs that would normally have been left staccato.

There was no frog in the kitchen, that first night. Lily scratched her temple theatrically and suggested that it might find a way out, in the end, and that as they were all awake anyway, wouldn't it be a nice idea to sit down for a cup of tea? Leo agreed and the three of them sat around a dining table that could have seated fourteen. He said nothing to indicate that he found this unusual or unsettling. Evangeline would later try to recast the night as charming, while relaying it to Ahk; but at the time had felt that it was sinister and foreboding. That time of the night was reserved for extreme drunkenness or family emergencies.

• • •

Over the last months of her pregnancy, Evangeline would look at her belly and wonder whether she'd been talked into keeping the baby or whether it was truly what she wanted. Was this really the best course of action? Had she received enough impartial advice to know? She alternated between feeling as though she was sharing her body with a best friend she had yet to meet and feeling as though she was carrying a merciless parasite who continually pressured her to make terrible decision after terrible decision.

She left her studies after a consultation with a student services officer, who assured her there would be no trouble in taking a break, though Evangeline had the sense that this was meant more in a logistical or legal sense than in terms of how easy it would actually be to pick back up the thread of her course after spending a year tending to a newborn baby.

When they gave Lily the news, she didn't appear at all surprised, to the extent that Evangeline wondered if Leo had already told her.

"You'll come here, of course," she said to Evangeline.

"That's what I told her," said Leo.

"I'm not sure," said Evangeline.

"If you're here, I can keep an eye on you," said Lily. "I can help too. I raised two of my own, I might be able to teach you a thing or two."

Evangeline went alone to Gloucester to tell her own mother, riding first class on the fast train at Leo's insistence, and drinking complimentary decaf coffee while reading an old Anne Tyler novel that made her ache with the pain of the kind of family she'd never had. Her family had never revelled in each other's company, never affectionately done much of anything to or with each other. Rarely bantered or shown affection. There were no rolling in-jokes or peculiar traditions. They had enjoyed each other, probably, for moments in the past, but since she and Emil had entered the clammy tunnel of puberty, the moments of light relief had been few and far between.

She kept two lists of baby names in her phone, adding to them both while reading novels or watching TV on her iPad. She was surprised and slightly embarrassed by the names that appealed to her.

Calliope/Aurora/Eugenia

Edmund/Wyatt/Armand

Stepping out of the train station, with its ugly, overpriced café and single bank of metal seats, Evangeline found the city she knew best changed in ways she hadn't expected. Her mother was waiting beside the red Mazda Evangeline dimly remembered from her last visit. Yara's eyes travelled directly to her daughter's belly and remained there, as though it was a screen sharing news of a still-unfolding tragedy.

"Good journey?" she said.

Evangeline nodded, her eyes clouding up, and her mum engulfed her in a hug unrivalled in the history of physical contact between the two of them. Evangeline was flooded with a kind of relief, as though up until that moment she hadn't been entirely sure she had a mother of her own. She wished she'd called her mother a month or six months ago. She wished she'd gone directly to her mother after taking the pregnancy tests and they'd spent an entire night giggling and sobbing and talking it all out.

But that wasn't her mother. Her mother would have been angry. Her mother would have been judgemental and cold and awkward. There was a reason Evangeline had not gone to her after the tests or after the scans or after the first time she woke up in the night and saw Leo Gaskill reading through the sent messages on her phone.

They disentangled and Yara's gaze fell back to the belly.

"Stop staring," said Evangeline.

"I can't believe my grandchild is in there," said Yara. "Have you chosen a name?"

"No," said Evangeline.

Indigo, she thought. *Edith, Thaddeus, Thor.*

"Have you decided what kind of birth you want? Home? Natural?"

"Mum, can we talk about this somewhere else?"

"Of course, we can, I'm sorry. There's just so much I want to know."

Evangeline sighed, suddenly eager to offload information. "I'm taking a year out," she said.

"Oh," said Yara. "Will you come home?"

"I might stay with Leo and his mum. They have a house near Lincoln."

"He's taking a year out too?"

"No. But he'll go back and forth. I'll be closer if I'm there."

"We haven't even met him," said Yara.

"You will." Evangeline tried to summon a reassuring smile. "You will meet him." As a consolation prize, she took her mother's hand and placed it on her belly. Yara squealed, despite the lack of any noticeable movement under her palm.

In the car, Evangeline only dimly registered the presence of a man in the driver's seat. The peppermint air freshener hanging from the rear-view mirror made her want to throw up. She added it to a mental list that now included liquorice, poached eggs, dill, gravy made with Bisto, mushy peas, indoor swimming pools, and coconut water.

"Is Emil coming?" she said, fingering a piece of the candied ginger she'd taken to buying from an Asian supermarket near her flat.

"You speak to your brother more than I do," said Yara, which was a hope, more than it was a statement with any truth to it. Evangeline hadn't exchanged more than a few memes with Emil for several months. The last she'd heard, he was taking some time to decide what he wanted to do, and he was no closer to reaching a conclusion than he had been back at school.

"But he's still at home?"

"No," said Yara. "As of last month, he's living with a couple of boys in a flat in Tredworth."

"Shitheads," said Luke Tapper.

"Bad influences," said Yara. "But I understand he needs his own space. He's still thinking about going to study."

"He's got a good head on his shoulders," said Luke. "It'd be such a waste to waste it."

It'd be such a waste to waste it? For the first time, Evangeline noticed it was Luke Tapper sitting in the front seat and felt bewildered by his presence in the car. Had he come purely as a driver? Surely this wasn't the branch of reality in which her mum remained with this man? It made no sense and when Evangeline was forced to think about it, she felt the familiar surge of anger toward her father; anger for breaking their mother so badly that she believed this Lynx-smelling person wearing a pair of Oakleys backwards on his buzzcut was the most she deserved.

"What's he doing?" she said. "For money."

They turned past the bus station, demolished and now in the process of being rebuilt from sheets of glass tethered by wire cables to the ground. Evangeline noticed an inexplicable proliferation of dessert shops with garish signs that professed to sell "freak shakes," "bubble teas," and "monster waffles." Their shopfronts were daubed with graffiti-style depictions of melting mounds of ice cream and multi-storey cakes.

"He's delivering food," said Yara. "For an app."

"He's a Deliveroo driver?"

"Well, a rider. He rides on a bike."

"Electric," said Luke. "We got it for his birthday. Top of the range. That thing'll take you to Timbuktu and back."

Evangeline decided she would go and see her brother, no matter how painful it was, and that she'd take her brother with her to go and see her dad.

"And Dad?"

"Your father's still your father," said Yara. "The less said about him, the better."

"That man," said Luke.

"Did something happen?"

There was an uneasy silence in the front of the car.

"No," said Yara. "But you know how he is."

Evangeline didn't know how he was, not really, not anymore. She wasn't sure any of them did.

The house was changed too. In Emil's bedroom, the bed had disappeared, replaced by a green screen hung from a plastic stand, and a series of ring lights aimed at an old machining stool that Evangeline recognised from the attic. A tripod awaited an iPhone. There were blackout curtains fixed by Velcro pads to the windows. When she saw the set-up, Evangeline's first thought was of hostage videos she'd seen of a journalist kidnapped by the Taliban.

Her room had remained recognisably her room, with the chalk-painted bed and desk and wardrobe as they were, though they'd been joined by a wicker basket of rolled-up yoga mats, an old iron kettlebell, and a set of adjustable dumbbells on a podium-like stand. The walls had been replastered and painted off-white. A plug-in deodoriser periodically blasted the room with the smell of straw and lilacs.

"Are you hungry?" said Yara. "We thought we could order. There's a new place in Moreton that does Vietnamese."

"I'm quite tired."

"Of course you are. We can order tomorrow. I'll let you have a lie down."

Evangeline waited until they were both asleep and slipped downstairs to make herself beans on toast, which she ate while watching reality TV on her computer. When she was finished, she turned the house over looking for some attractively packaged form of sugar. All she found was a cheesecake-flavour protein bar the size of her forearm that tasted of sawdust.

In the morning, after throwing up twice into the toilet, Evangeline managed to drink half a cup of Yorkshire Tea with sugar, then caught the bus into Gloucester and trudged across town to the address her mother had typed into her phone.

The flat was the basement level of a Victorian terrace near the park. Emil answered the door in a hoodie with sleeves that hung over his hands, chewed to rags. There was a roll-up in the corner of his mouth and he hadn't shaved. His acne was in the process of becoming acne scars, his cheeks cratered like close-ups of the moon.

"Hey, Lean," he said. "Nice belly. Can I poke it?"

"No. Why won't you come to Bourton?"

"Because there's a large penis living in our house."

He stepped aside and let her in.

"Welcome."

The famous electric bike had been brought inside and took up a quarter of the living room. There were half-full glasses of flat cola lined up on an upturned cardboard box and books stacked against the walls. Two Xboxes lay beneath a TV and a pair of computer monitors.

"Jack and Harv won't be up for a bit yet," said Emil.

"You're reading again?"

"Yeah," said Emil. "A bit. Sometimes."

"And delivering food?"

He shrugged. "Sounds bad but it's fine. I can just work whenever I wake up. And I listen to audiobooks while I'm cycling."

"Isn't that quite dangerous?"

Emil grinned and lifted up his hoodie, revealing a warped map of pearly bruises climbing the side of his ribcage like wisteria.

Evangeline recoiled in horror.

"It's fine," he said. "It doesn't hurt. I put Voltaren on it."

"Emil, that's not what Voltaren's for."

Emil shrugged again. "Feels nice, though. One sec."

He fled into a bedroom that Evangeline caught only a glimpse of, enough to see that it was unexpectedly tidy, with no crust of crumpled clothes on the floor, just his old bed and his old bookshelf, both pressed into the farthest corner of the room like anxious pets. There was no cover on the mattress and no curtains framed the windows. Evangeline wondered if she should say anything and told herself not to be motherly.

They walked from the basement flat to a tearoom along one of the medieval streets beside the cathedral, with low, bulging ceilings and undulating tiled floors. The laminated menus were cloudy with fingerprints and smears of ketchup speckled with salt. Both siblings ordered coffee, with milk but without sugar, and dishes that they referenced only by number. The waitress plodded through a pair of saloon doors into a stainless-steel kitchen where two other women in hairnets were reading news on their phones. She returned almost immediately with two chipped porcelain mugs.

"I can't believe you're pregnant," said Emil. "That's so weird." He took a gulp of coffee. "Is the dad a professor?"

"Very funny."

"Mum thinks that's why you haven't brought him over to meet anyone."

He said "anyone" as though there were a huge contingent of Candlewicks waiting impatiently to meet her boyfriend. Evangeline wished there was an "anyone," because then she would have had someone to go to when she'd realised that Leo wasn't the person he was in restaurants and dinner parties, or at least he wasn't only that person. She would have had someone to steer her gently away from the situation before it became this thing that she no longer had a way out of. She felt, suddenly, as though she wanted to fall to the floor and be given urgent medical attention. She ought to choke, she thought. She ought to be looked after by professionals.

"He's called Leo," she said. "I told you about him."

"Your boyfriend."

"Yes."

"Are you going to get married?"

"No," said Evangeline, so quickly her brother smiled.

"Did you think about getting an abortion?"

"Emil, you don't say things like that."

"Why not?"

"It's private."

"Oh," said Emil, in a tone that insinuated he now understood something beyond the inappropriateness of his question.

"Why did you say it like that?"

"Like what?"

"*Oh.*"

"Because you're keeping it for, like, moral reasons."

"As opposed to?"

"Well, you're not keeping it because you want a baby, you're keeping it because you don't want to kill a baby."

"You don't understand."

Although he did understand, perfectly, to such a degree that she wondered if she'd become transparent during her months at Elmwood, or her brother had developed supernatural perception. Of course she didn't want a baby, not really. She wanted to be back in her room on Aarkell Street, or in the Olisa Library, hunched over a selection of books meant to shed some light on the previous batch of books she'd fallen asleep onto.

The woman who brought over their food held the plates so limply that, as she lowered Emil's onto the table, a single sausage rolled off and landed beside his mug. All three of them stared at it, as though waiting to be told by a director which turn the scene ought to take next.

"Scusey fingers," the woman said, picking up the stray sausage, and dropping it back onto Emil's plate.

When the waitress was gone, Emil looked at his sister defensively, daring her to say something.

"How are you happy staying in Gloucester?" she said. "It's so depressing. There's a lot more to do out in the world. You'd like it." She was being hypocritical again, considering that she had spent the previous months almost entirely alone in some version of Satis House.

"Like what?"

"Expand," said Evangeline. "See things. Meet people who make sense to you."

"Because they're smart?"

"Because they're curious about the same things you are."

"I'm alright," said Emil. "But thanks."

They ate their food in silence. Emil decided that he wouldn't eat the sausage, then he worried that the waitress might be offended by the fact that he'd left it, or might be embarrassed or uncomfortable or worried for her job, so he ate it, washing it down immediately with the last of his coffee, and trying not to think about the neon talons of the woman and what they might have left behind.

Arthur had reduced his life to a minimum. He bought no new clothes, held no subscriptions, owned nothing worth over twenty pounds, and subsisted on around 1,500 calories per day.

He had no car and walked everywhere he went, regardless of the weather. When he needed something—Wellington boots, a raincoat, socks—he bought them at either the Oxfam shop or one of the other charity shops in the town centre. He was selective in which of these establishments he was willing to give his business to. He wouldn't patronise a shop dedicated to an organisation that helped animals, elderly Westerners, or diseases that had already been allocated significant resources.

His beard, once badger-streaked with grey, now became a complete wire brush, and his hair thinned into a brittle harbour that he took to hiding beneath a Marlboro cap bought for a pound from a car boot sale. He held his shoes together with electrical tape. To keep warm at night, he draped towels over his duvet and slept with hiking socks drawn up to his knees.

Once Evangeline returned to Hykeham, the days at Elmwood fell into a sluggish pattern of daytime TV and games of Scrabble, which she invariably won and which Lily Gaskill invariably sulked over. Friends of Leo's mother occasionally dropped by for hysterical afternoons that involved drinking artisanal gin and loudly discussing the achievements of other people's children. Lily sometimes left for a day or two at a time, to watch a play in London or visit her sister, who lived in Bicester and drank "like a sailor on shore leave." Whenever Leo's mother was gone, Evangeline would wander from room to room, soaking up her solitude, and speaking to her unborn child about the life that awaited it. She told her foetus about beach holidays and snow days, about reading under a duvet by the light of a torch, about making pancakes, about autumn, about asking at the cinema for them to mix the salty popcorn with the sweet.

Although Leo had encouraged Evangeline to invite over friends for company, the thought of bringing Ada or Ahk or anyone else to that place among the trees felt both absurd and anxiety-inducing. It would be like inviting someone into a dream. She couldn't imagine her friends reacting with anything but painful confusion to the situation. She couldn't picture them engaging with Leo's mother, couldn't picture them by the abandoned hives or the ant-speckled log pile or on the creaking stairs. They would want to know why she was alone in a draughty house with a mad woman. They would try to convince her to leave.

And it was hard but it was easy. Nothing was expected of her at Elmwood. Evangeline had been excused from participating in her own life. She was being looked after in every literal sense and it was easy to try and convince herself that this was more than enough.

Leo was meant to come and visit but he rarely did. Instead, he sent long text diatribes on subjects Evangeline had no interest in. He complained about academics being pilloried for misogynistic jokes. He sent her links to long papers on how diversity schemes were threatening to undermine the ability of physics researchers to access funding. Leo had promised to search for a rental house on the outskirts of Cambridge with a manageable garden and a room they could prepare for the baby, but once he managed to get her to Elmwood, Leo brushed off the subject whenever she brought it up.

Cloistered in the crumbling manor, Evangeline was no longer herself. She couldn't read anything longer than a single-page poem or sit through a programme longer than half an hour, unless it was a reality show about housewives, pregnant teenagers, or teams of people marooned on desert islands. She lay in deep baths until they turned cold and her skin broke out in goosebumps. She did not read the news or open any of the email newsletters arriving from causes she'd previously cared about.

For the first time in her life, Evangeline ate whatever she wanted to, hiding this development from Lily, who was puritanical about the diet that would trickle down to her unborn grandchild. Leo's mother never ate in Evangeline's presence. Every morning, a breakfast of porridge, seeds, nuts, and fruit awaited Evangeline in the outdated kitchen, with a clay jug of single cream stood at its side.

"Cream enriches your milk," said Lily. "When I was in hospital with Jeremy, they used to call me the Jersey Cow. They'd give my milk to the premature babies."

Lunch was some bland kind of salad, served in a copper bowl. Pre-cooked dinners were delivered by a catering firm, twice a week, in brown paper cartons sealed with plastic film. Lily's boxes were usually forced into the overfilled freezer. Evangeline ate hers while watching reality TV, laptop balanced on her swelling belly.

After lunch and dinner, Evangeline would sequester herself in her bedroom and eat pick and mix from the post office in the village until she felt close to throwing up. She did not know that it was the same tactic her brother was employing to overcome his chronic aimlessness and unshakeable sense of dread. A hundred and fifty miles apart, the two Candlewick siblings were both trying to plug holes in themselves with mountains of soft, sweet food.

Their final argument came at the end of a day when Evangeline had largely managed to avoid Lily by spending all afternoon in the village, peering into glass cases of medals and brooches in the antiques shop, and consuming three scones with clotted cream and jam in the café attached to the art gallery.

Lily cornered her in the kitchen, where Evangeline was waiting on the kettle to boil so she could bring a valerian tea up to bed. Lily held a tube of lavender-scented skin lotion out like a gift.

"Evangeline, darling, my shoulders are rather stiff again." She wagged the lotion. "Would you mind?"

"Sorry?" said Evangeline.

"Make your tea first, then I thought we could pop over to the lounge. I'll set myself up on the floor and you can sit behind on the sofa and give me a good old rub-down."

Evangeline looked at Lily Gaskill, trying to discern if she was joking. She wondered if Leo's mother was drunk. Her right hand was still holding out the lotion hopefully. She was dressed in a satin gown and sheepskin slippers, her calves embroidered with varicose veins.

"I'm sorry," said Evangeline. "I don't think so."

"What do you mean?"

"I mean, I don't feel comfortable giving you a massage. And I'm tired."

Lily lowered the lotion warily, like a policeman shifting a gun from the face of someone they weren't entirely sure was innocent.

"Of course," she said. "It's not like I ever do anything for you."

"Excuse me?" said Evangeline.

"Nothing."

"Well it's clearly something."

Lily took a deep breath and looked away. "You come into this house and lie around watching trash TV while I cook and clean and wash your clothes, but I ask you for a teensy favour, and you look at me with a face like a smacked arse."

"I didn't 'come into this house.' I was invited in."

"Oh, you don't want to be here?"

"Not particularly, no."

"Where is it you'd rather be, Evangeline? Because I was under the impression that your own mother is otherwise occupied with her new toy boy and your father has lost his marbles."

Evangeline almost laughed. "My father may have lost his marbles," she said. "But he's not batshit crazy enough to try and make a woman who's eight months pregnant give him a massage."

Without so much as a warning look, Lily lifted her wineglass from the countertop, cocked her arm, and sent it flying toward Evangeline. It sailed clean over Evangeline's head and broke apart into shards that tinkled like a cat pouncing on the high keys of a piano.

• • •

Even with his allowance and the money he made delivering damp pizzas and giant milkshakes, Emil became unable to afford his pill habit and he began reluctantly dipping into his portfolio of cryptocurrency and small-cap tech stocks. One night, while delivering pad thai to a security guard on a construction site, he was hit by a nineteen-year-old who'd commandeered his dad's Berlingo, and who promptly drove away into the hissing drizzle. His limbs seemed functional enough for Emil to forgo A and E, where he knew that he'd end up spending eight hours staring at a vending machine, surrounded by broken noses and sloppily drunk rugby fans. He bought a four-pack of Fosters from a petrol station and rode home through the rain.

He woke up the next morning and it hurt to breathe. His left leg was the colour of an aubergine. He popped the last of his pills and lay in bed, watching the ceiling, a podcast on supersymmetry playing in his left ear. When the warmth started to ebb away, he called Alice and arranged to meet at The Queen's Head.

It was early and the pub was dark and warm and filled with retired men at the bar and a young family awaiting food at a table by the window. Alice was reading manga on a high stool, with a man's brown leather jacket balanced on her shoulders. She'd written the word "NOMORE" on the back of her hand in red biro.

"Master Emil," she said. "How are we doing today?"

"Okay," said Emil. "You?"

Alice was high and she giggled, shaking her head, somehow managing to appear younger than she ever had to Emil. She was wearing make-up that had been applied with the precision of a paint roller. They hugged, quick but firm.

"You're walking weird," said Alice.

"I got hit by a car."

"Again?"

"I was listening to a book."

"And now you want something for the pain?"

"Yeah," said Emil. "I have cash."

The two of them picked up from an ex-army dealer who shared a bungalow with his demented mother, and hid in Emil's bedroom at the basement flat, watching *One Punch Man*, smoking cigarettes, and taking temazepam. He woke up later and Alice was gone. Alice always left, later claiming that she'd done it for his own good. There were times when Alice's life appeared to be moving in another direction—she'd talk about shaking down her uncle for university money or doing a TEFL qualification so she could teach English in Japan—but then they'd meet again and she'd be glum and quiet and the plans would have been abandoned.

For some time, Emil had been treading a border between maintaining something like a normal life and paying two- or three-day-long visits to a dark underland. Now he slipped and stayed below. He ordered pills online, in large batches that he kept in a locked box beneath a floorboard. He stopped delivering food. He stopped reading. He stopped visiting his father or his mother and he stopped responding to most of the messages he got from Deepesh or Alice or any of the people he'd worked with over the previous couple of years.

Emil never feared becoming homeless. This was, he had to acknowledge, mostly down to the fact that his mother had agreed to keep him afloat since he'd told her he was doing an unpaid internship as a data analyst at a management consultancy firm, which he most definitely was not. She paid his rent directly and sent money for food and clothes and a monthly bus ticket between Cheltenham and Gloucester. He slept for twelve or thirteen hours at a time, then stayed awake for six or seven. He ate once a day but in such monumental portions that he couldn't physically move once he'd finished.

In moments of lucidity or sentimental drunkenness, Emil scrolled his way through university courses on his computer. He imagined a life in which he'd left Gloucester to accept his place at UCL. He dreamt that he was pregnant and the baby belonged to Alice. He imagined all the ways they'd destroy their child's life and when he woke up, he took a pill and sat down in the hot shower for a full hour.

Leo came out to Hykeham on the morning train the day after the argument, forgetting to change out of his inexplicably paint-spattered electrician's overalls, and arriving to find Evangeline asleep in the bed of the guest cottage. He waited for her in the living room, legs spread, a mug of black coffee going cold in his hands.

Evangeline emerged from the bedroom with the duvet clasped around her like a cape. Her hair hung in greasy curtains around her face and there were whiteheads clustered like stars in the red sky of her forehead.

"Leo?"

She moved to kiss him but was stopped by the cold ferocity in his eyes.

"You've really upset my mother," he said.

"She threw a wineglass at my head because I wouldn't give her a massage."

"I don't think that's an entirely unreasonable thing to ask, Evangeline. She has problems with her back."

"And I don't?"

"That's a false dichotomy. I never claimed you didn't. But it would hardly have been a big ask, given that you spend every day horizontal."

"I'm pregnant," said Evangeline.

"Yes," said Leo. "Like the majority of women in history have been, at one point or another. Unlike the majority of women in history, however, you're getting to spend those months being waited on like Cleopatra."

"You're being cruel."

"We've been very good to you, Evangeline."

"Oh, you've been very good to me? How very good of you to be so very good to me. I'm not a charity you're patronising, Leo. We're supposed to be together. We're meant to be a team."

Leo put his mug to one side and leant forward with the impatience of someone whose interlocutor insists on missing the point entirely. "You know my mother's delicate."

"There's delicate and then there's throwing something made of glass at someone who has a human being growing inside them."

"Please, Evangeline. Get over yourself."

"Me, get over myself?"

"There's no need to be hysterical. I've spoken to Mother. She understands that you're hormonal and she says you've been gorging yourself on junk food in your room. I think if you could go back into the house and apologise, it'd restore the peace and she'd be perfectly willing to put all this behind us."

Evangeline stepped close and drew her hand back to slap him. He caught her wrist so firmly she could feel the blood beating against the barricade of his hand. She reared her head back and threw it as hard as she could against his nose, which gave way with a burst of radio static. Leo screamed and cradled his face, stumbling over to the sink while spouting insults that sounded like amateur acting.

Evangeline packed whatever was in reach, left through the back door of the guest cottage, and walked into the village across fields of furrowed mud and sheep who were only faintly curious about her passing.

It was Emil she called from the train. He turned up at Gloucester station on his electric bike and helped load her suitcases into a taxi that refused to accept the bike as cargo, given that the tyres were so encrusted with dirt. Emil shrugged and rolled the bike toward a hedge. His eyes were pinpricks and there were triangular sweat stains hanging from the armpits of his T-shirt.

Evangeline had booked herself a month at a holiday apartment near Gloucester Park. She didn't want to go home because she understood, on some level, that it was no longer home. She wanted to install herself properly in her hometown so that when she eventually made contact with her mother, she didn't leave herself open to being persuaded to return to Bourton. It felt important that she didn't go back to Bourton, that she remained in the outside world. Bourton was like the realm of the faeries; she was worried that if she let herself be lured back, she might never leave again.

This was going to be temporary. It was all going to be temporary.

The rented flat was part of a red-brick vicarage that had been renovated in the nineties and split into three separate holiday lets. Evangeline's floor had an open-plan kitchen-diner with framed lithographs of winter birds on the walls. There was an Aga beside the fridge, with a sign on it saying "Please Don't Use the Aga," and an arrow pointing to a cheap, white plastic oven caked in grease.

"It smells kind of weird in here," said Emil. "Are you sure you don't want to stay at Mum's?"

"Yes," said Evangeline.

"She'd do your washing."

"Emil, you can't tell her where I am."

"I won't."

"I really can't be told what to do by anyone else. This is my last month without a baby, I just want some time to myself."

"Yeah, fine."

Evangeline wheeled her suitcases into the bedroom and Emil wandered around the flat, opening and closing drawers and cupboards and rattling ornaments. He flipped through a guestbook that offered suggestions of things to do locally: "There is a cinema ten minutes by foot that shows all the latest films." "There is a very delicious Indian restaurant on Atherton Square." "You can hear live music at the Dick Whittington." "You can catch a train out to the beautiful Cotswolds, to see the fairytale villages of Painswick, Moreton-in-Marsh, or Bourton-on-the-Water."

They ordered from Balti Hut and sat on the sofa with trays on their laps watching *16 and Pregnant* on Netflix. When Evangeline woke up in the morning, draped in a blanket, Emil had left a note beneath a bowl of painted pinecones, which read: *Let the alone time commence. Sorry about your boyfriend. Call me if you need anything.*

Yara managed to deadlift 130 kg and Luke caught it on camera. When she saw that he'd uploaded it to YouTube with the caption "Age is just a number," she didn't speak to him for three days. He apologised to her with a video in which he green-screened Venice into the background, and explained that he'd booked a trip for the two of them to ride gondolas in Vienna.

"In Vienna?" said Yara.

"Yeah, babe," said Luke, grinning. "Excited?"

Evangeline didn't call anyone when she went into labour. She used an app on her phone to rent a car and drove herself to the hospital, sitting on towels from the flat to make sure she incurred no cleaning penalty.

Frowning and huffing and clutching her belly, she was ushered through the waiting room and into a windowless antechamber where three other women were already moaning on three other beds, each one paired with an awkward partner. The light in the room came from mirrored lattices embedded in the grey panels of the ceiling. There were monitoring devices bleeping in every corner of the room.

Evangeline curled up like a baby and was told to change position. The painkiller they gave her didn't kill the pain. As the contractions shuffled closer together, her pool of sensory input was reduced to a blur of pain and numbness and effort that she was told, again and again, was insufficient. Later, through a cloud of narcotic softness, she realised something was going wrong. She tried to claw her way out of the haze and ask what was happening. The midwife was bringing other people into the room. When Evangeline looked down, there were three and four and five people framed by her blood-smeared thighs, their heads angled like museum visitors trying to make sense of abstract art.

"Can you stop bringing new people in?" she said to the nurse.

"It's not bad," said the nurse. "Just interesting."

"Out!" said Evangeline. "All of you out."

"We can't all go out," said the midwife. "Someone has to deliver the baby."

Evangeline seized a pair of forceps from the tray beside her and hurled them at a poster on the wall showing a cross-section of a womb.

Frida Elizaveta Candlewick was born at 4:04 p.m., at the first glimmer of the hottest British July on record. She looked primeval to her mother, who was jolted by the sudden feeling that she would never again be truly alone.

14.

When Frida was thirteen months old, she began to see every object in the world as a potential telephone. She held half-eaten tomatoes to her ear, and mud-caked Crocs, and empty eggboxes. She said "hai?" into soup spoons and bottlecaps. She cautiously asked for her "muma" in toilet brushes, coasters, and the hardback memoirs of political prisoners.

At the age of two, she learned how to turn on the TV and navigate to what it was she wanted to watch—generally, David Attenborough documentaries or Japanese cartoons in which the protagonists were anthropomorphised eggs or trees or monsters with fuzzy blue coats and bulging eyes.

Every night, after putting Frida to bed, Evangeline would look at photos of her daughter on her phone. She would linger on each one, zooming in on her daughter's face, trying to make sense of the new set of emotions that were emerging from her exhausted mind. She occasionally cried in a way that she had not cried before, hurriedly trying to clear away the tears in case Frida became upset. Frida rarely got upset. She was a plump, pink stoic who nodded relentlessly at the events unfolding around her, long before she could walk or talk or laugh.

By the time she was three, Frida Candlewick could recite "The Jabberwocky" in its entirety and she wanted to know how sewage water was treated and why some grown-ups slept in sleeping bags on the street.

"Because they're not as lucky as we are," said Evangeline, trying to pull her daughter away from a cello-shaped sleeping bag in the doorway of a department store.

"Why not?"

Evangeline considered this for a moment. "When you flip a coin, it can either land on heads or tails." She shook her head, unsatisfied with the answer she'd begun. "Aristotle said there were four different types of cause."

"Who's Aristotle?"

"He was an ancient Greek."

"How old was he?"

Evangeline checked to see if her daughter was joking, and she never was; it just seemed too sweet, these tiny misunderstandings, spoken in a delicate little warble.

"He wasn't old, he just lived a very long time ago."

Frida nodded seriously. "Okay," she said. She stood on her tiptoes, inexplicably, because there was nothing to see over, just a person, cocooned in a tattered sleeping bag, with half a Styrofoam burger box collecting shrapnel beside them. "Maybe he could stay at Nan's house with Nan and Uncle Luke?"

"That's not quite how it works."

"Why?"

"Well, Nan doesn't know that person, does she?"

Frida looked uncertainly over at the person in the sleeping bag. "Could we lose our luck?" she said.

"No," said Evangeline. "You and I, we have very good luck."

Frida liked that. It sounded like a line from a song in *Mary Poppins*.

They spent their first years together in one of the semi-detached houses owned by Yara. Their furniture was all donated, gifted, or bought secondhand. In the weeks after Frida's birth, Ahk had driven down from Cambridge in a VW campervan and presented Evangeline with a record player and vinyl copies of several albums they'd listened to repeatedly in Cambridge. Phoebe Bridgers, The National, Bright Eyes. Ada visited whenever she came home from university and gave Evangeline gifts that her mother had given her to pass on: hats meant for newborns and wooden mobiles and rompers that wouldn't fit for another three years. Emil built a tepee out of wooden curtain poles, cream-coloured canvas, and a lambskin rug, which was set up by Evangeline's desk and filled with cushions and board books. Yara and Luke bought almost everything else that was needed in the weeks after the birth: the cot (that Frida never once slept an entire night in, insisting instead on sharing her mother's bed), the high chair (that Frida very quickly learned to climb out of), the changing table (that Frida would only consent to be changed on if she could "read" a picture book during the process), and the electric breast pump (that gave Evangeline an unwanted insight into how it felt to be a dairy cow).

Arthur didn't visit, although he asked after Frida in phone calls and emails, and showed a genuine delight when the two of them called round unannounced at his flat.

In order to make space for Evangeline and Frida, Yara had evicted a couple with their own child, a nine-year-old boy who made YouTube videos in which he talked at length about the relative merits of different Boeing jets. The parents had been understanding, due in part to the generous parting payment Yara offered and the help she gave them in finding somewhere new to live. The family left behind a room with wallpaper depicting the planets and a doorframe in which they'd cut notches to commemorate the various heights of their son.

Frida saw the notches in the doorframe as a challenge. Every few days of her third and fourth and fifth years she compared herself to Callum's height at the same age, waiting for the moment when she would overtake a person she'd come to view not as an enemy but as a kind of companion who grew up alongside her. At breakfast, she would tell her mother "I'm almost as tall as Callum now" or "Soon I'm about to get past Callum." And when she did overtake Callum, she came downstairs with the breathless excitement of a child on their birthday.

"Mum, I'm bigger than Callum!"

While they lived at the small house on Richmond Gardens, Evangeline worked her way through an Open University course on Global Development and Aid. She sat at a desk she'd procured through a freecycling website, read by the light of the old IKEA lamp from her childhood bedroom, and scrolled through case notes on a refurbished MacBook. Every month, her mother transferred a healthy allowance to her bank account, along with a separate allowance that came via Lily Gaskill, after a letter sent to Elmwood by the solicitor Yara had used during her divorce. The letter hadn't specifically asked for such an allowance but it had been offered nonetheless, in lieu of Leo ever being forced to pay child support directly.

Leo Gaskill didn't try to see his daughter and Evangeline tried her best not to hear any news of Leo Gaskill. She assumed he was still at Cambridge, probably teaching, maybe making and breaking relationships with students. She wished she could hang a notice around his neck like an animal being auctioned. "This man is clean and intelligent but cruel and strange," it would read. "Do not be fooled by him. Do not go near his mother."

She was in an odd situation: hating the person who had given her the thing she loved most in the world.

The love didn't come immediately. Evangeline would say that she fell in love with her daughter for the first time when she was nine months old. Nine months was the age that Frida began absorbing the world, reacting to the sights and sounds and smells, and wriggling and stumbling her way across the messy rooms of the small house. And she started sleeping for longer stretches, which meant Evangeline started to sleep for longer stretches too, and gradually, like a long winter thawing, her exhaustion began to recede.

By Frida's first birthday, celebrated at the Bourton house with a giant banana bread and gifts that included a baby grand piano and a wooden Robin Reliant, Evangeline had decided she would not be going back to Cambridge. She could not return to the experience she'd left behind and she was not willing to try and fight her way through the rest of her degree while simultaneously raising Frida. She realised she could remain where she was and spend the next years engaging with her child and completing the online course at her own pace, and that it might not be the end of her life, that it did not mean she had failed or fucked up or thrown everything away.

There were times when she wondered whether she was being petty or feeble by not going back to university and whether, as her mother would have put it, she was cutting off her nose to spite her face; but she knew that, even if she had desperately wanted to go back to Cambridge, the thought of returning to the place where Leo Gaskill might be waiting around any corner felt too horrendous to seriously consider.

Frida ran away from Acorns preschool twice in her first year. Both times, she was discovered at the local library attached to the nearby junior school, her face in a book meant for a child three times her age. They settled on an arrangement by which the librarian would call the staff at Acorns if Frida turned up again. And Frida did turn up again. And again. And again, ensconced in the giant beanbags by the back corner, her face hidden between the covers of a book about necromancers or escape artists.

"You can't just run away from school like that," said her mother.

"I wasn't running away," said Frida. "I was going to the library and I walked. I hate Acorns. All of the kids are boring and the books aren't even books." She shivered, as though recalling the deeds of a psychopath. "They all rhyme."

Evangeline had never really disciplined her daughter and never really found herself growing angry with her. There were moments earlier on, at four in the morning after weeks of exhaustion, that she swore, but she swore toward the ceiling, and Frida was quick to understand when her mother needed space to recover. She knew when to smile, giggle, or demonstrate a newly acquired skill at just the right moment in time that it imbued her mother with the strength necessary to carry on. Whenever Evangeline felt close to being overwhelmed, her new companion picked up the slack.

As soon as Frida could form two-word sentences, Yara took her granddaughter on an endless parade of outings; they saw the glittering hollows of Cheddar Caves, the maze in Bourton-on-the-Water, the wading birds at Slimbridge. They wandered through the convincing Victorian streets of the Black Country Living Museum, conversing animatedly with actors in hobnail boots and petticoats. They ate in ludicrously inappropriate restaurants where the waiters hesitantly pointed out that they didn't have a child's menu, only to be told by Yara that it didn't matter, that her granddaughter would have the glazed scallops, the goat tagine, or the coq au vin.

No matter how much they did together, Yara could never convince her granddaughter to fully relax in her presence. No amount of chocolate eclairs, gentle reassurance, or grandmotherly smiles could open Frida up into the person Yara knew she was when she

was alone with her mother. Frida remained alert around her grandmother, as though every excursion were a lesson she would later
be tested on. Yara suspected that her granddaughter had either discovered or been told that it was she who kept the two of them afloat
financially, and that it was her house they were living in, and that
the car they drove had been a gift from her on Frida's first day of
nursery.

She knew that the two of them shared a private world that she
would not be granted access to. Her heart had almost broken in two
the night she overheard them whispering to each other on the sofa in
the Bourton house, midway through a sleepover.

"Do you think Nan likes it when we're here?" said Frida.

"Of course she does, darling. What makes you say that?"

"Sometimes she goes quiet," said Frida. "Sometimes I think we
make her sad."

Spending time with Frida inevitably prompted Yara to return to
her own childhood. She considered re-engaging Dr. Weber but ul-
timately didn't, partly because she could no longer justify the expense to herself and partly because she did not want to concede that
the presence of her beloved granddaughter could, even on occasion,
cause emotional turmoil.

Some of the habits and patterns of thought that she'd worked at
taming during their years together crept back into her routine. She
dwelt on memories she'd considered closed books.

As a child, Yara's house had felt like a totalitarian state, in which
particles of her father inhabited every corner of every room. Her father was a gas that drugged them all into depressed submission. He
worked in a team of brusque men laying cats'-eyes in motorways
across the county. Sometimes he went away for two or three days
at a time. When his back surrendered, they gave him a job in the
Halifax factory, testing the rubber skulls that were popped out of the
injection moulds, and, without the physical work to exhaust him, he
came home with excess energy to unleash.

There was one memory in particular that Yara had been unpick-
ing with various therapists since her early thirties.

Yara is five, or four, or six, and she's walking in the rain, pushing
her two-year-old sister in a tiny plastic pram meant for a doll. Their

mother is walking ahead of them, the glowing ruby of her cigarette guiding the way through the darkness. It's too late, Yara knows it's too late. They aren't meant to be outside. They're supposed to be at home, bartering for more time around the TV—a dangerous negotiation because Yara wants to see the same shows as the other kids at school, but she does not want to see her father, who might arrive home at any moment between seven and twelve, looking for reasons to become a whirlwind of anger.

They come to a stop on the bridge and her mother lights a fresh cigarette. Yara holds the railings, pressing her face between them, watching the huge ropes of dark water sliding over each other like cobras. In the creaking pram, Opal shrieks until the sound of her crying is punctuated by the sound of her retching. Yara was allowed to name her sister and she named her after a witch from a book. The witch had great powers and could control the weather with a collection of three-word spells. Her baby sister cries until she pukes, laughs until she cries, and thrashes violently in her sleep.

"Mum?"

Her mother has pinged her cigarette into the water below. She's climbed up so that she's straddling the railing. For a moment, Yara thinks she's playing. Yara thinks this is a strange game played late at night between a mother and her two daughters.

"I don't know why the two of you can't just behave," says her mother.

"What?"

"'Pardon,' Yara, not 'what.'"

Yara doesn't know what her mother is talking about. The rain snatches away most of her words, hurrying them on in the direction of the rushing water.

"I don't know what's wrong with the two of you," says her mother. "I don't know what I did to deserve this."

A car comes to a skidding halt, the glow of its headlights fractured and warped by puddles on the road ahead. The hazard lights come on. The door snaps open and a man in a salmon-coloured shirt and a Paisley kipper tie staggers out. He marches toward the edge of the bridge, arm hung over his eyes to keep out the storm, and he stops in front of Yara, crouching to her height. She's never seen this man before and she thinks there must be some kind of mistake. The pattern on his tie feels like a complicated omen.

"Hey," he says. "Are you okay?"

Yara's mother remains where she is.

"Is that your mum?" the man says. "Is she okay?"

"Help!" shouts Yara's mother. "Pervert!"

The man straightens up.

"I just want to see you're okay!" he shouts.

"Rapist!" shouts Yara's mother. "Paedophile!"

"You're out of your mind," says the man. He crouches back down to Yara and she can see a round face with a cleft chin and a pair of rectangular glasses made of blue wire. "Is there somewhere I can take you?" he says.

Yara looks over his shoulder at her mother, who has climbed down from the railing and is watching her with an expression Yara can't read through the rain, her arms limp at her sides, her old wax jacket pinned to the bony angle of her hips.

"I'm fine," says Yara.

The man looks hesitantly between daughter, mother, and baby. He has a family at home, he's picturing them on a bridge in the dead of night.

Yara's mother strolls casually toward her.

"Come, Yara. It's time to get home."

The man bites his lip and taps Yara twice on the shoulder, as though completing a magic spell.

Yara has to push her sister home in the rickety pushchair, through puddles of oily water, while her mother chain-smokes, make-up smeared down her face in a sinister mask. The car driven by the man with the round face follows slowly along beside them until they're off the bridge and some way back toward Oxenhope. They don't speak but Yara has the feeling of having narrowly avoided something terrible, not because her mother almost heaved herself off a bridge, but because Yara almost betrayed her mother for the man in the car, and what would life after such a betrayal have looked like? She won't understand, until much later, exactly what it meant for her mother to straddle the side of a bridge.

Yara is terrified of her mother and terrified of her father and, as far as she can tell, her little sister has only made all of their lives worse. She draws macabre crayon sketches at school and her teachers recognise in her a certain type of child who comes along a few times per cohort. She's the child who loots her lunch from the lunchboxes of other children, and who comes in late or not at all, with shadows around her eyes and ketchup on her sleeves, listing like a ship in strong winds, whether out of exhaustion or hunger or shoes that are either much too small or much too large. She's the child who is reluctant to go home, who is often to be found curled up in a ball, snoring like a baby bear on the circular story-time rug, beside the shelf of picture books where talking animals teach each other about bullying and sharing.

But that girl was gone and Yara was relieved to see none of the same hopeless seriousness in her granddaughter. Frida was fearless and curious to a fault. She strode up to strangers and asked how they liked their jobs as parking attendants, plumbers, or bus drivers. She kissed dogs square on the mouth. In the cubicles of public toilets, she sang the hymns they practised in primary school assemblies. It was not unusual to find that she'd looked up the museum or the land registry office online and called them on her mother's phone, to ask about the intricacies of the job and the average salary and required qualifications.

Yara took Frida's hand outside the lopsided secondhand bookshop on Eastgate Street where the two of them had just spent an hour searching for a book to help with a school project on Cleopatra. She'd frozen. Across the road stood a hunched woman in a shredded mackintosh, the fabric billowing on her back like a sail as she addressed the cobblestoned floor through a rolled-up copy of the *Metro*. Yara was staring. She was seeing her own mother, alone in a street three streets from home, utterly lost. Alone in the nursing home. Alone in the beautiful box on the altar.

"Don't worry, Nan," said Frida, looking up at her grandmother. "You and I, we have very good luck."

15.

It started as a pain in the abdomen that Arthur attributed to his recent diet consisting almost entirely of basmati rice and kidney beans. He bought a handful of reduced-to-clear vegetables from the back chiller at the supermarket and boiled them in a scorched pan with red lentils, eating the meal cross-legged on the floor while listening to a Radio 4 broadcast about increasing the speed of broadband to rural communities in South America. There were snowflakes of white in his fingernails and when he woke up each morning, it felt as though a pair of invisible hands were trying to drive him back into bed.

He was no longer working at the charity shop, after an argument had broken out with the manager over pledging money in support of a co-worker's half-marathon for dementia. Arthur was surprised at himself for becoming so vehement, but he didn't regret any of the things he'd said. He believed them. He believed, still, that he had a duty to those less fortunate than himself and that a genuine part of that duty involved ranking the effectiveness of the causes he chose to donate to. For this reason, he did not give money to beggars or animal charities or organisations started by celebrities. He did not put money in collection boxes shaped like Labradors or into great plastic domes that spun his coins enjoyably into their bowels—he understood that good props were not a guarantee of the efficacy of a charity. He believed that his money would help more people when sent elsewhere and he fought the urge to give to the things that made him feel like crying.

He still acted as a donation consultant online for How to Save a

Life and gave business advice to several charities who mostly chose not to listen to him.

He hung up his headset after fielding a call from a fifty-year-old man who had wanted detailed information on the tax implications of donations. The man had been trying to discern whether it was possible to make money by giving money away and had asked Arthur whether illiquid assets could be directly donated or needed to be sold first, by him, in order to be validly written off. Arthur had asked the man to imagine that he was walking to work one day and he came across a child drowning in a pool of water.

There was a knock at the door and Arthur answered it to find Tony fidgeting beside a man named Mick and a timid, lanky twenty-year-old with holes in his trainers.

"Y'alright, Artie?" said Tony. "Mind if we pop in?"

"You're very welcome," said Arthur.

He stepped to one side and let Tony, Mick, and the boy enter the flat; each offered him a cursory nod en route to his bedroom.

"I'm just popping out," Arthur said to the closed door. "I'll be back later on."

"Thanks, Artie," said Tony.

"Help yourselves to whatever you need."

"You're a star."

In the time freed up by having lost his position at the charity shop, Arthur had begun walking the streets of the city, picking up litter using an old broom handle with a nail hammered into the end. He carried bin liners with him and sorted the rubbish into paper, plastic, and non-recyclables. At first, he'd carried glass with him too, but his load had quickly become too heavy to manage, and he'd been forced to rethink his method. Now he carried a trowel in the belt loop of his trousers like a dagger. When he came across broken glass in a park or a wood, he dug a hole and buried it. If he found intact wine or beer bottles, he brought them to the nearest house and snuck them into its green recycling box.

He followed his usual route through the town centre, past the Evangelical church, looping Robinswood Hill, heading back down Whitby Avenue, then Eastern Avenue, then along London Road until he was at the docks and keying in the code for his building.

He'd filled and offloaded six bags of rubbish: two plastic, one paper, three mixed.

By the time he reached his sofa, he was so exhausted that he lay there for two hours, unmoving, his skin flashing hot and cold, his feet throbbing, a gnawing pain in his gut causing him to bite down so violently on his back molars that they creaked like ice cubes under vodka. He could hear occasional bursts of chuckling and grunting from his bedroom and a syrupy, tar-like smell leaked into the living room.

There was another knock at the door and Arthur wondered if he was going to be able to get up to answer it. He looked down at his feet in their plaid wool socks, a sliver of toenail protruding from a frayed hole. He pushed against the sofa cushions and rolled off the sofa, landing with a thud on the thin carpet. After crawling several metres along the sticky floor, he hauled himself to his feet on the back of a chair and staggered the last few steps to the door.

It was Emil, dressed in a felt greatcoat, and holding a small bottle of cheap merlot and two tins of baked beans.

"Dad," said Emil. "What the fuck?"

"Language," said Arthur.

"You're yellow," said Emil.

Arthur turned his hand over and moved it toward his eyes. "Am I really?" he said. "I thought that might have been the light."

Emil marched into his dad's flat and was greeted by a waft of narcotic smoke. He pushed open the bedroom door and saw Tony with two other men holding valleys of tinfoil in their hands, lighters beneath them, and rolled-up tubes of cardboard clasped between their lips.

"Get out," he said. Tony glanced past Emil to Arthur, who was in the doorframe trying to read his own palms. "Yeah," said Emil. "Don't look at him. You've taken advantage enough already. Just go."

"Artie?" said Tony.

Emil took out his phone. "Go," he said. "Or I'll call the police."

The men sluggishly gathered together their sweat-stained coats and tobacco pouches, sloped past Emil and Arthur, and left the flat. Emil felt so hopped up on adrenaline that his hands were vibrating. He filled a mug with tap water, took two sips, and poured the rest away.

"That was uncalled for," said Arthur. "I often let them pop in and use the bedroom."

"You shouldn't," said Emil. "Dad, it's insane."

"It's not safe for them out on the street."

"That's not your responsibility. You can't turn your house into a drug den."

"It's hardly a drug den, Em."

Once the adrenaline had subsided, Emil called their family GP and made an emergency appointment for the following morning. He remembered that his father only kept herbal teabags in the house. He put the kettle on and became so agitated that he left the flat without saying a word to his father and knocked on the door of the next-door neighbour, a widow he knew as Mrs. Farnaby, who answered dressed in a chequered baking apron, with a Yorkshire terrier tracing what Emil recognised as a lemniscate around her feet.

"Hi, Mrs. Farnaby. I was just wondering if we could borrow a few teabags."

"Course you can," she said. "Arthur doing okay?"

"Yeah," said Emil. "Just needs a cup of tea."

"He's been looking a little peaky lately."

"Yeah."

"And there are comings and goings."

"Um, I need to get back over."

"Of course, of course."

The old woman smiled politely and returned a few moments later with a plastic jiffy bag stuffed with pyramidal teabags. Her dog rested a paw on the toe of Emil's trainer, like a queen presenting her hand to be kissed. Emil shook it off.

"Tell your dad I said hello," said Mrs. Farnaby.

"Yeah."

"And ask about the comings and goings."

"I'll ask."

As the tea brewed, Emil paced back and forth in the cramped flat like a caged animal. He opened the window and wafted out the stink of burnt lentils and heroin. The smell triggered a cascade of memories that weren't of people or places or things, but of feelings and states, of the unearned emotions he'd chemically conjured up in grotty flats and pub toilets over the preceding years.

"Do you really not feel unwell?" he said to his dad.

"I suppose I've been feeling a little low," said Arthur. "I thought I might not be eating quite right, you know. Not getting all my greens and so on."

"Fucking hell," said Emil.

"Em," said Arthur. "There's really no need for that language."

Emil took out his phone and snapped a photo of his father. He turned the phone around. Arthur moved the screen so close to his face, his real nose touched the nose of his three-seconds-ago self.

"Ah," said Arthur. "I do see what you're getting at."

Emil spent the night on the sofa, two beach towels clutched around his shoulders like wings. In the morning, he used an app on his phone to summon a taxi, and he drove with his dad to the same temporary-looking pebbledash building he'd been taken to when he first got tonsilitis and chickenpox and when he accidentally slammed his thumb in a car door and the nail opened like the window of an advent calendar.

He sat in the waiting room while his father shuffled after the old doctor. He wondered whether he ought to call his mother, but understood, on some level, that his father was no longer her responsibility. She had no connection to him anymore; marriage was a cord that could be cut, but Emil would not find another, more muscle-bound father, loitering near the bathrooms at the gym.

The diagnosis, tentative at first and then confirmed, was of metastatic pancreatic cancer that had already established outposts in Arthur's liver and abdomen. Arthur did not resist the news, didn't press the oncologist for his exact chances of survival or an estimate of the days he had left. Instead, he carried around the fact of his sickness like a piece of trivia. "Stage four," he'd tell anyone who asked. "A little tired, but I can't complain."

Yara and Luke were married on a thirty-degree Sunday, in the grounds of Hatherley Manor, surrounded by eighty-two people.

The night before the wedding, Yara and her bridal party stayed overnight in a nearby pub, with head-skimming ceilings and uneven stairs. The group consisted of Evangeline, her sister Opal, her programming friends Kerry and Amina, Luke's sister Cam, and a heavily tattooed woman from the gym named Kathleen Porter. Frida was spending the night with Luke's parents, who she'd developed a fondness for based largely around the fact that their bungalow was beside a small library, their kitchen possessed an ever-full biscuit jar, and they never told her off for reading too intently or saying too little. The Tappers treated Frida with the awed respect of a young monarch, almost as though they had never raised children of their own and had no real idea what such creatures were capable of.

The women were sat around a long table in one of several wood-panelled rooms clustered around the circular bar. They'd come to know each other very slightly, during a tame hen party that had involved drinking Aperol Spritz on a canal boat. The discussion had turned to weddings, having been steered there by Kathleen Porter.

"We did medieval," said Kathleen. "Paul was in a full suit of armour. I was done up like Maid Marion. Band played the wedding song on bagpipes."

"That sounds nice," said Kerry.

"It was tackier than a noddin' dog on the dashboard, but Paul was happy." Kathleen gestured at Luke's sister with her pint of bitter. "What about you, Merkel, how'd you tie the knot?"

Cam Tapper looked up from her gin and tonic. She'd tried resisting her nickname but had found that doing so only incurred further mocking from Kathleen.

"We got married in Lanzarote," she said.

"Cheap booze," said Kathleen, nodding.

"No," said Cam. "We liked the island."

"The island is nice," said Kerry.

"Personally, I don't have a lot of time for islands," said Kathleen.

"You don't like islands?" said Amina.

"Not particularly," said Kathleen. "First thing I do when I enter a room is find three exits. A country is no different. What if something happens? You go abroad, someone slips half a kilo of gak into your Trunki, and before you know it, you're serving thirty years in a Cambodian prison."

Evangeline caught her mum's eye and they both looked down into their drinks.

"What about your last time, Yaz?" said Kathleen. "Any of you lot there for that?"

Evangeline lifted her face and looked around at the random assortment of women her mum had chosen to share the occasion with.

"I was there," said Opal. "It was a very cold day. I had to wear gloves."

"That's all she ever says," said Yara. "That she had to wear gloves."

"Who has a winter wedding! It doesn't make any sense."

"We were hoping it would snow," said Yara.

"There was no way it was going to snow," said Opal. "It never snows when you want it to snow. That's just how it is."

Evangeline wasn't sure she'd ever heard much about her parents' wedding. She'd seen photographs but the people in them had been somehow unconvincing: her mother had been bulkier, her father much slimmer. Their clothes had betrayed the decade they were trapped in; the suit trousers her father wore were subtly flared and her mother's make-up was almost pantomime-y in its boldness.

"How about the reception?" said Kathleen.

"If I recall," said Opal, "there was finger food."

Kathleen grunted. "Well, that's a real vivid picture you've painted, sister of the bride. Yara, anything you want to add?"

Yara blinked. "I'm just nipping out for some air," she said, getting to her feet and carrying her drink underhand toward the door.

Kathleen called after her. "Yaz, did I put my foot in it?"

"No, Kath. I just need a breather."

Kathleen nodded, satisfied. "Always been a lightweight," she said to the others.

Evangeline watched her mother leave, drained her drink, and followed her out to the car park, where she found Yara sitting on a kerb and drawing on a cigarette, with her feet in a pool of flame-coloured leaves. She took a seat beside her and felt damp spreading through the back of her dress.

"Mum, what's wrong?"

"Nothing, Evie. I'm just being silly."

"You don't have to marry him if you don't want to."

"Evangeline."

"Joking."

Yara drew on her cigarette and blew the train of smoke down between her knees.

"I just didn't think I would be doing this again," she said.

"But it's not bad, is it?"

"No, Evie," said Yara. "It's not bad at all. Just different."

"There are sociologists who say marriage only made sense when our life expectancies were under fifty. If we're going to live till ninety, you can't be expected to devote the majority of your life to one person."

Yara looked at her daughter as though she'd missed the point entirely. "That's what makes it worth anything at all," she said. "It's hard but you do it anyway."

Back in the pub, shots had been lined up around the perimeter of the table.

"Down your gullet," said Kathleen Porter. "No excuses."

The next morning, Evangeline stumbled downstairs in a fog, wrapped in a complimentary dressing gown. She unlocked the front door of the pub, using the key attached to her room key and a hand-sized wooden paddle. The porch that led outside was occupied by a stand of leaflets advertising the kind of places Yara often took Frida to: farm parks, caves, museums, grand estates with large gift shops. What struck Evangeline, seeing all those places, was that Yara had not taken either her or Emil to any of them. There had been holidays, yes, but these had come as fortnight-long breaks in the midst of hectic months of work, during which there were days when the Candlewick children had only seen their parents for minutes each evening.

She stepped outside and dragged the fresh air of the morning into the dull ache of her hangover.

"Morning."

She jumped, clutching the dressing gown around her. Emil was supine on a bench with a paper coffee cup at his side and a book the size of a Bible open on his chest.

"Emil?"

"Walked over this morning," he said, rotating 180 degrees so that he was sitting up. He passed his coffee to Evangeline, who sipped at it and spluttered.

"Isn't the other hotel in town?"

"It was nice weather. I wanted to walk."

"What kind of coffee is this?"

"Triple-shot Americano."

"It tastes vile." Evangeline took a seat beside her brother and returned his coffee. "You weren't up late?"

"It's not really fun when you don't drink," he said. "When I left, they were mixing Luke a dirty pint."

"How was he?"

Emil grinned. "They started having pull-up competitions on the stairs and the hotel manager threatened to kick them out. Luke gave him a hundred pounds cash not to. Then Lucas started trying to make people take coke with him and they locked him in the cellar."

"Which one's Lucas?"

"Short and ginger."

Back inside, they found seats in the breakfast room and both requested more coffee from a teenage waitress, who told them to help themselves to food from a buffet laid out across two trestle tables pushed up against one of the walls.

"Where's Frida?" said Emil, as he used metal tongs to lower slices of bread onto a conveyor belt toaster.

"With Luke's mum."

"The tall one with big jewellery?"

"That's her."

As they ate, the rest of the bridal party slowly filtered down, fumbling with croissants and foil-wrapped packets of butter. Kathleen asked the waitress for a lager shandy and downed half of it, added a Berocca, and downed the rest. Opal carefully folded slices of ham in two and arranged them around the edge of her dish as though she was plating the breakfast for someone else.

The two Candlewick siblings ate toast, drank coffee, and stared at their phones for half an hour, until they both simultaneously received a message from Yara asking them to come up to her room. She was sitting on the blanket box at the foot of the bed, the plumage of her wedding dress piled up around her. She was biting on her lower lip and her right foot was beating against the carpet as though playing an invisible bass drum. The hairdresser had fashioned her hair into an opalescent pretzel.

"Mum," said Evangeline. "You look amazing."

"Yeah," said Emil. "You look nice."

Yara drew them both into a hug. Emil had never smelled so much hairspray and he fought the urge to gag.

"I love you both very much," said Yara.

Emil groaned.

During the ceremony, Evangeline and Frida sat beside each other in the front row, with Luke's tiny, gleeful parents, his sister Cam, and their Aunt Opal, who brought a full roll of toilet paper in her handbag and periodically used squares of it to dab sweat from her forehead.

Emil walked Yara down the aisle, eyes cast anxiously down at the floor as though he was performing community service. He looked up just in time to see his sister flinch as he passed their mother's hand to Luke Tapper. He wondered how much effort it was taking Evangeline not to start explaining to Frida how depressingly patriarchal the entire affair was.

He took his seat beside them and Frida patted his knee proudly.

Emil was surprised to find himself feeling quietly moved by the degree to which Luke's hands shook as he stuttered his way through the vows he'd printed onto a single sheet of the kind of dappled paper a child might use to create a treasure map.

"Yara," he read. "If I am reading this, then it means that you have not changed your mind. Thank you. I keep thinking to myself that you might have just forgotten to leave me. Well, I hope you stay forgetful for the rest of our lives. I may not be as smart as you, or as beautiful as you are, but I do love you, and I promise that I will try to take care of you, even though you do not need anyone to take care of you and you will tell me to stop."

Not knowing where to look, Emil traced the lines on his hands. He wondered what Alice would say if she were sitting beside him. He pictured Imogen in her grand house, painting a naked woman with her head burning like the wick of a candle. Would he ever get married? Did he want to? He didn't want to marry any of the people he'd met so far in his life, he knew that. Even his unbridled imagination couldn't come up with a kind of person he'd want to spend the rest of his life with.

Yara had memorised her vows and she spoke them with the measured confidence of a newsreader.

"Luke," she said. "I never expected to get married again. If I'm honest, I never expected to feel particularly happy again. You get to a certain point in your life and start believing you can see exactly how the rest of your years are going to play out. I could never have predicted what happened to me and I will remain eternally grateful you came my way. You are ten times the person other people see, and you make me feel the same way."

The reception, which was held in a converted barn on a dairy farm, had an open bar. The two siblings spent the wedding beside each other, whispering gossip and half-remembered memories about the guests who surrounded them. Frida leapt around the grand hall in a lilac dress, introducing herself to anyone who took her interest as "the granddaughter of the bride."

Emil left early, after several slurred speeches given by people he didn't know, in which they recounted anecdotes he didn't care about. Still dressed in his stiff black suit, he went to the cinema in Stroud and watched the last screening of a new DC film, feeling painfully sober and unprecedentedly alone.

Despite being invited, Arthur did not attend the wedding. He gave an envelope to Emil to leave on the table designated for presents and cards. When she opened it, several days later, Yara would find a handmade card with a terribly drawn picture on the front. The picture was of a wobbly-armed woman swimming among a sea of triangular waves, gripping the tail of a tiger with luminescent green eyes. "It's so strange that the days go by and nothing changes," wrote Arthur. "But then you look back, and it's all gone. Who knew! I will always love you, poppet, in one way or another. Have a wonderful day."

Yara put the card in the bin, retrieved it, then put it back in the bin again.

They left for honeymoon a week after getting married, embarking on a cruise that would take them around the Horn of Africa, across the Red Sea, past Egypt, through the Suez Canal, and, finally, to Italy, where they would see Venice for the first time and both fall asleep in a gondola.

A month later, Emil agreed to have dinner at Yara's and was caught off guard when he saw that the label slotted into the plastic space above the post box no longer read "Candlewick," but "Candlewick-Tapper," which sounded to Emil like a Christian rock band from Bible Belt America. The name change wasn't something he would have ever guessed could upset him, and it didn't, not exactly; it was more like unexpectedly receiving news that a famous person you had assumed was alive had died many years ago.

Yara kissed him distractedly as he kicked off his boots in the hallway.

"Are you okay?"

"I'm fine, Emil," said Yara, with such speed that he knew it couldn't be true.

Usually, he arrived to excited questions about what he'd been doing and what he had planned. Yara usually insisted on showing him videos on her phone of Frida doing wonky cartwheels or panting through Bach sonatas on the flute, despite the fact that he'd probably seen his niece more recently than she had and had amassed a photographic archive of his own.

The food was brown rice with tenderstem broccoli, edamame beans, pickled red cabbage, and slices of a kind of bread that had been made exclusively with chopped nuts and seeds. The kitchen had been remodelled, so that almost none of the old features remained. The old bulkhead lamps had been replaced by hanging Poulsen lights that made Emil think of UFOs. The pitted oak table was gone and a giant slab of pink terrazzo sat in its place, catching the merciless alien light in rings. The Shaker-style cabinets were now blank turquoise lacquer. Copper knobs adorned the cutlery drawers and the cupboards that hid the dishwasher, the bins, and the fridge.

"I need to ask you something," said Emil, once he'd consumed a polite amount of the unpleasantly grainy bread.

Yara set down her cutlery and drew her glass of wine close, lifting it but not drinking.

"We're not giving you any more money," she said.

"What?"

"'Pardon,' not 'what.'"

"I didn't even ask anything yet."

"You lived here rent-free for two years, Emil, need I remind you."

"Because it's my home. When did it stop being my home?"

"It didn't stop being your home but you didn't contribute even though you were making money at the time."

"Why are you saying this?"

"We paid for you to go to rehab, Emil. Do you realise how much that cost?"

Emil pushed his plate away so violently that several edamame beans leapt onto the dining table. He hated the new dining table, hated the new cabinets and the new sink. It was all money he couldn't even fathom spending, let alone spending on something so unnecessary. Where had their old kitchen gone? What had they done with it?

"I don't want money," he said. "I want a car. So I can drive Dad to chemo. He has to catch the bus and he refuses to ask anyone for help."

Luke tried to catch Yara's eye but she wouldn't shift her glare from Emil, who had pushed out his chest and planted his elbows on the table. He'd been listening to audiobooks about asserting yourself and was trying to eradicate the hesitant words he used to fill pauses. He had been told that he ought to allow himself to occupy space. He was working on unfolding himself.

"You can't even drive," said Yara.

"I can learn."

"And we'll pay for that too, will we?"

"I don't know."

"If your father needs help, he knows he can come and ask for it."

"No, he doesn't," said Emil. "That's an insane thing to say. Why would he come to you?"

"Because I care about him."

"No, you don't."

"Don't I?"

"No. You care about yourselves and your stupid holidays and making this stupid house as tacky as possible."

Yara left the table, carrying her serviette at her side like a bludgeoning weapon. She plodded up the stairs, her feet heavy.

Emil shrugged at Luke, scraped his plate into the compost bin, and left. Ten minutes later he was slouched at the bus stop, lighting his second post-dinner cigarette, when Luke reappeared, his toes wedged into Yara's too-small Birkenstocks, the foil of a protein bar poking out of his left fist.

"Hey," he said.

"I know," said Emil. "I'm sorry."

"It's not that, mate," said Luke. "I'll take the two of you to the hospital."

Emil lowered his cigarette, pulling a veil of smoke down off his face.

"What?"

"Don't tell your mum. Just give me a bell and let me know the times, okay? I can pick you up and drop you back. No problemo."

Emil stared at his new stepfather suspiciously. "Why would you do that?" he said.

"I know it's what your mum would want, really. It's just complicated. Things are complicated."

"Um," said Emil. "Okay. Thanks?"

Luke nodded and headed back toward the house. He stopped after a few steps and turned in a Columbo-style pirouette, one hand raised. He moved close to Emil, who for a moment became convinced that his mother's husband was about to hit him.

"You're not meant to know this," said Luke. "But I'm going to tell it you anyway." He took a bite from the protein bar and swallowed without chewing. "As part of their divorce thing, after your dad had his big fall, your mum made this deal so that he could get the money that comes in as rent from two of the houses, but through her. She knew he'd just spaff the lot away otherwise and end up out on his ear." He pocketed the remains of the protein bar. "She was always worried about that daft prick. Still is." Seeing the look of surprise on Emil's face, Luke ruffled his hair. "Go easy on your mum," he said. "She's a better sort than you give her credit for."

Part Five

Something for the Pain

16.

On hospital trips with his dad and Luke Tapper, Emil brought along hefty sci-fi books by William Gibson and Neal Stephenson and Ursula K. Le Guin, which he read in the waiting room, sipping bitter coffee from the sputtering machine and tapping his right hand with the impatience of a smoker on a long-haul flight. One afternoon, he became so irritated by a clumsy sentence in the novel he was reading that he put it to one side, and sat with his arms folded, staring at a woman feeding change into a vending machine stocked with chocolate bars that it refused to release. The woman was wearing a lurid purple tracksuit and quickly resorted to thumping the keypad of the machine.

"You absolute bastard," she said, with almost moving sincerity.

Emil took out his phone and scrolled over to the Notes app. It was where he jotted ideas as they occurred to him, only to reread them later and find them, for the most part, to be totally incomprehensible. He thumbed through his old thoughts.

Modular forms, explanation of everything, or . . .

An AGI that knows how little it knows, somehow? Hallucination problem. Socrates. Multiple agents—doubts.

Bertrand Russell said maths was everything, died saying maths was nothing. Because he was proved wrong? Or he saw something? Tautologies.

The line of best fit, Imogen.

Emil opened a new note and began writing. That morning in the watery, grey light of the oncology ward waiting room, he kept writing. He wrote in full sentences, sketching out the opening to a story that arrived virtually fully formed in his head as the woman in the tracksuit continued to berate the stubborn vending machine and the receptionist called security and a huge man in a lanyard arrived to threaten her with expulsion.

Arthur emerged from the chemo room two hours later, claw-like hands loosely clasping a copy of *The Economist*, a half-empty Evian bottle, and a dishcloth-sized yellow check blanket. Emil had no idea where the blanket had come from or what it meant; it had just appeared a month earlier and he had intuited not to ask about it.

"You okay?" said Emil.

"Never better," said Arthur.

Luke was waiting outside in Yara's giant Porsche, tapping out a drumbeat on the stitched leather steering wheel and scrolling through comments on a recent YouTube video he'd posted about when and how frequently he consumed a glittery muscle-building supplement.

"Everything okay, mate?" he said, turning down the pounding electronic music.

"Wonderful," said Arthur.

These twenty-minute drives were unpredictable affairs that ranged from silent, funereal ordeals to jovial trips in which they sounded more like a gang of schoolfriends than the male contingent of a complicated, blended family. That day, everyone was absent. Arthur stared at his right hand, willing it to move, even slightly, and finding himself amazed by its refusal to do so. Luke thought about falling subscriber numbers and lacerating comments on his last video. Emil was thinking of his story, of the people who inhabited it, of how they looked and moved and spoke.

When his father and stepfather dropped him at the basement flat near town, Emil set his moka pot on the hob, flipped open his laptop, and typed up the notes from his phone, drawing the sentences into paragraphs that grew into a living scene, at the edge of a flawless lawn, beside a neoclassical stone building in Princeton, New Jersey.

The story was set in the forties, at the Institute for Advanced

Study. It opens with four mathematicians huddled together at a garden party, eagerly discussing the feasibility of nuclear weapons and the progress of Heisenberg in Göttingen. The air is muggy with the smell of cut grass and cigarettes. Meat is being grilled, cans of beer are hissing open. The sun beats down on the pale, drawn faces of the mathematicians, the sleeves of their ink-stained shirts rolled up to their elbows.

One of these men is Artaud von Rosen, a man whose intelligence is beyond the comprehension of most ordinary mortals. At the age of two and a half, he taught himself to read using the instructions on a box of Borax. By six, he could solve simple equations using inverse operations and by ten he had a grasp on differential and integral calculus. He was admitted to Budapest's Pázmány Péter University at the age of fourteen.

At the barbecue on the lawn, four men in double-breasted suits and snap-brim fedoras turn up, their presence causing ripples of shock. They ask for Artaud von Rosen and the other mathematicians glance at each other questioningly. Among them, von Rosen is something of an outlier; a thinker who dwells so purely in the abstract realm of pure mathematics that there are rumours he can't tie his own shoelaces or make a cup of coffee. His wife, Kata, is a six-foot-tall Hungarian who shadows him like a bodyguard, mopping spills off his shirts and leading him out of situations which are liable to overwhelm him.

"May I ask what this is about?" says von Rosen.

"You may not," says one of the suits, aping the middle-European stiffness of Artaud's accent.

Kata inserts herself between the men and her husband. "He is not going anywhere," she says. "Not until we know what this is regarding."

All eyes in the garden are on them now. Martini glasses are frozen in mid-air. Conversations have wilted into silence. Somewhere, a lawnmower ticks and grumbles. A dog howls. The grill spits at rump steaks and burger patties.

Von Rosen plants a kiss on the taut, red skin of his wife's cheek. He is too curious to bother kicking up any fuss. Part of Artaud relishes the feeling of importance bestowed upon him by the arrival of the men. Although he comes across as someone with no ego, there is a small ember of vanity within him.

When he's gone, the mathematicians try half-heartedly to return to their conversation, but can't resist speculating on von Rosen's whereabouts. What would the government want with Artaud? They are both jealous and relieved. They have theories but no way of proving them. It cannot be about the bomb—von Rosen has been the least useful among them when it comes to weaponising the new physics.

Kata leaves, heading across campus toward the Cape Cod–style house she's shared with her husband for the last two years. In the kitchen, unsure of what else to do, she begins packing suitcases. She packs her husband's favourite jumpers and the socks he thinks are lucky and the childhood novel he treats like a Bible. She packs them all into the two leather suitcases they brought with them from home and lugs them out into the warm night.

She sits on the doorstep of her rented house. She has no idea where to take the packed suitcase. She is helpless now. All she can do is wait for her husband to return. In the distance, the lanky silhouette of Kurt Gödel limps across a lawn.

Emil wrote until the morning. When he finally stopped, his stomach was roiling with caffeine and his right hand twitched slightly if unoccupied. He scrolled through everything he'd written and found it clumsy and strange but filled with at least a semblance of the energy he felt toward the story. He wondered if he ought to break it up into chapters. He wondered if he ought to give it a name.

The last thing he did before leaving the kitchen was send an email to his boss at a telesales firm housed on an industrial estate in Brockworth. He told the boss that he wouldn't be coming in that day, or ever again, and that he was sorry to leave so abruptly, but some urgent family business had come up and there was no way of avoiding it.

One of his flatmates, Harvey, was in the living room, a joint dangling from the corner of his mouth while he button-bashed his way through a game of *Tekken 5* on the Xbox.

"Alright?" said Harvey.

"Yeah," said Emil. "Just going to bed."

"All-nighter?"

"Yeah."

"Nice."

As the days went on, Emil found he was no longer oversleeping. He set a run of alarms to begin at seven each morning and he took his laptop to the library in Gloucester, where he was less likely to be interrupted by Harvey or Ellis, and where he was surrounded by none of the distractions of his bedroom. He couldn't masturbate or smoke endlessly and he deliberately kept himself from seeking out the WiFi password so he couldn't watch YouTube lectures on AI developments or self-replicating machines.

His diet altered, largely due to him beginning to question which foods would enable him to keep writing for as long as possible. He knew that when he gorged himself on cake and biscuits, his stomach complained in a way that left him bed-bound for hours. Trying to stretch out what was left of his savings, he turned to his father's utilitarian recipes, emptying tinned vegetables and pulses into a colander in the sink, rinsing them, and dividing the mixture into old takeaway boxes. It was not lost on him that there were other respects in which his life began to resemble his father's.

He felt possessed.

He wrote like a painter: not from start to finish, but in daubs and patches that were vague at first, growing more distinct as he imbued them with details.

In the rotating set of AA meetings he'd been attending for the past year, Emil switched off and let himself drift away. He did his mandated duty bringing fresh packets of biscuits and washing up the coffee jugs and mugs, but he struggled to pay attention to the stories other people told of their daily battles and temptations, their previous lives of chaos and terror, lost as he was in his own newly unfolding story.

He no longer shared in the meetings. He sat in draughty church halls, on stackable plastic chairs, absorbing stories of other people. They recited mantras about accepting their own powerlessness and forging connections from the chaos of addiction. They confessed their sins and shared their successes.

He stole these people for his story. He attached their thin lips and coppery beards to his mathematicians. He filed away their turns of phrase for later use: "On a wing and a prayer"; "At the end of the day"; "I thought I'd be leaving there in a box."

After the Friday meeting at St. Mary's, Emil shook hands with Clive Lollard, as they all emerged blinking into the daylight, digging out tobacco pouches and vape pens from their pockets. Emil rolled a cigarette from a wig of Golden Virginia he was keeping wrapped in a shred of tinfoil after finding it down the back of the sofa.

He spotted a familiar face, smoking in the shadow of a hoodie, across the low drystone wall that separated the path from the grave-yard.

Alice looked both thinner and older than she had last time they'd met. It was the height of summer but she was dressed in a parka with a fur-trim hood, two bruise-dappled legs protruding from the ragged hem like a pair of stilts. There were pits in her cheeks and her eyebrows had been tweezered almost out of existence. A faint scum of yellowish-white clung to her lips.

Emil lit his roll-up and approached cautiously, as though Alice was a skittish creature he was liable to spook. She was sitting on a tomb, legs crossed at the ankles, and a tobacco tin open in her lap. There were pearlescent burns on her hands and scabs on her ex-posed ankles.

"You should come in next time," he said.

"But, Master Emil," said Alice, "if I get sober now, what'll I have to look forward to?"

"I don't know," said Emil. "Life?"

Alice whooped theatrically, holding her stomach. "Is that what life is, sitting around in crappy churches listening to old people talk about how they used to drink too much brandy?"

"It's not that bad. Some of them are nice."

"They're boring fucks."

"It's also kind of boring just getting wrecked every day."

"You're very high and mighty for someone who only used to call me because he was too afraid to go and pick up by himself."

"That wasn't the only reason I called you."

"Was it the scintillating company?

"We were friends."

"Were we really?"

"Yeah. And I don't want you to waste your life."

Alice's face shut like a slammed door.

"Nice," she said.

"I didn't mean it like that."

"No?" she said.

"You were being mean too." Emil pointed toward the cluster of frail-looking people lighting cigarettes outside the church. "This helped me."

Alice shook her head. "What helped you, Emil, is having parents who could pay ten grand for you to go and spend a month in some fancy hotel with people trained to dig around in your problems. It wasn't those old fucks in that dark room. It wasn't your incredibly inspiring reserves of inner strength. It was a boatload of money and the cushty future you'll have regardless of what you do."

She was right, of course, although it would take Emil an hour or two to realise it. Without being totally blind to the reality of his life, Emil had never felt happy enough to consider himself privileged. He knew, abstractly, that he had grown up in luxury, attending the kind of school that was a rarity even in one of the wealthiest countries in the world, but he had only ever been a child who felt out of place, and no amount of perspective would remedy that.

Alice disappeared into the streets of discount shops and chain cafés. Emil thought that if he were to chase her now, he'd catch her. She would no longer be able to outrun him.

To distract himself, Emil thought about the physicists and mathematicians in his story, and how they existed only in relation to one another, how they were defined by their relationships, their place within a pattern. If he was honest, he struggled to maintain all of the empathy he'd once had for his friend. Relatively safe now in his sobriety, he found it difficult to understand why she couldn't see that this peaceful, even-keeled life he now had was preferable to the terrifying ordeal of what had come before it. He wanted to shake her and tell her to stop, and he understood, finally, that this was how his mum had felt, back when he'd gone to live at home again, and she'd returned early from a holiday to find him passed out on the sofa, almost fully naked, surrounded by bloody tissues, a salad bowl filled with puke, and several empty cans of beer. She'd checked his pulse and gone up to his room. She'd found blister packs of alprazolam and baggies of ketamine and a small paper wrap of heroin, and the variety was enough that she knew at least some of the drugs were serious, and that whatever he was engaged in was beyond the casual giggly fun of a few friends sharing a joint.

When Emil had regained consciousness, he was in the back of his mum's car, dressed in a bathrobe, with puke crusted around his mouth. There were oak trees streaming past the window. He flipped over and wretched into the footwell. His mum said nothing. She said nothing when they pulled up outside a former monastery and she said nothing while a pair of smiling support workers looped their arms around his shoulders and helped him toward the great oak doors.

Watching her drive away, he felt a kind of relief. His fault had been discovered and he had been taken for repair.

Emil had thrown himself into the recovery process with a gusto that surprised even him. In circles of haunted people, he confessed to feeling overlooked and out of place. He told stories about manic binges and depressed hibernations and he talked about how, at the age of sixteen, he'd ordered his first batch of heroin from the internet and thrown up so violently after smoking it that he went temporarily blind in one eye. It was a relief to unburden himself of these moments. Emil was surprised to find that he had wanted something to change, he'd just never imagined it might be possible.

On Sundays, Evangeline took Frida to the car boot sale at the old cattle market on the edge of town, and the two of them would walk up and down the aisles of open cars loaded with the contents of attics and basements. They riffled through cardboard boxes of action DVDs and hardback books, searching for small things that brought them joy.

After several hours of browsing, they bought sugar-dusted dough-nuts from the royal green van and ate them on the sloped banks of grass that separated the cattle market from the dual carriageway. The first doughnut was generally eaten while playing a game, the rules of which decreed that the consumer could not lick sugar from their lips, not even once.

The smell of hot grease and sugar mingled with the exhaust fumes from the roads behind them. When Frida's hands grew sticky, she wiped them on the grass verge. Evangeline wasn't eating. She plucked whorls of lint from the fabric of her trousers.

"What would you think about moving?" she said.

It had been a long time since Arthur's diagnosis. Their loot for the Sunday consisted of a Folio Society edition of *Bleak House*, a brass candlestick carved into the shape of a stag, and a stuffed oyster-catcher with pearls for eyes.

"Moving where?" said Frida.

"To London," said Evangeline.

Frida turned away from her mother and yanked a handful of grass out of the ground, scattering it into the breeze. "I'd like it very much," she said.

She pressed another doughnut into her mouth but found herself unable to chew. She surreptitiously fingered the dough out of her mouth, flicking it a few metres away, watching as it tumbled down the grass bank.

Evangeline put her hand onto Frida's shoulder and turned her around. "Frida?" she said. "You're crying."

Frida nodded. "I'm sorry," she said.

Evangeline drew her daughter close and buried her face in the damp nest of her hair. She didn't think that she would ever get over the smell of her daughter. Frida would be fifty years old and Evangeline would want nothing more than to sit close, inhaling her. Did every child smell of buttermilk and pollen to their parents, even beyond their baby years? Was that how Evangeline smelled to Yara? Was that even how Emil had once smelled?

"What about Grampy?" said Frida, tilting her head back so that she was looking up at her mother from the soft nest of her lap.

"We'd still come back all the time to see Grampy," said Evangeline. "And Nan, and Uncle Emil."

"And my friends," said Frida.

"And your friends," said Evangeline.

It was a constant source of surprise to Evangeline that her daughter had not just multiple friends but a group large enough to constitute an unruly birthday party, a group seemingly without hierarchy, who generally didn't compete or quarrel, who didn't call each other cruel, imaginative names, or wear each other down until they were shadows of their former selves. Obviously, Frida was still young and had plenty of time to develop toxic relationships but for now Evangeline revelled in the uncomplicated joy of her daughter's friendships. She loitered quietly in doorways during sleepovers, eavesdropping on painfully sweet conversations about possible afterlives and future occupations. Frida's friends harboured old-fashioned ambitions; they wanted to be doctors and chefs and firefighters. On the news, Evangeline still watched interviews in which children professed to shoulder the burdens of climate change and global inequality, but her own daughter seemed only to want a life of quaint stability.

"Do you have a job offer?" said Frida.

Evangeline couldn't help but smile at Frida's choice of words. "Yes," she said. "I have a job offer."

"A good one?"

Evangeline took out her phone and made her way to the landing page for a think-tank dedicated to research tying democracy and sustainable development. The group was trying to explore ways in which economic policy ought to take into account subsequent generations and their current mission involved lobbying the UK government to form a Committee for the Future.

Frida read about the organisation, backhanding snot off her top lip.

"That sounds like it could help a lot of people," she said, passing back the phone.

"It does, doesn't it?"

"Nan's going to be sad if we go."

"She'll understand," said Evangeline.

"Yes," said Frida. "She'll understand."

They finished their doughnuts while watching the people below them move in streams down the rows of open car boots and buckling wallpaper tables.

When they were done, Frida solemnly emptied a gust of sugar from the paper doughnut bag, folded it, and slipped the wad of greasy paper into her pocket. "This is to remember when you told me we were moving to London," she said. "And to remember that I was sad at first, but I knew I would make friends there eventually."

. . .

Artaud von Rosen is brought to a building he's never seen before, hidden in the bowels of a much larger building made of buttery stone. He's shown into a windowless chamber with recording devices positioned along the walls. He takes a seat and is brought a steel mug containing bitter filter coffee.

The men in hats tell him that if he ever tries to make public what he's about to be told, his life will be over. He asks if he has the choice to leave. No, the men in hats tell him. There has never been a task more important than the one he is about to be given. The fate of the world is now in his hands.

"Is this about the bomb?"

"No," say the men. "It's not about the bomb. Forget about the bomb."

They have him sign several pieces of paperwork, upgrading his security clearance, and they bring him down a further set of stairs into a deeper basement, where a giant glass cylinder stands in the centre of the room, the size and shape of a phone box. There is a kind of fibrous gas in the chamber, repeating patterns in the air like a scarf being knitted by invisible hands. Artaud looks at the gas for long enough to see that the patterns are playing on loop. It's like nothing he's ever seen and he's at a total loss to explain it. When he places his palms on the glass in wonder, the men rebuke him.

"No touching," they say.

The men explain that the gas is a message that has taken many years to decode. It was only recently, with the help of computers developed by the team at Bletchley Park, that they were able to understand what the substance was trying to communicate to them.

They tell him that the gas contains a message from an alien intelligence, stating that their solar system is in the blast zone of a type of weapon that will be unleashed in a number of months. If they are capable of reading the message before the set time, they are free to send a delegate to lobby for their cause. If the delegate can prove they are of sufficiently advanced intelligence, certain laws decree they must be spared.

At first, Artaud believes that it's some kind of practical joke, either that or he's losing his mind. But once he's shown the work that de-coded the gaseous messenger, he has no choice but to believe what the men are saying.

They tell Artaud that he will be ferried away by a craft currently orbiting the earth, waiting for their signal. He'll be put into a bio-sphere somewhere beyond Pluto for a month, during which time he will acquiesce to all their requests. The message is long but the gist of it is that Artaud will be asked to demonstrate how advanced his species is. The intelligences seem to favour some form of mathemat-ics over any other kind of knowledge, which is why Artaud has been chosen for the job.

Artaud remains at a loss. "Why me over anyone else?" he says, finally. "Why not Jansci, or Gödel, or Einstein?"

"Einstein is too old," says one of the men. "Von Neumann and Gödel both recommended you."

Artaud looks down at his feet. Was it because the others truly believed in him or because they wanted to avoid shouldering such responsibility themselves? Artaud realises his shoes are untied.

"What do they mean 'how advanced' we are?" he wants to know. "Was Kardashev not right? Do they not simply need proof of our energy-harnessing capabilities?"

The men shrug.

Artaud already knows as much as they do.

As the disease closed in on him, Arthur narrowed his focus almost entirely to litter-picking. He wandered the streets and parks of the city with his stick and a roll of bin liners, collecting crisp packets and cigarette packets and packets that had once contained strawberry-flavour condoms, pre-made sandwiches, and sugar-speckled gela-tine shoelaces. Occasionally, he would be harassed or mocked, or someone would ask if he was performing community service or working for whichever building or premises happened to be nearby at the time.

On one occasion, someone threw an open milkshake at his head. A woman in a nearby bungalow hustled out of her house and blot-ted him frantically with patterned sheets of kitchen paper.

Getting home, Arthur would generally watch the news, lying horizontal on his bony sofa. He rarely washed and his skin accumulated a layer of sticky grease, like a wax jacket.

When his phone rang, he didn't answer. He didn't open his computer. He put on a thick dressing gown and didn't take it off for a week.

The only times he paid attention to himself was in anticipation of visits from his children or grandchild. Given enough advance warning, generally via text message, he could shuffle at least some of his mess into bin bags and take a brief shower. He could spray the corners of the living room with cheap deodorant. He could squirt bleach into the burbling toilet.

When Frida came, she would stomp around the bleak flat, emulating the parenting style of her mother. She'd tut at forgotten plates sprouting islands of mould. She'd run her finger along ledges and squint at the dust accumulated on her fingertip.

"We need to get some air in here," she'd say, shunting open the stiff windows. "Honestly, Grampy, it smells like a pigsty."

Frida and Evangeline would stroll into town with Arthur and spend their afternoons quietly browsing the new antiques centre or the chain bookshop, having afternoon tea in cafés, and discussing whatever Frida happened to be studying at school. They refamiliarised themselves with exhibitions in the two museums that Arthur had taken Evangeline and Emil to as children. Evangeline was reassured by the unchanging dioramas of medieval life and Celtic settlements, and she felt anchored to the city as she looked down through the glass floor that had been installed over an excavated Roman bathhouse.

Arthur grew tired quickly during such excursions but remedied his weariness with huge cups of coffee and slabs of 95 per cent cocoa cooking chocolate, which he kept in the inside pockets of his coat and consumed in the cubicles of toilets as though they were an illicit substance.

During one outing, a few weeks into his third bout of treatment, Arthur steered them all toward the cathedral, which sat at the medieval end of the town centre, ringed by a wrought iron fence, and clubbed together with rows of stone houses. Without warning, the sky had bloomed with black clouds that poured torrential rain onto the cobblestones. Shoppers hurried past under umbrellas or shielding their heads with rucksacks and magazines. It was early in the afternoon but soft orange lights flickered on in the upper-level windows of the timber-framed shopfronts.

Frida already knew Gloucester Cathedral, having visited as part of a school trip, and later as a member of her school choir. She'd developed a fondness for old religious buildings. Sitting on hard pews, thumbing the brittle paper of prayer books, she imagined the generations that had come before her, all the way back to a kingdom of knights and castles, and felt herself securely part of a grand and ongoing tradition.

Inside, the cathedral had the clammy, musty smell of a coastal cave. Incense trailed ribbons of smoke toward the distant, vaulted ceiling. Stained-glass windows cast watery scenes onto the flagstones. The patter of raindrops echoed endlessly.

They walked the perimeter of the nave and made their way along the raised ambulatory. Evangeline lingered over the stone effigy of King Osric, running her hands up and down the graffiti carved into the arms and legs of the bearded ruler. As a child, she used to fantasise about adding her own words to the decades of vandalism but could never bring herself to do it. What would she have written? On the eight-hundred-year-old folds of Osric's robe, someone had carved the words "Emma Monkton is Hungry for JIZZ."

Arthur paused and entered a chapel where he'd once come for the baptism of one of his employees' children. It had been a happy affair, followed by a trip to The Dick Whittington, where Arthur had set up a tab and let everyone get as drunk as they could before he left. It had been a rare moment of feeling as though he was bringing joy into the lives of these people who turned up every day to work for him, exhausted from forcing their children into raincoats, clutching curry-stained Tupperware containers of sandwiches.

Frida and Evangeline watched him from a safe distance. He looked terrifyingly small to Evangeline, who could remember when her dad had been the largest person in existence. There had been a time when Arthur had hoisted her up into trees and onto railings at the edge of zoo enclosures. Now his legs were like broom handles protruding from the tattered hem of his quilted coat.

"Do you think there might be a God?" whispered Frida, tugging on her mum's hand.

"We've had this discussion," whispered Evangeline.

"But maybe?" said Frida.

Evangeline sighed. "Maybe," she said.

Frida looked around and pocketed a receipt for two cucumbers and a jar of honey that had fallen out of someone's bag while they dug out change for a votive candle.

"What's that for?" said Evangeline.

"For remembering when you said he might be real."

In the giant craft beyond Pluto, Artaud finds himself installed in a strange room that is clearly an attempt by his hosts to mirror the Altbau apartments of Berlin. He has no idea how they've managed to assemble something that so closely resembles the living room of his childhood home. There are lace doilies on the side tables. There's a wicker magazine rack, sloppily stuffed with newspapers. The wireless stands like a great walnut memorial between bookcases crowded with clothbound editions of books that, Artaud will later realise, have no titles and consist only of blank, slightly foxed pages.

His hosts communicate with Artaud through the wireless. They adopt the voice of a young Scottish woman. She sounds rational yet somehow motherly, reassuring yet stern.

He's allowed to sleep as much as he needs to. When he wakes, he's fed fatty white bulbs that his hosts inform him have been created to satisfy all his bodily needs. The texture makes him gag but he never feels hungry or unwell.

After he wakes and eats, Artaud is brought to a room that feels like the gymnasium at his old school. The ceiling is high and there are no windows. Another wireless stands against a wall. He sits at a desk stocked with thick paper, facing a mobile blackboard in a wooden frame.

As he writes, the woman in the wireless responds to his jottings, like a backseat driver, giving him directions to a place he can't find.

Artaud tries again and again to convey the most beautiful mathematical theorems of his peers and academic ancestors. Having been convinced that Euclidean geometry would satisfy his hosts, he is surprised to find they have no interest in it whatsoever. They appear to have little interest in discrete numbers at all. They don't want to play his games with binary. They don't care about primes.

He gets slightly more of a reaction with continuous mathematics: topology over graph theory, differential equations over recurrence relations. When he spells out Cantor's proof, the woman in the wireless chuckles. A window opens in the side of the gymnasium and Artaud gets up to peer through it.

What Artaud comes to realise, after being shown a glimpse into a landscape of dimensions so complex that his mind registers it only as a kind of visual glitch, is that his mission is futile. There is nothing he can show his captors to convince them that his civilisation has achieved anything like enough complexity to be worthy of rescue.

His host informs Artaud that he will be permitted to write the message that will inform his people of their imminent extinction. The host expresses no regret. *There is but one route into the future*, says the voice. *This way.*

Evangeline drove herself and Frida to London in a rented Transit van. Except for their mattresses and the desk and eight cartons containing both of their books, their collection of belongings was so modest that everything slid around chaotically each time Evangeline hit the brakes. Yara and Luke had offered to accompany them but Evangeline declined, on principle. This was the second time she had climbed out from beneath her parents and she wanted to make a clean break.

As they approached the capital, she remembered buildings from the stuffy coach journeys that bookended school trips to echoing museums or dull performances of Shakespeare in theatres with velvet seats. She remembered sitting beside Ada, ears pressed together as they watched music videos on their phones. She looked over at her daughter, who was immersed in an Agatha Christie novel, and who glanced up to offer a reassuring smile, as though it was Evangeline and not her who was the uprooted child en route to a new life.

Their new flat was a one-bedroom on the second floor of an Edwardian terrace in Peckham. Frida immediately fell in love with the squeaky, pitted wooden floors, the crumbling coving that framed the ceilings, and the iron grate over the unusable fireplace. She liked that the cistern hung high on the wall above the toilet and was flushed by pulling on a burnished chain. She liked being able to watch the downstairs neighbour potter around the garden, kneeling on a skateboard, her grey hair tied in pigtails.

"I think we'll be very happy here," she said, after her first lap of the flat. She was trying to reassure her mother, who looked less convinced.

When Frida fished a paper clip out of a crack between the floorboards and stowed it in her pocket, Evangeline fought the urge to snatch her up like a puppy.

Artaud labours over his letter to the people of earth for as long as his captors will allow. He alternates between despair and awe. He wonders if there's any real point in communicating anything to a planet of people who will shortly cease to exist.

When he tries to ask the woman in the wireless questions about the nature of existence and the underpinnings of reality, she tells him that none of the answers she could offer in his language would mean anything. She tells him not to worry himself with such things. She encourages him to finish his letter.

I'm sorry to be the bearer of bad news, Artaud writes, *but we are to be collateral in a war that is beyond our comprehension. The beings who will extinguish us view us with little more interest than we view plankton. We have come up against a force many times more complex than ourselves. I did all I could. I showed them the fruits of our collective minds and these appeared to them as mere trifles. All I had, I gave, and they shrugged in the face of it.*

They say there will be the equivalent of thirty more days before the weapon that will annihilate our planet will be unleashed. I do not know why this will happen. Believe me when I say, these things are to us what we are to microbes.

I understand that I have been given a task of monumental importance and global significance but allow me to convey this brief message to my long-suffering wife, Kata von Rosen: Kitty, I don't know what any of it means, only that I am grateful to have shared it with you.

17.

As the disease progressed, it took Arthur longer to wake each morning and he found himself having to shake his limbs to life, one by one, like sleepy children. He'd taken to keeping an adjustable metal walking stick beside his bed, which he used to haul himself off the mattress and onto the floor. He slept in jogging bottoms, two pairs of nylon socks, and a scratchy Aran jumper that he'd discovered shoved down the side of the faltering boiler. Some days, he only got out of bed to pick up his laptop and empty his bladder. His urine had turned to golden syrup. Welts and wheals crawled like mould across his shoulders.

The winter advanced without hesitation, stripping all colour from the sky and chasing the blazing heaps of leaves into gutters and storm drains. On the days when he got out of bed, Arthur would drink chamomile tea while staring through the window at the unfolding rituals of the people in the street.

The jogger pulled on a snood that jiggled around his neck as he ran. The man in the suit scratched ice from the windscreen of his Fiat Punto. The young family tripped and stumbled toward the junior school, bundled up in puffy jackets and woolly hats, their noses glowing red in their pale faces like maraschino cherries on iced cakes. Only one person had moved away in the time Arthur had been there—the Bulgarian who used to perform tai chi at his window, in boxer briefs, with the TV set to the shopping channel. Arthur had overheard a pair of neighbours from across the street say that he'd moved to Alicante, to open a yoga retreat. Another neighbour, one who lived two floors below Arthur, said that the Bulgarian had died from a heart attack, and that his body had been shipped back to his family "at the taxpayer's expense."

Death didn't frighten Arthur like it once had. There had been a time when the thought of dying was enough to make him literally cower on the floor with his hands over his ears, as though it would arrive like a bomb, dropped from a passing plane. Now he imagined death as a glowing antechamber, which you entered to find a benevolent deity awaiting your arrival. The deity nodded to you as though you were conspirators about to execute a long-agreed-upon plan. You both knew your roles, both understood what came next. A swirling vortex of inviting darkness opened on the wall. Arthur imagined this portal would resemble the aurora borealis. He imagined it would lead nowhere.

The Candlewicks had once travelled to see the Northern Lights as a family. Evangeline had been thirteen, Emil eleven. They'd stayed at a lodge-style hotel on the edge of a pine forest in Norway, where wolves howled so loudly at dusk that both kids insisted on falling asleep with headphones on.

In order to see the lights, they'd signed up for a package deal that meant whenever the phenomena showed most visibly, the family would be woken in the dead of night, packed onto Skidoos, and driven out to a viewing point on the lip of a cliff. It had been expensive, especially considering there was no guarantee that they would see anything.

But the time did come, at three in the morning, after a long day spent arguing over the route to a hot spring in a rented 4x4 that neither Arthur nor Yara had proven particularly adept at driving. The guides woke Arthur and Yara first, instructing them to get the kids and meet them out front. Emil and Evangeline were slow to wake. Although Evangeline quickly perked up when she realised what was happening, her brother remained reluctant to emerge from beneath his duvet.

"I don't want to see any gay lights," Emil had said, shoving his mother away.

Yara, who had been half-asleep and wholly hungover, and who had been suffering her son's hormonal aggression the entire holiday, dragged him out of the bed by his ankle, so suddenly that his head cracked on the tiled floor of the hotel room. There was blood, not a lot, but enough to coat Emil's fingers as they explored the throbbing spot on the back of his skull. He looked at his mum with trembling, confused eyes. When she went to hug him, he pushed her away. He dressed with tears in his eyes and rode on a Skidoo with his dad, who had no real idea of how to go about repairing the rift.

"Your mother's tired," said Arthur.

"She hit me," said Emil.

"She didn't hit you, Em," said Arthur. "She pulled you, without warning. It was an accident."

As they rode along a path winding through the forest, clouds coalesced into a crashing sea of darkness overhead. By the time they reached their intended destination, there was nothing to see but banks of black fluff in the sky.

The Candlewicks stood beside each other, fidgeting.

"Are you happy now?" Emil said to his mum.

Yara said nothing.

They remained on the cliff for two hours, waiting for the clouds to clear, until their guides eventually relented and drove them back through the woods to their hotel, where the breakfast buffet had opened. Yara went directly to bed and stayed there for the rest of the day. Emil ate three croissants smeared with Nutella. Evangeline picked at half an apple and a handful of walnuts.

The holiday had cost a total of nineteen thousand pounds.

Arthur dropped the mug carelessly into his sink. Several of his mugs were missing handles but he didn't punish the limbless and continued to use them all equally. He stripped off his sleeping clothes, re-dressed in a loose-fitting fleece and old salopettes, and slipped into shoes which he understood were the shoes of an elderly person—felt sacks held fast with thick Velcro straps. Over the top of it all, he wore a fluorescent jacket that Evangeline had bought for him, citing concerns for his safety as he wandered in the darkness. The vest had the added benefit of bestowing an air of authority on him, thus warding off potential hecklers.

Outside, Arthur roamed the streets with his bin liner and the wooden broom handle hammered with a nail. He collected crisp packets and beer cans and cigarette butts. He collected banana skins and coffee cups. He collected plastic in all its bloated, twisted forms.

He didn't think about death or his ex-wife or the chill creeping in through his threadbare assemblage of clothes. The bag grew full and he switched to carrying it over his shoulder like a pitiable Santa.

On London Road, he came across Liklun So, the proprietor of the secondhand bookshop on Eastgate Street, digging a set of car keys out of his pocket.

"Arthur," said Liklun. "Out on your rounds again?"

"I am indeed," said Arthur.

"You're lookin' well. Lost weight?"

"Trying my best."

They exchanged smiles.

"Happy Christmas."

"Merry Christmas."

He carried on, along the tree-lined stretch of double-fronted Victorian buildings on Whitby Avenue that had once been homes but were now dentistry offices, physiotherapists, kindergartens, and yoga studios. Children on bikes squinted at him, trying to determine whether he might be a worthy target for any kind of abuse. His fluorescent jacket glinted in the passing headlights. No-one bothered him. Arthur was gaunt and sallow. His eyes peered out from his head like a pair of dice.

His shoes grew damp and his toes numbed into indistinct slabs of ice. He reached into his pocket, pulled out a brown glass bottle of Oramorph, and shook a few droplets onto his outstretched tongue. "Use as needed," Dr. Moreno had said. "When it stops doing the job, we'll bump you up a level."

At the square-towered church opposite the Robinswood roundabout, Arthur cleared the grounds of broken glass and submarine-shaped nitrous oxide canisters. The vicar emerged with two mugs of tea and passed one to Arthur, and they both took seats on a commemorative bench facing a holly bush.

"I should think it's rather a busy season for you," said Arthur.

"Births, deaths, and Christmas," said the vicar. "That's half the job these days."

"Not weddings?"

"Not so many as you'd think. Kids don't want to faff about getting married, anymore. Can you blame them?"

After the tea, Arthur knotted his first bin liner, threw it into the wheelie bins behind the church, and carried on toward town. It was early in the afternoon but close enough to Christmas for groups of middle-aged friends to be drinking in the day. Arthur saw reunited families ambling home with bulging shopping bags. He thought of days when the children had been young and they'd ventured into the city centre together, splitting into factions so that each child could buy a present for each parent, and vice versa. When had they stopped going on Christmas shopping expeditions? At some point they'd stopped. There had been one time that had been the last time, and Arthur had probably paid it no attention. He had probably been distracted and irritable and the kids had quietly graduated to ranked Christmas lists of electronic items and branded clothes, while Arthur and Yara had switched to giving each other only things that were obviously and entirely practical: new shoes, a hairdryer, an air fryer, a scraper for the windshield of the car.

Arthur now sent lists of recommended charities to his friends and family inside cards handmade from A4 sheets of cartridge paper. He copied illustrations of kittens in Santa hats from the internet onto the front pages. Inside, he wrote:

Happy Christmas!
From Arthur Candlewick

Please consider donating any funds that might
otherwise have been used to buy a gift to:

GiveDirectly
The Fistula Foundation
The Lead Elimination Project

A week earlier, Mrs. Farnaby from next door had brought him round a Christmas pudding she'd baked herself. "I know you don't like people buying things," she'd said. "So I thought I'd bake you something instead." Arthur ate nothing but Christmas pudding for three days. He used a selection of leaflets from the hospital waiting room to cut out paper snowflakes, which he strung together on a shoestring, and brought over with the empty cake tin. Mrs. Farnaby hung the snowflakes from the curtain pole in her lounge.

The streets in the centre of town were heaving with shoppers rushing to plug the holes beneath their trees. It was the year that the council had decided to replace the decades-old set of illuminations with a series of asymmetrical designs produced by local schoolchildren. The result was a city watched over by wonky stars and one-legged angels with faces like fried eggs.

Arthur made his way past shopfronts piled high with fake snow scattered over artfully arranged dioramas of hand soap and cashmere scarves. He tried to remember when they'd last had real snow on Christmas. Snow still fell, sometimes, but it seemed to shrivel to grey mush before anybody had a chance to do anything enjoyable with it. Arthur had endless memories of hurling snowballs and constructing towering snowmen as a boy. He couldn't remember his own children ever asking for a carrot or a scarf while three boulders of snow waited hopefully in the garden.

On the edge of town, he walked past The New Inn, and The Fountain Inn, and the Oxfam shop where he'd once volunteered, and where his marathon-running co-worker was squatting in the window, building a precarious house out of Christmas cards. He kept going, along the road past the train station, along the canal and the old antiques centre, past the new antiques centre and Tuxedo Junction and the office supply shop with its perpetually empty car park.

He walked until the town became a suburb of semidetached houses and he stopped picking up litter but kept the half-full bin liner clasped firmly in his sweaty hands. Occasionally, he stopped and shook a few droplets of Oramorph onto his tongue. He felt insubstantial. It barely felt as though his feet were meeting the ground. When he turned his head too quickly, the world turned too, as though he was wearing it in a headset.

Arthur crossed a bridge over a dual carriageway, electricity lines hissing and spitting overhead. The houses became smaller and then larger and further apart, set back from the road by longer and longer driveways, lined with leafless trees, their branches scribbled black against the blank grey sky.

He didn't know where he was.

He came to a kissing gate overgrown with brambles and sat down astride the rotting wood with his arms looped through the fence and his face rested atop it. Hugging the gate, he fell asleep.

Forty minutes later, a six-seater Mercedes GLS shot past Arthur, came to a stop, and reversed until it was level with him. A horn blared mercilessly. A window wound down. Arthur struggled to prise open his eyes.

"Arthur?"

Arthur lifted his stick, waving, though he couldn't tell who the person addressing him was. His vision gradually refocused. He saw the giant car and the pudgy face of his former business partner floating inside it. He extricated himself from the gate and stumbled forward, holding himself up on the rim of the window.

"What are you doing out here, Arthur?" said Brian Clinks.

"I was picking up rubbish."

"What do you mean?"

"I mean that I was looking for rubbish, picking it up with this stick, and putting it in this bag." He jiggled the black bin liner in his right hand.

"As community service?"

Arthur stared at his former business partner blankly. "No," he said. "Not as community service."

Brian snorted in disbelief. "Get in, ye' fuckin' nutter. I'm takin' you home."

"What about the rubbish?"

"Leave your rubbish where it is. Someone else'll get it."

Arthur gingerly abandoned his bag and climbed into the front seat of the Mercedes. Brian scrolled a dial on the dashboard and Arthur felt his leather seat grow warm. The interior of the car was spotless. A spearmint air freshener in the shape of a cloud hung from the rear-view mirror. Arthur thought of the antechamber and the gentle deity in his vision of death. He slid his hands under his thighs and wiggled his frozen toes in the damp felt shoes.

He could have owned a car like this. He had owned a car like this, once. A car in which the temperature could be controlled by the touch of a button. A car that cost as much as five years of education for one hundred girls in a Kerala boarding house.

Brian started to drive.

"So," he said. "How's tricks?"

"Fine," said Arthur. "Great."

"You're not lookin' too good, Arthur."

"No," said Arthur. "Well, I'm a little tired."

Brian honked his horn at a car ahead of them that had slowed almost imperceptibly. "Haven't seen hair nor hide of you since we sold up," he said. "Spoke to Yara a few times, back then. She was worried sick."

"Yes," said Arthur. "We've been on quite the journey."

"That's one fuckin' way of looking at giving away everything you ever worked for."

Arthur didn't say anything.

"You're not tellin' me you don't wish you could take that back?"

"Not at all," said Arthur. "I think it's by some margin the best thing I've ever had the privilege of doing."

Brian shook his head in disbelief. A bubble of spit formed and burst at the corner of his mouth. "We built that company, Arthur. We built it so we could have good lives, now you're sitting around like a fuckin' hobo on the street, with a sack of shit on your lap, like you're paying penance for some crime. Did you do something wrong?"

"Not in the way you're implying, I shouldn't think."

"Then what was it?"

For the first time during their journey, Arthur turned to look at his former business partner. Brian's nose was a boiled strawberry balanced atop a joint of ham. His lips were thin and parched and the pallid skin of his cheeks hung in pouches from his jaw. "I suppose I wanted to do something meaningful," said Arthur.

"Meaningful? We gave jobs to dozens of lads, all of 'em got their own families. We paid taxes. We contributed to the economy."

"I'm not sure that was entirely selfless," said Arthur. "And you can do much more good in the world than being a boss."

"Course you can," said Brian. "But a person can always do more. Give 'em the shirt off your bloody back if it'll make you feel right, but if the world is just a bunch of shirtless saints, who's goin' to work in the places that make iPhones or fuckin' McLaren parts, or serve lobster, or clean cruise ships on the Aegean, and what'll happen to the people who work in them places, or their families, or the places they buy their coffees and rugs and leather shoes?"

"I don't think that's a problem we're liable to have anytime soon," said Arthur.

"They might need malaria nets in fuckin' Africa, but people need jobs over here to pay for 'em. We can't all be litter-pickers, living off the state. Someone needs to fund the state. Someone needs to build the bloody state before we can use it to save everyone else."

"I'm sorry," said Arthur. "I think I'm going to fall asleep."

When he woke up, they were in Bourton, pulling up at The Old Rectory on Drybrook Lane. It had been strung up with tasteful, monochromatic decorations, and a vast wire Christmas tree had been erected halfway along the driveway. There was a wreath on the door, above a welcome mat on the front step that read "Santa Stop Here." Arthur realised that Brian had somehow missed the news that he and Yara had divorced years earlier, and that Arthur was living alone in an ex-council flat, and Yara was now married to a man who was half Arthur's age.

"I won't come in," said Brian. "Me and Debs are goin' up to Heston's new place on the Prom for dinner. Tell Yara I said hi."

"I shall," said Arthur.

"And give the kids my love."

"I will."

He wouldn't. He doubted the children even remembered Brian Clinks, who was never the kind of adult who stooped to their level to pull faces or make coins manifest from behind their ears. Brian looked at other people's children the way he looked at beggars or Jehovah's Witnesses—as though they were intruding on a world they ought never to have been granted access to.

Arthur climbed out of the car and watched as it backed recklessly down the driveway. He stood on the polished stones, not knowing what to do next. He hadn't spoken with Yara for years. He had promised himself a long time ago that he would keep out of her way, understanding fully that he had caused her a considerable deal of pain, even while he felt that this pain had been justified. It was why he had not attended the wedding or Frida's birthday parties or the primary school play in which their granddaughter had dressed up as a blundering Roman centurion.

Yara Candlewick-Tapper emerged from the house in a sports bra, Lycra shorts, and sheepskin slippers, carrying a full bin bag with both hands. She came to an abrupt halt.

"Arthur?"

"Sorry," said Arthur. "I didn't mean to be here."

"Arthur, you look like death warmed up. Come inside."

She tossed the bulging sack of rubbish into one of her four bins and held open the door like a bellboy, waiting for her ex-husband to enter. Arthur stepped into the house that had once been his home and unstrapped his sopping wet shoes while registering the first of many changes. The floor had been replaced by a deep, colourless carpet. The corridor had been painted a shade of grey that made him think of beached whales. There were canvases on the walls of spray-painted Disney characters engaged in un-Disney-like activities, with dollar signs and nuclear waste symbols scrawled behind them. The lampshade, which had once been a cosy Tiffany cone of coloured glass, was now a faux-industrial bulb housed in a metal grill.

He followed Yara into the kitchen. Gone was the bulkhead lamp. Gone were the zinc countertops and the Shaker-style cabinets. The taps had no handles, they had sensors. The fridge was a double-wide American-style colossus.

On the dining table, two huge spools of Sellotape lay beside a pair of scissors, several rolls of wrapping paper, and a mountain of expensive-looking clothes, gym accessories, filming equipment, children's toys, and hardback books.

"You were doing your wrapping," said Arthur.

"Sit down in the lounge," said Yara. "I'll put the kettle on. You still only drink that herbal tea?"

"If you have any."

"We might have some ginger somewhere." She nodded firmly at him. "Go and sit, Arthur. You look like you're about to keel over."

In the living room, Arthur lowered himself onto the sofa and hugged a cushion to his belly. The television had grown three sizes and there was a games console parked beneath it, a collection of shooting games stacked up to one side. A photograph on the fireplace showed Luke and Yara on holiday in Sri Lanka, both tanned to chestnut brown, both bleary-eyed and grinning. Arthur was surprised to see an older photo beside it, of him, Yara, and the kids on a beach in India. He'd imagined that Yara had systematically erased all traces of him from the house but there he was, over ten years younger and twenty kilos heavier.

Yara brought through two mugs, one of which she gave to Arthur, who held it from below, the fingers of his hands interlinked.

"Do you remember when we went to Norway?" he said.

"When we spent a boatload of money to not see the Northern Lights?"

"I thought it was going to be so magical, it'd stay with the kids their entire lives."

"All that stayed with them was how awful I was."

"That's not true," said Arthur. "They liked the reindeer. Evie kissed one, don't you remember?"

"He didn't forgive me after that," said Yara. "After that, I was the bad parent. You were the gentle one, too good to get angry. It was like that before, obviously, but I think that trip just drove it home."

"I'm really not sure that's true," said Arthur.

"Isn't it?" said Yara. "Wasn't I always the one storming off, while you stayed behind and talked about how unreasonable I was?" She shook her head, bringing herself back to the moment. "I'm sorry," she said. "It doesn't matter anymore."

Arthur felt another wave of irrepressible tiredness come over him. He wanted to tell Yara that it did matter, that she was colouring in their lives together using the wrong set of colours. They hadn't been upset with her, they'd been worried. They'd wanted her to be okay. They'd been plotting how to cheer her up.

"Is the book on Genghis Khan for Frida?" he said.

"Who else?" said Yara.

"She's not like other children, is she?"

"Not any I've ever met."

"Not even our two."

"No."

She took a seat not beside Arthur, but on the coffee table opposite, which was a slab of whorled green marble, framed by rosewood, and held aloft by iron legs. She was wearing a kind of perfume that was entirely unfamiliar to Arthur, and which made him think, for no obvious reason, of a Japanese bathhouse. Her toenails were painted the quiet orange of an apricot.

"I've just spoken to Dr. Moreno," she said. "He told me you haven't been engaging with any of the support they're trying to offer you. He doesn't even know if you picked up your prescriptions."

"There's not a lot they can do at this point," said Arthur.

"But there is, Arthur. They can make you more comfortable. They have a place for you at the hospice in Cheltenham. It's a good place. Luke's nan went there, last year. They have concerts and all sorts. It's not how you imagine it'll be."

"I don't want to go to a hospice. Those places are just death and more death. I'd rather be alone."

Yara remembered how he'd looked the first time she met him at the Rotary Club party in Warwick, toes pointed at each other, so clearly out of his comfort zone that she couldn't imagine why he'd come. He didn't look so different now. He looked, she thought, like a child expecting to be told off at any moment.

"Then you'll stay here," she said.

"I couldn't."

"You can. You will."

It occurred to Arthur to argue but he felt too safe in the arms of the sofa, with his ex-wife sitting opposite him, and a view through the patio doors of the wooden wagon on cinderblocks. A quarter of the garden had now been given over to decking on which several pieces of sculpture-like patio furniture appeared to be rehearsing a play, while another quarter was a bed of slate, in the centre of which stood a large hot tub. A speaker had been fitted to the exterior wall of the house, protected from the elements by a metal hood. Miniature replicas of gas lampposts stood along the path that no longer meandered around the garden but ploughed directly through it.

"The garden's changed," said Arthur.

"We had a nightmare with the landscapers," said Yara. "Feel free to hop in the hot tub, if you want to. It might do you some good."

"Thanks," said Arthur. "I think I might just rest a moment."

"I'll leave towels out on the stairs, in case you change your mind, or want a shower."

"Thank you, poppet."

The pet name made Yara hesitate for a moment before exiting the room, as though not quite sure whether she ought to correct him or not.

Yara spent the following hours on the phone, with a friend who worked at the GP surgery where they were both registered, and who referred her to Macmillan cancer support, an organisation who had tried to reach out to Arthur but not got anywhere. She managed to arrange for a motorised bed that had been offered previously to be brought out to Bourton, as well as securing the services of a Macmillan nurse who would come once a day, for an hour, to see that Arthur was comfortable, check his stats, and offer or alter his medication.

Luke got home at six, having been forewarned about the situation during a hushed phone call with Yara through his car dashboard. He mustered a more than passable impression of someone who was happy to find his wife's dying ex-husband dozing on their sofa. He was wearing a sleeveless hoodie, the sweat of his training session drying to grime on his forearms.

"Alright, mate?" he said, reaching over to slap Arthur's outstretched palm.

"Nice to see you," said Arthur. "I gather I'm to be your guest for a night or two, if it's not too much of an intrusion."

"Nah," said Luke, dropping into an armchair, and booting up the PlayStation with his big toe. "You wanna play?"

"I don't imagine I'll be much good."

"The taking part that counts, pal."

Luke tossed a controller into Arthur's blanketed lap and thumbed his way through a game menu, altering the settings at lightning speed, so that Arthur would begin the game with several advantages, including a full suit of body armour, unlimited ammunition, and a kind of automatic rifle so large it obscured his character's view.

"R1 to aim, right stick to move your gun, circle to shoot."

"And how do I move?"

"Left stick."

"And how do I shoot again?"

"R1 and circle."

When Yara returned to the living room, she found her current husband and her ex-husband chasing each other in circles around a virtual apocalypse of decimated buildings. Arthur looked gleeful, as though he'd been invited into a gang of boys much older and cooler than himself. She stood in the doorway, watching the two men who'd come to define the two halves of her adult life. It really was just one thing after another, with no logic, no obvious tether between what had happened and what would happen. Her arms slid around her midriff until she was giving herself a hug. There was something she needed to ask Luke and it was rattling around inside of her like a pound coin in the wash.

Part Six

Somewhere to Stay

18.

Arthur had been living on a motorised bed in the lounge of the house on Drybrook Lane for two weeks when Emil completed his novel. It ran to a total of 72,380 words over 341 double-spaced A4 pages. He was sitting in the kitchen, his stomach bubbling like a cauldron as a result of the three full moka pots of grainy coffee that had been sloshed into it during the preceding six hours. A plastic yoghurt pot to the right of his computer was overflowing with cigarette butts. He clicked open a grimy PVC window before stretching until his fingertips brushed the nicotine-stained ceiling.

There had been people over the previous night and their detritus was scattered around the living room: beer cans, bottle bongs, a copy of *National Geographic* covered in faint traces of white powder. When his flatmates hosted such parties, Emil would usually linger until he either felt himself growing tempted to drink or consume something, or until the attendees grew so incoherent that listening to their anecdotes and rants stopped being enjoyable.

The sun shone unobstructed in a sky like tropical water, melting the last of the slush that sat in divots along the kerb. Emil walked across town, to a copy shop wedged between a Chinese restaurant and a hairdresser. He printed off the entirety of his novel, a suggestion he'd taken from an online article titled: "You've finished the first draft of your book, now what?" The article instructed its readers to wait for a period between writing the last word of a story and commencing the redraft, in order to impart some distance between the writer and the work.

The writer is not the painter; the writer cannot physically step back and see their canvas from afar, so the writer must step back in time, and see their story with the perspective afforded them by a temporal distance of at least three months.

Emil had decided that he wouldn't wait that long, but that he'd give himself a kind of holiday, during which he'd spend time with his father, search job listings, and make at least an attempt to comply with his mother's wish that he browse Open University courses, even though he had zero interest in studying anything in an organised, official manner. She'd offered to pay, the same as she had for Evangeline. The one stipulation was that she paid for the course directly, which seemed only fair given the amount she'd shelled out for Emil's imaginary internship in the months leading up to his stint in rehab.

The sheaf of paper under his arm was surprisingly heavy. As he walked, he thought of other pieces of advice offered by the article. "Remove fifty per cent of adverbs." "Use only the dialogue tag 'said,'" "a character should never 'wail pleadingly' or 'ejaculate with pride.'" "Start as close to the end as possible." "Never tell the reader something you can show them." "Every character should want something, even if it's only a glass of water." When he'd read the last instruction, Emil had wondered if that had been his problem. That there were times when he wanted nothing at all, not even a glass of water. He supposed that was something that might be called depression, but he was suspicious of accepting labels written by other people for his own feelings. He knew that most appendixes probably burst in roughly the same fashion, but he couldn't imagine that the way he felt could be similar enough to the way anyone else felt for a diagnosis linking them to be worthwhile.

On London Road, he turned left, thinking that he'd take the scenic route down past the docks and the quays, and browse in Waterstones for something long and set in space before he headed home. As he went, he crossed a new-build estate, with a playground occupying half of the small rectangular park at its centre. The playground was small but recently installed, the paint still unchipped and the graffiti yet to crawl across the swings or the monkey bars. A young family were playing on the equipment, bundled up in cheap, bright winter clothes. Emil was almost directly beside them when he realised that the person he was looking at was his old friend Lewis, now apparently aged beyond comprehension, into a man who would have been indistinguishable from most other men, if it wasn't for their shared history of flicking bogeys at the back of other people's heads during assembly.

When had he last seen Lewis? Surely it can't have been long enough for him to have had two children? Lewis's acne was gone and he walked with his shoulders back and chest puffed out. His biceps strained out against a tight North Face fleece so carefully washed it looked brand new. He wore chinos with elasticated cuffs at the ankles and bright white tennis socks under an old but clean pair of Air Maxes.

Emil wondered whether he could get away without saying anything but he'd paused for too long and Lewis had seen him. The two of them locked eyes.

"Emil?"

"Um," said Emil. "Hi."

Lewis sauntered over to the playground fence. He looked happy to see Emil, which was not quite how Emil felt to see him.

"It's been a while, mate."

"Yeah."

Lewis tipped his head toward the woman standing beside him. Her eyelashes were heavy with mascara and there was an orange baby-size handprint on the green wool of her jumper.

"Emil, this is Luce. Luce, this is Emil. We used to go to Field Court together, then his parents sent him to fancy school."

"Ooh," said Lucy. "King's?"

"St. Isidore's."

Her mouth hung open in amazement. "You went to Isidore's?"

"Yeah."

"Is it true you had sushi for lunch?"

"Yeah," said Emil. "Sometimes."

"And you learned Chinese?"

"Yeah," said Emil. "If you wanted."

The three of them watched the two children chase each other in circles around the playground. The boy, dressed in a padded romper, was young enough to still be interacting with the world largely through his mouth. He knelt like a monk struck by the divine and began feeding himself chips of damp bark.

"Tyson," said Lewis. "Get that shite out of your gob."

Emil felt a stab of recognition. Lewis had always said gob, never mouth. He told people to "shut your gob," called a blowjob a "gob-job," and had once recounted a story in which "the dentist went pokin' around in my gob."

"What've you been up to?" said Lewis.

"Different stuff," said Emil. "Nothing, really."

"You're still living in Gloucester?"

"Yeah," said Emil. "You?"

"Nah, mate. We moved up to Cirencester. My brother—remember Will?—he manages a chain of pubs, I'm head chef in one of 'em."

"Cool," said Emil.

"It ain't bad. Shitty hours, but the pay's good. Free food. Plus it's somewhere to have the kids' parties without having to shell out."

"That's good."

"Heard from Cal Tobin that you was workin' telesales up Innsworth way with Danjit and that lot?"

"Yeah," said Emil. "For a bit. I stopped."

"The kitchen can get a bit much, but I can't imagine what it's like havin' to call old people and try to flog them stuff."

Emil grinned. "It wasn't fulfilling."

"Nah, but what is? You got LinkedIn?"

"No."

Lewis took his phone out of his pocket, glanced at the locked screen, and put it away again. "I never imagined you'd do some shit like that, no offence. I always kind of thought you'd be, you know, some genius in London or whatever."

Genius, Emil wanted to point out, wasn't a job. It was a sobriquet given to people who happened to be born in the right place at the right time. Plant Steve Jobs or Grigori Perelman in a rural Cambodian village and see if they still came up with the iPhone or solved the Poincaré conjecture. (With a kind of detached curiosity, Emil recognised the influence of his dad in this thought.)

"Your parents still living out in Bourton?"

"Yeah."

"That house is crazy. I always remember thinkin', when I grow up, this is the house I wanna live in. I remember they had all those old pattern pictures of flowers on the walls. Me and Lucy got one of those, off Etsy. Makes me think of your place every time I look at it."

"You're so soppy," said Lucy.

Lewis shrugged. "I just felt kind of safe in your house, you know? Like it was always so warm and the tea tasted different and the carpet was real soft."

"Really?" said Emil.

"Yeah," said Lewis. "Everything was so nice and old and peaceful. Man, was I jealous of your house. Then you went off to fancy school and I guess I didn't come over anymore."

The manuscript under Emil's arm looked suddenly like a badly made stage prop and he felt preposterous carrying it. He wished he could drop it and run away. He wished he could set it on fire.

"I have to go," said Emil.

"I'm grabbin' a drink with Etchells and Ben later at The Brewhouse, if you fancy it?"

"Okay," said Emil, backing away, slowly at first, then turning and breaking into a run that felt so pathetic it only urged him to go faster, until he was moving so fast that he tripped on a loop of root that had broken through a paving slab, and landed on his chin. The wound stung with grit and the coarse salt cast out to melt the ice on the roads.

Later, reflecting on why exactly he'd gone from the playground to The Water Poet and ordered a pint of Stella and a double Absolut, Emil would struggle to piece together an answer he truly believed. He didn't envy Lewis, not consciously at least. He had never wanted a family of his own. One sentiment he'd absorbed in rehab had been that the relapse begins long before the drink or the drug is picked up, and Emil took this to mean that Lewis had simply been the triggering force on a trap set by his father's rapidly deteriorating health.

Unlike Arthur, Emil felt horrified by the prospect of death. Not just the endless nothingness, but the way he'd spent his single opportunity to exist within it. It was his failure to get to the bottom of what was to come that shook him; everything else he'd ever wanted to fathom, Emil had been able to teach himself. He'd learned quantum field theory and geometric algebra and how to install a new GPU into a gaming computer, but there was no amount of lectures, papers, or textbooks that would enable him to grasp the meaning of death. Either it was nothing at all, or it was contact with an incalculably expansive and complex superhuman presence. He felt so unprepared for either eventuality that even the prospect of sixty or seventy more years on earth felt like a woefully inadequate amount of time to prepare.

He sat alone at a table in an alcove of the pub, with his manuscript next to him, its title staring at him accusatorily. He had called the book *The Proof.* He sipped and then glugged at his pint and the rush of adrenaline at breaking his sobriety was followed ten minutes later by a sickly, fuzzy tipsiness that wasn't anything like the unbounded euphoria his mind had spent the last year trying to convince him alcohol would bring.

Emil scanned the bar, recognising some faces. Kyle Newborough, one of the guys he'd occasionally picked up from, was hunched over the fruit machine, dressed in an Ellesse tracksuit, with a cigarette tucked behind his ear. A group of men in their fifties were eating burgers around three tables that had been pushed together. Emil recognised two other men at the bar, dressed in rugby shirts, with big, cheap watches and gelled hair. They were men he'd worked with for a brief period at an auction house out in Innsworth that mostly handled foreclosures and emptying the houses of people who died without relatives.

He moved toward them, lifting his empty pint glass in greeting.

"Emole," said Luke Padsworth. "You don't normally drink in here, do ya?"

"Sometimes," said Emil.

"What's that you got there?" said John Trevaskis, pointing to the manuscript.

"Nothing," said Emil. "Some work thing. It's just stupid. I don't know." He realised he was talking too much and pressed his thumbnail into his thigh through the pocket of his right trouser leg.

He thought they might pry but they didn't. The three of them bought new drinks and relocated to a settee by the patio doors, where a wall-mounted TV was showing the preamble to a rugby premiership match between Exeter Chiefs and Saracens which didn't seem to have attracted much of an audience, largely due to Gloucester having fared so badly earlier in the season. The game was scrappy and slow and neither of the men bothered to grumble or cheer at much of what was going on. Instead, they yawned through TikTok on their phones, occasionally showing videos of painful falls or bizarre culinary creations to Emil or each other.

"Emole's on a mission today," said Luke, watching Emil return from the bar with his fourth pint in an hour.

By the end of the match, Emil was so drunk that when he used the toilet, he tipped forward on the seat, until his head was rested on the night club advert on the back of the cubicle door, and he momentarily fell asleep, spraying piss over his trousers. He woke up with a jolt and dabbed the urine off his legs, left the cubicle, and balanced awkwardly with one leg up on the sink, so that he could dry his jeans on the hand-dryer.

Staggering back out into the pub, Emil felt determined to continue getting drunk. His experience had been that inebriation came in waves and if he could keep pushing forward, he might once again find himself on an island of relative sobriety.

He closed his eyes and thought of fractals. He wondered if he smelled of piss. He wondered if the universe was an unfathomably large consciousness of which he was a single quark in a single neuron.

Alice was at the bar with a six-foot-four man in a Tupac hoodie and motorbike trousers. Emil frowned in confusion and turned around, realising his only other option was to go back into the toilet. He moved defiantly to Alice's side and placed his hands flat on the bar.

"Emil," she said.

"Hm?" said Emil, doing an unconvincing impression of someone who had only just realised she was there. "Oh, hello."

"Ky messaged me," said Alice, nodding toward the tracksuited man still hammering the fruit machine. "Told me you were sitting in the corner with two brickies getting shitfaced, telling them you'd just relapsed because the world was about to end."

"I'm ordering a drink," said Emil. "I, am, just, ordering, a, drink."

"Might not be best," said Alice. "You should get home and sleep it off. You'll be upset in the morning, Master Emil."

"I'm upset now."

"It'll be worse."

"You're a hypo, a hypocrite."

"I know," said Alice. "I'm a terrible, horrible hypocrite." She pointed to the man at her side. "Anyway, this is my friend Big Ted, I'm not sure if you've ever met."

"Hi," said Big Ted. "Don't think we've had the pleasure."

"I'm just getting a drink," said Emil. "Do you want one, Ed?"

Alice looked up at the giant beside her and nodded and he lifted Emil off his feet and threw him over his shoulder. Held aloft in the tattooed arms of the large man, Emil felt so small that he couldn't bring himself to call out or fight back, understanding that he'd only lose and fail, and that anyone watching would think him even more pitiable than they already did.

The ensuing journey was a blur in which Emil occasionally giggled and occasionally sobbed. He watched the upside-down world flash past in a blur of bare trees, dirty bus-seat moquette, and a spinning ceiling of dark sky.

Eventually, he was in his bedroom, in his flat, pawing at his eyes, while Alice and Harvey and Ellis and Big Ted looked over him like a flock of doctors.

"Try to get some rest," said Alice.

"What about you?"

"Don't worry about me, Master Emil. I'll be just fine."

Emil blubbed, suddenly overcome with emotion.

"It's not my fault you're poor," he said. "I'm sorry. I wish you weren't."

A grin spread across Alice's face and she leant down and planted a kiss between his eyebrows like a proud parent.

The hangover that arrived the next day was so painful that Emil crawled across the living room floor and into Harvey's bedroom and rummaged around in the old Neapolitan ice cream tub his flatmate used to store his pot, speed, and stash of pills. He took three Valium, tried to write an IOU using a spent promotional biro, climbed back into his bed, and fell into a sweaty half-sleep that lasted ten hours. He was woken at six that evening by the persistent ringing of his phone.

"Emil?" said Yara.

"Yeah," said Emil. "Sorry. I'm here. I was sleeping."

"Can you come home?"

"Why? What's wrong?"

"Your father's had a slight turn. The nurse says it won't be long now."

Before he left the basement flat, Emil searched his room for the manuscript like a burglar hearing the crunch of tyres on driveway gravel. It wasn't below the bed or on the desk or wedged into the bookshelf. It wasn't in the kitchen or the living room. Harvey hadn't seen it and Ellis had left to visit cousins in Monmouth. Emil made a coffee and splashed own-brand Baileys into it from a bottle he knew had been forgotten among the random assortment of bleaches and degreasers dumped under the kitchen sink. He put on an Aphex Twin album he'd listened to during his school years and stared at his reflection in the toothpaste-spattered bathroom mirror. Death, he thought, would be like a gang of bullies surrounding you, throwing punches and kicks until you were unable to discern one blow from the next. Death would be like a dream that made less and less sense. Death would not be like any of the other things he'd ever seen or heard or felt, so he wouldn't be able to see it or hear it or feel it; death would be like hypersonic noise or ultraviolet light.

Together, Evangeline and Frida had transformed their Peckham flat into something that resembled a cross between a dive bar and the set for a Saturday morning children's TV show.

They bought their furniture from flea markets and car boot sales, hauling it home in rented cars and on sweaty tube journeys. They ordered paint samples and daubed them onto the walls of the hallway so that it became a patchwork quilt of autumnal shades. They rescued torn lampshades, broken chairs, stained rugs, metal bookcases and a wooden vitrine from various skips, and painted them pastel shades of blue and yellow.

The primary school Frida attended was in an old clinker brick schoolhouse, ringed by a rainbow-coloured fence. Almost half of the students received free school meals, which was a fact Evangeline quietly and proudly filed away, like a good joke. She prepared bean salads and grilled vegetable sandwiches for herself and her daughter, and on Fridays she gave Frida money to buy fish and chips from the school canteen.

The school was a six-minute walk from their flat and although the two of them walked together at first, by their third week in London, Frida was commuting with a new best friend named Adeola. The girls shared a love of fantasy books in which good triumphed over evil, passing them between each other like contraband. They split their lunches equally. Like nineteenth-century criminals, they tacked hidden meanings onto everyday words, so they could converse openly without being understood by teachers, parents, or their fellow pupils.

Frida was bullied once, over a two-day period, by a boy who'd overheard her explaining the origin of her name and taken to drawing a monobrow onto the laminated photograph beside her coat peg. Among the traits Frida inherited from her mother was an ability to remain unflustered in the face of other people's spite. Frida arrived at school early one morning, while her teacher was sleepily marking a stack of English essays she'd put off over a weekend of clubbing, and she presented her with a DVD copy of the Salma Hayek film about Frida Kahlo's life, purchased from a car boot sale several months earlier. Miss Ellacott was grateful for the excuse to escape two hours of hungover teaching. Although she later received several complaint letters from parents in the days following the screening of the film, the pictures stopped appearing beside Frida's coat peg, and the fact that she'd been named after a Mexican painter was never again mentioned with anything but reverence.

Frida told her mother all this only after it had transpired and Evangeline squeezed her daughter so hard that Frida had to fight her off.

Evangeline's work was more administrative than she'd expected, but at least it felt like a step in the right direction. She struggled to imagine that the emails she sent, cajoling policymakers, climate scientists, and sociology professors into attending their conferences and engaging with their proposals, were having any real effect. But the project the IDCA had been painstakingly working toward—encouraging the UK to establish a Committee for the Future—had been granted a date for a vote to be held in the House of Lords.

Evangeline was now in the process of doing everything she could to give their motion its best chance of success. Despite this being the organisation's focus, there was increasingly little optimism among the staff, with many having reduced their expectations to that nebulous, unfalsifiable crutch used by celebrities who didn't want to part with their own money—raising awareness.

They'd been in Peckham for a little over a month when Frida passed on a dinner invitation to Evangeline.

"Adeola's mum wants to know if you want to come over to her house with me tomorrow, after school. She's really nice."

"Where do they live?"

"On the other side of the overground. By the big church."

Evangeline didn't hesitate before agreeing. She hadn't had time to form any real friendships in London and the majority of her socialising occurred in the form of hours-long phone conversations with Ahk and the occasional game of chess with her elderly neighbour, June Williams.

A week later, after buying a ten-pound pinot noir and a box of Milk Tray from the nearest corner shop, Evangeline and Frida walked for fifteen minutes, cutting across Telegraph Hill Park, with its view down into the great glass towers of the City, and walking down into Nunhead until they came to a well-tended townhouse on a tree-lined road with the remnants of a street party still clogging the storm drains.

They were let in by a tall woman in pinstriped pedal pushers and a long-sleeved blouse, her arms outstretched to reveal an impressive wingspan and a treble clef tattoo on her right wrist.

"It's lovely to meet you," said Imani Kwepile. "If we got on even half as well as our daughters, my husband will be incredibly jealous."

The back of the house had been cut out and replaced by a huge glass extension, housing a gleaming marble-topped kitchen. One corner of the room had been given over to a patch of rubber matting at the foot of a rock-climbing wall that stretched from the skirting board to the skylight. Rugs in deep, earthy colours overlapped each other like computer windows and a vitrine showcased pieces of brass trench art and large ammonites. The built-in bookcase was

almost entirely stocked with sheet music, A3 design books, and biographies and memoirs of musicians. Evangeline resisted the urge to
go and inspect the library.

"This house is beautiful," she said.

"Thank you," said Imani. "It took us a while to get it into this
state."

"How long have you been here?"

"We moved a few years back, when I stopped working."

"Did something happen?"

"Nothing too harrowing: I retired. But I try not to say retirement,
because it sounds kind of wanky."

"I don't think it's wanky," said Evangeline. "My mum did the
same thing. What kind of work were you doing?"

"Live events. Bringing artists over and sending them on tours.
It was exhausting and after Brexit, it was too painful to be worthwhile."

"You must have been good at it."

"I'd say good is necessary but not sufficient. You need to be good,
perseverant, and incredibly lucky. Book a run of unreliable musicians and you'll be saddled with debt like you wouldn't believe."

The two of them sat down at the kitchen island while the girls
pelted around the garden, Adeola pointing out the chicken coop, the
wooden pagoda, and the miniature waterfall cascading into a small
pool of goldfish that had once lived in a tank above the fridge. Evangeline felt a stab of longing for her childhood home, the way it had
been before her mother and Luke Tapper had gutted it of everything
familiar. Her current flat, with its patchwork walls and ragtag collection of shabby furniture, suddenly seemed embarrassing and incon-
sequential, and having had the thought, Evangeline felt as though
she'd somehow betrayed her daughter.

Outside, the girls were playing at something that involved lining
up and saluting, cocking guns, and firing into the sky. Imani tutted
and shoved open the patio door.

"Hey," she said. "No army games."

"We're not army," said Adeola, as though that ought to be bla-
tantly obvious. "We're UN peacekeepers."

Unconvinced, Imani ducked back into the kitchen and topped

up Evangeline's wineglass, before topping up her own, despite neither of them having had more than a sip. The wine was viscous and plummy and gave Evangeline gustatory flashbacks to the expensive bottles she'd nonchalantly pilfered from her parents.

"Addie said you moved from the Cotswolds?"

"Gloucester," said Evangeline. "But I grew up in a village in the Cotswolds."

"You moved here for work?"

"Yes, I'm at a place in Lambeth called the Institute for Democracy and Climate Action."

"Sounds proper. What were you doing before?"

"Studying," said Evangeline, hoping she wouldn't have to elaborate. By the second leg of her Open University course, she'd managed to convince herself it was as worthwhile as sitting in an old building at a hallowed institution, but since finishing, she'd found herself being vague and cagey when asked about where she studied. When the time had come to assemble her CV, she couldn't help but imagine how it might have looked had she never met Leo Gaskill. She pictured a leaner, faster-moving version of herself, who spoke French and travelled to conferences across Europe on sleeper trains. She saw that version of herself the way Frida had seen Callum—as a kind of ever-present, unmeetable companion who would age alongside her.

"You're just a baby," said Imani.

Evangeline looked down at her chest, as though doubting it. "It doesn't feel that way."

"It will, in a few years' time."

"I thought children were supposed to make you feel young."

"They make old people feel young," said Imani. "They make young people feel old."

There were photographs on the walls of Imani and Adeola, posing in front of swirled mauve backgrounds, with a handsome, bearded man, whose forearms were snaked with raised veins.

"And your partner?" said Evangeline.

"He's a solicitor. Family law mostly. Lot of legal aid, nothing showy. But he gets too involved and we don't always know when we're going to see him."

The photographs were surrounded by shaky drawings of isosceles houses and stick figures with faces like Halloween masks. Evangeline envied them. Most of Frida's artworks were scrunched up and thrown away before they had chance to be displayed, having failed to meet her own exacting standards. The only work she allowed to survive intact were sketches of maps and diagrams she copied from textbooks and atlases. There was a biro rendering of Antarctica on their fridge, its blank mass bisected by a blue line labelled "Amundsen's route to the pole."

Evangeline's phone rang and she drew it out of her handbag, hesitating, watching the word "Mum" on her phone as though she couldn't understand how it had come to be there. The girls in the garden were passing each other stones from the flowerbeds. The fridge rattled and hummed as it pressed fresh cubes of ice. Evangeline bounced her knees off each other, a knot forming in the pit of her stomach.

"Sorry," she said.

"Take it," said Imani. "I'll keep a lid on the insurrection."

With an apologetic nod, Evangeline took her phone into the corridor. She stood with her back to a wall the colour of matcha, surrounded by framed illustrations cut from hundred-year-old children's books.

"Hey, Evie," said Yara. "Do you think the two of you can come home?"

"Is he dead?"

"No," said Yara. "But things aren't looking too good."

"How long?"

"We don't know exactly. Not long now."

When she shuffled back into the Kwepiles' kitchen, looking as though she'd just donated several pints of blood, Imani instinctively looped her arms around Evangeline and drew her in for a hug. The gesture was so unexpected that Evangeline burst into tears, clinging to the pale chiffon of her host's blouse, thinking about her skeletal father in his robotic bed. The two women broke apart and realised they were being watched by two tiny peacekeepers at the patio doors, questions written across their faces.

"Is Frida's mummy okay?" said Adeola.

"Why don't you ask Frida's mummy?" said Imani.

Adeola looked expectantly at Evangeline, who forced a smile out, tasting the salt of her own tears. "I'm a little upset," she said. "Someone I love very much isn't very well."

"It's my granddad," said Frida, stepping into the centre of the group. "My nan doesn't speak to him anymore because he sold his company and gave all of the money to poor people."

Amused, Imani looked to Evangeline for clarification.

"She's right," said Evangeline. "More or less."

Frida nodded. "More or less," she said.

Evangeline and Frida dashed back to their flat and hurriedly packed a rucksack each with a random grab of relatively clean clothes, books, and a sculpture that Frida had made for her granddad at the after-school club she attended so that Evangeline could work until five. The sculpture was of an anatomically correct human brain. Although the various lobes and folds had been rendered convincingly using a combination of papier mâché and humps of masking tape, the colour was a too-bright shade of pink that gave the object the air of a Barbie bike helmet.

They caught a taxi to Paddington and sat opposite the departures board while gangs of ravaged pigeons hopped between the great steel rafters. As well as her sculpture, Frida had brought along a stuffed toy shaped like a tardigrade that she'd been allowed to buy at the gift shop of the Natural History Museum. The brain and the tardigrade sat together in a canvas Waterstones tote bag at her feet. Evangeline eyed it unsurely, wondering whether she ought to have deterred her daughter from bringing the brain with them. It felt too pertinent, as a metaphor. It felt like a bad joke.

"Darling, I should warn you that your granddad might not be able to appreciate your sculpture."

"Will he be unconscious?"

"He might be. But that doesn't mean he won't be able to hear us. Hearing is the last sense to go."

"What's the first?"

"I'm not sure. Taste, maybe."

Frida lifted the plush tardigrade out of the bag and hugged it to her chest. "We should think of a good story to tell him," she said.

"That would be very sweet," said Evangeline.

"I'll describe the sculpture to him, too. I'll say the colour is realistic. He doesn't have to know." She looked down sadly at the canvas bag. "Some people's brains might be that colour," she said, hopefully.

On the train, they shared a pair of earbuds and listened to a podcast about the life of Clara Schumann. Frida was asleep by the time they passed Didcot Parkway. Evangeline bought crisps and a canned white wine spritzer from the food trolley and consumed them while staring at her daughter so intently it was as if she'd been told the evening would involve having to draw her from memory.

She had not, she knew, ever really forgiven her father for doing what she still believed to be the one thing any privileged human being ought to do: give until it hurt. She had not fully allowed him back into her life and he had made it easy to keep him largely out of it, by never imposing himself on anyone, never inviting himself anywhere or insisting that anyone take time out of their lives to go and see him. When she asked herself why she'd behaved that way, she still struggled to find a satisfying answer. The conclusion she drew from that failure was simply that she was selfish; that she was either in denial or deluded about who she was and what her own values really were. She had come to the conclusion that a value was not a value unless you acted on it: it was an affectation, make-up, the T-shirt of a band you've never even listened to.

Emil arrived at the house and crept into the living room in his socks, like a child in the night, hoping not to wake his dad. As he lowered himself onto the seat beside the bed, Arthur's eyelids flickered open and he exhaled in a manner that seemed more to Emil like leaking than breathing air.

"Yara?" said Arthur.

"It's me, Dad."

"Emil."

"Yeah. You okay?"

"Oh, just wonderful, poppet. And yourself?"

"Fine."

Emil twitched and fidgeted in the seat, his mind softened into sentimental porridge by the now relatively unfamiliar throb of drunkenness becoming a hangover. "Actually," he said. "I think I kind of messed up. Or, I don't know. I'm sorry." He watched as his dad fought and failed to shift his upper body into a sitting position. "It's okay," he said. "You don't have to sit up."

Arthur relaxed back into his nest of sheets and pillows. "What happened?" he said.

"I don't know," said Emil. "I saw Lewis, in town. And he has kids now. And a wife. And his whole life is laid out and he knows what he's doing. I just thought I'd have done something by now. Or at least know more about what I should be doing. But I'm just . . ."

Arthur lifted one of his hands and gripped the metal railing at the side of the bed. When he started speaking, the words came out of him so slowly that Emil occasionally dug his phone out of his pocket and checked the time. "Poppet," he said. "There were times when I thought I knew exactly what I was doing, only to find out I'd been heading in the wrong direction all along. A few hundred years ago, the most intelligent people on the planet believed phlogiston was the fundament of everything and drilling a hole in your skull was the best way to cure a headache. None of it is set in stone. Just because you don't know now, doesn't mean you'll always feel that way. And when something changes, you just have to make sure you've managed to stick around long enough to see it happen."

Emil nodded uncertainly, his hands so deep in his pockets he could touch his knees.

"What have you been reading about lately?" said Arthur.

"I don't know," said Emil. "Just sci-fi mostly. And stuff about how AI could help solve some of the big maths problems because of, like, automated proof checkers."

"Interesting," said Arthur. "So they'll take over the grunt work?"

"Yeah," said Emil. "And there are like loads of people online already who are building these libraries together that will be able to do it."

"And you're involved?"

"Kind of. Sometimes."

"Fascinating," said Arthur. "I do start to think, though, that the abstract questions, the big thoughts, the impossible numbers, they're only worth something in the way that they relate to human beings. Sometimes they seem to wander off somewhere else entirely and forget that. You could discover a grand unifying theory alone on a desert island and what good would it do you? Knowledge is only ever about something. It is not the something. The something is the people, the feeling, the universe with you in it." Arthur tapped his railing. "This is the something." He blinked, exhausted by the effort of speaking at length. "You don't belong to a realm of forms, poppet. You belong here, whether it feels that way or not."

Emil stared blankly at a spot on the wall. Occasionally his You-Tube algorithm recommended him self-help videos in which men who looked like Luke Tapper implored him to make his bed and chat up women in public places, and his father's speech was veering toward the same territory. He didn't feel like a child of the universe or a magical constellation of love and beauty. He felt like a thing among things, biding his time until the next period of unconsciousness arrived to relieve him of his thoughts.

"This isn't helping much, is it?" said Arthur.

Emil shrugged, wishing his father would stop talking, and feeling guilty for wishing his father would stop talking, given that it would not be long before his father stopped talking forever.

"Can I ask you one thing?" said Arthur. "After that, I promise to shut up."

"Dad, you don't have to shut up."

"I will, I know I'm going on. But first tell me: what is something you've done that felt like the thing you ought to be doing?"

Emil let the question roll around his head several times before he understood exactly what it meant. When had he been doing something that felt like the thing he ought to be doing? He mentally scrolled through all of the jobs he'd held in the preceding years: telesales marketing, food delivery, cleaning at the gym on Barton Street, serving beer at the rugby club. None of them had ever been anything but a way of keeping himself in narcotics and microwave meals. He'd been writing, up until recently. And that had made sense. But the story he'd been left with at the end of it all felt like a botched piece of DIY—an embarrassment that he knew needed to be torn out and rebuilt by a professional.

"I don't know," said Emil. "I like reading, I guess; but that feels more like forgetting you exist."

His phone vibrated and he glanced down abruptly, like someone awaiting biopsy results.

"Who's that?" said his dad.

"No-one," said Emil. "I thought it might be this friend, Alice. I think, probably, she's not speaking to me anymore."

"Who's Alice?"

"You don't know her."

"Tell me about Alice."

So Emil, with nothing else to do, and feeling guilty for not being able to find any suitably solemn or emotional words for his dying father, recounted the history of his friendship with Alice, who he had first met some nights after Arthur's fall, and who had become a complicated person to know, given that she, in some respects, had the same set of problems as he did, with far more excuses for having ended up there and far fewer ways of escaping.

Emil had pieced together a blurry and incomplete picture of Alice's life over the time they'd known each other. As far as he could tell, she'd bounced between foster homes and a residential centre on the edge of town since her mum had gone to jail for assaulting, with a meat tenderiser, a boyfriend who had threatened her with a nine iron. By the time Alice's mum had come out of the prism-shaped prison opposite the canal marshes, they'd both been so altered by their time apart that they had little use for each other. Alice had already graduated from the care system and been supplied with a council flat on Bruton Way, which played host to a rotating cast of addicts and the people who supplied them; while her mother, mentally deteriorating from prison drugs and an undiagnosed personality disorder, followed a cruel welder to Leicester and found herself working night shifts in a care home, subsisting on off-brand energy drinks and expired prawn mayo sandwiches.

One night, drunk and high on gritty ketamine cut with Nesquik powder, Alice had told Emil that she only chose terrible boyfriends because she didn't trust the other kind: why would they want to be with her? She had grabbed Emil by the jaw and moved his face to hers until their noses were squashed together. "Should I have fallen in love with you instead?" she'd said. "Would that have been bet-ter?"

The memory of it felt like stale milk in his stomach. Emil brought his legs up and held his knees pressed to his chest. He told his dad about the night when he'd found himself locked out of the house and walked into Stroud and the night when he'd driven with Evangeline to pick up Alice from the man so covered in piercings he looked like the villain from a horror film.

"You helped her," said Arthur.

"I don't know," said Emil. "I guess."

"Why?"

Emil wasn't sure how to answer. He rewound through the night when he'd threatened a man with his replica crysknife and lifted a lifeless Alice off the bathroom floor. He remembered how it had felt to have her head in his lap as they drove across town at four in the morning, knowing that she was safe now, at least for the next few hours, at least while he was there with her.

"Because there was no-one else," said Emil.

"There you go," said Arthur. "And how did that feel?"

"I guess good," said Emil.

"You guess good," said Arthur, a smile emerging from the grey-ing folds of his face. "I don't care what you achieve in your life, Emil. There's no-one to answer to at the end of it, there's no form you get to fill out saying that yes, you managed to buy a house and raise a pair of kids: the only thing you'll have to answer to are the feelings you're left with." He pointed to the ceiling, his index finger skel-etal and trembling. "We worked so hard to make enough money to buy this whopping great place that stood so far away from the other houses, with its big fence all around to keep everyone out, but why?" He shook his head. "All I'll ask is that you check in with yourself when you find your life heading in a certain direction: is this making me happy? Do I want the things that will make my life better? Or do I want the things that I've been tricked into wanting? If the answer is yes, might I suggest you find a nice deep hole to fall into, for a little perspective."

"Thanks, Dad," said Emil.

"Thank you too, poppet."

As Arthur fell asleep, Emil put in his headphones and listened to a podcast from a Yale professor called *The Science of Happiness*, while occasionally dabbing at his father's head with a damp flannel. He placed his hand on top of his father's hand and felt the undertow of his hangover pulling him back toward the dim warmth of the Wetherspoons in town. He turned from the feeling as though it were an evangelical missionary preaching a gospel he didn't want to hear. *Sorry*, he told it. *Not today.*

Luke Tapper was waiting at the station in a candy-apple-red Mustang, with chrome accents and tail-lights that jutted out from the protracted boot like wings. Evangeline was struck by the memory of that day years ago when she'd come home to tell her mother she was pregnant. She wanted to somehow reach into her mind, lift out that memory, and pass it to her daughter. She wanted for her daughter to hold all of the moments of her life, without quite being sure why. It was a kind of narcissism, she supposed. Evangeline wanted someone else to keep her company in the lonely hours of her past.

"Hi, Uncle Luke," said Frida, wrapping herself around the firm muscle of his stomach.

Luke had never been dubbed Granddad, simply by dint of not looking enough like one. By that point, he was working as a personal trainer alongside running his YouTube channel, and building a fitness app with Yara's help, meant to help people who felt intimidated by entering a gym for the first time. The app tried to set people at ease by speaking gentle reassurances to them. "You are good enough," it told them. "You are worth no less than these intimidatingly chiselled athletes. Every one of these people had to start their journey somewhere. Every one of these people once felt the way you feel now."

They climbed into the car, with Evangeline sitting in the front and Frida taking the middle seat in the back so she could wedge her face between the front seats and not miss any of the adult conversation.

"How's he doing?" said Evangeline.

"He's in and out," said Luke. "More out than in, the past few hours." He checked his watch. "One of the nurses is coming again at nine, just to check in. Deirdra, she's called. She's a good sort."

Luke turned down the volume on a playlist of nineties dance

music and turned up the heat until the car was so warm Evangeline wound down her window.

"Is he in considerable pain?" said Frida, from the back seat, when they stopped at a set of traffic lights.

"No pain at all," said Luke. "They got your granddad higher than a kite. You could stick a pin in his foot and he wouldn't notice."

Frida nodded. "The miracles of modern medicine," she said, so solemnly that both Luke and Evangeline laughed.

19.

As Arthur's illness entered its final stages, the living room was gripped by a sludgy, fleshy smell that thickened the air like steam. Yara aired it three times a day, lit scented candles, and drew shapes in the corners of the room with bundles of burning sage. The fug refused to shift. She filled vases with bouquets of fresh roses and hung bunches of dry lavender from the sconces. She bought a waist-height, O-shaped air purifier that glowed in pulses like an organism from the ocean floor.

"It looks like a portal," said Arthur, sleepily, when Yara first plugged it in.

One night, before the nurse had numbered his days, Yara woke up at four and tripped downstairs in her dressing gown to find Arthur awake and staring at a spot on the wall. His hands, shrivelled to fragile matchstick models, sat pathetically at his sides. His body was so thin its contours were barely visible from beneath the duvet.

"You can't sleep?" she said.

"Sorry, poppet. Did I wake you?"

"By staring silently at the wall?"

"Sometimes, I'm no longer sure what I'm saying out loud and what I'm only thinking."

She took a seat on the armchair which had been positioned next to the bed for guests. She didn't know whether to look at him or not. It felt too intimate, watching him shrink and wither like a huge root vegetable.

"What were you thinking so loudly?" she said.

"I suppose I was thinking about my childhood," said Arthur.

"About Hatfield and how we used to pick blackberries. About the kids from over the way, the Fords, and how we'd spend half our time scrapping, the rest playing shops or Roman soldiers."

"You make it sound more idyllic than it was."

"I believe the place was idyllic, even if our lives were anything but. We had all the ingredients for a wonderful life but I suppose my parents hadn't the faintest clue how to assemble one."

"We weren't those kind of parents, were we?"

"I shouldn't think so," said Arthur. "I suppose we shook them up, in our own way. But I'd like to think we've done okay."

Beside the bed, there was a wheeled tool cabinet that had been brought in from the garage and filled with medicines, syringes, bandages, and candles. An empty clay bowl sat on top of the unit, beside a glass bottle of mineral water and a stack of clean flannels, folded into neat squares.

"Yoghurt or water?" said Yara.

"Neither," said Arthur. "But thank you."

They both sat looking at the garden, illuminated in stretches and slivers by half a silver moon. The gypsy wagon had been sanded down and repainted cornflower blue. Arthur had noticed one other remnant of their old life, relocated to a discreet spot near the back corner of the fence: a blazing red acer that he'd planted in a fit of energy one spring Sunday morning more than a decade earlier. For no discernible reason, he could remember that day almost from start to finish. There had been an intifada on the news. A hurricane in the Philippines. They'd eaten roast lamb and Emil had asked if they could build a murderous robot out of scrap metal and bring it on *Robot Wars*.

"I always thought I'd be a fount of wisdom on my deathbed," said Arthur.

"Arthur," said Yara. "You don't have to worry about that."

"I wouldn't mind a few more weeks to come up with some half-decent last words."

"Arthur, please."

"But then I suppose my last words will probably be 'water' or 'make it stop.'"

A squirrel dashed from the foot of the magnolia to the fence and disappeared through a gap between the slats.

"Years ago, when we came out of that horrid office in Cheltenham, my solicitor asked what was wrong with me. He said that as a father, I ought to have been thinking of my children above all else, and he couldn't believe I really thought what I'd done was sane."

"I believe it now," said Yara. "I think I believe it now." She opened one of the drawers of the tool chest, took out a rolled bandage, and began running it up and down the outside of her thigh. "Do you remember the night you went missing?"

"Of course," said Arthur.

"During the hearing, you called it a 'road to Damascus moment.'"

"It was," said Arthur.

"What happened?"

"Could you pass me some water, please?"

"Flannel or cup?"

"Cup, I think."

Yara took a plastic beaker from the tool chest and filled it with mineral water from the glass bottle. "Here." She lifted it to Arthur's mouth and he sipped, gently, even the small amount of water causing him to splutter. He wiped his mouth on the duvet.

"When I fell," he said, "I hurt so incredibly, I wasn't sure how I could even continue to exist. The pain was just relentless, and what hurt all the more was realising that there was a very real chance no-one was going to find me."

"Someone would have found you," said Yara.

"I didn't know that. Really, I didn't. So to try and distract myself, I read dubbin's book. Of course, I could only read when light fell into the mineshaft at just the right angle, which meant I could read for a while, then would spend some time thinking about what I'd just read. I read about a tropical disease that causes the face to swell to three times its normal size, and women who leak faeces and urine after giving birth because they can't get fistula operations. I read about people who were suffering as much as I was in those few days, but every day of their lives. People who brought children into the world and had to watch them waste away without food or water, or with diseases that could be prevented by mosquito nets that cost a pound or vitamin supplements or surgeries that are so simple you could teach a new doctor how to do it in fifteen minutes."

"Don't get yourself riled up," said Yara.

"I finished the book, but the pain was still there. I was passing out and coming around and I couldn't tell how much time was passing. Which is when, I confess, I took a small amount of those drugs."

"I knew you took the acid," said Yara, clapping her hands. "You told me you didn't."

"I knew you'd say I'd lost my mind if I had. But I knew I hadn't. I knew that I'd found it. When I took the acid, I scrolled back through all the moments of my life, which I understand sounds almost ridiculously cliched, but it's what happened. I went through feeling overlooked and somewhat insufficient at home, going to university because it was what was expected, meeting you, dropping out, starting Riverwild, almost losing Riverwild, deciding we wanted the kids to grow up surrounded by nature, finding this beautiful house, doing everything we could to buy it, then watching the kids retreat to their rooms and stay there for the next ten years." Yara smiled weakly. "Then I saw a kind of dark, endless ocean, with all these tiny cotton bubbles bobbing on it. Inside each bubble was a translucent baby, curled up with its hands at its mouth. And some of these bubbles were tied to all the bubbles around them, and some were just floating out there, entirely on their own."

"Arthur."

"And then I came back to the mineshaft but I saw all of these people stood around me, the people from the book, and they looked so concerned. They were asking if I was okay. They were telling me everything was going to be fine. But they were also asking why I hadn't helped them. Why I'd left them to suffer, while we sat in our great big house, being sad in separate rooms. I told them I was sorry. I told them if I survived, I would do all I could to help them."

Arthur gestured for the cup and Yara brought it to his mouth again. This time, when he drank, he didn't splutter. "It's either true that we ought to be helping people using all the excess we have," he said. "Or it's not true. There's no in between. There's no world in which occasionally throwing five pounds into a charity bucket is enough, I'm afraid. If we can save the lives of people without so much as putting ourselves in the slightest bit of danger or discomfort, then I think we have to do it."

"I'm sorry, Arthur," said Yara. "But I really don't want to get into this."

"Why not?"

"Because I don't want to upset you and I don't think my opinion matters anymore. You chose your path and you're happy you went down it."

"I don't think 'happy' is the word, but I'm glad I did what I did. I think it was right."

"Then there we go."

"What's wrong, poppet?"

"It just wasn't the deal, Arthur."

"Well," said Arthur. "No, perhaps not. But I think what I really felt was that we had so much, but we weren't happy, so what was the point?"

Yara wanted to argue but she didn't know how. What could she tell him? That they had been happy but none of them had realised it? That happiness was only ever something you could see from a distance?

"How about this," said Arthur. "*And now, I bid you adieu.*"

"Sorry?"

"For my last words."

"It's a little bombastic."

"You're right, poppet. I'll keep thinking."

Three days later, the Macmillan nurse signalled for Yara to follow her out of the living room and told her that Arthur probably only had a few days left. He'd been lapsing into unconsciousness for longer and longer periods of time and was beginning to eschew food, asking only for the occasional spoonful of raspberry yoghurt, in a voice that became so thin and hoarse that it sounded villainous.

Yara made herself a French press and sat down at the living room table. She wrote a list of people she felt ought to know, or ought to want to know, that her ex-husband was almost gone from the world. It took half an hour to call them, one by one, the news of Arthur's imminent death becoming a streamlined set of sentences which set out the facts as succinctly as possible.

Arthur's cancer has moved into the final stage. The nurse says he prob-

ably has days. He's in good spirits, when he's awake. You're welcome to visit any time.

An hour after the last call, a woman arrived at the house carrying a wicker basket filled with artisanal cheeses and foil-wrapped bottles of olive oil. She was in her mid-sixties and draped in knitting: leg warmers and mittens, a headband and two scarves.

"Your daughter let me know what was going on," she said. "I hope it's okay to pop round. I didn't come before because I was visiting my sister up in York. Beautiful place, York. Have you ever been?"

"Oh," said Yara. "No?"

"You should. There's the Viking centre, for starters. Lots of lovely cafés too."

She passed the basket of gifts to Yara, who wondered whether she ought to show it to Arthur, despite the fact that he wouldn't be able to consume anything in it. Perhaps he could smell the cheeses? Use the olive oil like hand cream? Yara showed the woman through to the living room, where Arthur was sleeping so deeply that his guest span around to Yara with a look of panic.

"It's okay," said Yara. "He's resting."

The doorbell rang again a few minutes later. It was Brian Clinks and his wife Debbie, holding a bottle of champagne and a metre-long box of Lindt pralines. Yara wondered whether all these people really thought Arthur was fit to get drunk and gorge himself on dairy products. What did they think dying entailed? Eating and drinking until your heart stopped?

Arthur was still sleeping. Yara invited Brian and Debbie to wait in the living room until he woke up and, feeling like they had no other choice but to accept, the Clinkses took seats on the sofa next to the wool-covered woman who'd brought the cheeses.

By ten o'clock that evening, the living room was crowded with people. They sat on stools and cushions and chairs brought in from the dining room. They had all brought useless gifts: history magazines and red grapes and paperback novels. Several had brought flowers, which Yara ran out of vases for and resorted to jamming into spaghetti jars and an asparagus pot. Someone had brought a large cigar, as thick as a hockey stick. Someone else had brought a tartan scarf, which Yara draped across the foot of Arthur's bed. All were waiting

for Arthur to wake up, having been told by Yara that Arthur did occasionally regain consciousness, and not wanting to leave without
having had the chance to say hello and goodbye, and to prove to him
that they had come.

Emil was reading *New Scientist* online. Brian Clinks was asleep.
The woman who'd brought the cheeses was engaged in an enthusiastic discussion about Chatsworth House with the vicar. Opal was
tidying. A woman named Wing-Yan Harper was typing on an iPad
affixed to a rubber keyboard. Mrs. Farnaby was in the toilet, which
she visited reliably at fifteen-minute intervals, having apologetically
told everyone that she'd eaten onions that morning. Arthur's brothers were in the kitchen helping Yara to make tea and sandwiches.
Two former employees of Riverwild Timber were sat on the floor
with their backs against the wall, watching the same horse race on
separate phones.

Evangeline and a sleepy-eyed Frida inched apprehensively into
the room at quarter to eleven, having arrived from the train station
with Luke. Frida's hand shot out and gripped her mother's jumper.

"Mum," she said. "Who are all these people?"

"They're people who want to say goodbye to Grampy, darling."

"His friends?"

"Some of them, I expect."

The sea of faces smiled at the tiny girl with sympathy. Frida
climbed up onto the robotic bed beside her granddad and lifted his
hand. She rested her head against his chest.

"Grampy," she whispered. "I made you a brain."

Arthur's eyes fluttered gently, before snapping open in abject horror as he took in the inexplicable crowd of people occupying his living room. He screamed. It was a horrible, keening sound that tore
through the muggy peace of the previous hours. Frida rolled off the
bed like a TV policeman tumbling off the bonnet of a car.

"Everyone out," said Yara.

"Grampy?" said Frida to herself, on all fours.

"It's okay," said Evangeline, lifting her daughter off the carpet
like a tortoise and carrying her out of the room. "Grampy just needs
a second."

The crowd of people were ushered through to the dining room, while Yara knelt beside the bed, and moved her face so close to Arthur's that all he could see were her big hazel eyes, unblinking, the only two objects left in existence.

"I'm here," she said. "It's me. You just had some visitors and they all wanted to wait until you woke up."

"Water," said Arthur.

"Of course," said Yara.

She unfolded one of the flannels, dipped it into mineral water, and pressed it between Arthur's cracked and peeling lips. He closed his eyes and shivered in gratitude. His right foot twitched defiantly beneath the duvet. She pulled the flannel away and draped it over the rim of the clay bowl. Arthur drew a frail, rattling breath into the brittle cavity of his chest.

"I thought they were ghosts," he said.

"No," said Yara. "They just wanted to say hello."

You're the ghost, she thought.

"Okay," he said.

"Okay?"

"Perhaps they can come back in now, poppet."

"Are you sure you're up to it?"

"I should think so."

When the visitors were brought back into the living room, they looked tense and apprehensive, as though scared Arthur could begin screaming again at any moment. They took it in turns to hesitantly hug him or kiss him or lift his limp hand and make a pretence of shaking it.

"Sorry for the hullabaloo," said Arthur, once everyone had paid their respects. "You gave me a fright."

A ripple of laughter passed through the assembled visitors.

"Luke?" said Arthur.

"Yes, mate?"

"Do you think we might open some wine?"

"I'll see what I can dig out. Your pal also brought some champers."

Luke left for the kitchen and Yara flicked Radio 4 to Radio 2, which was playing eighties synth pop that put her in mind of the sticky-floored discos she'd haunted as a teenager.

"I wasn't aware you all knew each other," said Arthur.

"We were waitin' for you to wake up, you nutter," said Brian Clinks.

"Apologies," said Arthur. "I seem to have developed a fondness for napping of late."

Wine was passed out in tumblers and mugs and Emil excused himself to smoke in the garden. He sat on the step of the wagon, watching the awkward horde of people in his mum's living room attempt to work out how exactly they were meant to say their last goodbye to his father. The vicar appeared to be tapping his foot in time to the music. The two former employees were still trying to follow the horse race on their phones. Emil smoked cigarette after cigarette until he felt nauseous and stopped, clutching his shins and resting his head upon his knees, as a kind of party sprung up around his father.

By the time Emil stepped back through the patio doors into the house, it was clear Arthur was worn out and the visit was coming to an end.

"Well," said Arthur. "Thank you all for coming. Sorry for all the screaming. I think I'm going to rest for a bit now."

It would be three more days before Arthur died. During those nights, Yara lived in the seat at his side, only agreeing to spend a few hours in bed when one of her children took over.

She kept Radio 4 whispering from an old radio/cassette player slotted onto the bookcase. A salt lamp was left on in the corner of the room. The curtains were opened just enough for the meagre hours of daylight to fan out across the carpet. Occasionally, a candle smelling of bergamot or cedarwood was lit for a few minutes and blown out.

Luke Tapper excused himself almost entirely, spending long days at the gym, and preparing meals for whoever felt hungry, leaving them stacked in Tupperware boxes in the fridge and freezer. He labelled these meals in a manner he'd learned from Yara: "lentils, halloumi, broccoli, so spicey"; "mega protein chili"; "pasta and houmouse, not very nice."

Evangeline and Frida slept upstairs and periodically tried to convince Yara to leave the room and take naps and showers. Emil came in and out of the house at odd hours, reading his father articles on

witch trials and the Carthaginians from years-old *BBC History* magazines he'd excavated from the attic.

With Yara unwilling to open the windows or the patio doors for
more than a few seconds in case Arthur grew cold, the room was
overcome by the damp, animal smell of decay. Emil was unable to
shake the feeling that the smell was caused by particles of his father
escaping into the air. He breathed in the clammy fog and imagined
he was inhaling specks of his father's silver beard and flaking lips,
of his long, restless hands and complicated knees and the blue-black
moles on the back of his neck.

Arthur slipped rapidly from speaking hushed sentences to single
words—"water," "light," "music"—to groaning when he woke up
or opened his eyes to saying nothing, just blinking like someone
emerging from a long film in a dark cinema.

The drugs that were dripped directly into his spine conjured vi-
sions and summoned long-forgotten memories, welding them together into impossible stories that flowed with the flawless logic of
dreams.

Each time he closed his eyes, Arthur was somewhere else, the
voices of his family sounding down on him like gods.

"Does he look okay?"

"Does he need water?"

"Is he cold?"

He is sitting in the kitchen of this same house, so many years
earlier. His children are still children, on the cusp of crossing the
threshold into what comes next. He is the only person in the room
but he can sense his family's presence on the upper floors and he
knows that he is not alone. He sees his face in the glass panels of the
cabinets. His hands are steady, his wedding ring is a gleaming band
of rose gold. The sky is not dusky pink, but an apocalyptic orange,
like the raging flash of a nuclear explosion. There is a glass of wine
in his hand, the viscous red liquid leaving traces of itself behind
as he whips it into a vortex. The wine breathes out hints of maple
syrup and ozone. A slim book is on the table. A manila envelope is
on the table. Four bowls of unfinished feta salad are on the table. He
empties his wine glass and stuffs the book and the envelope into his
pockets, crumpling them both like crashed cars. He leaves the house

with the wine bottle hanging loose in his right hand. He climbs into his BMW.

The village is empty. Bulky cars sleep in gravel driveways. Forested hills loom over fields of baled hay.

Arthur abandons the car and begins to walk. He walks and walks, beyond the pain of his knees and lower back and the ache behind his eyeballs. He keeps walking, knowing that he has a destination, without knowing what that destination might be and why it's imperative that he reaches it.

He enters a dense thicket of trees and ploughs on, briar and nettles lashing out at his ankles, leaving behind welts and crazed scratches. The wine bottle, empty, falls from his hand into a crib of moss and doesn't break. He counts his steps in packs of ten. When he thinks he can't go on, he convinces himself he can reach another ten, and another ten, and another ten after that.

And then he falls, without warning, so far that he has plenty of time to think: I am falling.

He lands in a heap with his legs somehow higher than his head and one arm pinned behind his back as though he's being arrested by the earth.

He looks up at his feet and wonders if he's dead. Can a body be arranged like this and later brush itself off and continue about its day? It is, he thinks, too dark to be the afterlife, and it smells too much like mulched leaves and wet slate. There are already ants winding paths up his crooked legs. He sees a woodlouse and thinks, with surprise, that he saw woodlice very often as a child, and almost never in adulthood.

"I think I might be in something of a pickle," he tells the woodlouse.

He tries to move and a pain, originating between two of the links in his lower spine, explodes outwards in all direction. He pictures a star collapsing in on itself, its glow expanding before sharpening into a single thread that stretches from one end of everything to the other. As his eyes adjust to the gloom, he can make out kinked, hairy fingers of root protruding from the packed mud of the shaft. There are sounds like heavy machinery at war with formations of ancient stone.

He is back down in the belly of the planet. His legs and chest, aching with the exertion of the journey, are now reduced to a reminder that this body is something he has borrowed from the great, unfeeling mass beneath him. He has an impulse to try and defy the inevitable, to try and keep all the parts of himself together, as though he were an unravelling mummy with nothing inside but the desire to keep existing.

He plunges his hands into the dirt.

He sees an endless network of mineshafts filled with an endless number of bodies. Every body lies on its back, looking up at the hazy loop of light through which it fell, waiting for a rescuer to materialise. The light dims and brightens and dims again. Arthur tries shouting. A face appears, round and frowning, and is joined by the forgiving eyes and slick nose of a Labrador.

"Hello?" booms a voice.

God has a dog, thinks Arthur.

The blue halo tears open. The sky engulfs him.

Arthur Candlewick passed away some time in the early morning of the last Tuesday in January, while his son was asleep beside him in the armchair. After holding a pocket mirror over his father's mouth with a trembling hand, Emil went to wake up his mother in her bed and they shared a hug while Luke Tapper called the Macmillan nurse, who told them someone would be over shortly to take away the body.

The body, thought Emil.

20.

Given that the arrangements had been made several months earlier, Yara and Luke decided to attend their appointment at the Falling-water Clinic on Harley Street. They stayed at a hotel on the eastern edge of Hyde Park, on a street of minor embassies and renowned plastic surgeons. At the buffet breakfast, Yara ate a croissant stuffed with sliced apple and cream cheese, while Luke filled two plates with French toast, stubby, shrivelled sausages, and glistening discs of black pudding.

They arrived at the clinic early and spent twenty minutes leafing through outdated gossip magazines. Luke read about a former glamour model having her breasts reduced then enlarged then reduced again and spending three months in a Thai rehab centre where she converted to Mahayana Buddhism. Yara read about footage being leaked of a male politician who'd voted against gay marriage giving blowjobs to three young escorts in a Felixstowe Travelodge.

"These people are outta their fuckin' minds," said Luke Tapper.

After the appointment, the pair of them sat in a café decorated like a steel foundry where the coffee was served in tin camping mugs. Yara kept excusing herself to smoke cigarettes outside, while Luke tried to cheer her up despite having no real idea what had caused her mood to plummet. He was—he had been—very happy. He thought they were celebrating.

"Is this really okay?" Yara said to Luke.

"Of course it's okay, babe," said Luke, genuinely confused by the sudden onset of his wife's sadness. "Why wouldn't it be okay?"

"I don't know," said Yara. "I'm not sure."

Luke dropped to his knees and Yara wondered if he was about to propose before remembering that they were already married, that they had already stood opposite each other in front of everyone they knew and promised to do the thing she had promised to do once before and failed at.

"After everything you've done," said Luke, "you deserve this."

There were two weeks between Arthur's death and his funeral, which was scheduled to be held in Robinswood Evangelical Church, on a Saturday morning in early February. The arrangements were taken care of by Mortimer & Son, whose premises in Bourton, wedged quietly between the river and the mini-supermarket, Emil had walked past countless times without once wondering what went on there.

Luke set up a Facebook page to try and inform as many people as possible about the arrangements for the service. Emil monitored the page, surprised to find a number of totally unfamiliar names posting condolences and messages to Arthur. He assumed some of them were connected to his father's charity work and that some might have been former employees or school friends or the men that made use of Arthur's flat to smoke drugs.

Arthur,
You'll be very much missed by this community. Our thoughts are with your family at this difficult time.

Hey, A.
Won't be able to get up from Penzance for the service, you know how it is with kids. Catch you on the otherside.

Artie.
Remember the Perugia tour in 03? You were on top form then, lad. Sorry about the way things went.

Sorry to hear the news, Arthur. Big love to the fam. Say hi to Tone when you see him up there.

Arthur, there are no words. I'll be thinking of dear Emil and
Evangeline. You're in our prayers.

It was a surprise to himself that Emil didn't drink or consume anything intoxicating in the days or weeks after his father's death. He
finally had the perfect excuse to retreat into chemical oblivion and
he did not take it. Instead, he returned to the grunting camaraderie
of NA and AA meetings, forcing himself to mumble a few words,
even if just to say that his dad had died, and he felt lost, and he was
grateful to have somewhere to come and say that.

Following one meeting, two days after his father had died, Emil
made his way to the big library on the outskirts of town, stopping
off at the McDonald's on an industrial estate to buy a Big Mac and a
chocolate milkshake, which he ate alone in a reading booth, scrolling through an article on his phone about quantum field theory
and the plethora of applications it might prove to have in a few
years' time. Since the night Alice had brought him home from The
Water Poet, he hadn't tried to write again. Instead, he'd gone back
to reading with a newfound appreciation for the way certain writ-
ers could build worlds that he cared about more than the one he
currently occupied.

It was while he was sequestered in this booth, alternating between skimming science articles on his phone and rereading a tattered James Morrow novel, that Emil noticed a very badly designed
poster reading: "Silver Surfers—tech savvy volunteers wanted to
teach OAPs how to navigate the online world." He immediately
heard his father's voice in his head: *What is something you've done
that felt like the thing you ought to be doing?* Once he'd finished his
milkshake, he introduced himself to a twitchy librarian in a wool
beret, who told him to come back on Saturday at ten in the morning, and not to prepare anything because he'd likely find himself
disappointed.

"You sure you want to do this?" she said, as though he was
contemplating having a rhinoplasty or adopting a malevolent pit
bull.

"Uh, yeah," said Emil.

The librarian sighed. "Alright. Just remember not to go overboard."

Last girl put together a PowerPoint about romance scams and ended up leaving in tears."

When he arrived two days later, there were three elderly people waiting by the bank of ancient computers in the back corner of the building. One was holding a green highlighter like a cigarette, another had peroxided his shoulder-length hair, and the third, the only woman, was sketching in a spiral-bound notebook with the solemn concentration of a bureaucrat.

"You our new teacher?" said the one smoking a pen. "Last one was about as patient as a rhino." He exhaled imaginary smoke. "Are you patient, young man?"

"I think so," said Emil.

"We'll see about that."

"I'm Emil," said Emil.

"Raymond," said the pen-smoker. "Karl Lagerfeld over there is Eric, and scribbling away at the end is Audrey."

"Enchanté," said Eric.

Audrey glanced up from her notebook. "You're not going to do a PowerPoint, are you?"

"Uh, no," said Emil.

He sat between them, feeling like an imposter, and watched as they all haltingly typed their library card numbers into the login screen. Once they had logged in, the silver surfers all swivelled their chairs to face him, like the crew of a starship awaiting orders. Emil opened his mouth but no sound came out. Eric smiled at him encouragingly, his lips the royal purple of beetroot.

"Do Raymondo first," he said. "He's always easiest."

Raymond's central problem was that he had a chain of email addresses with different providers, none of which he could remember the passwords to, and each of which, when he attempted to reset the password, directed him to another email address, which he also couldn't remember the password to. Emil helped him draw up a list of phrases he was sure he had used at one point or another.

ORANGUTAN1!

RORYMCELROY1!

LUCYCARTWRIGHT1!

SORRYRUPERTFORWHATIDID1!

By trying the entire list on each account, they eventually managed to gain access to a single account, which enabled them to unlock several others, in one of which they found an email with an attached photo of a young man dressed in a leather apron hung with chisels.

"That's my grandson," said Raymond, pressing his forefinger against the screen until it warped. "He's a carpenter."

"Cool," said Emil. "Like Jesus."

"Exactly," said Raymond. "Except I don't think Jesus ever knocked up a kitchen cupboard."

"Why not?" said Eric, who was using a single finger to type the word "kaftan" into Google. "They had kitchens in Bible times."

Raymond scrunched his hammy hands into fists. "Jesus did not have a kitchen," he said, turning in his swivel chair until his back was to Eric and he was facing Emil. "He talks utter poppycock, that one."

"If they didn't have kitchens, where did they cook, Raymondo?"

"Don't call me Raymondo, Eric. I told you my name is not Raymondo."

"It's called a nickname," said Eric. "It's affectionate."

"I'll affectionately clip you round the ear in a minute, if you don't give it a rest."

Eric was dressed in a cashmere muumuu with chunky-soled Chelsea boots, as though he was due to sit front row at Paris Fashion Week. He wanted to ask Emil how it was that he could go to a site, be shown a price for a certain piece of clothing, then return to the site a few hours later and find the price had increased without explanation. Emil showed him how to clear his cookies and introduced him to a price comparison website on which he could set email alerts to arrive when certain items dropped below specified thresholds.

"Oh, now that's wonderful," said Eric. "You'll save me a small fortune."

Surprised by the cost of the clothes the elderly man had been browsing, Emil tentatively asked whether he'd considered buying clothes secondhand.

"You mean like eBay? I don't do eBay. My sister bought an iPhone, only when it turned up it was just a printed-out photograph of an iPhone."

"Not eBay," said Emil. "There are other sites specifically for clothes." He navigated to the homepage for a vintage reselling app then left his hands hovering over the keyboard like a pianist waiting for his cue. "What are you looking for?"

"Try searching for culottes," said Eric. "Plaid culottes. Twenty-eight waist." He glanced down at his stomach. "No, twenty-nine."

Emil dutifully typed in the request and the screen was suddenly flooded with images of stubby, wide-legged trousers, in various fabrics and patterns.

"Oh my giddy aunt," said Eric. "Those are gorgeous. As are those. And those." He eagerly elbowed Emil. "Try searching for Maison Margiela, men's."

After several attempts, Emil got the spelling right, and the screen was filled with ludicrously proportioned shoes and dark, angular garments of clothing. Eric was transfixed.

"And these are really the prices? Or is it a scam?"

"It's just secondhand," said Emil. "I don't think it's a scam."

"Try typing in Hermès scarf," said Eric. "Try typing: Hermès scarf fox pattern."

Once they'd searched for several more increasingly specific items of designer clothing, Emil turned his attention to Audrey, who had opened a program with a familiar interface, and was intently rotating a polygon while glancing back and forth between the monitor and her notebook.

"It's okay," said Audrey. "You won't be able to help me. I'm more here for the company."

"She's in love with us," said Eric, scrolling through an endless catalogue of designer cardigans.

"She wants us to propose," said Raymond, pasting a meme of a llama into the body of an email to his son.

Emil shifted his stool closer to Audrey. "I can try and help," he said.

"This is called Blender," said Audrey, impatiently. "It's a program for making animations. It's quite technical."

"I know Blender," said Emil.

"Do you heck," said Audrey.

"Really," said Emil. "I used to use it to make, like, little games and stuff."

Audrey eyed him suspiciously. "My problem is that when I try to shade smooth the mesh in this one, everything goes kaput."

"Can I?" said Emil.

Audrey shifted to one side and let Emil take control of her mouse. "Interior faces," he said, some dim recollection of the issue coming back to him. "You might have accidentally stuck another polygon inside this one, if you pressed fill while you were in it." He deleted the extraneous element with a swift double click. "If it happens again, just go up here to trait, click interior faces, and get rid of any that come up."

Grinning, Audrey performed a celebratory drumroll on the rickety computer desk.

"Righty right," she said. "This one's a keeper."

After his first session with the silver surfers, Emil left in an odd mood that he struggled to decipher. He went to the bookshop and bought a copy of *The Little Prince*, which he posted to Frida in London, along with a postcard showing a choirboy stood outside of the cathedral. He smoked three cigarettes while watching his own reflection in the canal. He bought a hot chocolate from Starbucks and drank it while scrutinising war medals through the window of an antiques shop.

The next week, he turned back up at the library to find Raymond, Eric, and Audrey, all sitting in exactly the same places, waiting for him, like stuffed toys on a window ledge. Eric was dressed in a turquoise gilet while the other two were wearing outfits so similar in cut and colour to the previous meeting as to be identical.

They spent the first half an hour working together to help Raymond complete an online puzzle in which as many words as possible had to be discovered within a wheel of six letters. Once the puzzle had been largely solved, Eric performed a twirl to show off his new attire and asked Emil whether it was possible for him to learn how to list his own old clothes for sale on the reselling site. Emil's phone interrupted the lesson a few minutes in.

"One sec," he said, carrying his half-full bottle of Coke outside with his ringing phone, under the watchful gaze of a frowning librarian.

The number, which his phone failed to identify, was a London landline. Emil trawled through his head for anyone in London who might want to speak to him but he could only think of his sister, whose poky flat had no housephone, and who had switched to communicating primarily through meandering voice messages in which she let her thoughts unspool like poems.

"Emil Candlewick?" said a woman's voice. It was definitely not Evangeline, nor was it Frida, who did occasionally call to ask her uncle for help when stuck on particularly troublesome maths homework.

"Yeah?" said Emil.

"Felicity Ward here."

Emil assumed it was one of the recruiters or employers he'd emailed during one his fits of job-searching. He'd applied for jobs ranging from full stack developer at a mobile gaming company to Roblox tutor to university admissions administrator. By the time any responses or interview offers came, he had usually graduated to another plan for his future.

"Sorry," he said. "I'm not looking for work at the moment."

"I'm sorry?"

"I'm not looking for work anymore. Something, um, came up."

"Are you saying you've found other representation?"

Emil unscrewed the cap on his Coke. "What do you mean?"

"You are Emil Candlewick?"

"Yeah," said Emil, growing increasingly nervous. "Who are you?"

"I'm Felicity Ward. We emailed, you said you'd rather speak by phone."

"I don't think so," said Emil.

"I'm sorry," said the woman. "I'm slightly confused."

"Me too," said Emil.

"Did you submit a novel called *The Proof* to Ward & Hackett?"

Emil put down his Coke.

"What's Ward & Hackett?"

"A literary agency."

"You're a book agent?"

"I'm sorry, Emil, I'm struggling to see what's happening here."

He thought back to the morning when he'd woken up crushed by the weight of a hangover, when he'd stumbled around his bedroom, searching for his manuscript like a burglar. And it hadn't been there. Had he even brought it with him from the pub? Or was that when Alice had taken it? Because who else would have bothered to read his story? Who else even had a copy? No one could get into his computer. Could he have submitted it while blackout drunk? He hurriedly checked the sent folder of his email on his phone. He'd sent it nowhere.

"Emil? Are you still there?"

Through the windows of the library, he could see the silver surfers, spinning in circles on their chairs, holding biros like swords.

"Sorry," he said. "I have to go. I'll, uh, call you back."

Emil hung up and clamped his teeth around the mouth of his plastic bottle, while shuffling his thoughts like a newsreader trying to order a sheaf of papers. He tried to call Alice but she didn't pick up. He sent her a message that read: "Did you take my story?" He wasn't expecting a response. There had been no responses since she'd ordered a giant man to carry him back to his flat and he'd passed out after loudly informing her that it wasn't his fault she was poor.

Back inside the library, the silver surfers were already heaving themselves out of the swivel chairs and gathering up their loose printouts and half-read crime thrillers. Emil was surprised to feel a twinge of disappointment.

"There he is," said Eric. "The boy wonder."

"We're knocking off early and going for ice cream," said Raymond.

"You in or not?" said Audrey.

Emil grinned. "I'm in," he said. "I'm definitely in."

Together, the four of them moved through the town centre at a pace that felt to Emil to be ludicrously slow. Raymond pointed out shops that he wished were still other shops, and buildings that had once been grander, less soulless buildings. They paused to watch mutilated birds bicker over the flaky remains of a Cornish pasty. Outside a betting shop, a man was lying prostrate on the ground like someone anticipating a bomb.

They followed Northgate Street to the cross, passed the parade of charity shops on Southgate Street, and turned right into the narrow opening of College Court, where a velvet-curtained place selling birthstones and incense sticks stood opposite a glass-fronted café called Lily's Tearoom. Emil realised this was the place where Imogen had broken up with him.

"My favourite gang of terrorists!" said the owner, bustling over to greet the group as they pushed through the creaking door.

"We have a new recruit," said Eric. "He's only a baby."

Emil sat wedged between the silver surfers on the comfy sofas and was passed a laminated menu listing various ice cream dishes. *What is something you've done that felt like the thing you ought to be doing?* Strangely enough, it was this.

The reading of the will was held in a cold solicitor's office above a hairdresser on Westgate Street. There was very little suspense, given that Arthur owned nothing but the contents of his rented flat and slightly over two hundred pounds in a Halifax current account. He did, however, leave behind a handwritten note giving a number of unusual requests about how his funeral ought to proceed. The note was read out, haltingly, by the solicitor, to groans, sighs, and giggles from the remaining Candlewicks.

Evangeline and Frida returned to London and ordered a colossal amount of sushi, which they ate over two days while watching two full seasons of *Gilmore Girls*.

Yara signed up for the Paris marathon, due to take place in six months.

Luke Tapper stuck a note to the fridge which read: "Sweat is just fat crying."

Emil caught the train to Paddington for a meeting at the offices of Ward & Hackett. He stayed with his sister and niece in Peckham, sleeping on the sofa and waking to find three bowls of overnight oats pitted with blueberries waiting on the kitchen counter.

As the short, dark days slowly began to expand, Patrice let himself into The Old Rectory and went to check for any instructional notes on the kitchen island. Yara intercepted him in the corridor. She asked if he could follow her into the living room. Her arms hung limp at her sides as if they were heavy objects that took some effort to carry.

Patrice wondered if he was about to be accused of stealing something. This happened with upsetting regularity. Over the years since he'd become self-employed—meaning complaints were no longer handled by the agency—he'd been accused of stealing wedding rings, vibrators, wads of cash, vetiver root hand balm, a Louis Vuitton teddy bear, a Chinese Crested dog, a first edition copy of *The Lord of the Rings*, and a signed photograph of the Dalai Lama blowing a neon pink bubblegum bubble.

But Yara Candlewick didn't look angry as she gestured for Patrice to take a seat. He noticed that she'd hoovered and dusted and made an attempt to clean the windows with some ineffectual method that had left arabesque streaks on the glass. He lowered himself warily onto the firm, Scandinavian sofa, lodging a rectangular bucket filled with floor polish, microfibre cloths, and an electric toothbrush between his feet. Yara smiled sadly at Patrice, as though it was him and not her who had recently suffered a bereavement.

"Patrice," she said. "You don't know how difficult it is to have to do this." Her hands, one on top of the other, drifted up to her heart. "Over the years, you've come to feel like part of the family."

Patrice closed his eyes, which Yara took as a sign of overwhelming emotion, and which was really an attempt to conceal a combination of irritation, exhaustion, and slight amusement.

"You don't need a cleaner anymore?" he said, to keep her from fumbling around with the words.

Yara smiled again, in a way that looked as though it was physically painful. "I know it won't make this easier, but here's a little something to say thank you."

She passed him a bulky manila envelope. Patrice stood up. It was immediately obvious to him that Yara was expecting a hug and he thrust out his hand to shake hers before she pounced on him. Her palm felt like chamois leather. The gold chain around her neck was as thin as angel-hair pasta.

"Okay," he said. "Thanks, Kara."

At the end of Drybrook Lane, Patrice counted the money in the envelope. It came to eleven hundred pounds. It would be enough to cover two months' rent and pay for his daughter to go on a week-long school trip to Italy that she'd magnanimously assumed wouldn't be within their means. Patrice felt a stab of regret for having pretended not to know Yara's name but he was tired of being told how treasured he was by the people who paid him minimum wage. If he really seemed to Yara like a member of the family, Patrice felt awful for her two kids.

21.

On the day of the funeral, Emil put on a pinstriped suit he'd gone with Frida to buy at a charity shop in town. It was two sizes too big and hung from his shoulders like a barber's cape. He wore a scuffed pair of old school shoes that his mother insisted on blackening with boot polish and a plaited leather belt that had once belonged to his father. On his mother's orders, he shaved with calamine lotion and a pink Venus razor he found in the cupboard under the sink.

The family, including Arthur's brothers and their wives and children, and Yara's odd cast of Northampton relatives, met at the Bourton house before the service. Despite it being only eleven, Yara's side of the family drank beer and cider from cans, and smoked and vaped in the kitchen, which Yara had decreed would be allowed for one day only, given the circumstances. Everything smaller than a plate but larger than a cigarette butt was recruited as an ashtray: the plastic lids of protein beakers, chopstick holders, Easter egg foil, the empty Ziploc bag from a block of mature cheddar.

Emil was trapped between two of his cousins and a console table crowded with plates of mini sausage rolls and devilled eggs. The two cousins were drinking black tins of fruit cider. They were both so pale as to be almost translucent and topped with ragged clouds of strawberry-blonde hair.

"Sorry about your dad," said Tom.

"Yeah," said Ryan. "Sorry."

"Didn't you have a cousin who died?" said Emil.

"Fell off her horse," said Tom.

"Now we ent allowed to ride horses whatsoever."

"Do you want to ride horses?"

"Dunno. Probly not."

Luke Tapper dug two pairs of fingers into the corners of his mouth and cut through the gentle chatter of the room with a piercing whistle. His suit was specially tailored to fit his bulk and made him look, to Emil, like a rugby player attending a court hearing.

"Alright, boys and girls," he said. "Time to get this show on the road."

Emil, Evangeline, Frida, and Yara travelled together in the hearse, while another funeral car followed along behind them, containing Luke, Opal, Arthur's brothers and their wives, and an incredibly elderly man who the Candlewicks called Uncle George, who wasn't really an uncle but the best friend of Arthur's mother.

The cars crawled slowly through the village and toward Gloucester. The back windows were blacked out and Emil was grateful that no one could see inside, even though the remaining Candlewicks weren't putting on a particularly entertaining spectacle. Yara was texting about serviettes with the woman organising the catering for the wake. Frida was humming the theme tune to a BBC series about food through the ages. Evangeline was biting into her index finger and scratching an itch on her left ankle with the toe of her right foot.

Their destination was St. Barnabas, the church at the base of Robinswood Hill. They walked in past modestly occupied pews and took their seats at the front. Emil was reminded of having to sit in a similar position during his mum's wedding to Luke Tapper. He wondered, vaguely, whether it would be a more appropriate tradition for the living to give away their dead, the way a father was meant to give away his daughter to a groom. He imagined walking a zombie version of his father down the aisle and handing him over to an aloof and impatient angel.

They had declined to supply their own team of pallbearers and the men who carried Arthur into St. Barnabas were a group of stooped, grey-haired undertakers in rumpled suits, who trembled like stilts beneath the pale wicker coffin. As the box was lowered onto a plinth draped in a cotton sheet, Emil gripped the arm at the end of the pew as though he was on a rollercoaster.

He barely heard the opening remarks of the vicar, or the hymn that he dumbly mouthed along to, or the reading from Ecclesiastes about there being a time for everything, including death. He was staring at the box, trying, unsuccessfully, to transmit a message to his father. "You're just knowledge now. How does it feel? There was a person called Dad and now there's the body without a name and everything will carry on." When he broke away, he realised his sister had been crying so heavily that Frida was feeding her tissues as though they were ammunition.

"Emil," she whispered, through a mouth choked with phlegm. "Will you read this?"

She held a folded piece of A4 paper out toward him. Emil didn't take it.

"What?" he said. "No."

"Emil, please."

"Evangeline, no. I can't read a speech."

"Someone has to read it."

"You wrote it."

"Exactly. Just this once, Emil, please."

"What does that even mean? When else would this be happening?"

The vicar cleared his throat.

"And now, Arthur's daughter, Evangeline, will say a few words."

Emil glanced at his sister and at the empty space behind the podium and sighed inwardly. His sister was pinching a snot-withered tissue to her face.

"Fine, Phyliss, give it here."

Evangeline smiled behind her tears. "Fuck you."

Their Aunt Opal, in the row behind, caught the offending word.

"Evangeline," she said. "This is a funeral."

Emil grinned. "Yeah, Phyliss, you potty mouth."

"Uncle Emil," said Frida. "Quiet voices."

"Yeah, Uncle Emil," said Evangeline.

"Sorry," said Emil.

The vicar was looking expectantly in their direction.

Dragging his feet across the stone floor of the church, Emil ascended the podium and unfolded the speech his sister had written. He tried to scan down and absorb everything before he started but there was too much of it and the text was too small and his hands were shaking too much for the words to come into focus.

He scratched at a burgeoning spot between his eyebrows.

"Hi," said Emil. "In case you can't tell, I'm not Evangeline Candlewick, I'm Emil, Arthur's son. I'm going to read the speech my sister wrote now because she's a little, um, yeah."

He started to read.

"During the last days of my father's life, I met a woman named Wing-Yan Harper, who works for a charity called How to Save a Life. The aim of the charity is to identify and promote the most effective charities across the globe, so that when people donate, they can be sure their money is helping to alleviate as much suffering as is possible.

"I first came across the charity as a teenager, in a book written by an Australian ethicist named Peter Singer. When I read it, I thought: isn't this common sense? Isn't this what we already do? It's not, of course. We let our hearts choose which causes and organisations to donate to, and the majority of organisations are not running trials or evaluations to research which of their interventions are most effective. My father came to believe, as did I, that this is not a matter where we ought to be guided by our feelings. If we are going to give, we ought to give well. One pound given to an effective organisation can do more good than a thousand pounds given to an ineffective organisation.

"After the sale of his company, my father donated a total of two point three million pounds to the four organisations most recommended by How to Save a Life. He did not tell my mother he was going to do this, nor did he tell me or my brother. Needless to say, it came as quite a shock."

There was a gentle gale of laughter. Emil paused, taking in the faces. He was looking for someone who might reassure him. He saw his Uncle Hugo, who inexplicably seemed to be filming the events on his phone.

"According to Wing-Yan Harper, it's likely this donation saved over one thousand lives, through a combination of cash incentives for vaccinations, malaria nets, and vitamin supplements. It's the charity's policy not to comment on individual donors, but I was told that the donation my father made was significant enough for a number of groups to expand their projects into villages that otherwise would not have fallen under their remit. In this case, one thousand is not just a number. One thousand is an attempt to signal toward the huge number of thinking, feeling, loving human beings who can continue thinking, feeling, and loving because of the help they received through this organisation and my father." Emil pondered this for a moment and went off-script, thinking out loud. "One thousand is more than ten times the number of people here today," he said. "It's a lot."

He read on.

"For a long time, I was angry at my father for what he did. Strangely enough, I thought what he'd done was selfish. It wasn't necessarily the money but that, without warning, he'd thrown a grenade into the centre of our family. It has taken me some time to come to terms with those feelings and to accept that I am proud of my father, even if I believe what he did may not have been fair to me, my mother, or my brother. My father was so good he made us feel bad. He made a moral choice on our behalf and we resented him for it. My father made me feel as though no matter what I chose to do with my life, I could never match up to him.

"We had an unusual relationship, in that I believe my father taught me as much in the last years of his life as he did in the first years of mine. Most crucially, he taught me to remind myself daily of a few key things: I am alive and I am healthy. I am warm at night. I do not fear for the physical safety of my family. When unexplained pains arise, I go to the doctor. When my stomach grumbles, I go to the fridge. It is easy to get lost in the accumulation of small stresses that constitute our lives; in shopping for a rushed dinner, reading celebrity gossip on a cracked phone screen, or fretting at the rising price of petrol. We struggle, yes. We struggle but we are also blessed with an opportunity to help our cousins, countries and oceans away; their lives fraught with problems we never even have to consider. As my father discovered, this is not a burden but a gift. We are the ones who get to give help, not the ones whose lives are dependent upon receiving it.

"I will never be like my father was. I will never have such a grand sum of money to give away and even if I did, I don't know if I could do it, knowing the uncertainty my daughter will face as she comes of age in a world that is changing faster than anyone can keep pace with. I want my daughter to have new shoes and all the books she wants. I want her to someday have a home that can't be snatched away from her by a changeable landlord. I want her to live in peace and comfort. But this is balanced against the thought that when she goes on the internet or flicks on the TV to witness unimaginable poverty and suffering, I want to be able to tell her that we don't bury our heads in the sand and assure ourselves that this is simply how the world is. That we look outside of our community and give at least some of what we've been blessed with to others.

"Before my dad passed, we had a conversation over coffee about how far our individual moral responsibilities extend. Who are we responsible for? Our families? Our friends? The people in our town, our country, our continent? The people living in misery because of historical atrocities committed by our ancestors? Everyone who exists now? The people of the future? No-one but ourselves? I don't know what the answer is, but it's clear what Dad came to believe.

"My father took the whole world into his heart and now he's gone back to join it, in the mud, air, ash, and water. No matter what kind of world lies on the other side of this one, I'm sure its residents will welcome him with open arms. My father is gone now, but there are people across the planet who remain with us because of what he did."

Emil turned slightly to address the coffin on the starched sheet at the front of the church.

"Goodbye, Dad. You were a huge weirdo, and we're going to miss you very much."

When Emil finished reading, he lingered at the podium, lifting the inside flap of his blazer to wipe snot off his face. There was audible crying from several members of the audience. He returned to his seat and pushed the speech back into his sister's lap.

"Thank you," said Evangeline.

"Yeah," said Emil. "Thanks too."

A hand reached forward, gripped Emil by the shoulder, and shook it gently.

"Well done, mate," said Luke Tapper.

Once the vicar had taken over and led them through another few Bible passages and a hymn that felt only loosely relevant, a speaker was placed at the front of the church and switched on. It began to play an incredibly grainy 1928 recording of a song called "Prends Donc Courage" by the Cajun musician Cléoma Falcon.

"What even is this?" said Evangeline.

"I don't know," said Yara. "It's what he asked for."

The blacked-out funeral cars took the close family members to a crematorium fifteen minutes away, where they sat on chairs even less comfortable than the pebble-smooth pews, facing a hatch framed by velvet curtains. The wicker coffin was carried in and set on rollers. Yara thought of a weekend break she'd taken with Arthur to Paris, when they'd loaded their luggage onto the conveyor belt at security and he'd tipsily said, "Poppet, did you remember to pack the explosives?" They'd been forced to accompany an apologetic security guard to a windowless room where their underwear was unrolled and their toiletry bags were turned inside out.

The wake was held at a social club in Innsworth, with a skittle alley running parallel to the bar and neon paper stars scrawled with special offers tacked up to the mirrored shelves of spirits. In accordance with Arthur's wishes, the family arrived to find a local pub-rock band tuning their instruments on a knee-high stage. The band consisted of four men with ponytails, two of whom were wearing leather jackets, one of whom was in a leather waistcoat. There were balloons tethered to light fixtures and the old TVs that were usually set to show cricket matches.

"This is so weird," said Emil.

"Remember," said Yara. "It's what your father wanted."

The four of them sat together at a table in the back corner, surrounded by sepia photos of forgotten rugby teams and shelves bearing old trophies and horse brasses. There were photographs of Arthur pinned to a giant corkboard in the centre of the room: Arthur as a child in the grounds of Hatfield Hall, triumphantly naked on the roof of a plastic car being driven by his older brother. Arthur during a rugby match, his head taped up, a green gumshield obscuring his teeth as he grimaced. Arthur on his wedding day, flanked by his brothers, the top hat on his head cocked like Willy Wonka. Arthur and Brian Clinks at the gates to the second set of premises Riverwild had taken on.

Emil drifted away from his mum and sister to go and smoke outside. He didn't know how to deal with the condolences that kept coming his way from people he couldn't recognise but who recognised him.

Evangeline remained beside her mother in the alcove, receiving the occasional relative like royalty. They were both drinking heavily but finding themselves unable to get drunk. Nothing would soften the edges of the occasion. Nothing would make it hurry along any faster.

Kathleen Porter appeared once the waves of family had eased. She was dressed in a black romper with Doc Martens and holding a pint of Stella to her chest.

"Not a bad turnout," she said.

"He knew more people than I'd imagined," said Evangeline.

"Hey," said Kathleen. "Your dad was a charmer, in his own way. "Course your mum's a saint too. If my hubbie gave away two mil, he'd be carrying his own cock to A and E in a bag of frozen peas."

"Thank you, Kathleen," said Yara.

"Either of you want a shot?"

"Yes," said Yara and Evangeline at the same time.

There were rugby pitches attached to the social club, as well as a playground missing several components, their absences marked by steel stumps as though great metal trees had been felled between the monkey bars and the seesaw. Emil took a seat on a swing and lit a cigarette. It was near total dark and the night was still and biting.

He tried to call Alice, as he had done numerous times since hearing from Ward & Hackett. This time, she answered.

"You sent my book to an agent," he said.

"And your dad died," said Alice. "I'm sorry."

"It's okay," said Emil. "I mean, it's not okay, obviously, but it's, I don't know. It's what happened." He swung, back and forth, watching his shadow distend across the chips of bark. "Where have you been?" he said.

"Cardiff," said Alice. "I'm staying with my aunt. She's loopy but she's alright really."

"Oh," said Emil. "Okay."

"I needed a change of scenery. You know how it is."

"Yeah," said Emil.

"Hard to change when nothing else does."

"Yeah."

"Sorry I didn't let you know."

"It's okay. I just wanted to say thank you. I was going to burn that book."

"And now you have an agent?"

"Not exactly. She said the book had potential, then she sent me a lot of notes, and said if I had time, I should give it another go and send it back to her."

"You think you can do it?"

"I don't know if I want to. It was cool, hearing that she liked it and stuff, but I don't know if that's really the thing I want to do. I think it's like learning or coding or something, it's not really fun when you're doing it for someone else. It's like being at school again."

"I think you're nuts, but I get it." He heard the clatter of pans and a pained shout in the background. "I have to go, Master Emil, but *Naruto* and pizza when I'm back?"

"Yes, please," said Emil.

"Nice."

He hung up and continued to swing, higher and higher, the mourners in the soft light of the social club blurring like smeared paint.

Yara and Evangeline had been sitting in their dark corner for several hours and had finally managed to break through the wall and become deeply drunk. Though Evangeline's mind felt sharp and uncompromised, when she reached for a glass or her phone, her hand appeared slow and over-exposed. She had an urge to start running and a competing urge to curl up and fall asleep on the floor.

There was an order of service on the neighbouring table, with Arthur's face staring up from the cover. The picture they'd chosen was taken on a walk in the Brecon Beacons. Emil and Evangeline are both dressed in padded suits with wool mittens draped around their necks on pieces of red string. Yara is in a matching scarf and bobble hat, both of which were Christmas gifts from Arthur, and which are such a vivid shade of indigo that it looks like a printing error in the photograph.

Yara stared through the window at her son, alone on the playground. She scanned the room for Luke and saw that he'd been cornered by Hugo's three sons, who were excitedly probing him for tips on how to acquire a similarly impressive amount of muscle mass.

Yara's phone plinked and the screen revealed that a picture had arrived of a smiling, pregnant woman, clutching her belly. Evangeline frowned and moved her face closer to her mum's phone. Yara snatched it away.

"Who was that?" said Evangeline.

"No-one," said Yara.

"What do you mean, no-one? Who is it?"

"Just leave it, Evie."

"What? Why?"

"Because I'm asking you to leave it."

"Why are you being so aggressive?"

"I'm not being aggressive, Evangeline, but this isn't the time or the place."

"The time or the place for what?"

"I'll tell you another time, in another place."

Evangeline took a sip of her drink, entirely bewildered and driven by her drunkenness to keep pushing. "Is that Luke's secret daughter?" she said. "Or Dad's secret girlfriend? Am I going to have a new brother?"

"Don't be ridiculous."

"I'm sorry my guesses about your mysterious pregnant friend aren't hitting the mark."

"Just shut up, would you?"

"Don't tell me to shut up. What's wrong with you?"

"Oh, for god's sake. Come with me."

Yara took her daughter by the hand and led her behind a fabric curtain that sectioned of part of the club being used as storage for rugby balls and tackle pads and plastic crates of water bottles, and opened a door into a cleaning cupboard that was doubling as a lost property office. Filthy clothes were heaped in the centre of the tiny, damp space. The cupboard smelled of radiator heat and stale sweat.

Yara explained, as quickly as she could given her level of inebriation, that she and Luke were having a baby, via surrogate. They had been working toward it for several months. It was something she had thought long and hard about and she was sorry for not having mentioned anything sooner but she was worried that it wasn't the right time, that Evangeline and Emil were already too burdened by their father's death, that they didn't need this other emotional thing laid on them.

She watched her daughter absorb the information.

"I'm sorry," said Evangeline. "But I think that's repulsive."

"Excuse me?"

"I'm sorry, Mum, but I do."

"What the fuck is wrong with you, Evangeline?"

"Wrong with me?"

"How on earth is it repulsive that I want to have a child with the man I love?"

"Did you listen to nothing Dad said? There are children who die from not having access to one-pound malaria nets, and you're going to spend fifty grand to bring a third child who looks slightly like you into the world."

"That's not how it works. That's not how anything works. And I have a right to build a life. Men are free to—"

"Don't try and frame this as feminism. It's basically *The Handmaid's Tale*, you paying a poor woman to grow your baby inside of her."

"You were happy enough for our money to keep you comfortable while you studied what you wanted to study."

Evangeline felt a rush of blood to her mouth, as though a tooth had just been knocked out. "That was completely different," she said. "You fucked up my life and then you paid to pick up the pieces."

"We fucked up your life, did we? Really? Enlighten me, Evangeline, how exactly did we manage that? By taking you on beautiful holidays? By sending you to an incredible school? By paying for you to go to university, only for you to get pregnant and drop out?"

"By not being there when I needed you," said Evangeline. Yara took two steps back, as though she'd just been slapped. "I love Frida more than anything, but she was the result of an abusive relationship that I should have been able to come to you for help with."

"You never came to me for help!"

"Because I didn't feel I could."

"Why not?"

"Because it never felt like you were on my side."

"How can that possibly be true, Evangeline?"

"Everything I ever cared about or showed an interest in, you diminished and patronised. You never thought anything that I was doing or thinking was worthwhile. All you cared about was making sure I was some kind of girl-boss who got good grades and went to university and made plenty of money. You were so obsessed with making sure we were successful, you never checked to see if we were happy."

Yara wrapped her arms around herself. "I'm sorry," she said, "but I don't recognise anything you're saying as true. I think you're drunk and you're upset about something but it can't be the way I've treated you. In case you didn't notice, it's been left to me and me alone to care for the fucking lot of you. I kept your dad from living on the fucking street. I kept Emil from dying of an overdose. I put you and Frida up in Richmond Gardens. And you stand there and tell me that I was always too selfish to listen to your diatribes about how we should be doing more for kids in fucking Africa. I'm sorry if I didn't have time to save the world while I was looking after my family. I'm sorry if there aren't enough hours in the day. I'm glad you've decided to spend your life helping other people, Evangeline, I really am. And although I can't for the life of me understand what was going on in his head, I can't deny that your dad was happier in the last years of his life than he was in the last years of our marriage, but you have to see that you're only able to do what you do because of my help. I've always cared for you and loved you and maybe that didn't take the exact form you'd hoped, but if you sit down and have a long, hard think about the way things really are, you'll realise that I honestly don't know what more I could have done. I'm a fragile person, Evangeline, I know that, but I had to grow hard these past years, and it didn't come for free."

Yara took a breath.

Evangeline opened her mouth and closed it again.

Frida stumbled into the room, holding a sausage roll on a red serviette with the seriousness of a pageboy bearing wedding rings.

"Oh," she said. "Sorry, I was looking for somewhere to be on my own."

"That's okay, angel. You can come in here."

Frida took two steps backwards, the sausage roll raised like a relic. "Were you talking about something I'm not supposed to know about?"

"No," said Evangeline, crouching until she was the same height as her daughter. "But I think Nan could maybe do with a hug."

Frida passed the sausage roll to her mother and ran full pelt toward Yara, who lifted her off the ground and held her close. "What were you talking about?" she said, her arms roped around the sinewy neck of her grandmother.

"Just how we always want you to tell us everything," said Yara. "And that you should never think you can't come to us."

"I know that," said Frida. "Why wouldn't I tell you something?"

"Because you think we might not listen, or we might be angry with you."

"I know you'd listen, obviously. You'd probably even listen too much. And Mummy's never angry. She's just disappointed."

Together, the three of them headed back out into the rugby club, where the band were playing Oasis and Brian Clinks was dancing wildly, as though he was a guest at a wedding, and not the funeral of a man who'd died thirty years too early. The bucket collecting money for How to Save a Life was filling as people became drunker and forgot they'd already given or decided they ought to give more in honour of Arthur's memory. The song came to an end and the band announced that the following track would be a slow one.

Yara set Frida down on a barstool and turned to Evangeline.

"Do you think we could dance?" she said.

"Mum," said Evangeline.

"Please, Evie."

As the two of them bobbed hesitantly to a growled rendition of Celine Dion, Evangeline looked over her shoulder at the people who had gathered to celebrate the life of her father. A huddle of men in tracksuits. A table of elderly women in large hats. A woman typing ceaselessly on a keyboard affixed to an iPad. They were a visibly random assortment of people, with only her father connecting them, like a dissolved stitch.

In the playground outside, her brother was standing on a swing, staring up at the moon. He released a jet of smoke into the sky.

Evangeline stepped on her mother's foot.

"I didn't even know people danced at funerals," she said.

"What did you think they did?"

"I don't know," said Evangeline. "Cried?"

22.

The morning after his father's funeral, Emil woke in his childhood bedroom, surrounded by video recording equipment. There was a green screen occupying one wall; a blank expanse of canvas the colour of watermelon rind, waiting to become whichever skyline or landscape Luke wanted to appear behind him. A microphone pointed to Emil like an accusatory finger. A ring light hovered over his head like a halo.

The radiator had been left on overnight and drawn the moisture out of the room, so that Emil's cheeks felt parched and scraped. He took deep glugs from a bottle of water he'd had the foresight to wedge between his air mattress and the wall. He drank until he felt bloated and awake.

Snow was falling in spirals over the garden. A blanket of white lay on the roof of the vardo wagon and the paths, flowerbeds, and lawn had all become a single lumpy sheet of plaster-white, extending from fencepost to fencepost.

Downstairs, there were ashtrays and half-empty cans covering the terrazzo dining table. Emil could see his niece through the patio doors, sitting straight-backed on the bench, watching the falling snow with rapt attention. He pushed open the bifold doors.

"You're outside," he said, words turning to smoke in the air.

"It smells like cigarettes in there," said Frida.

Emil brushed snow off the bench and took a seat beside his niece, pulling his hands up into the chewed sleeves of his hoodie.

"We're the only ones up," said Emil.

"Mum and Nan are going to be hungover," said Frida. "They stayed up really late, talking about serious things."

"How do you know?"

"I started to sneak down to listen but then I felt guilty and I went to bed again. They drank two more bottles of wine. I counted."

"That's okay," said Emil. "It's a funeral. Adults are allowed to get drunk at a funeral."

"You didn't get drunk."

"No."

"Because you have addiction, which is a disease."

"Is that what your mum told you?"

"Yes. And she said you're even smarter than she is but you never know what to do with it."

"Your mum's being modest. Anyway, neither of us is as smart as you are."

"I have high emotional intelligence but I'm not academic."

"Did she tell you that too?"

"No, I did a personality test online. I'm also an overthinker, a classic Cancer, and a Monica."

"That's good to know," said Emil.

Frida squinted, as though suddenly finding it difficult to see her uncle.

"Are you really writing a book?" she said.

"I write sometimes, if I feel like it."

"When you're not helping the old people?"

"When I'm not helping the old people."

"But can you imagine how amazing it would be if one day you could go into a bookshop and your book would be sitting on a shelf next to all the other books?"

"Kind of," said Emil.

"Kind of what?"

"Kind of yes and kind of no."

"Why?"

Emil cracked his knuckles, wondering if he had some duty to try and instil optimism in his niece. "Nothing ever feels like you think it's going to," he said. "Some things you think are going to be like the end of the world just happen, and it's as normal as the clocks going back or whatever. It's not like the grand climax of a story, or something that changes everything, it's just a day, like the days that happened before, and you get hungry and you eat something, and you drink coffee and you take a piss."

"Piss," said Frida, joyfully.

"Wee," said Emil. "I meant wee."

"I think you're wrong anyway," said Frida. "I was really sad when we moved to London and for a while I only ate tangerines. I put on my headphones and listened to music and it felt like I was a character in a film, which is good because in a film something always changes. The sad bit isn't the end, it's the beginning or the middle."

"Sometimes the sad bit is the end," said Emil. "It kind of depends what kind of film it is."

"Fine," said Frida. "What type of film do you think life is?"

"I don't know," said Emil. "A satirical horror film?"

"What does 'satirical' mean?"

"It's when you copy something in a funny way to show people how silly it is."

"Oh," said Frida. "Okay."

Emil rubbed his hands together. The bitter cold had made its way under his skin and his teeth were clicking like typewriter keys in his mouth.

"Does your mum let you drink tea yet?" he said.

"If it's really milky and not with any sugar."

"I'll see what I can do."

Emil got up and stretched and went back into the kitchen. He filled the kettle and set it boiling and turned the oven to 180 degrees. As he waited for the water to boil, he tore a page of baking paper off the roll, unfurled it in a metal tray, and covered it in pricked sausages, rashers of bacon, and halved tomatoes sprinkled with basil and white pepper. He cracked six eggs into a mixing bowl, whisked and seasoned them, and set them next to a frying pan smeared with butter. He added water and milk to the mugs and fished out Frida's teabag before the contents had darkened beyond the colour of marzipan. Before he went back outside, he paused at the window to watch her. She was doing nothing at all. She wasn't playing on a phone or reading a book or scrolling through a computer. She was just sitting and staring at the snow as it fell, as though nothing else existed.

Emil carried the cups of tea outside and returned to his seat, which had already been covered over again by a thin layer of fresh snow. Steam climbed in twists of lace from the mugs in their hands.

"When you were my age," said Frida, "what did you think would happen in your life?"

"Good question," said Emil. "I don't think I ever thought I'd get older. Every day felt so slow."

"That's very relatable," said Frida. "Sometimes, at the start of the summer holidays, I think it's impossible that the last day of the summer holidays will ever come. And then, on the last day of the summer holidays, it feels impossible that it was ever the first day of the summer holidays."

"Yeah," said Emil. "I think that's probably what life's like."

"What do you think happens after you die?"

"I used to think the universe might just be a giant piece of maths. That maths wasn't the thing we were using to describe things, it was the thing itself."

"I don't really get it."

"That's okay, I'm not sure I do either."

"But you don't think that anymore?"

"No," said Emil. "I don't think it explains why it feels like something to be us."

"It feels like a lot, sometimes, doesn't it, Uncle Emil?"

"It does, Niece Frida."

"If you don't think we're maths anymore, what do you think happens after we die?"

"I'm not sure," said Emil. "I think, maybe, it's like what you said about feeling like you were in a film: that life is whatever story you choose to tell yourself about what's happening, and death might be like that too."

"So you get to decide?"

"Yeah, maybe."

For a reason he wouldn't have been able to articulate, Emil set his tea down on the patio and threw himself backwards onto the white lawn of unspoilt snow. He swished his arms and legs up and down, shifting the white power into piles at his head and feet. After a few seconds, his cheeks were burning with cold and his clothes were soaked through. He returned to the bench and wrapped his cold hands around the warm mug. Frida was staring at him, aghast.

"What did you just do?" she said.

"What do you mean, what did I just do? What does it look like I just did?"

"Laid down on your back and wiggled around?"

"Yes, to make what?"

Frida glanced uncertainly over at the shape her uncle had left behind in the snow. "A farfalle?"

Emil thumped his forehead. "No," he said. "It's a snow angel. Didn't your mum ever show you how to do a snow angel?"

Frida shook her head. "I don't think we had snow like this before," she said, adding defensively, "She's showed me lots of other things."

"Anything good?"

Frida thought for a moment then moved the flat of her hand in an arc until it connected lightly with Emil's Adam's apple. "That's where you hit a predator," she said. "There, or in the testicles."

They sat in the snow and finished their cups of tea and, when no-one else had woken up, they went back into the kitchen and cooked together. Emil fried the eggs and Frida buttered toast and they played Radio 2 from the restored old radio. When the table was fully laid out, they sat at opposite ends, like rival kings, and waited for three minutes until it became clear that there was still nobody else about to come down the stairs.

"Shall we just start, Uncle Emil?"

"It's what they'd want," said Emil.

They ate until they were both painfully full and slouched in their seats with their bellies stuck out. After a half-hearted attempt at clearing things away, they relocated to the living room and Frida browsed the selection of sun-faded DVDs stacked below the TV. She picked out the Disney version of *101 Dalmatians* and slid it into Luke's PlayStation. As the opening credits played, Emil was possessed by the unshakeable feeling that he was still just seven years old, sitting beside his sister on a Sunday afternoon, in the cramped, damp living room of their first house in Abbeydale. Tomorrow, they'd go to Field Court Juniors and practise joined-up handwriting and times tables and reading comprehension, and Arthur would pick them up in his old silver Citroën, and dinner would be fish fingers and mash, eaten while Yara tapped tirelessly at a whirring desktop computer in one corner of the room. All this death and responsibility, this raw change and its accompanying shadow of nostalgia, would still be to come, and Emil would not long for it this time, he would gratefully absorb every fleeting moment of childhood, every sticky ice cream eaten among piles of cut grass, every sweaty shoulder ride, every exhausting trip to a distant zoo crowded with listless animals.

Within a few minutes, they were both fast asleep, which was how Yara and Evangeline found them, an hour later. Their hangovers were tender and surreal, and they stood in the doorway watching the two peaceful sleepers with envy. Emil was snoring gently, hands tucked beneath his cheek. Frida had curled up kitten-like at the end of the sofa.

"Should we wake them up?" whispered Evangeline.

"No," whispered Yara. "Let's let them sleep a while longer."

ACKNOWLEDGEMENTS

Thank you very, very much to Renata, Mischa, Wyn, and Damir, for making home *home*. Thank you to Anna, for seeing something in this book first. Thank you to Chris and Margo, and everyone at Scribner and Avid Reader Press, for wanting to bring it out in the world. Thank you, as always, to Jan, Alice, and Rebeca—Long Live Blackie. Thank you to Jessica, for doing so much to help start a new chapter. Thank you to Beth and Guy. Thank you to Jackie and Alex. Thank you to Crispin. Thank you to Dan, for straightening up the maths. Thank you to Katy, without whom I'd never have been in a place to write another novel. Thank you to everyone at the Hygrove. Thank you to Spanish Love Songs, Petey, and Phoebe Bridgers for the soundtrack. Thank you to Peter Singer, Will MacAskill, Toby Ord, and everyone working toward a better world.

ABOUT THE AUTHOR

BEN BROOKS is the author of books for children and adults, including *The Greatest Possible Good* and the million-copy series Stories for Boys Who Dare to Be Different, which is both a *Sunday Times* (London) and *New York Times* bestseller that has been translated into twenty-eight languages and received a British National Book Award. He received a Somerset Maugham Award and the Jerwood Fiction Uncovered Prize for his debut novel, *Lolito,* and a Kelvin 505 award and a Torre del Agua award for *The Impossible Boy.* He also writes for television and is developing original TV projects in the UK and Germany.